The Awakening of Navi Septa

Book Two

The Mountain Mouse

By Linda Williams

CheckPoint
Press

THE AWAKENING OF NAVI SEPTA
BOOK TWO: THE MOUNTAIN MOUSE

ISBN-13: 978-1-906628-32-1

PUBLISHED BY CHECKPOINT PRESS, IRELAND

CHECKPOINT PRESS

DOOAGH

ACHILL ISLAND

WESTPORT

CO. MAYO

REP. OF IRELAND

WWW.CHECKPOINTPRESS.COM

The Awakening of Navi Septa

Book Two

The Mountain Mouse

A Fantasy of Reality

by Linda Williams

This book is dedicated to the many men and women
who have devoted their lives, and often given their lives, to making our
world a better place

CONTENTS

Part One - The Tiger's Sword

Part Two - Uncrowned King

Part Three - The Wheel of Fortune

Part Four – Ends and Beginnings

PROLOGUE

The first part of this story is related in The Keys of Wisdom. Raynor, then eighteen and the oldest of us seven, found an ancient prophecy which said some young people would travel to a northern country, where they would find spiritual powers to help them overthrow the evil Sorcerers, High Priests as they called themselves, then ruling Teletsia, where we lived. We had to run away from these devilish rulers and finally reached Sasrar, much further north, two years before this part took place.

By this time we had figured out that we were the young people foretold in the prophecy. Raynor married the oldest girl, Tandi. Lee, my intelligent cousin, Ahren, a formerly a wild country boy, and I, had now finished our education. My brother Derwin and his contemporary, Conwenna, a girl of eleven now, were still at school. We always had certain abilities, which in Teletsia we had to conceal. We could go into a state of inner peace, joy and stillness, and could not be hypnotised or terrorised by the Sorcerers. We also discovered that when we were in this state and asked ourselves a question, if the answer was 'yes' we would feel a coolness on the palms of our hands and if 'no', it would register as heat. This saved us time and again.

We also discovered that everyone had a subtle, inner 'Tree of Life'. The root of the tree is at the base of the backbone and its top at the crown of the head, and in between are five subtle centres placed at various points in the body. These centres correspond to different parts of the body and different aspects of a person's personality, but the tree had to be awakened for one to be conscious of it and to use its subtle powers, and in Sasrar everybody knew about this. The first thing we learnt there was that the Mother Earth has a Tree of Life and different countries corresponded to different subtle centres. Then there were the Keys of Wisdom, that we had come upon in extraordinary ways, and each key had the power of the subtle centre and country it matched. They were vital for the success of our journey. In Sasrar we learnt more about our inner selves, our powers and how we could use them to help ourselves and others.

As in the earlier book, I, Asha Herbhealer, am the narrator, and again there are some chapters where I was not personally present, so they are written in the third person. This second book begins just over two years after the end of the first one, I have also done some more pen drawings, which hopefully give the idea of the scenes better than a description could, and below is a map of the lands involved in this section of the trilogy.

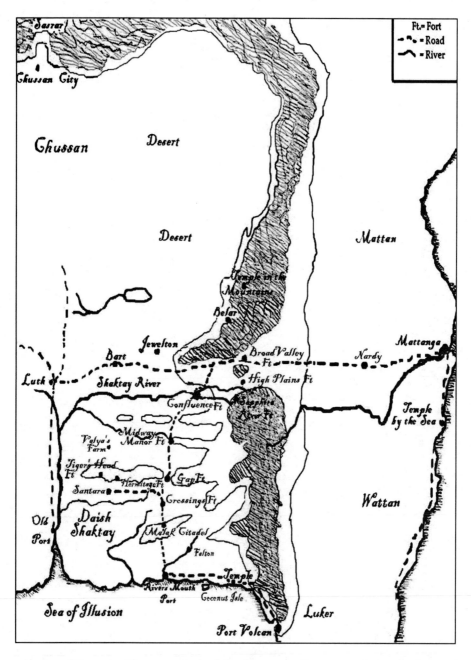

A map of Eastern Chussan, part of the Mattanga Empire and Daish Shaktay

PART ONE

THE TIGER'S SWORD

CHAPTER 1

AN OVERPROTECTIVE FRIEND

I had a vivid dream. I saw a road running through a narrow valley and along it came a baggage train – mules loaded with goods, and a number of fine horses being led and ridden. Some soldiers were guarding it and I recognized the livery of the official Chussan army – Chussan being the country to the south of Sasrar, where we lived. A band of young men appeared from behind some rocks, ambushed the soldiers and put them to flight. The grooms attending the horses also ran away, leaving the baggage train and most of the horses behind. One of the attackers had been killed and their leader, distraught, knelt by the body. This young man had beautiful vibrations, especially from his subtle heart centre. I knew my friends and I had to help him in some way.

I woke up, damp and cold from sleeping in a flimsy tent in the mountains, because we were spending a day or two at the southern end of Sasrar, high up in a small valley surrounded by snow covered peaks. Above us were some pine trees, and our tents were pitched up against the steep mountainside. Our ponies were tethered nearby, happily munching the short grass. This range spread along the north of Chussan and all the life giving rivers flowed from it onto the dry plains below.

I was now eighteen. Lee and Ahren were also both nearly eighteen and were sitting on the ground talking with Robin, four years older. He had straight, coppery brown hair, brown eyes and the light skin of the northern people. He was tall, strong and fit, and had an open, smiling face. With his quiet, courteous manner, one would not have suspected that he was the chief freedom fighter of Lord Albion, the rightful king of Chussan, at present living in exile in these same mountains. His flying horse, which he used to fly over the mountains between Chussan and Sasrar, was not with him and like us he had come up here on a pony.

Since coming to Sasrar Lee had grown up and although still stocky he was now taller and brawny. His dark hair still stuck out like a brush and our honey coloured skins contrasted with those of the locals. Ahren, another of our group from Teletsia, was no longer the tall gangly youth of two years before and he too had filled out and was well muscled. Raynor was also with us. He was now a schoolteacher at the local school in Kedar, but it was holiday time so he was not working. Tandi, Raynor's wife, had not come, because she was not feeling well, but Conwenna and Derwin were with us.

'The astrologers want to see you,' began Robin, after we had finished breakfast some time later, and Conwenna and Derwin had gone off somewhere.

'That's all very fine, but how are we to get out of Sasrar?' asked Lee. 'You've got your flying horse, but Ahren's might not want to take him over the mountains yet and I haven't even started training one. There's no other way out that I know of.'

'There is,' Robin went on. 'That's why I asked you to come up here on this border patrol. I had a message the other day from a shepherd on our side of the mountains, who was looking for some lost sheep and discovered they'd strayed right into Sasrar, through a cleft in the rocks. It's round the corner there, under those crags. We can go out through it and then blow it up, because if shepherds can get in, then others who are less friendly could as well.'

'I thought evil people could never get through these mountains.'

'In theory they can't, but you never know. Anyway, do you want to go and see the astrologers?'

'If they've asked us, we must,' said Raynor.

'There are problems in the countries above the Sea of Illusion,' Robin continued. 'Something about an evil king, who has dreadful ogrous creatures doing his dirty work, and he also has a large army. Trouble is, it means any groups of people trying to come to Sasrar will have a hard time getting through, especially if they come from the Eastern Ocean.'

'Being as those countries are connected with the subtle centre of the heart, it's no wonder I've been feeling a dull ache there,' I added.

'You're not the only one. I reckon the astrologers want the boys to help fight these ogres. This isn't for you, Asha.'

'Did they actually say that?'

I looked at the beautiful ring I was wearing, a present for my recent birthday. It was gold, and engraved with the four petalled flower which represented the first centre of the inner Tree of Life. One of the qualities of this subtle centre was the ability to overcome all obstacles, including, I thought, those created by this over-protective young man.

'No, but girls don't go to war, do they?' Robin turned to the others, 'We should leave soon. Asha, can you take the young ones home?'

'I suppose so.'

The conversation moved on and I sat listening in silence, plotting my next move. Robin might have been a brave and ingenious partisan, used to outwitting the forces of the Chussan government, but I was not going to let him get the better of me so easily. A little later I went to find Derwin and Conwenna. They were now down the valley, gorging themselves on the plentiful wild fruit they had found. Our dogs, Nog and Kootie, were with them, playing with each other and chasing the occasional hare or rabbit they put up in the heather and other bushes.

'Listen, I want you two to help me,' I munched some plump, tasty raspberries.

'OK. What's it this time?' asked my brother.

'Robin says the astrologers want us to go and help in one of the countries further south. He doesn't want me to go, but try the vibrations: should I? I felt cool, but see if you feel the same.' Conwenna and Derwin put their hands out and asked the question in their hearts.

'It's so cool for you to go!' insisted Conwenna.

'You've *got* to!' agreed Derwin. 'How are you going to get there? We can't get out the way we came in. The door shut tight and became part of the mountain after we'd come through it.'

'Robin has found a sort of cave. He'll go out through it with the boys, then blow it up behind him so no one else can get in.'

'So?' said Conwenna.

'I'll go through it some time before they leave and hide until they've blown it up. Then they can't send me back.'

'But surely they'll go along with the vibrations if it's cool for you to go?'

'Don't be too sure. They always want to protect me from danger.'

'Why can't we come?' asked Derwin.

'You've got to finish your schooling. You can't go through life semi-literate,' I did my big sister act.

'I suppose you're right,' Conwenna, put her hands in front of her again. 'There aren't any cool vibrations when I ask for us - my hands are warm and tingling. What do you want us to do?'

'First, get yourselves and the dogs home without me.'

'That's easy! It's not far to the Channum's farm and we can stay with them any time,' said Derwin.

'Secondly don't tell the boys or Robin my plan. They'll leave soon, on their ponies. I'll pretend to feel a bit ill and say goodbye now, and tell them I'm going to ride slowly on down the valley with both of you. In fact, I'll take my pony through the cleft in the rocks. I don't want to lie, but the vibrations are the highest truth. They always try to stop me doing what they call wild and dangerous things, especially Robin; he can be a bit too much sometimes. He doesn't know what we went through on our journey here.'

I won't repeat what Lee said to me when I appeared from behind a boulder on the path beyond the rock cleft and cave after Robin had blown them to smithereens. Lee always looked after me like a brother, so had some right to be incredibly angry. Robin was also extremely short and not his usual congenial self. Raynor, so extraordinarily honest, simply couldn't believe I'd been a bit free with my definition of 'down the valley'. Only Ahren was amused.

'If the vibrations were cool for you to come,' he chuckled, 'come you will. I know you, Asha.'

The next day, after a fearsome ride on narrow tracks that clung to the sides of deep valleys, we trotted into the yard of the astrologers' summer home.

Some of Robin's friends came from the village of Upper Dean to help us with our ponies and then we went to see Mrs Pea-Arge in her kitchen. She greeted us as if we had only been away a month, not two years, and sat us in the staff hall with hot drinks.

'My goodness, you've grown, Lee!' she began. 'And you Ahren. You look like one of those partisans young Robin's been training. And Asha, pretty as a spring dawn now you've put on a bit of weight!'

She was a bit too flattering about my looks, but I no longer had the tense expression and skinny beanpole body of two years before. Mrs Pea-Arge asked warmly after Derwin and Conwenna, and about Tandi's marriage to Raynor. When we told her we were possibly going south again, she said, 'Raynor, you can't just go off and leave Tandi alone like that. You might be away ages.' Raynor was silent because he had forgotten to test on vibrations to see if it was cool, therefore alright to come.

The next morning we were in the rose garden in front of the rambling mansion on a warm summer's day. Robin and the three astrologers joined us; Lord Albion was not there because he was off on some partisan quest. We stood up, bowed our heads slightly and pressed our palms together in the gesture of respectful greeting, then we all sat on the lawn between the flower beds, surrounded by fragrant roses of many colours. The valley stretched out below us, and far above were the high, snow covered peaks.

'It's a pleasure to see you,' began the eldest, who had a beard and a dark skin.

'It's a great honour that you've called us, sir,' replied Raynor.

'Sasrar has done you all a power of good,' continued the middle-aged man, who always wore white, 'but now, if you like, it's time to go south again. Not to Teletsia; you're not ready for that yet, but to Daish Shaktay, above the Sea of Illusion. What are your commitments in Sasrar?'

'Ahren and I have been doing our share of border duty, as has Raynor,' contributed Lee.

'I'm working as a school teacher,' said Raynor.

'I've been looking after my brother Derwin and the little girl, Conwenna,' I added.

'And the older girl?' asked the youngest astrologer.

'She's now my wife,' Raynor replied.

'This mission is not for you,' he continued. 'It could be a one-way trip, because it will be dangerous. There are problems in Daish Shaktay. The young man who should be king there is called Rajay Ghiry. He's an awesome freedom fighter and his enemies can't catch him, so far. They call him the Mountain Mouse.'

'What can we do?' asked Lee.

'The vibrations indicate that you three, Lee, Ahren and Asha, could help him. For you boys there may be some fighting. Are you up to that?'

'We'll do our best, sir,' said Lee. 'Robin has been training us.'

'Good. What about you, Asha?'

'Robin is adamant that as I'm a girl I shouldn't fight.' I looked at Robin but he avoided my gaze, staring pointedly at an eagle wheeling far overhead. No one commented so I went on. 'The most important thing I've learnt in Sasrar is how to awaken the Tree of Life.'

'Could you give this to people in Daish Shaktay?' asked the middle-aged man.

'Yes, I think so, but I'm nervous of making mistakes.'

'Don't let that stop you – we all make mistakes,' laughed the youngest astrologer.

'How are we going to get you there?' mused the oldest man.

'I'll take them across the desert,' Robin was looking increasingly worried when it became clear that I was going too. 'It's the best way, but they couldn't make it alone.'

'So, young warriors of truth: this is your first assignment!' said the youngest of the three. I wasn't sure I could be a warrior of truth, but I'd let myself in for it now.

The middle-aged man turned to Raynor, who looked embarrassed. 'You did a great job getting your friends to Sasrar,' he said encouragingly. 'You need to be there a bit longer and you can go back through the mountain.'

That evening we were in the staff hall, enjoying strawberries and cream. We sat round the long wooden table and behind us a fire burned in the grate, because it was sometimes chilly here in the evenings, even in summer.

'We're going to have to disguise you again,' Robin chuckled, gleefully.

'Oh no! That awful hair dye took ages to grow out,' wailed Ahren. On our journey to Sasrar we had been transformed from brown skinned, black haired Teletsians into people vaguely resembling the fairer folk of this area.

'That bleacher really dried up my skin, and made me as wrinkly as an old apple for weeks,' I moaned.

'The Chussan troopers may still be after you,' explained Robin patiently. 'If *you* insist on coming, Asha, *I* insist you disguise yourself. I'd never forgive myself if you got caught.'

'OK, you win,' I conceded. 'Where's the beauty parlour?'

'I'll deal with Lee and Ahren, and Mrs Pea-Arge will transform you.'

There was no escape.

The next morning three brown haired, light skinned young people, and Robin, who always looked like that, set out for the plains south-east of the mountains. The story was that Lee, my brother, was taking me to my husband-to-be in the south, and the others were guarding us from outlaws. Robin had been in hiding recently and now lived with the astrologers when not travelling around the country secretly organising bands of partisans.

We wound our way through the high valleys and finally reached the plain, where we changed our woollen clothes for flowing cottons and kept one cloak each, to keep out the night chill. We travelled light and only took absolute essentials: two or three changes of clothing, money, weapons, food and water bags, in case any of the wells or water holes in the desert were dry. Often there was a day's journey between them.

We set off through the arid lands, where only coarse grass, aloes and cactuses grew, along with thorny bushes. It was dry, unfriendly and searingly hot. Well, hot in the day and freezing at night, so we travelled mainly at night. This empty, desert-like land was so still under the bright moons' light that we often talked as we rode steadily south and east. We had many interesting conversations and one I particularly remember concerned the nature of the guardians. Robin explained that they were highly evolved souls from another planet, who took their birth on this earth, but were neither invincible nor incorruptible and were susceptible to all the temptations that anyone else had to face.

Lee asked Robin how he first met Lord Albion. He told us that from childhood he felt a deep dissatisfaction with Chussan and longed to make things better, and knew he had to find someone to help him. When he was fourteen, a well-spoken young man came into the yard in Chussan City where Robin's father, Mr Markand, had their animal dealing business. He wanted to buy some horses and asked if someone could ride up into the mountains with him to help deliver them, so he and Robin set off, and once they were out of the town he introduced himself as Albion, the king in exile, and told Robin that he had come to find him, and the animals were only an excuse. He had been guided to the Markand's yard by the cool vibrations. After this Robin frequently went up into the mountains to be with Lord Albion. They often went to Sasrar on flying horses, Robin became a partisan and they went all over Chussan on secret missions.

True to his word Robin guided us perfectly. He led us to the often hidden water sources and we did not get lost once. We barely spoke to anyone except each other until we approached the southern side of the desert. Some rain fell on these mountains and there were a few villages on the banks of the streams that flowed from higher up and were used for irrigating the dry land. The people there told us that the two brothers who ruled Chussan had made an alliance with the ogre king and on one occasion, when Robin had gone to see some partisan friends for a short time, Chussan troopers had waylaid us three Teletsians and asked us our business, but our excuse, that they were taking me to my future husband, had been believed. By now our disguise had begun to wear off, but fortunately they did not notice, as they accosted us late in the evening when it was nearly dark. Another evening we were camping in a farmer's barn. The farmer knew Robin, but we stayed in the barn to hide ourselves, because this was safer.

'Asha, you must look more demure and shy,' Robin advised, 'like a village maiden going to meet the man she's to marry. You're much too open and confident.'

'Sorry, but we three have been around, a good way round the world, in fact,' I joked.

'It'll be some time before any of us really get married,' said Lee.

'Yes, we've got so much to do,' Robin replied. 'Me in Chussan and you - the astrologers said this mission will be a training, before you go back to Teletsia. We all have our vows to fulfil. Our lives are going to be dangerous for some time, and if we were married, that could hold us back.' We had told Robin about our vow, made in Teletsia, to try and free our country of the Sorcerers, and he had made a similar one. 'I'm going to leave you soon. We're across the desert now. The land around here doesn't belong to Chussan, although they do try to control it. I don't know it very well so I'm not much use as a guide.'

'You're always such a help and I feel so safe when you're with us,' I said.

'Thanks for the compliment, but I'm needed up north. Lee and Ahren can look after you.'

We rode on for another day and mercifully did not come across any more Chussan troopers as we crossed the parched plain, down a good road made of packed earth. Robin was wary and told us to watch out for the people who lived here, because they were a rough lot. 'We kill 'em first and ask their names afterwards,' chuckled one man, when Ahren asked how they got along with the troopers. Lee wondered if we had been foolhardy to come into this lawless area without any definite plan, and then we saw a village nestled up against the eastern hills in a valley, among some green, irrigated fields. We approached it and Robin said this was where he would have to turn back. He told us to go on to the village, where he would catch us up and we could have a meal together before he left. Meanwhile he wanted to see a mule breeder who lived nearby, one of his network of partisans. He went down a track onto the plain to behind a rocky outcrop, where the mule breeder had his farm.

We rode on into the village square in the late afternoon. The ground was dry and dusty, with a few tired trees eking out a living near the small stone houses surrounding the square. In one corner was a bullock, walking in a circle around a pole attached to a device for raising water from a well, into a channel which led to troughs and gardens. We went over and asked for a drink from a boy whose job was to hit the bullock with a stick periodically and urge it on when it got fed up with its endless circular quest. After being given water for ourselves and our ponies we walked over to a rail at the other side of the square, hitched them to it and went into the one food shop, as our stores were low. Some of the villagers who were standing together eyed us suspiciously, then looked away and went on with whatever they were doing. We bought provisions for ourselves and grain for the ponies and as we packed our shopping into the saddle bags we overheard the villagers talking.

'The Chussan troopers are after him and his gang…'

'They say he's from a royal family...'

'Yet another band of outlaws, I reckon...'

'He comes from Daish Shaktay. He captured a baggage train that was being sent to the ogre king, Karlvid of Mattanga, as tribute, from Chussan. He said, "Both Chussan and Mattanga have stolen so much from us and I need the money to pay my army."'

'Sounds like our man,' whispered Ahren.

'How do we find him?' asked Lee.

At this moment a farmer arrived in his bullock cart, beating his lumbering animals into a reluctant gallop. He saw us, jumped off his cart and ran over to where we were standing.

'Come here, quickly!' he cried, and grabbed the boys. He pushed them round the corner of a house at the side of the square. I followed.

'The troopers are just down the main road, coming this way,' he began. 'Get on your ponies and leave, right now. They know about you, because that young man with you is the most wanted rebel in Chussan.' Ahren looked horrified. Robin had been risking his life for us, yet again. 'Where is he?'

'He's gone to see a friend who breeds mules,' Lee pointed in the direction that Robin had gone.

'Don't worry, we'll hide him,' the farmer added.

'Which way do we go?'

'Up into those hills. Follow the path by the stream bed, it's quicker than the road. After three villages you'll come to an old temple. Don't be afraid of the weird shrieking noises, it's only the wind in the rocks. We tell 'em troopers it's ghosts so they keep away. Off you go,' he hustled us towards our ponies.

'But....' protested Lee.

'If anyone stops you, say old Pahari sent you. I'm the headman here and they all know me. Now go, and go fast.' He took off to find Robin and we galloped up the hillside.

Afterwards Pahari returned to the square and called the villagers together. 'We're all enemies of those Chussan troopers, aren't we?' he began. There was a cry of approval. 'So, if they ask, those strangers went along the road into the desert. If anyone tells the troopers where they've really gone, you all know what happens to people who betray us.' He fingered the long dagger by his side.

CHAPTER 2

BECOMING PARTISANS

It was the dregs of dusk when we reached the large, partially ruined temple. It was in a compound of a number of buildings and was surrounded by a wall which was tumbling down in places. Behind it we found a large cave with an old wooden door, in the side of the rocky valley. We hid our ponies there, after giving them water from a cistern and some of the grain we had bought, then walked through the gateway into the deserted temple compound.

'Watch out for snakes,' called Ahren from behind.

'There goes one now!' I warned, as a long thin tail disappeared into a hole at our feet. Fortunately all three moons were up and we could see where we were going. We stamped our feet as we walked and a variety of other reptiles and small animals slithered and scuttled into their homes. We explored the abandoned buildings around the edge of the walled compound and found the main shrine, a large domed building in the centre of the courtyard, sat on its steps and had our supper: bread, spiced dried sausage and some fruit.

'I hope Robin's all right,' began Ahren. 'I don't feel any fear when I put my attention on him.'

'You wouldn't. He's as brave as a lion,' Lee put in, 'but let's ask on the vibrations: is he safely away from the troopers?'

'It's very cool,' I said, 'He's OK.'

'He's – so selfless, so modest,' said Lee philosophically.

'He's great company,' Ahren was more down-to-earth. I was silent, but realised he had now saved our lives more than once. What a friend!

We fetched our bedrolls, lit a candle and went into the temple. In the centre of the hall was a dais and on it was a lifesize statue of a lady, made of silver and copper. The face, hair, hands and feet were of copper and the robes were silver, glinting in the candlelight. At her feet was a tiger, also made from silver and copper. Someone cared for this place; the flagstone floor was swept clean, the statue had been polished and some flowers had been offered.

'Do you think we should sleep here?' asked Ahren.

'Yes,' I replied, 'as long as we're respectful.'

'I agree,' added Lee. 'Let's bed down behind that marble tracery, so if anyone does come we won't be seen. Asha, you go that side of the statue and we'll be here.'

'Let's say a short prayer, that we can somehow meet up with this Rajay Ghiry,' I proposed.

'You're hopeful,' Lee replied.

'Yes, I am. That's what my name means – hope – remember?'

We duly knelt in front of the statue and I made the request on behalf of all of us, after which we laid out our bedrolls. Lee and Ahren were soon sound asleep, but I just tossed and turned. The more I looked at the statue, the more invigorated I felt. After a while I noticed something in the doorway. At first it looked like a large dog or pony, but then I saw the silhouette clearly. It was a tiger. I clutched at the key around my neck and it turned to look directly at me, hidden behind the tracery. It walked towards me and stopped close by, on the other side of the marble screen. It had a gold collar and I realised it was a guardian tiger. Meeting it here did not surprise me; when I saw the statue of the tiger, I was reminded of them. I stood up quietly, put a shawl around my shoulders and went towards it. It took my shawl in its mouth and led me out of the temple, through the ruined gateway and into the rocks at the side of the valley. The moons were all nearly full, making it a very bright night.

Behind one of the rocks it began digging, and after pushing some stones aside, revealed a sword in a scabbard inlaid with gold and decorated with rubies and sapphires, with the twelve petalled flower of the fourth subtle centre embossed on the hilt. The tiger picked it up in its mouth and gave it to me. It was magnificent, and I drew the sword out of its scabbard. As I did so I felt a gust of cooling wind flow over me and it seemed to come from the sword. There was some writing on the blade in the classic language, which I could now understand, and just about read, in the bright moons' light: 'The sword of the rightful king of Daish Shaktay, by the grace of the goddess who protects his land. May all those faithful to him swear allegiance on this blade, symbol of his right and fitness to rule, as the instrument of truth and justice.' There was more, but that was enough for me to realise the tiger had given me something incredibly important.

While I read this the tiger disappeared. 'So,' I thought, 'I've been given this beautiful sword, we know who we have to find, and he might even be in the district, but however are we to put it all together?' I decided to wait until morning, when I could talk to the others, and returned to my bedroll.

Later I heard voices and some young men came in. They were tough, unshaven and walked fearlessly. Not the sort you'd want to get on the wrong side of. They carried weapons, and their clothes, although worn and dirty, were of good quality. I was well hidden, but was scared. Were these the troopers? Were they bandits? Their vibrations were very cool, I knew we were safe and my fear was replaced by curiosity.

Lee and Ahren woke up immediately, but like me kept dead still behind the marble latticework so as not to be seen. The moons' light filtered through the doorway and we watched. The young men laid their weapons reverently at the feet of the statue and knelt in obeisance, then stood up and one, presumably their leader, turned to face them. He was medium to tall in height and his piercing eyes lit up his face when he smiled. My inner Tree of Life jumped as if in recognition when I put my attention on him, and I felt his subtle heart centre: brave, powerful, compassionate. I recognised that face – I'd seen it in my dream of the ambush. He was the person who had been kneeling over his fallen comrade.

'Those of us here tonight are party to a solemn oath,' he began. We looked at each other from behind our screen. 'We swear, before this image of the goddess who protects Daish Shaktay, that we will not rest until we have freed the whole of our country from its wrongful rulers, or died in the attempt.' The others solemnly repeated his words. 'It's been dangerous to come this far north, but only with divine help can we succeed. Let's get some sleep now. The old guesthouse by the gate is a good place. I'll take the first watch and stay in here.' Although his attitude was relaxed, he was evidently used to giving orders. Another young warrior stepped forward; I later learnt his name was Danard.

'We must make another oath, that we'll accept Rajay as our leader until he releases us from his service, or we die in the attempt to make him crowned king of a free Daish Shaktay.' They all made this second promise and I remembered the writing on the sword.

I looked at Lee and Ahren, and assumed they would stand up and introduce themselves, but Lee indicated we should watch and wait a bit longer. The young men, meanwhile, took their weapons and left, apart from Rajay Ghiry, who sat down cross-legged in front of the statue. He had dark hair, a dignified, straight nose and a determined chin, at present covered with a ragged beard, and on his cheeks was a thick stubble. I also noticed his hands, with their long, strong fingers resting palm upwards on his legs. He radiated a feeling of absolute peace, joy and benevolence; his outer appearance was that of a hardened partisan and his inner self that of a saint. Some time passed and I wondered what to do, not wanting to disturb his serene meditation. Lee solved the problem. He dropped off to sleep again and turned noisily. Rajay Ghiry was instantly alert and grabbed his sword from in front of the statue. I was sure he wouldn't harm me so I stood up and walked out from behind the marble grill holding the sword I had been given, bowed to him and presented it. He looked at me in amazement.

'What a gift! My prayer has been answered. I was praying for guidance, for some sign,' and he took the sword.

'Please, unsheathe the sword and read the writing on the blade,' I asked shyly. He did so.

'It's too dark to read in here,' he pointed out sensibly. 'What does it say?'

'It's for the king of Daish Shaktay. That's you, isn't it?'

'Yes, if I'm worthy to be so,' he stared at the blade in wonder. 'Are you an angel, or something?' He looked at me with a hint of a smile. I wasn't looking very angelic – my hair was unbraided and fell untidily down my back, and my travel stained shawl covered the long cotton shift, frayed and worn, that I always wore at night.

'No way, that, she is most definitely not!' grinned Ahren, standing up. He and Lee came nearer, their hair tousled from sleep and not looking remotely threatening.

'We've come from Sasrar to help you. I'm Lee, this is my friend Ahren and my cousin Asha, Your Highness. She has a way of finding important things at the moment they're needed.'

'That's for sure! Call me Rajay. I'm hardly a king yet, only a freedom fighter. But this sword! An old rhyme says a maiden will give a sword like this to the one destined to make our country great again. There's even a tiger mentioned.' He looked at the statue of the goddess with the tiger at her feet and reverently placed the sword at its base, then gave me the traditional blessing: 'Most auspicious lady, may you always bring such good fortune, in all places and at all times.' He put his right hand on his heart and bowed his head. I had just enough composure to give the expected reply.

'I bow to you too, my lord. May such blessings as you give return to you a hundredfold,' and also put my hand on my heart in the gesture of humility.

'You are my most honoured sister!' he smiled, broadly this time.

Rajay's friends heard our voices, came running to protect their leader and as they entered the temple he raised his hand, indicating we were not dangerous. 'The fact that we've found each other and this sword has come to me cannot be a coincidence,' he went on, and I felt a blast of coolness coming from the statue, or maybe from the sword lying in front of it.

'Where *on earth* did you get that sword from?' Lee took me aside and whispered.

'A tiger gave it to me.'

'I believe you, although not many would.'

The next morning I slept late and only woke up when Lee brought me a hot drink. Generally I was the cook and looked after the boys but today was an exception. I sat on the steps of the shrine and sipped the amber coloured tea, and noticed the young men had undergone quite a transformation. They were clean, had either shaved or their beards were neatly trimmed, and no longer looked like outlaws.

'We found a great bathroom near the monks' dormitory,' Ahren pointed to it. 'It's a cave with two little springs, one warm and one cold: hot and cold running water for a change! We're all finished there now, so you can go and clean up if you want.' I went off and as I passed the dormitory, now our stable, I overheard two of Rajay's friends talking together.

'Those lads are going to be a great help. They look like they can fight; no wonder Rajay was so pleased, but I don't know about the girl. She's a nice lass, but we'll have to leave her somewhere safe in the next few days,' commented the first, whose name was Varg-Nack. He was a strapping heavyweight and made even Lee look puny. He had light brown skin and his black hair was very short.

'Rajay was thrilled with the sword,' explained Valya, the other one, 'and it was the girl who gave it to him.' He was tall and slim, with dark brown hair and honey coloured skin, strong features and a sensitive expression that transformed into a shy smile.

At least someone is on my side, I thought gloomily, not relishing the idea of being offloaded on the first hospitable family we came across. I washed, was given some breakfast by one of Rajay's friends and decided to do a bit of exploring. I checked on the vibrations it was safe and set off through the gateway of the shrine and down the steep twisting track to a farmhouse some way below.

Rajay, who was an excellent climber, led Ahren and Lee up to a rocky ledge, high on the cliff beside the temple. He kept watch and talked to them, because they needed to get to know one another.

'Those horses,' began Ahren, 'some of the finest I've ever seen.'

'Yes,' replied Rajay nonchalantly, 'they were from the baggage train we took, part of the tribute from the Chussan brothers to the ogre king of Mattanga. The Mattanga thieves have stolen goodness knows how much from us, along with whole slices of my country itself, and the Chussan government encourages their raiders to attack our trading caravans. Now I've taken a little back. The money and precious stones should be safely at my capital, Malak Citadel, in Central Daish Shaktay by now, and I'll use some of the spoils to compensate our hard-pressed merchants they've almost bankrupted. We needed some decent horses and there they were, waiting to be taken. I've chosen that mouse-brown one with the black mane and tail - she's the fastest, most sure-footed and most intelligent animal I've ever ridden,' he paused for a moment, scanned the horizon, and then went on, 'I'm at war. So far it's a guerrilla war, but still a war. We'll go home via a family friend, Count Zaminder, who rules the area south of here. We'll leave Asha there, because I don't allow any girls or women on my campaigns, it's one of my strictest rules.' Lee caught Ahren's eye, because the vibrations had definitely indicated that I should go with them to Daish Shaktay. They didn't say anything though, and Rajay went on speaking.

He told them his family had ruled Daish Shaktay for generations, but the ogre people had invaded Mattanga, to the east, many years before and had recently overrun his land too. As they grew older they transformed from humans into a form that suited their nature, and many developed a scaly skin, little horns on the top of their heads, and so on by the time they were middle aged. These were the cruel, power loving individuals who played the same role as the Sorcerers in Teletsia. They made sure they stayed on top and everyone else suffered. Rajay's father had eventually given up opposing them and taken service under their king. In return he had been given back some of his depleted kingdom, provided he paid a heavy annual tribute. What remained of independent Daish Shaktay was ruled by Rajay's mother and the Council of Elders. This half-free land prospered but the northern part of the country, ruled by Mattanga, suffered under unjust laws and unbearable taxes.

'Two years ago,' Rajay continued, 'with the approval of the Elders and my mother, my friends and I started our guerrilla operations. Daish Shaktay has broad valleys intersected by lines of high hills. On many of these hilltops are forts, and whoever holds the forts controls the country. Even in the area administered by us, the Mattangans had put fort commanders sympathetic to them, but recently we've replaced them with men loyal to us. This soon came to the ears of the Mattanga king, far away on the shores of the Eastern Ocean. I meekly sent word to him saying I was improving the administration by placing more competent people in positions of power, but that excuse won't last long. Recently my father was murdered and I've come here not only to make the vow, but also to pray for guidance as to what to do next.'

'What *are* you going to do?' asked Ahren.

'I'm not sure.'

'When we came from Teletsia to Sasrar, we had advice from many wise people who are the spiritual guardians of the world.'

Rajay was silent for some moments, and scanned the ravine below. 'I'm also a guardian, but these ogres are powerful and it's going to be downright difficult to get rid of them. Plus I don't yet have a Key of Wisdom. I have to prove myself before I get one. My mother has the Daish Shaktay key at the moment.'

'The astrologers of northern Chussan asked us to come and help you. They wouldn't have sent us if it was impossible.'

'That's encouraging! One thing I'm certain, it's important to have a spiritual guide - for me, and especially for my friends. The knowledge of the Tree of Life and the vibrations are so much part of me that to know right from wrong is automatic, but they don't have this awareness yet. I'm waiting for some sign before I tell them. I operate from a deep level, the universal unconscious, in that I may not consciously know why I do something but it usually turns out for the best.'

Just then they saw a peasant girl staggering up the track in the ravine bottom. She had a brass pot on her head and was not walking with the usual rolling fluency of the country women. She entered the temple complex and put the pot clumsily on the ground, and they realised that it was me.

'Now what's she up to?' Lee sighed.

'Let's go and see,' Rajay didn't sound pleased.

I had bought milk, coffee and sugar, and gave my shopping to Witten, the cook. He was of medium height, had a plump, smiling face, narrow slanting eyes, a dark skin, shoulder length dark hair and a comfortably rounded body.

'Where have you been?' demanded Rajay. They had climbed down the cliff and I went to greet them.

'I've had a very productive morning,' I replied apprehensively, sensing something was not right. 'Let's go into the shade and I'll tell you.' We sat under a tree, which had grown up at the side of an old pool, its sides and bottom made of decaying masonry, meant for pilgrims to wash in before entering the temple. These days the pool was green and stagnant, but the tree enjoyed the moisture and we sat on the steps at the side, under its spreading branches.

'So?' continued Rajay sharply. I couldn't figure out what I'd done wrong.

'First I went to that farmhouse down the gully. After some bartering, and help from the farmer's wife, I came away dressed as a local woman. She gave me a skirt and a veil, and I bought that pot from her too. It's not so easy to carry them on one's head.'

'We noticed,' Lee smiled.

'And then?' Rajay glared at me.

'I went down to the village. The local costume was in case there were troopers around. It was a run down place, with a dozen or so single storey stone houses built round a square, and some more behind on the hillside. There were a few small terraced fields, hardly more than gardens, at the back of the houses, and a stone water trough in the square, presumably fed by a spring, and the excess water flowed down the side of the track to the valley. I went into the one shop and the shopkeeper asked who I was, so I said my family were visiting the temple and I'd come to buy food. As I was leaving, with a few things I had bought, I noticed some merchants arrive with cooking pots for sale, loaded in large baskets on the backs of mules. They laid their merchandise on the ground in the square and soon a number of people gathered round. The merchants told everyone the latest news before getting down to business. I walked over to where I could hear them.

'There are some Chussan troopers around,' the boss began. 'Not that they were interested in us. It's Rajay Ghiry they're after. Hopping mad they are, that he pinched all that stuff they were sending to Mattanga. I'd rather he had that loot than the ogre people. They call him the Mountain Mouse because he knows the country like the back of his hand and disappears into the hills when they try to catch him. They've offered a large reward for him, dead or alive.'

'I wouldn't give him away for all the gold in the world,' said a villager, 'I hope they never get him.'

'Have you heard of the great hermit who lives in the mountains south of here?' asked another merchant.

'Naturally,' replied a woman, 'what do you take us for? Dull-witted city folk who don't know what's important? It's because we have the holy temple up the hill, and that saintly hermit fair nearby that we have any peace around here at all.'

'One of his disciples is in Belar. He's well worth going to hear. What words of comfort he speaks, and how beautifully he sings the praises of our Creator!'

'How long is he there for?' asked another villager - prosperous, judging from his clothes and the fact he wore shoes.

'A week or two......' At this moment a man came running into the square.

'Tigers! Lots, at least twelve!' he shouted, and everyone stood up and prepared to make for cover.

'Calm down,' the prosperous villager urged, 'no one has seen any tigers around here for years.'

'I saw them with my own eyes. I was on the hill and looked into the ravine, where the road goes through it. A band of Chussan troopers came galloping up.....'

'When?'

'Just now, and suddenly these tigers appeared and attacked them. One man was wounded by them, and another two were hurt when they fell off their horses.'

'Where did the troopers go?'

'They turned around and galloped back down the road. The strangest part was that the tigers had golden collars around their necks.'

'You must have been seeing things,' joked a merchant. 'Wild tigers never have gold collars!'

'Don't be too sure,' said an older villager. 'I've heard there are magical ones guarding the temple.'

I finished my story, and continued speaking. 'Then I came back here, after I'd bought some nice fresh milk for all of you from the farmer's wife,' Rajay was still glaring at me.

'Asha, I have to talk to you. Come over here,' he demanded, and I followed him to the other side of the tree.

'Have I done something wrong?'

'Don't you realise how dangerous it was, going off by yourself like that?'

'No I….'

'If you'd been caught, we'd have had to rescue you. Didn't you understand the vows we made, or the writing on the sword? I'm fighting a war to get my country back, and it's not some childish game. Another of my vows is to protect women – and even foolish and irresponsible girls like you. Why do you make it even harder for me?'

'Asha, you'd better apologise,' Lee came up behind Rajay.

'You're going back to Sasrar as soon as I can arrange it. I *cannot* risk having you around at this time.'

'But I have a job to do in your country,' I persevered.

'The only job *you'll* do is to lose me the lives of some of my most trusted followers.' Rajay clearly saw me as immature, irresponsible and an added burden.

'I'm sorry,' I murmured, without conviction.

'You're not. You're in your ego, thinking you're right.'

'But -'

'But what?'

'I have to try to awaken the Tree of Life of your people in Daish Shaktay, and show them how to use its powers and blessings. Don't you want my help?'

'Not if you get us all killed.'

'Don't you understand how much it can change everything, if people's level of consciousness changes?'

'You've forgotten who you're talking to, Asha,' said Lee brusquely. 'Try to have some respect, at least.' At this moment, luckily, Witten arrived with a pan of hot, milky coffee and some horn cups.

'Thanks Witten. Leave it there,' said Rajay calmly. 'Ask Danard to come here immediately.'

'I'm sure Asha checked with her subtle power that it was safe to go to the village, right?' Lee tried to smooth things over.

'Yes, obviously,' I replied.

'So maybe Rajay will forgive you, if you promise not to go off alone again.'

'Indeed. What's done is done,' Rajay conceded. 'For all your rash behaviour, you've brought me the great news that we've been saved by the guardian tigers, and my prayer for a spiritual guide may also be answered.'

'You were right to be angry. I didn't realise the danger I was in, and the danger I've now put you all in. Please, have some coffee,' and I poured it out for him.

'Asha, you're too much!' Rajay laughed, accepting the coffee, and to the boys, with good natured resignation asked, 'How *do* you put up with her?'

'We're used to it,' sighed Ahren. 'We've learnt to accept each other's shortcomings by now.'

'What's going on?' Danard arrived at the run.

'Make sure everything is packed and hidden in the big cave,' Rajay ordered. 'Saddle the horses. We must have our weapons ready because there may be troopers around. We should be able to fight them off if they attack, because we can easily hold the ravine. I take it you two can use a bow and arrow, and a gun?'

'Well enough,' said Ahren modestly, considering he was the Sasrar archery champion.

'Actually, guns are too noisy, and take too long to reload. In case of attack, Asha, hide, and if it goes badly for us, escape when they've gone. The local partisans under that village headman will protect you.'

All was peaceful until early evening, by which time I had climbed up to the high vantage point with Lee, and was watching the track, which twisted down the valley. As it became cooler a wind got up and did make strange shrieking noises in the rocks, but it didn't bother us. Then I saw them – a dozen or so mounted troopers approaching fast, quite far away. I called to Danard, down below in the temple courtyard, and warned him.

'Lee, come and help us. We'll give you weapons,' he shouted back. 'Asha, stay up there, out of sight, and let us know when they're getting close.'

Within almost no time, all the young men were concealed behind rocks at the sides of the ravine in its narrowest place. Lee joined them. I did my bit and signalled when the troopers were nearby, but couldn't resist watching. As they came round the corner of the track, the tiger I had seen the night before jumped out from some rocks and swished its tail angrily, standing in the path of anyone approaching. It was dusk, and the troopers' horses skidded to a stop, panicked and shied, and maybe the troopers did not know there was only one tiger, not a whole group. The wind was making strange noises, also scaring both the troopers and their horses. One trooper saw me, jumped off his horse and began climbing the cliff up to where I was now attempting to hide.

The troopers in the front were momentarily distracted by the tiger. Rajay and his friends, concealed behind rocks in the poor light, shot them with arrows, silent and deadly. Ahren, lightning fast and unerringly accurate, brought down two. I screamed for help because I was about to be caught. Ahren looked up and aimed an arrow - that trooper probably never knew what had hit him – Ahren caught him in the heart, from behind, and another in the neck. Unfortunately as Ahren's attention was on saving me, one of the troopers charged him with a sword. I could not see what happened, only that it didn't look too good, but then Witten pulled the one attacking Ahren off his horse, and killed him, also with a sword. It was all very confusing but soon the leading troopers were done for, and those behind turned round and fled. The tiger also disappeared.

Rajay's friends looked at their fallen enemies, and I noticed the heavyweight, Varg-Nack, casually finish off one who was still alive. I didn't feel right about this, but it could easily have been us, and from what Robin had told me of these types, our fate would have been the same if they had been the victors.

'Are you all right?' Lee called up to me.

'Yes, thanks to Ahren,' I stuttered as I climbed down to join them, shaken and scared. Ahren was nursing a slight wound and Rajay looked at it, and asked Valya to fetch the medicine and bandages bag.

'You've got good bodyguards,' Danard said to me with a smile, by way of complimenting Lee and Ahren. 'And we'll also do our best to keep you safe.'

'Those troopers were quite pathetic, the way they ran off,' added Witten, cleaning his sword. 'You three didn't see us at our best. It was hardly a fight, even.'

'Easy, Witten, we could all have been done for. It's lucky they were such cowards,' cautioned Rajay, while tending Ahren's arm. 'That tiger made all the difference! He appeared at exactly the right moment,'

'You're good at this – how come?' asked Ahren, as Rajay worked at his wound with confident efficiency.

'I've had to learn how to kill people, so decided to also learn a bit about healing them too. Keep still, or I might hurt you. We'll leave for Count Zaminder's right now, in case the troopers come back with reinforcements. I wanted to wait until tomorrow, and give the horses a full day's rest, but it's not safe. We've got some extra ones and we'll travel fast, so you'd better let your ponies loose. Asha, can you ride a warhorse?'

'I'll try. We stole some Sorcerers' horses and escaped from Teletsia on them.'

'Really? You have the makings of a partisan.'

CHAPTER 3

VISITING THE ZAMINDERS

We left soon after, taking a narrow, winding pass through the mountains in the moons' light so as to avoid the main road through the plain. Riding a powerful horse throughout the night was no joke, and we must have covered a good three or four days' walking distance. The country was dry and deserted and the track was often steep and rough, so my horse stumbled occasionally, nearly throwing me off. Our new friends took turns to lead the way as they had come by that route the day before, and I had never been so tired as I was the next morning, but I wasn't going to admit it to anyone, least of all Rajay.

At dawn we reached the pleasant valley where Count Zaminder lived, in the hills north of Belar, the town where the hermit was staying. As we approached the Zaminder's estate we stopped in a wood some way before the gatehouse, and could see their home in the distance, at the end of a driveway through fields. Danard went to see if everything was alright and we watched him ride on ahead, cautiously. He was taller than Rajay, and they both had dark hair and dark eyes, but Rajay's skin was lighter. Danard's face was angular and his features were sharper, but nevertheless sometimes people mistook them for relations.

'Danard is like a brother to you,' Lee observed while we waited.

'Yes, we spent time together as children,' replied Rajay, 'when I was about six years old, the Mattanga forces were, as usual, giving my mother and me a hard time. This was before my father gave up fighting them, so my mother and I were always moving from one fort to another for safety. Danard's father hid me on his farm in the hills for some time and people thought I was his cousin. He's a bit older than me, and Namoh is his brother, three years younger.' I looked at Namoh, standing by his horse and talking to Ekan. Namoh had the same sharp features as Danard, but was wirier, as if he hadn't finished growing and would fill out in a year or two. 'Here's Danard; it's safe to go on,' continued Rajay, who as always was keeping a sharp eye on the road ahead.

The Zaminder family lived in a low stone house behind their fort, that was kept ready in case it was needed. Their staff, including a small army, lived in cottages up and down the valley. Count Zaminder ruled this area, but the ogres

23

of Mattanga and the Chussan brothers both claimed to be his overlords. A crowd of people greeted us in the yard at the front of the fort, because Rajay was a celebrity round here. We were introduced to the count, a paunchy man in late middle age with an enormous moustache, a beard, straggly greying hair, mid brown skin and a somewhat fearsome expression. We also met Countess Zaminder, a jolly, roly-poly lady with lots of chins who looked as if she could keep her husband in order, if anyone could; their tall, well-built son Bukku and their daughter Melissa, a pretty girl of about my age with a pale skin, a warm smile and a mop of curly reddish-brown hair. In colouring she took after her mother.

I was dead tired, and was only too happy when she showed me to a comfortable bedroom in the house, which was built round a courtyard, with delicate wooden balconies on the inner side, flowers and fruit trees in large pots and a chuckling fountain in the middle. Rajay and the others stayed in the fort; he expected them to be able to live anywhere. I collapsed on a bed just as I was, and the next thing I knew was Melissa, knocking on the door and asking to come in.

'I've brought you some herbal tea. It's afternoon,' she said, standing over me with a mug in her hand. 'Would you like to borrow some clothes?'

'That's very kind.'

'I've got masses you can choose from, and some I've never worn.'

We were instant friends, and I was soon wearing a pale yellow dress with a long skirt and colourfully embroidered sleeves: a gift, Melissa insisted. Around my neck I had my golden key of Sasrar with its many jewels winking from the petals, and she gaped at its beauty. I knew its potent vibrations would have a good effect on her, so took it off for her to look at. After this, she suggested we go outside, as it was pleasantly cool, and she took me to her large herb garden behind the house.

'Lee told me you know a great deal about herbs,' she began, as we sat on a stone bench under a tree.

'Yes, but you grow different ones here from either Teletsia, where I used to live, or Sasrar, where I've been recently.'

We talked on. She had a good feeling when I put my attention on her inner side, and I wanted to give her awakening, as the astrologers had asked me to. I prayed to the great Mother of the primordial Tree of Life to inspire me.

'Can you feel the joy of the plants and flowers, as they bask in the sunlight?' I asked.

'Yes, and I wish I had that joy within me. It's not easy living here, never knowing when the next gang of soldiers is going to attack us and maybe wipe us out completely. My two older brothers were killed last year, leading our little army against one from Jewelton.'

'I'm sorry, it must have been a great shock,' I paused, but she did not reply, so I went on, 'In Teletsia my life was also full of insecurity and fears, and then I discovered I did have that peace, hidden away inside. I can show you how to find it within you, if you like.'

'Really and truly?'

'That's what I've learnt in the secret kingdom of Sasrar. We all have an inner Tree of Life, with seven subtle centres, like jewels of power or spiritual flowers at different points up our back, and in our head, and they each have a special beautiful quality that you can start to live once it's awakened. Put your right hand on your heart, and your left hand outwards, palm upwards. Ask, "Am I pure, eternal spirit, full of joy and peace?"'

'All right, I'll go along with that.' Melissa was surprised, but eager to try and did so.

'Keep your eyes closed, put your right hand on top of your head and ask, "All loving Mother of Creation, You who are reflected in me, please awaken my Tree of Life, and let me be a conscious part of the whole, and feel that thoughtless peace and joy."' As she did this, I raised my hands up behind her back, rotated my right hand in a clockwise direction above her head, and the air just above her felt cool, even in this warm garden.

'Put your hand above your head. Do you feel a cool breeze?'

'Yes, and I feel peaceful and still.'

'That coolness means you are now consciously connected to the power that created us, and you can find that inner peace any time you want, by putting your attention on the top of your head and letting the thoughts float away.'

'It's so easy! Is there more to it?'

'Lots, but later, we have company.' Danard and Valya came towards us.

'I hear you're a great herb gardener, Melissa,' Danard began.

'I'm learning.'

'Back home on our herb farm, we do a great deal of research,' said Valya. 'Will you show us round? Danard is a farmer, and he also understands plants.'

Valya had been the heir to vast estates in Daish Shaktay, but his father, who collaborated with King Karlvid of Mattanga, had disowned him for joining Rajay. I left them with Melissa and went to find Lee and Ahren. They were in the main hall of the house, practising music on some instruments. Since living in Sasrar, a land where music flowed constantly, like the ever-present waterfalls, we had learnt to sing, play and dance quite well.

'You're looking nice,' Lee complimented me.

'The dress was a present from Melissa. And guess what, I just showed her how to awaken her Tree of Life.'

'That's brilliant!' Ahren congratulated me.

'The first to be awakened by someone who's not a guardian, and not in Sasrar,' added Lee. 'Good for you.'

'There's a big do for Rajay this evening,' said Ahren. 'We've been asked to play some music. That's why we're practising.'

'Could you try to awaken the people's Trees of Life? You know how we learnt to do it through music in Sasrar?' I suggested.

'Since you've already awakened Melissa's, you should do it,' Lee replied.

'All right, but you do the talking,' I was desperately nervous of speaking in front of a crowd. It was bad enough to be asked to play and sing.

'No problem.'

'Lee and I had better go and spruce ourselves up,' Ahren grinned.

'What about your arm wound?'

'It's fine. I had a narrow escape.'

'I know, I was watching.'

'Rajay warned me that one must always be very careful of an unexpected counter attack like that. He's going to teach us a lot.'

'I sincerely hope he is. I don't want to lose either of you. By the way, is he still angry with me?'

'He wasn't angry with you, just concerned for your safety, but you were an idiot, going off like that,' added Lee.

'Mmn, I can see that now.'

'He felt responsible for you, like, if anything had happened, he'd have blamed himself. He's a caring soul underneath that tough exterior.'

'How's the fort?' I changed the subject.

'Noisy and smelly,' Ahren put in, 'because they keep masses of animals in the yard there - cows, horses, hounds and so on. We're upstairs, but we're partisans now, so who's to complain about a little discomfort?'

In the evening Rajay wore rich brocade clothes and a jewelled turban. Dinner was in the Great Hall, and he had the seat of honour, covered with a silken rug of many colours. He, his friends, we three and the men of the Zaminder family sat at a high table on a raised dais at the top end of the hall. The tall ceiling was vaulted stonework and the walls were decorated with frescoed battle scenes. There were lines of lighted candles on high ledges around the walls, and behind each of them was a simple mirror, which reflected the candlelight out into the room. A large number of men, women and children sat at long trestle tables, waiting for the feast to begin and eager to catch a glimpse of the young king.

'We are grateful that you visit us again, Your Majesty,' began Count Zaminder.

The Countess and Melissa served Rajay first, with an assortment of exotically spiced and flavoured dishes: venison, mountain goat, roasted birds, and all the usual vegetable accompaniments, and when he complimented them on the delicious food, the reply was, 'It's our pleasure, if only we could do more.' Although the hospitality was spontaneous, Rajay was also their lifeline. If he could re-establish a strong Daish Shaktay they could become protected allies.

'I'd like to visit a holy man who's in Belar at the moment,' he mentioned to Count Zaminder.

'He's called Baktar – we all respect him enormously. Might it not be safer to invite him up here?'

'Let's try.'

When the tasty desserts had been served and eaten, and the meal was finished, the trestle tables were taken down and everyone sat on the floor. There was a call for music and we listened to Melissa, who played a stringed instrument, sitting on the dais where the high table had previously been. The rhythm and melody combined perfectly and we experienced an inner dancing joy; she later said that since I had awakened her Tree of Life, her playing was transformed.

Next we were called up onto the dais. Lee played his flute, Ahren was on the two-toned drum and I played Melissa's instrument. We sang songs from Sasrar about the awakening of the Tree of Life; they had catchy tunes, and soon everyone joined in the rousing, easy choruses - including the Zaminder's staff, Rajay's friends and the families of the locals.

'Let's see how many of them have got it,' said Lee. We stopped singing and he stood up. 'Can we do an experiment? In Sasrar we use music to awaken the eternal spirit within us. That's what those songs were about. Stretch your hands above your heads and ask, "Is this the power of divine love?" If we feel coolness flowing on our hands – that's how the power says 'yes' to us. Do any of you feel it?'

There was an ominous silence.

'I feel it, like a fresh mountain wind on my hands, and such peace and joy!' Rajay came to our rescue, and then it started.

'Yes, I feel it too!' or 'Isn't it wonderful?' and the hall was full of excited voices and shining faces and sparkling eyes.

When the evening drew to a close, Rajay came over to me. 'Lee told me you began this by giving awakening to Melissa. They got it well, didn't they? I could feel the coolness from them, but none of them dared speak up, so I helped you along a bit.'

'Thank you. I hope we did the right thing.'

'Obviously! That's your role. It was a surprise for me, that your music could touch their souls. Will you do this in Daish Shaktay?'

'Yes, that's why I came, but I apologise for being so disrespectful yesterday.'

'Forget it! If there's one thing I admire, it's people with depth and courage, like you three have,' he bowed slightly, gave me a kindly smile and said goodnight.

I breathed a sigh of relief.

CHAPTER 4

FINDING A MASTER

The next morning Ekan and Ahren set off for the town of Belar on borrowed horses, as theirs were resting, to invite the saint up to the Zaminder's. They rode down the valley, enjoying the scenery – houses here and there surrounded by fields on the flatter valley floor and orchards on the slopes. Above were higher hills covered with forest, and as they approached the town these were replaced by a broader valley which opened out onto a plain. They were leading an extra horse for the saint, but all the horses were very badly behaved. They tossed their heads, started at every bird that flew by, and snorted and suddenly stopped in their tracks every now and again, for no apparent reason. Their riders, both competent horsemen, coaxed them on and assumed they would soon settle down.

Ekan told Ahren about his friendship with Rajay as they rode. Like Danard, he had known Rajay from childhood. He was strong and fit, with a prominent nose, reddish hair and the coppery skin of the people who lived in the lands on the eastern coasts now ruled by the ogres. His mother's family had fled from there to Daish Shaktay. Rajay and Ekan had been on many escapades when they were boys, such as pursuing a leopard that had turned man-eater into the rocky crags above Santara in Daish Shaktay. Later they helped clear the land of a terrible plague of wolves that appeared one winter and scared the farmers horribly by attacking their animals and even their children. They oversaw hunting parties which had finally got these creatures down to manageable numbers. Like Ahren, Ekan understood animals, but whereas Ahren was especially good with horses and donkeys, Ekan was more interested in dogs.

By the time they reached Belar they realised all three horses were hopelessly unruly beasts. They found Baktar sitting in a shady grove outside the town and Ahren recognised him as one of the followers of the mountain hermit he had met two years before. He was wore simple white cotton clothes, had grey hair, a wispy beard and a kindly smile. He was talking to a crowd of people, but broke off when he saw them.

'One of the Teletsian boys! What a change!' he cried. 'What brings you to

Belar?' They tied their horses to a hitching post and went up to him. Ahren explained, in an undertone, that they were from Rajay Ghiry.

'He humbly begs you visit him at the Zaminder's,' said Ekan.

'If he wants to see me, he can come here,' Baktar was adamant.

'It was felt it might be dangerous.'

'He'll be all right.'

At this moment their horses created a major disturbance. Ahren ran to help, but nothing would calm them. Baktar, who was not only short and slim but also had a slight limp, fearlessly went up to them, their hooves and teeth flashing viciously. The moment he approached them they became still.

'I'm not a fighting man,' he explained. 'Even these fierce creatures become docile in my presence. Tell Rajay Ghiry that if he comes to see me, no harm will come to him.' Baktar returned to his seat and the horses started to misbehave again, so Ekan and Ahren left as quickly as possible.

'That was a complete failure,' observed Ahren once they were alone.

'Here, you lead this extra horse,' added Ekan gloomily. 'It's a bit less awful when you take it.'

They returned to the Zaminders and the following day Rajay, his friends and we three from Sasrar went down to Belar. When we reached the grove, Rajay went up to Baktar and knelt before him.

'Young man,' he began, 'I've heard about your courage and high ideals, but you must never forget you are only the instrument of the Goddess of Daish Shaktay. You can contact her through quiet meditation and only then you will be able to help your country.'

'I understand that, but I need your advice,' Rajay replied, and they talked together for some time. The rest of us stood back, watching respectfully.

'Rajay is a man of action, not a recluse,' I whispered.

'Baktar's not telling him to withdraw from the world,' Lee replied, but I wasn't so sure, especially as the day wore on and Rajay continued to sit reverently at the feet of the saint. In the afternoon Lee, Ahren and I went to a shop to buy some food, and a young girl was serving.

'I don't believe it!' cried Ahren.

'You've grown up!' said the girl. She was about twelve years old, wore a bright red dress with multicoloured embroidery on the hem and sleeves, had long black hair braided in a plait down her back, and a light skin. Her dark eyes had a depth about them, and she looked long and hard at the two boys.

'Great to see you again,' smiled Lee.

'Hey! Let me in on this,' I begged, puzzled.

'This is Pulita, who saved my life when I was bitten by the snake,' Ahren grinned.

'If you're going to be here for the evening,' she went on, 'you'd better come and stay the night. Mum and dad, who own this shop, would be happy to have you. The Zaminders have a house here, but maybe you'd like to be with us.'

'Ahren and I had better stay with – our leader,' concluded Lee tactfully, 'but I'm sure Asha would love to.'

Later we listened to Baktar singing devotional songs until past midnight, after which I went to stay with Pulita and the boys went with Rajay and his friends to the Zaminder's house. Unknown to them, a man who was an informer for the Chussan troopers left town for the north, to look for them and tell them about Rajay, because word had got around about his identity.

'I want to sit alone in the forest,' said Rajay the next morning. 'Don't disturb me.' He walked off into the trees, the beginning of the wooded foothills behind Belar that stretched to the mountains south of the town. He spent the day there and went to listen to Baktar in the evening. The next day was the same, so his friends and we three had a serious discussion.

'Now what?' asked Ahren. 'We didn't come all the way from Sasrar to watch Rajay meditate.'

'It may be a passing phase,' Ekan explained. 'He's a fighter, but there's another side to him. We lost one of our group recently and he took it very hard. It may be something to do with that.'

'I made an oath to fight, if necessary to the death, to free Daish Shaktay,' said Varg-Nack. 'That's not going to happen if he's sitting meditating. Those Chussan troopers might find us and Rajay's a sitting duck. He'll never win back his country without some fighting and deep down he knows it. He may be the elusive Mountain Mouse, but he shouldn't push his luck too far. The troopers are after our blood and won't give up in a hurry. I heard in the town this morning that there's a price on all our heads, especially Rajay's.'

'Let's leave him be for a day or two, and keep a sharp eye out for the enemy,' suggested Danard. 'The only one who can influence him is Baktar, or possibly his mother, so we'll send her a message. She's fairly near here, trying to arrange an alliance between us and a warlord, Lord Chandan of Jewelton. She knows we were going to the Temple-in-the-Mountains, and said she would try to stay in the district in case we needed her help.' Ekan, the best rider of Rajay's friends, rode off at speed to find Queen Jansy.

The next day Pulita's mother cooked a feast of a lunch for us – rabbits roasted with herbs, vegetables from their garden, an open tart filled with berries from the forest, bread, cheeses and a home made cordial flavoured with the white flowers of a bush that grew profusely in this area. Pulita took some out to Rajay, who was sitting cross legged under a tree, his back against the trunk. She quietly put the food down, spread a cloth, laid out the meal with love and care, then stayed nearby to make sure no animals or birds helped themselves, because Rajay was deep in meditation, his eyes closed and his expression peaceful.

'This is too much! Is this all for me?' he asked, opening his eyes.

'Yes, Your Highness,' she got up to serve him.

'I'm trying to be a recluse and you've brought me a feast.'

'That's because you're a king. We know you're going to free our lands of our enemies. We've heard what a brave fighter you are and how clever you are. At last someone's going to help Count Zaminder!' Rajay smiled, which she took as an indication to go on. In fact he was thinking she was an innocent child who was merely repeating what she had heard from her elders. 'My great uncle, the hermit in the mountains, says that if a man has taken his birth as a king, the only way he can please God is to protect all the good people, even if he has to kill the bad ones to do it.' She paused, then added, 'I wouldn't like to be a king.'

'I have to be ruthless sometimes. It's not so bad when the enemy is evil and murderous, but when my own people suffer and my friends get killed…. that's why I'm here in the forest, praying I won't have to do it any more.'

Pulita jumped up to chase away a crow which was trying to steal some food. She felt she had said too much and they were both silent. He finished his meal, after which she cleared it up and quietly withdrew. Rajay knew that the most unlikely people sometimes bring important counsel and he pondered her words. Nevertheless he returned to his meditation.

I continued to stay with Pulita's family and we moved some brooms, buckets and coils of rope out of a back room to make a place for me to sleep. In the daytime the boys and Rajay's friends stayed as close to him as they could, in an effort to guard him. We didn't waste our time. Rajay's friends soon found out that Ahren was the best archer they had ever seen and the most accurate shot with a gun, whereas Lee had an extremely strong wrist when he used a sword and was virtually unbeatable in hands-on fighting. He always seemed to know what his opponent was going to do next and had the edge on everyone, even Witten, who knew some extraordinary wrestling tricks. When the boys tried to work out why they were so effective, they came to the conclusion that it was because of their state of mind.

'It's like this,' said Ahren. 'When I aim an arrow, my mind is free of thoughts and I'm totally one with that still, powerful attention. I only see the target. Nothing else exists for me at that moment and I rarely miss.'

'I also go into a still, thoughtless state,' added Lee, 'and something seems to guide me to defeat my opponent.'

As a result Lee and Ahren had a group of tough partisans wanting to know how to use the powers of the Tree of Life. Rajay meditated by sitting on the ground with his hands on his knees, palms upwards and we explained that now their Trees of Life were awake, they could feel as good as he looked if they did the same. The boys told them to sit like this, close their eyes and put their attention on the top of their heads and let any thoughts float away, and showed them how to reawaken their inner subtle selves. They were to place both their hands in front of them, at the level of the base of the backbone, then raise them up and twirl them round each other as they rose. Then they were to make a gesture like tying a piece of string on the top of their heads. Lee demonstrated how to protect the subtle energy and prevent any negativity affecting them.

'Watch,' he put his left hand out with the palm upwards and with the right hand made an arc over his body, seven times each way. 'Now you try. That's more or less it, Danard. No Valya! Ahren, show him.'

Although they were brilliant fighters, they did some mighty strange things when waving their hands around. Eventually they grasped it, but the only one who got it immediately was Pulita, who had also come to join us. They took it very seriously, especially Valya and Namoh, and the boys promised that if they did this every day they would start to develop the still, sharp attention and lightning fast reactions they both had.

That night I had a dream. Rajay was on a throne in a large hall and someone came in and gave him bad news. He looked at me with a commanding expression and said, 'Have you taught my friends the bandhan of request?' I replied that I hadn't. 'Then please do. They're going to need all the help they can get.'

The next day we were again in a forest clearing, the young men surreptitiously guarding Rajay, who they could see sitting deeper into the trees. They were resting after shooting practice.

'Meditation time,' I called out hopefully. No one took much notice and they went on talking to each other.

'Right everyone,' Danard took over, 'this morning Rajay told me we should listen to Asha. She comes from a place where girls also tell folk about this spiritual wisdom, so I know it isn't our tradition for women to do this, but I guess times are changing.' They gathered round, seated in a circle on the ground. It had not occurred to me before that this was unusual, because in Sasrar everyone: boys and girls, men and women, knew how to share the wisdom of the Tree of Life. I was shy with Rajay's friends, but realised they would do what he asked.

'I'll show you something else really useful, called the bandhan of request.' I demonstrated what Robin had shown us long ago and which we had used hundreds of times since. 'It only works if what you ask is in tune with the flow of creation. Write something on the palm of your left hand that you want to happen, or the name of someone you want to help, with your right index finger. Then make a circle in the air above the left hand, with your right one. Witten, go clockwise or it means the reverse. The longer you go on circling, the deeper you go, like a deep pool of desire and divine love.'

I wondered how many of them asked something about Rajay. Initially it was as much as I could do to figure out their names, but now I began to see them as individuals. Danard had something approaching hero worship for Rajay and although the others had great respect for him, I felt they had taken the oath in the temple primarily because they realised he alone could help them free their country. Maybe I was wrong – only time would tell. Valya and Namoh

were interested in the wisdom of the Tree of Life for its own sake and not
because it would make them more effective partisans. Valya could have been
a Teletsian; he had such a strong awareness of the divine power as manifested
through the Mother Earth and Namoh had a dogged determination, even though
he was overshadowed by his elder brother Danard.

By this time Ekan had managed to locate Queen Jansy. Like all Rajay's
childhood friends, he had known her for years and she was delighted to see
him. Ekan's family, comfortable farmers from the south of Daish Shaktay, did
not approve of his having joined Rajay, but the queen was right behind this
young man who had given up an easy life to serve her son. When she heard
his news she was very concerned.

'Rajay is the only one who can lead our people to freedom! He was born
to fight and there's no other way he can regain the kingdom from Karlvid of
Mattanga. Surely Baktar understands this? I'll come at once.'

Queen Jansy did not like riding horses but on this occasion she, Ekan and
a few trusted bodyguards rode as quickly as possible to Belar, where after
nearly a week nothing had changed. She met Baktar and greeted him with great
respect. She was an elegant lady of medium height and build, her long, thick,
dark hair was lightly streaked with silver, and she had the same straight nose,
determined chin and piercing but compassionate eyes as her son, but her skin
was fairer. She wore a simple but elegant brown cotton dress with long sleeves
and a high neck, which reached to the ground, and no jewellery that I could
see. Whereas Rajay radiated enthusiasm and confidence, she had a wistfulness
about her.

'Your songs of praise are beautiful and your lectures are inspiring,' she
complimented Baktar, 'but my son must turn the Mattanga invaders out of our
lands. Who else can unite our country? Who else has the intelligence to outwit
our enemies, and the charisma and courage to lead our people?'

'Your Highness,' replied Baktar, 'I'll speak to him tonight.'

'If you can put him back on the path of action, I'll never be able to thank
you enough.'

Word got around about this conversation and the evening programme was
well attended. There was thunder in the air, so it was held in the local temple,
a large building with only one entrance. When everyone was settled, seated on
the floor or on benches round the walls, Baktar asked for quiet so he could
speak. Rajay was in a corner at the front near Lee and Ahren. I had come in
late with Queen Jansy and we sat at the back with the local ladies.

'Today,' Baktar began, 'is the festival when we celebrate how the all
merciful Creator has made the different parts of the world, animals and people
in a perfectly interlocking pattern. When He made the universe, He assigned
various duties to different people. No one can attain eternal salvation, or even
inner peace, if they don't do their allotted duty. What would happen if a bird

suddenly decided to live in a cave and never came out into the light, or a tiger curled up, refused to hunt any more and expected the deer to come willingly to it?' As he said this he looked at Rajay, who was keenly aware of his gaze.

Baktar invited everyone to start singing. Ahren, Lee and I, along with Ekan, who played a wooden xylophone and Namoh, who had a perfect sense of rhythm with small hand-held cymbals, went to the front to provide the accompaniment. Baktar called Rajay over and spoke quietly to him.

'My son, a king should not hesitate to attack, conquer and if necessary kill the enemy if his country is threatened, and he must protect his subjects. Only then can he know fulfilment, like a father who sees his family contented and prosperous. Not for you the seclusion of the forest; you were born to free Daish Shaktay.'

'But I need a spiritual guide. A king must always bow before a true saint, and accept his advice.'

'I'm giving you advice. I'm not the one for you.' Here Baktar was interrupted by Danard, who had been standing outside the temple keeping an eye out for anyone hostile, and now struggled through the people to the front.

'Rajay,' he whispered, 'Chussan troopers are surrounding the temple. They know you're here. I overheard their leader, he said, "If we can't single out Rajay Ghiry, we'll kill the lot. It'll be like killing chickens in a hen run."'

'I'll give myself up.'

'Don't say or do anything, or everyone will panic,' Baktar ordered and told us musicians to stop playing. He took up his stringed instrument and sang in a loud, clear voice.

'Oh Lord, have mercy on these men who know not what they do,
As for myself, I have no fear, for I am one with You.
But if these others suffer pain, I cannot bear the sight,
And if our praise is not complete, my heart is sad as night.
And so, Great God, make haste to help, and save us from our plight.'

He closed his eyes in prayer. I made a bandhan on my hand, noticed Lee and Ahren doing the same, and interestingly Namoh. The vibrations were cool and strong. 'Our prayers are answered. Musicians, go on. It will be all right,' Baktar declared.

I concentrated on the music to try and quell my fear, but my hands shook as I played. I could not see Rajay and assumed he had gone back to his place. I wished I had not heard the conversation. Ahren made another bandhan on his hand and indicated to me that it was cool but I couldn't help wondering if it had been suicidal to leave the safety of Sasrar. The melody flowed, the drums throbbed and over a hundred voices rose in praise of the Creator, but outside something very different was going on.

Pulita's mother had been feeling hot in the temple and was sitting across the street under a veranda, fanning herself. To her horror she saw the soldiers approach the door of the temple and prepare to enter. They got off their horses and drew their swords. She was about to run round the back of the building, then she saw a young man, seemingly Rajay, leap from a window at its side. He dropped onto the back of a white horse she hadn't noticed before.

'May the tigers who guard me destroy you!' he shouted, and galloped off.

'That's him, the Ghiry boy!' yelled the soldiers, who jumped on their horses and charged after him. Their pounding hooves woke some of the dogs of Belar, who joined in merrily and barked the soldiers out of town.

Every now and again the soldiers caught sight of the white horse and took a shot at its rider, but none of the bullets or arrows found their mark. They careered down the main road to the south. It led through woodland and open fields, over a hilltop of dry grassland, then into trees again, and much later the fugitive took a track through the woodland in the foothills which led up to the high mountains to the southeast. The chase went on and on, and the track led over more hills and valleys, into thicker and thicker forest, and slowly the soldiers gained on their victim. The animals were tiring but the soldiers raked their sides with spurs to urge them on. They saw the white horse turn off the track into the forest and crashed after him. Some horses fell, their feet entangled in roots, and some soldiers were thrown off when branches whipped back in their faces or across their bodies.

The white horse stopped. They could see its hide glinting under a tree, its sides heaving with exhaustion and flecked with foam. But where was Rajay Ghiry? Ahead towered a steep cliff, rising above the trees, a narrow path clinging to its side. 'May the tigers who guard me destroy you!' a figure taunted from above.

'There he is! Up the cliff!' ordered the captain. 'Leave the horses here while we kill him!' They scrambled up, looking for footholds, but instead found thorn bushes, loose rocks and even the occasional furious scorpion. The soldiers' hands were sore and bleeding and still they hadn't caught the Mountain Mouse. Down below their horses took fright and galloped off, so whatever happened the soldiers were in for an extremely long walk home. When they reached the top of the cliff they glimpsed the man they were chasing darting through the distant trees.

'Now we'll have him!' they shouted, and staggered after him.

The chase went on but soon the fugitive was exhausted, and collapsed on the ground by the side of a stream, under a waterfall. Sunrise was near, the darkness gone, but the closer the soldiers came the less like a man he looked and when they reached the waterfall what they thought was their victim was nothing more than a trick of the light on the spray rising from its foot, as the morning sun shone through the trees.

The soldiers were in a bad way. They had lost their horses and themselves, were worn out, and two were in great pain from scorpion stings. Their captain was in a tremendous rage, like the thunderstorm that soon broke over their heads to drench them. Rajay Ghiry and his white horse had been a miraculous illusion which had lured the soldiers away from Belar to this out of the way spot far from anywhere.

The night was over, day had come and I could hear thunder and rain drumming on the roof of the Belar temple as a flash storm joined in the music. I turned around and saw Rajay sitting behind me, and Ekan was there too, telling him that the troopers had disappeared. 'Let's sing the final praise song, kneel in gratitude for our deliverance, and leave,' Rajay advised. Ekan gave the thumbs up sign and in different parts of the temple we breathed a sigh of relief.

'My son, you have my blessings,' said Baktar, after the programme was finished. 'I've had a message from my old friend Luth. He's most disappointed that no one has asked for his help in freeing Daish Shaktay. You've got to contact him.' At this moment a tired man came into the temple and went up to Baktar. 'Hello Gumnar, I thought you were out of town.'

'I was, but last night I was riding home and a young man on a white horse came careering past me, and on his heels were a company of troopers. They took off into the forest and I saw them on the further hill some time later, still chasing him. But - I don't get it – he looked exactly like you, sir,' and he nodded at Rajay, who was sitting nearby.

'I understand now,' Baktar went on. 'My prayer was answered. While we were singing that final praise song, a voice came from the statue in the temple, saying the soldiers have been lured away from here by a magical illusion, and won't be back today, but you, Rajay, must be gone by this evening. I'm leaving now and no one will find me.'

Baktar put his little pack and stringed instrument on his back, took his staff and ambled off into the thick woods behind the town. The rain had stopped and Rajay asked us to meet him in the clearing where we would sit while guarding him meditating.

I went back to the grocer's house to wash and change before going there.

'Today is the festival of the brotherhood bands,' Pulita said as I was about to leave her house. 'Why don't you give some to those young men and make them your honorary brothers?'

'I'd like to, but I don't have any.'

'We've got masses in the shop. Here, take some,' and she pressed a bunch of brightly coloured cords into my hand. I rejoined the others. The rain had left the trees, grass and other plants clean and sparkling, and soon the sun dried up the ground well enough for us to sit on it.

'I've been saved from death by a miracle, but we must leave today,' Rajay told us all. 'Valya, go up to the Zaminder's fort and collect our spare horses and other things. Ask Count Zaminder and his men to come down, as my mother and I need to talk to them.' Valya left and Rajay called me. 'Stay with the Zaminders until it's safe to leave, then go to Daish Shaktay with my mother and start to awaken the Trees of Life of my people. You'll find them honest, on the whole, and moral, but they like to do things the way their ancestors did, even if those customs make no sense. Because my father sold out to the ogre peoples they allow themselves to be dominated by these devils.

'Traditionally women don't take an active role in public matters, but don't let anyone stop you giving awakening because you're a girl. My mother will make sure everyone knows I'm behind you, so if anyone gives you a hard time they'll have me to face when I get back. Some of the wealthier people and nobles have thrown in their lot with the enemy because it's easier in the short term. Maybe if their Trees of Life are awakened and they're in touch with universal truth they'll improve. Let's see. Do I see brotherhood bands in your hand?'

'Yes. May I tie them on your friends?'

'Of course, but what about me?'

'Well, yes, but....' I did not presume to make the King of Daish Shaktay my brother.

'Until I marry, every woman and girl is either my mother or sister. Doesn't that include you?'

'Yes, if that's really all right.'

He called his friends and I tied a band around each of their wrists, and also Lee and Ahren's. It was a completely chaste, binding and sacred relationship.

'Now Asha is our sister and we must look after her like one,' Rajay said when everyone was wearing a coloured thread.

We went off to get some sleep, but Rajay took his mother to the Zaminder's house, where they had breakfast and discussed affairs of state.

I was grateful that I had tied the brotherhood bands. In our world young people are not so troubled by an overwhelming desire to pair off at the first possible opportunity, as I gather, from what the Grandmother in Sasrar told us, used to happen on the planet where the guardians came from. It is something to do with our having three moons, which helps us to be more balanced. When we marry this usually happens in a relaxed manner, with the advice of our parents or elders. Nevertheless, here I was, a girl of eighteen among a group of dashing and delightful young men, and one had to be realistic. We three from Sasrar were here to learn - we weren't sure what - to help free our own country and it would be better if nothing came in the way. Pulita later admitted that Rajay had bought the brotherhood bands and asked her to give them to me.

CHAPTER 5

OLD FRIENDS REVISITED

A little before midday Valya came back. Count Zaminder, his son Bukku and a number of their soldiers came too, because they, and quite a number of the youth of Belar wanted to join Rajay. However, he asked them to join the Zaminder's army, so that when he needed them they would be ready. Count Zaminder told Queen Jansy that Karlvid of Mattanga was demanding even heavier tribute from him than previously and he was eager to shake off their domination.

Valya was busy and I didn't manage to give him a brotherhood band. He brought the spare horses and baggage, along with Rajay's precious sword, and had been told on no account to unsheathe it. Rajay was the only one to do that, so the prophetic rhyme said, and he discovered a dire warning on it – no one should handle it without the permission of its owner. I had, but Rajay reckoned that was all right. I sincerely hoped so. He decided to wear the sacred sword and gave his old one, also a fine weapon, to Bukku Zaminder as a way of sealing his alliance with the family.

Rajay sat on a simple chair under a tree, the new sword on his knees. One by one his companions and Lee and Ahren came up and touched it, as a symbol of their allegiance to him. He would not allow anyone to kneel before him, but asked them, by way of a salute, to touch their forehead three times: once for the supreme Creator and his power, the compassionate Goddess who cared for the entire universe, once for their own father and mother, who had given them life, and once for him as king. All of them had awakened Trees of Life and felt a coolness radiating from the blade when they touched it, and also it kindled great courage in their hearts. Many young men from the Belar district took their turn as well, and any fears or doubts disappeared the moment they touched the sword.

After this there were farewells and thanks for hospitality.

Lee, Ahren and my new brothers galloped north and once out of sight of the town turned westwards into the plains, away from the forested hills, down a temporary stream that was flowing over the road as a result of the previous night's storm, being careful not to leave any hoof prints. They rode over a plain that was a carpet of flowers after the recent rainy season, then stopped for a rest near some shallow pools of water, already drying up in the sun. They let the horses drink and looked around for some shade as it was still hot, despite being late afternoon. Ahren and Lee sat under a lone tree with a trunk like a barrel and a few straggly branches.

'Looks like someone planted it upside down,' commented Ahren.

'No matter, it gives some shade,' added Lee.

Rajay joined them, sat on the ground and stretched out his legs. He had checked the horses and made sure the water skins loaded on the spare ones had been filled.

'These plains are beautiful after the rains,' he looked at the incredible variety of flowers, multicoloured and stretching to the horizon, and listened to the buzzing of a billion bees, collecting enough honey to last the whole year. 'I don't think we'll be chased out here. Let's hope the troopers have decided that pursuing me, or someone who looks like me, isn't a good idea. We need to find Luth quickly because I must get back to Daish Shaktay soon.'

'He has a hermitage to the west, beyond these plains,' said Lee, 'but he may not be there, because he travels a lot.'

'I feel cool on vibrations when I ask if he is,' Ahren declared.

'We'll go and see,' said Rajay. 'Can you lead us?'

'Yes, but we should hit the road south of here. Will that be safe?'

'We'll chance it.'

'Excuse me for asking, but why did you go off into the forest like that?'

'I wanted to meditate for inspiration to free Daish Shaktay without violence. I sometimes see flashes of what may happen in the future, and what I've foreseen recently isn't all pleasant. I now realise we'll have to go on fighting, although what I did in Belar felt right at the time. It gave Asha a chance to teach my friends about the Tree of Life, you a chance get to know them better, the locals a chance to join me - and we experienced an extraordinary miracle, yet another proof that we're being well looked after. Added to which Asha met my mother, so we can get her to my country to start her work there. Does this make sense?'

'Yes, I hope you don't think I'm questioning your judgement.'

'Not at all. I'm glad you asked.'

'Forgive me if it's out of place, but why don't you teach people about the Tree of Life and the vibrations?' asked Lee.

'Up to now, that's not been my role, but things will change now. The desire for this wisdom has to come from souls of this world, especially those who've been to Sasrar. Then it's like a candle - one can light the next.'

'I never realised our journey was so important,' said Ahren.

'Well, now you do, and that's another reason why my lands have to be free, so others can make the journey. You don't think you got all that help from the keys and guardians for nothing, do you?' smiled Rajay. The boys had told him about the prophecy and our journey from Teletsia to Sasrar.

'I think we did, even if not consciously,' said Lee.

'May I ask you another question?' Ahren went on.

'Yes, and then no more. At least for the time being!' laughed Rajay.

'You won't let people kneel before you, but you knelt before Baktar. Why?'

'It's necessary to show respect for his age and sanctity, but I want my subjects to grow, so they can eventually take full responsibility for Daish Shaktay. Then I can step back. If everyone is in the habit of kneeling at my feet, and blindly doing what I tell them to, that won't be so easy. I'm often setting an example. As you grow older you will be too, so watch out!'

'I'll go back to being a dairyman after we've finished this fighting.'

'Thank you for being so open,' said Lee.

'Let's move, we don't have time to waste,' concluded Rajay.

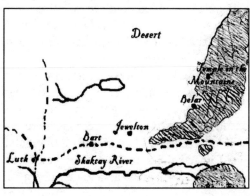

After two days of difficult travel through the semi-desert, pitted with deep ravines and rocky outcrops, they skirted a sizeable town, Jewelton, the capital of this area, ruled by the crusty old Lord Chandan. It was rich, on account of the diamonds found nearby, and well defended, on account of the wealth, which paid for a strong army. It was surrounded by high wall, and some crops were grown under irrigation near the town. It had been the northernmost part of Daish Shaktay, but had been lost to Lord Chandan, who had carved a little state for himself some thirty years before and kept the ogres of Mattanga quiet with tributes of gemstones.

'My mother tells me he's not interested in allying himself to us against King Karlvid of Mattanga. We'll deal with him in good time, but not yet awhile,' explained Rajay.

Soon they reached the road. They rode along it, passed through a number of villages and the next evening reached the one where the boys had met Kanta, the kind farmer's wife, two years before. It had been rebuilt and looked peaceful and prosperous.

'I'm sure we can spend the night here,' said Lee.

'You two go on ahead to make sure it's safe, and remember, we're travellers, armed for safety. For the time being my name is Ray Horsetrader,' Rajay cautioned, 'that's why we've got such good horses.'

Lee and Ahren walked down the path to the farm and the others hid in the small wood. The boys entered the farmyard, which had become much neater and more prosperous looking since they were last there. On one side was a large barn, on another low sheds which from the sound of mooing contained cows, on the third side was the farmhouse with a fruit tree, climbing roses and vines trained up the wall, and in front of the house was a picket fence and a small flower garden. On the fourth side was a wooden henhouse with a fenced in hen run behind it. Someone was shooing some hens into their house, and as she heard the boys and turned round they saw it was Kanta. She had put on some weight and was evidently pregnant, but was glowing with good health. For a moment she looked scared, then recognised them. Hens forgotten, she came over and greeted them.

'Wonderful to see you! Are you on your tigers?' Not waiting for an answer she continued, 'Here's Bart, my husband,' as he came round the corner of the barn, carrying a bucket of chicken food. He was tall, strongly built and bearded.

'Great to see you again,' he began.

'And you, sir. No tigers this time, but we've got some friends over the hill,' said Lee. 'Would it be possible to spend the night in your barn?'

'Go and fetch them at once. We've got room for you all in the house, because I've done some building since you were last here.'

Bart and Kanta wanted everyone to go indoors immediately to enjoy warm family hospitality, and urged them to give their horses to the farmhands. Nevertheless Rajay told Varg-Nack and Valya to take charge of them. He didn't want strangers looking too closely; they had weapons, and the linings of the saddles were filled not only with the usual stuffing but also gold coins and jewels for buying their way out of trouble if the need arose. The others went into the large farm kitchen and Bart went to the barn to help with the horses.

'Everything OK?' he asked, patting Rajay's friendly mouse-brown mare.

'Yes thanks,' replied Valya, busy with his powerful black horse, nervous in a strange environment.

'Help yourself to hay and whatever you want for your animals,' Bart continued. 'Fine horses, but you've been in rough country recently and some of them need reshoeing,' he looked at the horses' hooves. 'I'll do it for you tomorrow if you like.'

'It's kind of you to offer, but my father is a blacksmith,' explained Varg-Nack. 'If I could borrow your forge I'll do it myself.'

They all had supper together in the kitchen, sitting around the large table and enjoying a generous meal. Kanta now had a servant girl, who helped her pile the delicious food onto any plates that became empty, until they could not eat another mouthful. The guests didn't speak much and Rajay especially kept a low profile. Bart told them his service to Prince Osmar's father, King Orzon, in his war against the ogre peoples had been a success in every way and the king had paid him well. He had bought another two farms, taken on some more workers, and was becoming quite a landowner. This area was in Lord Chandan of Jewelton's state and Bart complained about the high taxes they were forced to pay, the price of peace, Chandan's men told them. The guests went to bed as soon as was polite because they were exhausted and Bart, like many farmers, rose with the birds and usually went to bed early too.

Early next morning Bart, Varg-Nack and Valya were in Bart's forge shoeing horses. It was at one end of the barn, and a fire, fuelled by charcoal, was burning in a fireplace against the wall. Various tongs and other farrier's implements were laid out ready, and Varg-Nack made the fire hotter with the help of the bellows at one side, then used it to soften and shape the new iron horseshoes Bart gave him from his stores, ready to put on the horses.

'Have you heard about this young rebel, Rajay Ghiry, who's standing up to the ogre peoples?' Bart mentioned casually, as he held the head of Ekan's fiery chestnut brown firmly and Varg-Nack reshod it.

'We did pick up some gossip along the way,' Valya answered in an off-hand manner, holding the next horse to be dealt with.

'This area used to be part of Daish Shaktay and I wish it was still,' continued Bart. 'From what I've heard of this Mountain Mouse, as they call him, I reckon he could win it all back. I'd join him any day, but the trick is to find him. They say he's as elusive as the wind. I'd hoped you might have come across him.'

None of them noticed Rajay come in behind. He liked watching skilled craftsmen and Varg-Nack was an expert. He took one of the red-hot horseshoes he had hammered into shape from the fire and tested it on the horse. There was a sharp smell of scorched hoof and then he plunged the shoe into a trough of water to cool it. Clouds of steam rose.

'Bart Charval, your wish is answered,' Rajay declared.

'Ah, Mr. Horsetrader,' Bart turned round.

'I'm Rajay Ghiry! I'd be honoured to have you join me.'

'Indeed, Your Highness, I thought there was more to you than met the eye – a veiled nobility,' Bart grinned mightily. It was tradition that when a warrior gave his allegiance to anyone, he would place his weapons at their feet, but Bart's weapons were stored away, so he took a large hammer and reverently knelt with it at Rajay's feet. Rajay put his hand on Bart's shoulder.

'Don't kneel, but I accept the hammer. You'll hammer the enemy and rise high in my service. Raise and train a company of freedom-loving men and be ready when I call you.'

CHAPTER 6

RAJAY'S TESTS

At midday they left the farmhouse, hoping to find Luth, and two days later reached the crossroads where Lee and Ahren had first met him. Rajay told them the menhir which towered over the four roads had been put up by his ancestors, when Daish Shaktay had been the largest state in that part of the world. He had a feeling they should get out of sight, so they hid themselves and their horses in a thicket nearby. It was early afternoon, not a time for sensible travellers to be on the road. There was silence, and in the heat of the day even the birds and insects were having a siesta.

'Let's see if there's any sign,' suggested Lee, looking up and down the roads as he left the thicket. They were deserted, but the landscape shimmered in the heat and he wiped some sweat from his forehead.

'I'll come with you,' said Rajay, and told the others to stay hidden. They walked up to the great carved stone and looked around, not knowing what they might find.

'Nothing,' sighed Lee. Then, at the base of the massive rectangular column, he saw something, intentionally indistinct but recognisable to Lee and Rajay. Half hidden behind the spiky grass was a newly carved design of a twelve pointed flower, the same as Lee's Key of Wisdom had been. Underneath was the letter 'L' in the classic script and an arrow pointing towards his hermitage. 'That's it!' Lee pointed at it.

'The twelve petalled flower, like my mother's key!' Rajay was thrilled, but at that moment they heard sounds; the jingling of harness and the tramp of marching feet. 'Hide! We don't want to be caught unprepared.' They darted behind some cactuses and crouched down, avoiding the prickles.

A platoon of foot soldiers, with two officers on horses and an obese, ogrous looking man swaying perilously on the back of an elephant came along the road from the north-west going in the direction of Mattanga, the ogre's capital. Lee recognised the livery. He had worn it once himself, extremely unwillingly. It was that of General Khangish, who had been killed two years before by Raynor's key, after Khangish had kidnapped the three boys. Lee had heard that the general's second son had recently collected his father's sympathisers together and offered their services to the ogre king. The soldiers stopped at the crossroads in front of the menhir.

'Listen up,' shouted the leader, from his elephant, 'We've had a message that Rajay Ghiry and his gang may be somewhere near here. We have orders to kill him if we can find him and there's a big reward for his head. King Karlvid is fed up with his childish pranks and wants to give a warning to the people of Daish Shaktay.'

Lee looked at Rajay, who put his finger on his lips in the gesture of silence, then made a bandhan on his hand. Unfortunately, at this moment, the elephant walked towards them both, and the leader could easily see them. Lee froze and Rajay chanted some words in the classic language which Lee did not recognise.

'Hello, you two,' said the man on the elephant. 'Why are you hiding there?'

'We've also heard about this dangerous Rajay Ghiry and his followers, and when we saw you coming, thought maybe you were them. We're road repairers – we work for Prince Osmar, and we're waiting for the rest of our group. We're in charge, and do the surveying. Did you see a number of workmen, by any chance? There's been a mix-up. We arranged to meet here but they must have got delayed, or something. They were working on the road to the south of here, this morning, so actually you probably wouldn't have seen them. But you don't want to know about our problems! Is the road to the west in good order, sir? We try our best but funds are so short – if only we could impose a small toll it would enable us to ……'

'I haven't seen your men, and the road we came on is in a dreadful state. However I don't have time to discuss that with you now,' the leader was bored by Rajay's long rambling speech. 'If you want to make some money, either for yourself or your ruler, I suggest your people find this Ghiry and his followers – there are about ten of them, riding high quality horses, armed like the bandits they are – and deliver either them or their heads to the agents of the Mattanga Empire. Then you'll have enough money to do something about this road.'

'Thank you sir, for your excellent advice. I'll report back to my superior as soon as I can,' Rajay bowed and the man turned his elephant away. The platoon set off again, trudging along the Mattanga road, too hot and tired to be on the lookout for Rajay Ghiry, stray travellers or anyone else.

'That was close! He must have had a description of us all, and you're wearing your jewelled sword. How come he didn't recognise us?' said Lee when they had gone.

'You're with the Mountain Mouse,' laughed Rajay, 'and mice know how to hide. This mouse can also fight, but at this time I'd rather be incognito. Those words were the command for him to be confused, and unable to recognise me. I didn't know if it would work for you too, but it did, fortunately.'

'May the Mother Earth be praised, as we would say in Teletsia,' Lee murmured, in awe of this outwardly very normal young man who had just saved his life.

'Long ago, I was blessed with the knowledge of how to make use of powers such as this, but it's vital to be completely detached from them, and not to assume they'll lead you to some higher level of spiritual awareness. On the contrary, they can lead one horribly astray. Also, I can't use them too often; once or twice per lifetime at the most, and my mother and I used that one when I was with her as a child, escaping from my father's enemies. So let's hope I don't need that again in the near future. Anyway – enough of philosophy, let's get moving.'

'We found a sign,' explained Lee after they returned to the others, who had kept the horses quiet so as not to give them away. 'I think Luth may be expecting us.'

'Let's go,' said Danard, and they set off towards where Luth's hermitage had been. From the top, this dry plain looked flat, but in fact it was intersected by deep valleys and canyons.

'We'll take a short cut,' Lee led them, but unfortunately it turned into a series of long detours, because he forgot that last time they had been on tigers, which were much more agile than horses. The group kept coming across gullies that were too steep for them, but finally reached the top of the ravine wherein the hermitage lay. Lee and Ahren went ahead and climbed down the path at the side. They saw some blackened ruins and nearby a new cottage with wooden walls and a thatched roof, some other new buildings, a garden with rows of vegetables and a stockade around the whole settlement. Two monkish looking men, with shaved heads and simple robes, came out of the cottage, collected water from the stream running past the garden, and went back indoors.

'They're harmless enough,' said Ahren quietly.

'Yes, let's fetch the others,' agreed Lee.

They all led their horses down the narrow path and when they reached the bottom the monks came to meet them.

'Greetings, holy ones,' began Rajay politely, walking ahead with Lee and Ahren.

'And greetings to you,' replied the older monk uneasily. Perhaps, thought Lee, he assumed they were bandits, because they were armed.

'Please, come in so we may refresh you,' added the younger one nervously. Bandits or not, the laws of hospitality were sacrosanct. He led them into the front room of the cottage, gave them water to drink and they heard a moan in the other room.

'Is there someone here who is unwell?' asked Rajay.

'Yes,' replied the elder monk, 'there's not much hope.'

'I have some medicines in my pack. My life is full of falls and wounds; perhaps I can help,' Rajay went on, concerned.

'I doubt it.'

'What can we do for you?' enquired the younger monk.

'We're looking for Luth, the great saint.'

'Why?'

'I'm a warrior, but I need a spiritual master.'

'You may be too late. Master Luth is dying.'

'I can't believe it,' said Ahren. 'He'd never die at a time like this!'

'Master Luth has been waiting for so long now. He's spent years setting things up for the one who is prophesied to free Daish Shaktay, but he hasn't appeared,' said the older monk.

'Please let us pay our respects,' Rajay begged.

'I'll go and ask him.' The monk disappeared into the other room but soon returned. 'You may go in, but don't stay long. He's very weak.'

Lee, Ahren and Rajay went in and there was Luth, looking very frail, lying on the bed.

'*This* is my master,' Rajay declared to the boys, and all three knelt before him.

'Lee, Ahren, great to see you!' began Luth feebly. 'From your faces, I'm sure you made it to Sasrar.'

'Yes, we did,' Ahren affirmed.

'What brings you to this seething cauldron of problems?'

'We've brought you Rajay Ghiry of Daish Shaktay,' said Lee.

'I'd almost given up hope!' Luth sat up and perked up enormously.

'Master, I know you,' Rajay was overjoyed. 'I saw you at the festival at the Temple-by-the-Sea, in Mattan Province. I'll never forget the look you gave me, years ago.'

'And now you're here. At last!' He flopped back on the bed. 'But you're going to have to help me get my health back.'

'What can I do?' Rajay was dismayed; everything was so nearly coming right.

'Tiger's milk,' groaned Luth, his eyes closed. 'I must have tiger's milk. That's the only thing that will cure me.' Lee and Ahren looked at each other. How was Rajay to come by that?

'Is that all, master?' his dark eyes shone.

'Go, and hurry. This body won't last much longer without it.' Rajay left and the others made to follow, but Luth ordered, 'You two stay here.' When the monks had gone off to show Rajay's friends where to put their horses, Luth spoke again. 'Do you know how to allow the vibrations to flow through you to heal the sick?'

'Yes, we learnt in Sasrar,' Lee replied.

'We sort of knew before we got there, but we learnt how to feel the problems on our fingers. That's much more accurate,' added Ahren.

'You don't have to convince me, lad. I know well enough how it works, but come here and give an old monkey man some healing, because I've been very ill. I've taken so much negativity, so much evil and so many problems on this body. It needs the vibrations of the compassionate healing power that you Teletsians worship as the Mother Earth and Rajay bows to as the Goddess of Daish Shaktay.'

'It would be easier if we could be behind you,' said Ahren.

'I'll sit on the edge of the bed.'

Luth placed his hands on his knees, palms upwards. Lee and Ahren first reawakened their own Trees of Life, and made the bandhan of protection over their bodies, then put their hands towards Luth.

'But your vibrations are so cool!' exclaimed Ahren.

'Feel a bit more. The heart centre is not all right.'

Lee felt tingling rather than coolness on his little fingers, which corresponded to the fourth centre of the Tree of Life. He and Ahren made a circle in the air at the level of Luth's heart. Gradually the tingling left their fingers and they felt cool vibrations flowing on them.

'This is the part of the world which corresponds to that centre and I'm one of the guardians, so the load falls on me. The pain is too much sometimes, but if Rajay works out as he should, it will improve. Give me more vibrations to strengthen the heart area.' Lee and Ahren put their left hands towards the evening sun outside the window and their right hands towards Luth's back at the level of the heart. 'That's better,' he sighed.

'You're radiating a tremendous cool breeze now!' cried Ahren. 'Let's give you another protection bandhan and you can lie down again.'

'Thanks, lads. You've learnt well in Sasrar.'

'Asha came with us and she's gone to Daish Shaktay with Rajay's mother, Queen Jansy, to tell people there about awakening the Tree of Life,' said Lee.

'Now you're really talking! You young men can fight and maybe defeat the evil forces for the time being, but the only way to make things better permanently is to transform people's level of awareness, and the only way to do that is to awaken the Tree of Life in everyone. Good for Asha.'

'She said the vibrations were so cool she had to come too,' added Lee dubiously. 'We couldn't stop her.'

'Queen Jansy will keep an eye on her. Now listen, I've got one or two more things I need you to do for me,' Luth went on, 'but don't tell anyone. You'll see why later.'

'How can we help?' asked Ahren.

'Go into the yard and from the tree pick me a large, ripe mango - if there's one that's fallen on the ground, so much the better. Bring it here. Then, go to the older monk for a slice of raw meat – we always kill a goat when a group of visitors arrive, especially if they're hungry young men. Bring the slice to me here, and the more blood it has the better. And ask the other monk for some clean bandages.' Lee and Ahren brought Luth this odd assortment of requests and he told them to come back later.

Rajay had done many outrageously brave things but he had never tried to milk a tigress. Nevertheless if this was what would help Luth, he was determined to try. He knew well enough how to kill a tiger, but a dead one would not yield milk, and anyway he would never kill one of these beautiful animals unless it had turned man eater. As he went up the valley to look for a tigress, Valya, who was feeding the horses, saw him. The others were sitting around a fire some way away.

'Where are you going? asked Valya.

'I've got to milk a tigress, because Luth says that tiger's milk is the only thing that can save him, and I may find one by the stream, coming to drink.'

'I don't believe you!'

'Tiger's milk is what he's asked for and that's what I've got to get him.'

'At least let me come with you.'

'No, I'll be fine, and don't tell the others. Here, take my sword, because I don't want a tigress to think I'm going to kill her.'

Valya took the sword and knew better than to argue further. Rajay walked away and although he would have a dagger on him, it wouldn't be much help against a furious tigress. Sometimes being Rajay's friend was quite a test of detachment. Valya said a prayer to the Goddess of Daish Shaktay that he would survive the night.

By the light of the moons, Rajay searched up and down the stream and eventually found a place where there were large tiger prints going down to the water. He looked more closely and realised his luck was in, because he also saw many small prints of cubs. It could have taken days to even locate a tigress with cubs and therefore milk. He sat silently and half hidden at the side of the ravine to wait for the tiger family to come and drink. Some deer came and then a wild pig. He wished he had his mother's key to the area, because with it he could call the tigers it governed, but when he thought about it, even that wouldn't help. He had never heard of one of those tigers having cubs.

He felt uneasy, even though he knew words of power which theoretically controlled animals, even wild and ferocious ones. One could never be sure of anything with tigers though. It was quite some test, but no tigress appeared and after a long and fruitless wait he dropped off to sleep. This was most out of character for someone who could sit up on the watch all night if necessary, his attention as sharp as his sword. He had a vivid dream: he was in the Temple in the Mountains, kneeling before the statue of the Goddess with the tiger. It came to life and spoke to him and was not pleased.

'Why are you so worried?' it asked.

'I've got to get some tiger's milk for Master Luth,' began Rajay, in the dream.

'We guardian tigers are there to serve you, as the rightful king of Daish Shaktay. Use your heart, your intelligence and most of all your finely tuned vibratory awareness to get us to do as you want.' The dream faded.

Meanwhile, down the valley, the others were sitting around trying not to be anxious, because Valya had told them what was going on. They kept their ears peeled, in case Rajay should shout for help. They decided it was not the moment to roast the goat and instead had some biscuits and cheese for supper, gifts from Kanta and Bart.

'He's been gone a long time,' said Danard.

'Let's do that request bandhan that Asha told us about,' suggested Namoh. They wrote Rajay's name on their left hands and circled above them with their right one. 'It's cool. He'll be all right.'

'We must go back and see Luth,' said Lee. 'He wanted to talk to us again.'

'I wonder what he'll want this time,' Ahren added. They went and Luth thought it was Rajay, come back with the tiger's milk.

'Why is he taking so long?' asked Luth.

Lee and Ahren were silent, not wanting to be impolite and say, 'It's not every day you get asked to milk a tigress.'

'Lee, you'd better go and help him,' Luth advised.

'How?' asked Lee.

'Your Sasrar key works as well as the twelve petalled one you had on your journey. Blow through its stem and even if you can't hear the whistle, the tigers will, and they'll be there for you.' Lee left and Ahren stayed with Luth.

Lee walked up the wooded valley, the light of the moons filtering through the tall trees as he put some distance between himself, his friends and their horses. Then he blew and soon a tigress, accompanied by three tiger cubs, came up to him. She knelt at his feet and he recognised her as being the tiger Conwenna had ridden two years before.

'So, my old friend, I see you're taking some time out to raise a family,' he said in the classic language as he stroked her head. She purred in agreement and her children tumbled playfully around his feet. 'Come, I'll introduce you to your future king. Luth has set him a test – he's got to ask you for some milk.' The tiger looked at Lee uncertainly, snarling slightly. 'Please don't eat him, because Daish Shaktay is depending on him.' She swished her tail and set off at a smart pace up the valley, along with the cubs. Lee was left behind and followed more slowly.

Rajay woke up and felt something warm and fluffy on his hand and what seemed like a very small tongue licking his cheek. To his horror he saw one tiger cub standing on his hand, another licking his face and the third pulling at some cheese he had put in his pocket in case he got hungry. Behind them a large and fearsome tigress was standing staring at him and he was in shock for a moment because with her cubs she would be mortally dangerous. He slowly picked up the pot intended for the milk and moved towards her, expecting her to pounce at any moment.

'I need some of your milk, please, mother tigress,' he said slowly. 'I have to take it to my master, who is very ill.' Amazingly, she stood stock-still and seemed to understand what he was saying. His heart thumped as he milked her. Then he saw Lee approaching, his Sasrar key in his hand.

'I told her not to hurt you,' he called out. 'None of them will, in fact those little chaps are probably your future bodyguards.' The cubs were treating Rajay as if he was some sort of wonderful toy. It was only then that he noticed the tigress was wearing a gold collar and knew she was one of the tigers that helped protect Daish Shaktay. His mother had told him that these tigers had been given gold collars by Prince Osmar's father.

Some time later Lee and Rajay returned to the hermitage. Rajay was holding the brass pot containing the milk and saw Danard sitting alone on watch over their horses and belongings. He looked at Rajay and smiled; Danard would never rest unless he was certain his friend was safe. The milk was delivered to Luth and Rajay assumed his test was over. He went to sleep and this time did not dream.

In the early morning he was again outside Luth's cottage. In his hands he had a large and flawless diamond he had cut out of the lining of one of the saddles and which he wanted to give to Luth. The older monk was padding around doing domestic chores.

'The master would like to talk to you again,' he said, so Rajay went into Luth's room and presented his gift.

'This is exquisite, but what am I supposed to do with it?' asked Luth as he held the jewel up to the sunlight coming in through the window, and the light split into all the colours. 'Actually I could make use of it, if you don't mind it being sold.'

'It's yours, master.'

'I've been doing a bit of preparatory work for you, since I saw you at the temple some years ago. I've been founding hermitages like this one. To run them does cost money, so the jewel will come in very handy. Men come and stay in them for a time. They study good and virtuous living, but also learn to fight, so all over this area, as far as Mattanga, there are groups trained in guerrilla warfare. Some are monks and some are living ordinary family lives, but they are all waiting, waiting for you.'

'That's why I had this incredibly strong feeling I had to find you!'

'Yes, but we still have a big problem and I don't mean the enemy. My will to live has returned, thanks to your timely arrival and the tigress's milk, but I have a grievous wound. It may be necessary to amputate my leg.'

'May I have a look? I have some medical training and might be able to help.' Rajay was alarmed, because amputations could be fatal. Luth drew back the bedclothes and there was a bloody bandage covering an immensely swollen leg. Yellow pus was seeping through a gap in the bandage and it was extremely septic.

'Don't come too close!' he cried, as Rajay was about to remove the bandage.

'But master, I must look at it.'

'To lead people and give orders, you must first learn to take them,' Luth objected tetchily, and covered himself with the sheet once more.

'Is there nothing I can do?'

'The only way to save the leg is to suck the poison out. I've asked these monks here to do it but they refused.'

'That's easy!'

Without hesitation he brought a dish that was lying in the corner of the room, knelt by the side of the bed and put his lips to the suppurating wound. He sucked and spat, sucked and spat and the swelling went down considerably. Luth ordered Rajay to stop.

'My son, you have passed your tests. When you brought the tigress's milk, you passed the test of courage, and when you were prepared to suck out the pus you passed the test of compassion. The pus was the pulp of an over-ripe mango and the blood came from a dead goat. Here, take this away.'

Rajay took the mango pip and skin, and the bloody bandage, then walked off into the forest and sat alone under a tree in meditation with a look of utter peace on his face. Some time later the tigress came up and lay at his feet. He stroked her and she purred in appreciation, but her children became too rough with him so she batted them sharply with her paw and took them away. He lay down and drifted off to sleep but later opened his eyes with a start, because he heard the sharp crack of someone treading on a dry stick and breaking it. It was Valya.

'Where's your woodcraft? You should be able to walk more quietly than that!' laughed Rajay.

'I know the quickest way to get *you* on your feet. I can walk silently in a forest if I want to. Witten sent me to say you must come and eat something.

He's roasted the goat.'

'Yes, I'm famished,' and Rajay followed his friend back to the hermitage. Valya was skilled at living in the forests and mountains, despite being the son of a nobleman. He had revolted against the decadent life his family led and like Rajay, from an early age had been much more at home living on the land he knew and loved. He had come up silently and stood watching Rajay for a while before intentionally standing on a dry twig to alert him. As they walked, they talked.

'There's one thing worrying me,' began Valya.

'What's that?'

'Lee says this Luth looks like a monkey – a sort of half monkey. I mean, how can you bow to a monkey as your master?'

'Feel his vibrations - right now.' Rajay stopped walking and indicated for Valya to put his hands in front of him.

'Very, very cool and I feel joy in my heart.'

'Doesn't that answer your question?'

'I suppose so. It's up to you who you have as a master.'

'Luth is a great soul who's chosen to take his birth in the body of a race of beings who are another strand of evolution. His powerful Tree of Life can manifest just as well through that body. Are the others bothered about this?'

'No, only me.'

'That's something. Try to get over your aristocratic conditioning, cousin. It doesn't help you one bit.'

'Forgive me.'

'Naturally! At least you're beginning to understand how to use the vibrations, which is going to be enormously helpful when we've won back Daish Shaktay and you become one of my ministers. We were all monkeys not too many lifetimes back. Eventually you'll remember your past lives and then you won't get so upset by this sort of thing. And by the way, Ahren told me the most sensible member of their party when they made their journey from Teletsia to Sasrar was their dog.'

'Point taken.'

Luth wanted to make sure Rajay's friends were thoroughly competent fighters and watched them as they practised all forms of combat. He told them to learn the finer points of archery from Ahren, who, for example, could shoot at night by the sound of the target. He asked Lee and Witten to share their wrestling tricks and suggested they should take lessons in sword fighting from Varg-Nack. Ahren could ride like a circus performer, if necessary without saddle or bridle, and could cling onto the side of his horses' flanks so he could not be easily seen from the other side. This could not be learnt quickly and needed practice, but he did what he could to show the others.

Luth also pointed out some of the shortcomings in their characters and told them to always have complete trust in Rajay, not only because he was their leader, but because he was a guardian and had a very strong Tree of Life. He asked Lee and Ahren to teach Rajay's friends more about it, so in the stillness of the early evening the young warriors sat on the ground, cross-legged with their hands on their knees, palms upward, for their next lesson in inner wisdom. Ahren explained that everyone's subtle system became a bit dirty or damaged at times, especially in a negative environment, and this affected one's character and physical well-being. For fighters this could mean the difference between life and death.

'Everybody, reawaken your Tree of Life,' began Lee. 'Once you've done that, put your attention on both your hands and feel which one is cooler.' They all felt cooler on the left hand and warmer on the right. 'The right side is the side of action, and if you overdo it or get into your ego a bit, you strain it. Also, strong feelings of anger or aggression can damage this side. To cool it down, or as we say, bring it into balance, put your left hand towards the sky to let the heat flow up into the air. Keep the right one on your knee, palm upwards. Let your attention go to the top of your head, the thoughts will float away and your attention will become still and strong.'

Ahren showed them how to cool down their over active right sides by putting their feet in the cool stream or even a bucket of water with some salt in it. 'We can use the power of the elements, and that's how to use the water element,' he said.

Rajay joined in some of the training sessions and he was a master of every aspect of both combat and the subtle wisdom, but mostly spent his time with Luth. A few days later they wanted to leave and everyone was packed and ready to go. Luth came out to see them off.

'You've done well to bring Rajay to me,' Luth congratulated Lee and Ahren, 'and I can see you young men are having a great time together.' He gave words of encouragement to everyone and lastly came to Rajay. 'Is there anything more you need to ask?'

'Yes. You're not tempted by vices like greed and ego. If I do manage to unite Daish Shaktay and become the crowned king, I may get lost in a love of wealth or power. So let me, while there's still some common sense in my head, offer my kingdom to you. I'll rule in your name.'

'My son,' Luth put his hand on Rajay's arm, 'your heart is pure and your mind is clear. You'll never fall prey to those vices! The last thing I want is your kingdom, but I'm always here if you need advice. Take that red cloak everyone has seen me wearing. It will remind you that you're fighting for freedom and justice, like me. You must lead your people and destroy your enemies – they've asked for their deaths by either invading your land or supporting those who've done this. Forgive if you can, try to transform people first, and these young people from Sasrar will help. They can awaken the inner Tree of Life, which will enable everyone to change from within. However, if you have to destroy those who are beyond redemption, do so.

'I'll get my groups of men ready to help you and create some diversions, to draw the interest of the ogre kings' troops off Daish Shaktay for some time. Don't waste the breathing space it gives you, because you won't be able to play cat and mouse forever. I'll see you again soon, but now go, and my greatest blessings go with you.'

CHAPTER 7

QUEEN JANSY

Back at Belar, life soon returned to its easy, small town rhythm. The soldiers who had chased the illusion of Rajay into the forest did return, and very bedraggled they were too. They looked for Rajay and his friends, but not for Queen Jansy and me, safe at the Zaminders' fort. Tracks of horses were found leading into the plains but the soldiers didn't follow them. As it was they were the laughing stock of the district and the story of the magical white horse and its phantom rider got more incredible with each retelling, so they gave the whole thing up as a bad job and admitted that Rajay Ghiry had got away from them yet again, and returned to Chussan. After some days Queen Jansy decided to leave for Malak Citadel, and we set out for the south, with a sizeable escort of mounted soldiers borrowed from Count Zaminder. She was eager to leave as soon as it was safe to do so, because Rajay had told her he might plan more guerrilla operations in that area and didn't want us to get involved. Queen Jansy invited Pulita to come with us, but she refused.

'Mum is not healthy and dad needs me to look after her and the shop. Also, Lady Melissa has asked me to help her to do awakening programmes. She says she doesn't have the confidence to do them alone, but if we could go to the nearby villages together I know we'd do well.'

'You may be right,' agreed Queen Jansy. 'Just as the young men of Belar must train for war, you and Melissa should awaken the inner side of people. That will also help transform this part of the world.'

It was a long, hot ride and the first part was on rough tracks which led through wooded hills and open plains, which were sometimes wild and empty, and in other places farmed, with villages here and there. Queen Jansy ordered our bodyguards to avoid the high roads, where we would be more likely to be attacked. Until we reached Daish Shaktay, at night our retainers would put up a tent for us and the soldiers kept guard, both from wild animals and dangerous people. There were good roads, with inns, forts and manor houses to stay in when we reached Central Daish Shaktay, the part administered by the Ghiry family, and once there we were welcomed with honour wherever we passed.

To begin with I was very shy, only said anything when spoken to, and called the queen Your Majesty. I longed to ask her more about herself, Rajay and Daish Shaktay, and after some time she opened up and told me, but first I had to tell my story. When I got to the bit about riding the tigers and how Lee would call them with his key, Queen Jansy took out hers, telling me she was a guardian. It also had twelve petals and the stem was hollow like a miniature flute, but the leaves were a little different. I showed her my Sasrar key.

'You're very blessed to have a Sasrar key,' she observed. 'You must use the power it gives you or it will diminish.'

'Please, Your Majesty, could you explain?'

'You must use your ability to awaken the Tree of Life in people and tell them all the techniques, so they can strengthen and grow. Rajay spoke very highly of what you did at Belar and with the Zaminders, but you must take it further. Did you tell his friends how to clear their subtle centres if they are damaged and weakened? And how to understand the language of the fingers: what the sensations on each finger mean and which subtle centre they each correspond to?'

'I didn't get that far.'

'Well, you must. Those young men are risking their lives every day they spend with my son and they have a hard fight ahead. They might not all survive, and if their subtle centres are strong, and their connection with the all-pervading power is well established, they're more likely to have good fortune.'

'I'm not sure I'm capable of this.'

'Always remember you're only the instrument of that higher power, and then you'll do fine.'

The next day, as we rode steadily south, she told me about herself and I discovered her life had been the opposite to the one of the ease and luxury I'd assumed a queen would have had. 'I, and now Rajay, are the only descendants of the family that formerly ruled the land north of Mattanga, on the eastern coast of this continent. When I was a little girl, the ruling family of Daish Shaktay came on a visit. It was the time for the yearly festival when mock battles are fought with coloured powders, and the son of the king of Daish Shaktay and I had a wonderful time playing together.'

'Don't they make a lovely couple?' my father said jokingly, but the king and queen of Daish Shaktay took this seriously and insisted on a formal betrothal. This was only grudgingly accepted, because my country was then much more prestigious than Daish Shaktay.

'A year later everything changed. The Mattanga armies invaded us and although it was hopeless, my people fought to the last man. After a day of bitter fighting, a wounded messenger brought the news to the ladies of the court: they had lost their husbands, brothers, fathers and sons. Worse, the enemy soldiers were coming to claim them as spoils of war. Some would be thrown to the crocodiles in the Mattanga River as a sacrifice to the Crocodile God of the ogre peoples and the rest would become slaves. There was no escape, so the ladies decided to end their lives and save their honour. My old nanny and I hid under the steps in the main courtyard. I shall never forget the sound of the roaring fire in the yard and the muffled screams and prayers as they bravely died. Soon the ogres' men arrived.

'There's the treasury, but first let's find the women,' shouted a harsh voice.

'What's that?' demanded another. 'I see a vast heap of glowing ashes.' Among them were bones, and the remains of gold and silver jewellery. They searched the palace and returned with a crippled old cook, dragged from the kitchens.

'That's all that's left of them,' she said between sobs.

'You mean,' barked the ogrous soldier, 'they burnt themselves when they knew their men had been killed?'

'Yes. Something your crowd could never understand,' she retorted. The soldier drew his sword then we heard a blow, a groan and a thud as the old cook fell to the ground. She had been killed for her brave and truthful words.'

'That's too terrible,' I felt quite nauseous.

'It made me determined to oppose them with every breath I take. My dear, I think you've also seen things which made you determined to try to change your country.' It was true. I had seen the Specials in Teletos take friends away screaming in terror, knowing they would either be used for dreadful experiments or sent to the slave farms, where they would be worked to death.

'Did things get better for you after that?'

'Slightly,' the queen sighed. 'When the ogres had gone, my nurse and I fled, and lived with some of my mother's cousins until I was older. They insisted the betrothal was still valid and that I should marry the heir to the throne of Daish Shaktay, which I did.

'At that time, my husband, King Partap, was still trying to get the Mattangan invaders out of Daish Shaktay, and when Rajay was born in a hill fort a year later, I knew he was the one we'd been praying for. I kept him hidden as much as possible, because a wandering holy man was heard to say that the child who would free Daish Shaktay had been born. Our enemies were looking everywhere for him.

'Rajay and I constantly moved from one fort to another and also stayed with the country people to escape the ogres, but finally my husband realised it was hopeless. Our citizens were being slaughtered, the lands desecrated and the starvation and disease that follow war were everywhere. He surrendered in order to save his people, and to stop the Mattanga agents pursuing Rajay and me. My husband was forced to cede large tracts of land and give vast tribute from what remained and we lost our most precious possession: our independence. He had to take service under the ogres and move to Mattanga. I refused to go or to allow Rajay to be brought up there. After my own experience, I never trusted the ogre peoples and Rajay grew up with an iron resolve to defeat them.'

'Lee told me he's known his friends almost all his life.'

'Yes, as a child, he spent most of his time with the country boys, and the nobles referred to his friends as his 'cow dung company', but they're the brave, faithful young men who are becoming masters of guerrilla warfare - and that's the only way we're going to regain our freedom, because we don't have the manpower to face Mattanga in open battle.

'Three years ago Rajay's father managed to persuade the ogre king that his son was capable of being responsible for Central Daish Shaktay. Rajay was summoned to Mattanga and I had to go too. It's run on cruelty, slaves, other people's money and an efficient system of spies and oppression. My husband was delighted to see his son after so long. King Partap was one of King Blagart's leading generals and Rajay was allowed to roam around the city. One day he was at the docks and a gang of slaves were being particularly badly treated while unloading some cargo. Rajay recognised one, the brother of a friend, who'd been captured some time before. He ordered the slaves released, had the overseer of the gang soundly beaten, and because Rajay's father was so important no one questioned his authority. Then, to everyone's amazement, he took off the thick gold chain around his neck, a present from his father, broke it into bits and gave each slave some links to buy his way home.

'The next day Rajay was summoned to an audience with King Blagart, the father of the one we now have, Karlvid. The courtiers all went through the expected ritual of bowing to the floor before their overlord, but not Rajay. "Do you seriously expect the Crown Prince of Daish Shaktay to bow to that scaly ghoul? If anyone is the overlord, it's you and also me, seeing as so much of his so-called empire is rightfully ours, and I'm also heir to my mother's kingdom, now her family have been killed by these devils," he complained to his father. Partap managed to calm everything down and convinced Blagart that Rajay was a good boy, but given to occasional fiery outbursts. He felt the further Rajay was from Mattanga the better, so we left the next day.

'On the way home we stopped at a famous temple during the festival in praise of the Supreme Creator in his form as king and warrior. At one point, I noticed an elderly man with a monkeylike face standing near Rajay. I heard the old man whisper to the person next to him, "It's him; a fine young man - the bearing of a prince and the humility of a saint." I knew this older man to be one of us guardians. We looked at each other, bowed our heads in recognition and left without speaking. I'm fairly sure he's the one your friends are taking my son to see.'

'Is your husband still at Mattanga?'

'No, Karlvid had him murdered. Officially he was killed in a hunting accident, but in fact one of his officers did it.'

'I'm sorry.'

'He was a good man, and kind, but we never spent much time together, because we had to put the needs of the country before our personal lives. Our spies tell us the ogre peoples, not content with stealing Northern Daish Shaktay, are going to overrun our part as well now. That's why we're starting the freedom struggle in earnest.'

Soon we sighted the grim but strong walls of Malak Citadel. On the plain below was a town, but the Citadel dominated the landscape, built on a flat-topped hill and surrounded by ramparts.

'Home at last,' Queen Jansy said. 'You'll be safe here. This is where we're starting to fight our war from, although Karlvid doesn't realise that yet.'

We were respectfully greeted by Deradan, Rajay's friend, who had brought the stolen baggage train here, down the Old Forest Road and across the Shaktay River on barges to avoid Northern Daish Shaktay. The people of Malak Citadel town turned out to welcome us as we passed through, and we were escorted up the hill to the Citadel by the castle guard. It was a warren of ammunition and weapon caves and treasure cellars down below the main buildings, and above were watchtowers, storehouses, granaries, wells and water cisterns, and administration offices. These were ranged around a number of courtyards, and there was also a barracks for a fair sized garrison, and living quarters for a number of officers and their families. The largest buildings were the Royal Palace with its Great Hall, which were on the sides of the main courtyard. Rajay had a modest suite of rooms on the top floor of the palace, and the queen had a comfortable flat at ground level, overlooking a garden behind, with flowerbeds and some shady trees. To begin with I stayed in one of the guest rooms in the palace.

Queen Jansy introduced me to her lady-in-waiting, Amber. Her father, Commander Aydriss, was in charge of an important fort and she had recently married Saber Rizen, captain of the powerful Malak Citadel Guard. Amber was tall, a little plump, had straight dark hair, a dark olive skin, a round face and talked a lot. Everyone was her friend and she generally saw only the good side of people. Like Melissa Zaminder, I immediately felt at ease with her and very soon we told each other our life stories. After hearing mine she wanted me to awaken her inner Tree of Life and learn how to use its powers. Word got around that the girl who had come with 'our Queen Ma', as Queen Jansy was known, 'could make you feel really happy inside'.

Within days I had a group of people with awakened Trees of Life: some of the castle guards and other members of the Citadel staff, who always wanted to know more about the subtle knowledge I had learnt in Sasrar. We had a few meetings in the garden, in the evenings. I showed them how to reawaken the power, do the two bandhans, balance their left and right sides and various techniques for clearing the different subtle centres, so they could feel inner peace and joy and maintain their physical health. I also showed them how to ask questions on the vibrations, cool on the hands was a 'yes', and if warm, or tingling on the fingers a 'no'. And most important, to spend a short time each day in meditation, allowing one's attention to float to the top of the head, the seat of the connection with this inner peace and joy. I was amazed at how easy it was once I had the confidence to speak out, and everyone was so responsive.

I wanted to give this to more people, and Deradan came to my aid. Like Valya, he was a bit older than Rajay. He was a tall, slim man with a light skin. He had a slight stoop; a high, broad forehead, a long thin nose and tied back his long, dark hair. Lawyers, professors and the like often wore their hair like this in Daish Shaktay and as Rajay's First Secretary he did the same. Nevertheless, Amber's husband told me he was fearsome with a sword and kept fit in case he had a chance to go out fighting. After Amber he was the first to ask me to awaken his Tree of Life, and he would sit in meditative bliss whenever he had the time - which wasn't often, because Queen Jansy kept him very busy helping her run the country.

His father was a roving minstrel who wandered from court to court singing ballads, and who loved to sing songs to the perfect lady, a metaphor for the eternal mother, the timeless feminine. Deradan had lost his own mother young, so from early childhood he travelled with his father and was used to court life and its intricacies. When Deradan's father, his stringed instrument under his arm and his son by his side, had walked into the palace at Santara where Rajay spent some of his childhood, they went no further for a few years. Later, his father moved on, but Deradan became a close friend of Rajay and stayed. His skill in writing got him the job as Queen Jansy's and Rajay's secretary, an important position requiring discretion and intelligence. Deradan, like his father, was a poet and musician and I soon taught him the songs we sang in Sasrar to help awaken the Tree of Life. One morning, Amber, Deradan and I were having a mid-morning snack in Amber's kitchen.

'A lot of people in the town have heard about you, Asha,' he said. 'You're getting a reputation as a miracle worker.'

'I just show people how to help themselves.'

'There's the woman in the laundry who had a fever and you taught her how to cool the right side of her subtle system, and she got better. And that guard, Bonor, who had such bad headaches that his vision was affected. You waved the candle behind his head, had him look through the flame and asked him to put the back of his head towards the rising sun every morning, and now he's fine too.'

'So what's next?'

'We should borrow the Covered Market in the evening, when it's empty, and you and Deradan can do a music programme like the one you did at the Zaminder's,' suggested Amber.

'Where is it?' I asked.

'In the main square of the town,' explained Deradan. 'It's a large building with vaulted stone roofing and columns, open at the sides. By day it's used for selling farmers' produce but at night it's cleaned up and the stalls are taken down, so you can fit in as many people as you like. I'll organise it and we'll put a notice in the local news sheet. The gossip about you is already round the district. It helps that you arrived with our Queen, and Rajay is right behind you. The place will be packed.'

'OK, but I'm not going to stand up and speak. I'm so nervous in front of a crowd of strangers.'

'I'll do that. I often give official proclamations for Queen Jansy and Rajay, and everyone knows me. You tell me what to say.'

We arranged our first mass awakening programme, and when we told Queen Jansy, her comment was, 'It's an excellent idea. I wish I could come as well, but if I do, the townspeople will be too much in awe of me and won't put their full attention on you.'

As predicted, the Covered Market was full. Some people just came to see this new curiosity, me, but it didn't matter. Our music group consisted of Deradan, me, Bonor the Citadel guard, who played the xylophone, an elderly gardener who was an excellent drummer and two girls from the palace kitchens who sang like nightingales and learnt the Sasrar songs. Tall conical lamp holders, made of carved stone, held scores of oil lamps, and were placed at each side of us on the raised dais at one end, and in front of us benches had been placed in rows for the large audience. Some people also stood at the back, and others sat on the ground at the front on mats laid on the flagstones. Deradan introduced me, spoke about the Tree of Life, we began the music and soon everyone joined in the choruses. We went through the same routine as we had at the Zaminder's and again nearly everyone felt coolness flowing, and inner peace and joy.

After that most people went home, but some came and asked us if they could know more. We arranged a follow up programme in the house of Mr Ricemaize, a corn dealer, who said we could use his front parlour. One man asked how this fitted with the various religions practised in Daish Shaktay and I told him that this was the fulfilment of all religions, because you actually experienced the divine power flowing through you, and at this point I noticed some older men talking among themselves in the background. It was getting late and those of us from the Citadel left soon after, and walked up the hill. The next morning I was in the yard; a number of people came and thanked me and then Deradan appeared.

'We've got problems,' he said.

'What do you mean?' I replied, puzzled.

'The Guild of Priests has sent an official complaint to the queen and they're coming for an audience this morning.'

'Who are they complaining about?'

'You, me and all of us who were singing last night.'

'Were we too noisy? It wasn't late.'

'It's not that. They reckon you're taking their business and the salvation of souls is their job. Plus it's absolutely unheard of for a girl like you to give such important wisdom.'

'Rajay warned me about this.'

'Queen Jansy will see them in the Great Hall and you can listen out of sight, in the Minstrels' Gallery. Take it easy! Her Majesty is clever and she'll come up with something.'

The queen made the delegation from the Priests Guild wait. She finally entered the large, bare hall accompanied by Deradan and her armed bodyguards. She wore a gold circlet on her dark hair, a robe of a rich dark red material embroidered with gold, her twelve petalled key was visible around her neck, and she looked stately and imposing. I watched unseen as she sat on a divan on the dais, and behind her was the empty throne. This made it clear that she was merely standing in for the absent head of state. The bodyguards flanked her, their weapons at the ready, and Deradan stood on the floor below, between her and the supplicants.

'Forgive me gentlemen, for being delayed, but while my son is away I have much to do,' she began. 'How can I help you?'

'Your Highness, it's very kind of you to see us at such short notice,' said a black-cloaked man, the head priest at the temple dedicated to the formless aspect of the divine. He had an appointment with his accountant after this, to discuss the healthy profit he had made on some business deals using money belonging to his temple. They were going to work out how he could avoid paying any tax on his new-found riches and he hoped this inconvenient little meeting would not take too long. 'Your Ladyship, we'll come straight to the point. This young girl, from the land of the Teletsian Sorcerers, has been inciting the good people of the town and claiming to give them a direct connection with divine power.'

'You mean Asha Herbhealer? Is that a problem?' replied Queen Jansy, ingenuously.

'Well, yes,' added a tall man with a scarlet robe, the head of a sect that revered the Goddess-of-the-Mountains. 'With respect, madam, you know as well as I do that women simply do not involve themselves in this sort of thing. This is men's work, and qualified men at that. How can a young girl like that achieve, with a few songs and prayers, something we train for years to do?'

'You went to the programme in the Covered Market?'

'We did stand at the back....'

'And did you follow her instructions, and experience the cool wind of the spirit, the inner joy?'

'Of course not! That would take years of study, or penance, or enormous donations to your place of worship,' said the priest who had a meeting with his accountant.

'I suggest you try. My son did, and said it was one of the most profound experiences he's ever had.'

'But if everyone does this, no one will come to our temples any more. Then how are we to make a living?' objected the man with the red robe.

'So you're saying that even though she can show people how to find themselves inwardly, which she claims is a gift to be shared by all, she shouldn't do this, because it will deprive you of money?'

'It's not quite like that,' continued the man in red.

'This girl risked her life to travel to the faraway kingdom of Sasrar, the home of spiritual wisdom. After she had learnt some of the secrets, she left the security of that place to come and help us. Then, while in the temple of the goddess who protects our land, she found the fabled sword of Daish Shaktay. It is prophesied in your own scriptures that when this is given to the rightful heir to the kingdom, our country will become free and strong again. Miss Herbhealer met my son and gave it to him. He has the highest respect for her.

You might do better to consider her a useful ally; if anything she'll encourage people to be more religious. And try to get over your prejudice about her being a woman, or a girl. You're speaking to the person who's running Daish Shaktay at the moment and I happen to be a woman. Don't be deceived by Miss Herbhealer's youth. She's an instrument of the greatest power on earth, the power of innocence and compassion. She won't threaten you, any more than the young men who came with her will threaten my son - they've come to help, because they understand that unless there's peace in this part of the world, it will create problems elsewhere. They're global personalities: neither selfish nor mean minded, like your scriptures exhort us all to be.' Queen Jansy paused and the priests shifted uncomfortably, because they couldn't disagree. 'Unless you can bring me definite evidence that her work is creating problems in our land, that is all I have to say to you.'

The priests shuffled off, silenced but not satisfied. The queen called me over.

'Just as Rajay has more problems from those people who should help him most, the nobles and wealthy businessmen, we'll have the stiffest resistance to developing spiritual awareness from the very people who are supposed to do precisely that. Don't worry, you're awakening the power of the Tree of Life and against that, nothing can stand for long. We'll make sure that our intelligence service keeps an eye on those men, and that they don't trouble you any more. Deradan, see to it immediately, will you?'

'Yes, Your Majesty.'

'Come Asha, and tell me in detail how it went last night. This evening I'd like to hear those songs you sing, to help awaken the Tree of Life, and maybe Deradan can accompany you. We'll meet in the garden outside my apartment.'

Deradan and I spent a delightful evening with the queen, playing music and singing to her. She also invited us to supper, and afterwards Deradan said he had not seen her so happy and relaxed for a long time.

Daish Shaktay showing Malak Citadel and the principal forts

Part Two

Uncrowned King

CHAPTER 1

FRIENDLY PERSUASION

Rajay and his friends rode along the high road until they reached the Charval's farm, then left it and took a smaller one which led southeast through villages and farmland. The land sloped gently down towards the south and eventually they reached a forested area, beyond which they could see a wide valley with a large river snaking through it.

'That's Daish Shaktay, on the other side of the river,' Rajay pointed out as they halted on the brow of a hill. 'This side used to be too, but now the river is the northern border and regrettably all that part is a province of Mattanga. Not for much longer though.'

They rode on and turned up a lane. Ahead were some ruined walls and towers - a temple which usually housed one of Luth's groups. He had suggested they stop there on their way home. However, if there was any problem in the area his monks would move elsewhere for a while.

'Lee and I'll go ahead on foot and everyone else hide in those trees,' indicated Rajay. They left the others with the horses and walked towards the temple complex. The outer buildings, once pilgrims' lodging houses, were deserted and tumbled down, the forest was taking over and only monkeys gibbered furiously as they passed.

'This must have been impressive, once,' Lee peered at the ruins. 'Did your ancestors build this?'

'Yes,' Rajay looked around carefully, 'but lesson one: keep your attention on the job in hand. Don't talk, keep feeling the vibrations and asking, is this place safe to enter? If you feel heat or tingling on your hands tell me fast.'

They walked on, Lee felt coolness on his hands and they reached a courtyard in front of the main shrine. An elderly man appeared holding a broom, saw the strangers and pointed to a fountain in the corner.

'Let's have a drink and see what he does,' Rajay whispered.

The man started sweeping a sandy area of the yard, his broom making a rhythmic swishing sound. Rajay walked over to him and traced a design of the twelve petalled flower on the ground. The old man disappeared into the temple. Then another man, tall, his long hair tied in a knot on top of his head and a single piece of cloth wound around his muscular body, came towards them.

'Good evening. My name is Athlos. We received word from Luth, by messenger bird, that a group of travellers might come this way, but you are only two.'

'The others are in the trees,' said Rajay.

'Is, eh, His Highness with you?'

'That's me.' Athlos dropped on one knee before Rajay. 'Please, I kneel before saints, but no one kneels to me.'

'We've been waiting a long time for you, sire,' Athlos stood up and smiled broadly.

'I'm honoured. Lee, go and get the others.'

'Sire, when you've refreshed yourself, my cook will prepare food. I need to talk to you. We are thirty-two fighters here, at your service.' Everyone arrived and another monk showed them where to stable the horses.

'Athlos looks more like a professional wrestler than a monk,' said Ahren to Lee. 'I bet he could teach us a thing or two.'

The monks could certainly cook, and a spicy meal arrived in due course – roasted meat and wild roots. It was a bit too spicy, and soon the guests were gasping for water and laughing with their hosts. Afterwards the travellers were looking forward to a good night's sleep, because they had been on the road since dawn. Lee and Ahren laid out their bedrolls in a pleasant spot under an open portico at one side of the courtyard which caught the night breeze. One of the monks walked over.

'His Majesty wants to see you.'

'Doesn't Rajay ever get tired?' moaned Ahren.

'Not when his kingdom is at stake,' yawned Lee. 'Come on, the sooner we go the sooner we get back.'

Rajay and Athlos were in a cloister. Above, from the point of an archway, hung a brass lamp and the flames flickered in the breeze from the nearby river. A map was laid out on the ground between other lamps.

'Sit,' Rajay began. 'Athlos has some information about a fort and you might be able to help.'

'We'll do our best,' yawned Ahren. Rajay did not take the hint and continued speaking.

'We've recaptured or regarrisoned seven forts in Daish Shaktay recently and they now offer their allegiance to me, not Mattanga. They're all in the centre of the country, but I want control of the northern ones, because forts are the key to success. It will be a declaration of war.' Lee and Ahren sat down at a respectful distance. 'Come closer, you need to see this map. This is the Shaktay River,' Rajay pointed to a line on it, 'and we're here, on the northern bank. About two day's journey upriver is Confluence Fort. It's high up on a cliff, where another river joins this one: the Sapphire River, so called because further up are sapphire and ruby mines; the source of much wealth if it can come to us, not Mattanga. The Shaktay River is fordable there when the water is low and there's a ferry too. The Sapphire River has made a deep gorge and the road goes up it into Daish Shaktay. It's the only easy crossing round here, but that fort is in the hands of Mattanga. Are you with me so far?'

'Yes, but what do you want us to do?' asked Lee, still shaking off his sleepiness.

'Athlos tells me they have a new commander. He's a tribal chief from the plains to the northeast of the mountains who's taken service under the ogre king. His wife and son are with him and the son has recently returned from the famous school in the Sea of Illusion.'

'Maybe we know him!' cried Ahren.

'That's what I'm hoping. I want you to pose as merchants, to get into the fort. Once inside, try and meet this boy and ask him why his father has taken service under these devils. Attempt to bring him over to our way of thinking. Feel his vibrations. They're not too bad, are they?'

'Could be better,' said Lee, putting his hands in front of him and his attention on this boy, 'but yes, they're basically sound.'

'Witten will come with you. He'll have a close look at the fort in case we have to storm it. His family are business people, so he'll help you there too. I'll give you some silver jewellery to sell. With luck we'll win back this fort without too much bloodshed. All right?'

'Absolutely! This is what we came for,' Ahren, now wide awake, smiled enthusiastically.

'The Captain of the Guard there is a relation of Athlos's. He may help us, but we're not sure. In any event, I need allies, not corpses. Athlos's men will come along behind to give you backup if you need it. They'll turn up in the role of a troupe of singing monks, wanting to offer entertainment.'

'I don't mean to be rude, but can they sing?'

'Yes, very well, and they also do a good turn as an acrobatic troupe. I'll come with them,' Athlos put in.

'They'll help protect you if things get violent,' Rajay continued,. 'Athlos was an officer in my father's army, but resigned when he surrendered to Karlvid of Mattanga, so he'll look after you if anyone can. He's tough, clever and brave. Don't be foolhardy, because if we have to use force we'll think of another plan, but gather as much information as possible. Are you still game to go in?'

'Of course,' Ahren reiterated, and Lee agreed.

'We'll leave tomorrow morning. Now go and sleep, because you're both dog-tired.' In fact the conversation had woken them up.

'So, now our real work starts,' said Lee, when they were back in their bedrolls.

'Who'd have thought we'd be doing this when we were in Teletsia - me the milkman's son and you at your dreadful school in Teletos, both praying we wouldn't be sent to the Sorcerers' Special Clinic?' mused Ahren.

'We've got so much to thank Raynor and Asha for. Namoh told me what Rajay's been doing in the last couple of years: how they captured the first fort, Hermitage Fort, above their old capital at Santara. Queen Jansy told Rajay about a hoard of treasure, hidden there by Rajay's father before the ogres took the place. The treasure was bricked up in a wall, but she knew exactly where. She told Rajay to either capture the fort or the treasure, preferably both, because they would need a great deal of money for their freedom struggle.

'Hermitage Fort is a long way from any village and in the rainy season none of the local food sellers would trek up the hill to deliver stores, so at that time the garrison was reduced. That year even the commander, a lazy man appointed by Mattanga, had gone away, leaving only a handful of disgruntled soldiers to guard the place.

'Rajay's friends told him about this and one night he, Danard and two hundred or so hill men Rajay had known from childhood slipped into the fort and occupied it. They bribed the guards, who wanted to defect anyway, because they were wet, hungry and underpaid and that was it. If they hadn't done as he demanded they'd have been killed, because even though Rajay was only eighteen, he was a strong leader, right from the start. He and Danard found the treasure and paid his helpers well, before taking the rest back to Santara for future use. Word got around that Rajay was good to work for, because he had money and used it generously.

'He wrote to Mattanga complaining about the lazy commander and said he'd replaced him with someone more reliable. The new man was very reliable as far as Rajay was concerned: he was Danard's uncle, but the ogre king lost his first fort in the area under the direct control of Mattanga.

'Queen Jansy and Rajay moved the capital to Malak Citadel about a year back, because it's easier to defend. Rajay ran his operation at a profit - less and less tax went to Mattanga and he sent a stream of letters explaining that this was due to incompetent officials appointed by them, that he wanted to replace. He also blamed bad harvests and made sure the agricultural returns were meticulous, but wildly inaccurate, to prove this. Finally he regretted bitterly the many bandits who seized the tribute money sent to his overlords. The raids took place well into Mattanga territory, but Rajay supplied the bandits, so the money went back into his treasury. He got away with all this for some time.

'He was extremely lucky in one respect. King Blagart died recently and his son Karlvid became king. While the old king was suffering his final illness no one was too bothered about Daish Shaktay. Meanwhile Rajay and his friends quietly took over more forts in the border area between Central and Northern Daish Shaktay, built up a standing army and trained a good number of partisans. King Karlvid wants revenge and since they captured that baggage train things will become much trickier.'

At dawn Rajay woke Lee and Ahren and asked them to lead a meditation session, which they duly did. They told the others that they must always give themselves the protection bandhan before going out on a mission and should allow themselves to go into this inner thoughtless peace for a short while before getting involved in their daily activities. In that state their attention would be sharp and they would be more likely to be protected from danger. Rajay's friends now realised he had been doing this ever since they knew him, early every morning, just before the sun rose.

Later they all left - Lee and Ahren rode with Witten, and Athlos and his men came along too.

'How come you live in Daish Shaktay?' Lee asked Witten.

'My father was a spice dealer in a town called Port Volcan,' he began. 'It's near this country, but part of the Mattanga Empire. The Mattanga sympathisers who ruled the place suspected him of being a spy and put him to death most cruelly. He was completely innocent. My father only knew how to make money, and lots of it. He wasn't interested in politics. The rest of our family were forced to board a ship bound for Tong, but on the way it put in at River's Mouth Port in southern Daish Shaktay. My uncle has another branch of our business there and my mother got word to him. Uncle Elychi sent an agent aboard and he bought us as slaves from the unscrupulous captain. So we lived comfortably, but I was bitter about my father and soon left home to join Rajay. Our family has connections with business houses and bankers all over the continent, but I prefer to help Rajay run his business, the country itself.'

'I didn't realise,' apologised Ahren. 'I thought you were his martial arts expert and cook.'

'My main job is cooking the books of Daish Shaktay. With the help of Deradan I do this fairly successfully - it keeps the Mattanga crowd quiet and makes us a bit richer. As far as martial arts are concerned, in Tong most young men learn wrestling and all our family can cook – we're spice traders and we like good food.'

'According to Rajay you have the best financial brain in the country,' added Lee.

'He's too generous with the compliments. Daish Shaktay isn't a country of businessmen. In my land of Tong I'd be pretty ordinary.'

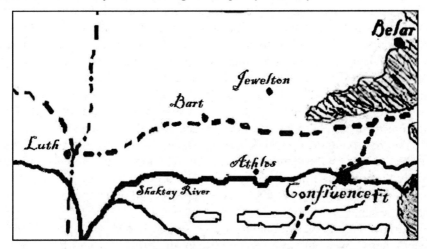

When they neared Confluence Fort they split up. Rajay and his friends made a risky crossing downriver from the fort and swam the horses across the deep swirling water. They were going to raise the local partisans on the south side, in case their help was needed. They would hide with a farmer known to Danard, who lived in a secluded valley. Witten, Lee and Ahren exchanged their battle chargers for the monks' more homely beasts, including one for the merchandise. Its saddle was stuffed with jewels and gold coins for bribery, and Witten showed the boys how to cut them out in a hurry. They crossed the river via the ford, where it was broad and shallow, and Athlos and his men would follow some time later.

To Witten it was just another fort, another day's work. Of the many forts that had come over to Rajay recently, Witten had been there every time. Sometimes they had won over the commanders by persuasion, otherwise by bribery or tricks and only in the last resort used brute force. Rajay had no qualms about fighting, but deeply respected life and set much store by his power to forgive. Many of his enemies became his friends in this way. Witten wondered how these untried Teletsians would fare, but realised that at least no one would recognise them as being Rajay's followers. He had disguised himself with a turban and a long robe, had not shaved for a few days so had a short beard, and hoped for the best.

They forded the river in full view of the fort high above, its ramparts casting a shadow on the water. The fort looked large and imposing and Lee and Ahren began to feel small and vulnerable. They climbed up the path with their unpretentious looking horses, the guards stopped them at the main gate and after a quick look for weapons were about to let them through, but then the Captain of the Watch went up to Witten and looked searchingly at him.

'Come in here,' he ordered. 'Bring one of your friends too.' Witten and Lee followed him into a small room in the gatehouse while Ahren held the horses. The Captain closed the door behind him. 'Her Highness Queen Jansy and her retinue came through here some days back. Very respectful she was, but didn't stop to meet the commander – just paid her dues and went on south. Her son Rajay Ghiry – he's another matter altogether – unpredictable and dangerous as an ocean tempest, and now there's a price on his head. By the way, I recognise your face,' he said to Witten. 'I had to collect the annual tribute for Mattanga from Malak Citadel last year. You work there, don't you? And you're one of Rajay Ghiry's friends, right?' Lee wondered if this was the end of his career as a partisan before it had even begun. Witten was unfazed.

'You're mixing me up with Witten the Tong. Good job he's got, well paid and secure too, by the standards of the day. He doesn't have to go traipsing around the country selling cheap jewellery for a living like I do. I'm also from Tong, but my family are jewellers. To you people, all of us Tongans look and sound the same.'

'Alright then. If the Mountain Mouse walked in here tomorrow, he'd be given a hero's welcome by everyone except the officers from Mattanga. It's my job to guard this place and I know exactly what the talk is in the barracks,' commented the Captain.

Lee felt the vibrations and they were cool. The boys had arranged with Witten that if this was so, they would give a nod. Witten did not trust his feeling of the vibrations yet, although he was sensitive to them. Lee nodded and Witten acknowledged him.

'If Rajay Ghiry did appear, how would *you* react?' Witten asked.

'I'd not hinder him.' Witten took two large gold coins from his purse and put them on the table. The Captain went on, 'Oh no, sir, you don't need to do that. You can be sure of our loyalty. We've been waiting for - what shall I say? - a visit from His Highness.' He nevertheless picked up the coins and put them in his pocket. 'I'll put the word around, discreetly mind you.' He opened the door and said loudly, 'As I was saying, you can't be too careful these days, can you?'

'No, indeed,' agreed Witten.

Lee's heart was pounding. Rajay's friends were cool and resourceful. He was very impressed. He hoped the Captain was as good as his word, or they were in deep trouble.

Once inside the fort, Witten asked to see the officers' wives and soon the supposed silver traders were seated in a comfortable living room, surrounded by twittering ladies. First they asked for news, because merchants always brought the latest gossip. Witten fed them some nonsense and then the selling began; he laid out the silver jewellery and was soon driving his first hard bargain, while Lee kept an eye on the stock.

Ahren was standing at the back and noticed a light skinned, sandy haired youth come in. He immediately recognised him as Persheray, whom he had met at the school on Theon's Island. His friend looked depressed, but brightened up enormously when he recognised Lee and Ahren. Ahren put his finger on his lips indicating silence and meanwhile Lee noticed a bracelet disappear up the sleeve of one of the ladies, but said nothing. Rajay's fort was worth a trinket or two and this was the vital moment.

'What on earth are you two doing here?' whispered Persheray.

'Selling jewellery,' Ahren whispered back.

'Come outside, this is unbelievable!' Ahren followed Persheray out into a small walled garden and they sat down on some steps. 'You look great. Did you make it to that place you were trying to get to?'

'Yes, but - you look awful. What are you doing here? I thought you lived much further north.'

'We did, but, Ahren, it's so abysmal! Sometimes I want to throw myself over the cliff into the river and my father and mother aren't much better off. Those Mattanga people, I wish - oh - I don't know what I wish!'

'Why not start at the beginning and tell me what's going on.'

'Last year, those wretched creeps invaded our lands for no apparent reason and captured nearly all our flocks and herds - and they were our wealth. Then they burnt our houses down, so my father went to Mattanga and complained to King Karlvid, but all he said was, "Sorry, it was a mistake, we received some intelligence that you were about to attack us". It was absolute lies, but my father was conned into accepting this job as commander of this fort and we've been here ever since. I hate Daish Shaktay, I hate the ogres and in fact there isn't much about my life I don't hate. I just want to go back to our beautiful plains and our flocks and houses that aren't there any more, but we don't even have enough money to buy food, let alone leave. Our overlords in Mattanga hardly ever pay us and rarely give us money to pay the troops, so they're on the point of mutiny.'

'Persheray, don't give up hope. We didn't, and everything worked out for us. Don't hate. Be detached; it's less wearing and more effective in the long run.'

'You - you have an inner stillness and depth, yet you bubble with life. You're so different from when we last met!'

'That's what we learnt in the mountain country. First you get all right inside, then things get better outwardly.'

'It's easy for you to say that.'

'No, seriously, I'll show you the first bit. Put your right hand on your heart and say to yourself, "Deep inside, am I calm, joyful, eternal spirit?" Close your eyes and say it. Go on, try. Put your left hand out as if asking for something, palm upwards.'

When Persheray's eyes were closed, Ahren raised his right hand up behind Persheray's back to the top of his head and rotated it above his crown. 'Raise your hand, put it above the top of your head and say, "Please, all loving, mother energy that powers the universe, awaken my spirit in me so I can know peace and joy."'

All this time Ahren was moving his hands anti-clockwise in the air near Persheray's subtle centres, behind his back, feeling on his corresponding fingers where the problems were and directing the power in his hands to heal them.

'What do you feel above the top of your head, if you put your hand there?'

'A hot wind flowing, but I'm more at ease than I've been for months. Whatever did you do?'

'Tell you in a moment. Close your eyes again and put your attention just above your head.' Ahren went on giving vibrations to his friend's damaged heart centre and the one in his forehead, to settle his fear, anger and aggression. He had felt pain and a pricking sensation on his little fingers, which corresponded to the heart centre and accounted for the fear. Then he felt heat on the fourth finger on the right hand, which corresponded to the front part of the sixth centre, in the brain. This was because of Persheray's feelings of aggression. 'Put your hand above your head again. Do you feel a cool wind now?'

'Yes, and I'm less angry. What's going on?'

'I've awakened your subtle spiritual awareness, so you can know inner peace. Come down to the stable with me and we'll sort out your other problem.'

While they were walking towards the stable, where the packhorse and its precious saddle were waiting, Ahren checked various things on the vibrations. If he got this wrong it could cost them their lives. Once there he took out his knife, slit the lining of the saddle and out fell gold, emeralds and diamonds.

'There's your escape route.' He put the jewels and gold in Persheray's hands. 'Those are for you and your parents, if you'll leave this place. I'm with Rajay Ghiry and he wants his fort back.'

'You mean you know the Mountain Mouse?' Persheray's face lit up. Whether it was the fact that Ahren had awakened his Tree of Life, or whether it was the mention of Rajay, Ahren realised he was dealing with a very different personality from the one he had recently met.

'I'm one of his freedom fighters.'

'Now you're talking! He's my hero. I'd give anything to meet him. Any chance?'

'Yes, definitely. He'll help you every way he can, if you'll help him. If you don't, you've had it, because he knows his country, his people love him and you'll not escape alive. He sent me and Lee here to try and sort out this whole thing peacefully. Put those jewels out of sight, somewhere safe. So, what do you say?'

'I'll go and talk to my father, right now. Go back to the ladies and meet me in the garden when you're through with selling bangles. I'm tempted to call you a saint.'

'We've met some saints recently,' Ahren pondered. 'No, I'm just Ahren, the boy from Teletsia, or Sasrar.'

'Whoever you are, thanks, friend.' Persheray left to talk to his parents, his face glowing. He soon returned and asked Lee, Ahren and Witten to come into the garden, where they could talk in private. Once there he continued, 'Dad wants to escape. Mum's a bit scared, but she'll go along with him. Dad would like to talk to you.' Lee and Ahren checked the vibrations and nodded at Witten.

'That would make sense,' said Witten.

Persheray took the three of them up to the family's apartment.

'So, you're my son's friends,' began Lord Plainsman, his father. He was a tall, slim man, with shoulder length blond hair, a bushy beard and a long, whiskery moustache. His blue eyes were piercingly intelligent.

'Yes, and this is Mr Lato Tong, who's helping us sell jewellery,' Lee introduced Witten.

'Really?' said Lord Plainsman cynically, not believing a word. 'Persh, stand by the door and make sure we aren't overheard,' and to the visitors, 'My son just brought me some very welcome news, and a handful of the most valuable gems I've ever seen, so let's get straight down to business. If I wanted, I could have had you thrown in the dungeons already. I'm also well aware that most of the lower ranks here would much rather have Rajay Ghiry as their overlord than me, or shall we say Mattanga. The questions we have to consider are firstly, how are my family to get out of here and secondly, where do we go then?'

'I think we should report back to you tomorrow,' Witten suggested.

'How can I be sure you're in good faith?' asked Lord Plainsman.

'I'll stay behind as a hostage,' said Ahren.

Lee and Witten looked searchingly at him. They had not planned this, but Ahren put one hand above the other, palms together and little way apart, as if to say – the vibrations are cool.

Lee and Witten left and saw Athlos on their way out. He had just arrived for a singing session in the evening, so his group would be staying in the fort overnight. Lee went up to him as if to beg a blessing, and mentioned that they should try to stay the next day.

Witten led Lee to the farm where the others were hiding.

'We'll forge a letter from Mattanga,' Rajay decided, having heard how the meeting had gone. 'We've got writing materials and a stolen Mattangan seal, but our best writer is Deradan and he's gone back to Malak Citadel. Those orders would be in the classic language and none of us are much good at writing it. I can speak it, more or less, but writing is hard.'

'I can write it fairly well,' said Lee.

'What luck!'

Rajay and Lee created a convincing document late that evening, by candlelight, in the farmer's front room. Rajay had seen numerous official dispatches and communications from Mattanga, so knew what it should look like.

The next morning Ekan swam his horse across the Shaktay River well below the fort and approached the ford from the north. His mother had come from Mattanga and he was posing as a messenger, because his reddish hair was common in those parts and he could put on a Mattangan accent. When he reached the fort he asked to see Lord Plainsman and was taken to their dining room, where the family was finishing lunch. Ahren had been telling them of his adventures.

'So, you're another of them, are you?' Lord Plainsman said, as Ekan handed him the letter.

'This is from Mattanga and requires urgent attention, sir,' he replied blandly.

Lord Plainsman read the letter. 'I see I'm to return to Mattanga immediately, with all my senior officers and five hundred loyal men. Temporary command of the fort is to be given to – what's this? My son?'

'I am merely a courier, sir.'

'And a few officers are to stay here and support him – ah! I get it now. There are some who might change sides if there's money involved and others who are utterly useless, so I won't have to leave many who'll actually help defend the fort.'

'Sir, my leader feels it would be better if you don't go straight back to your country. When some monks meet you at the ferry, they'll escort you to an ally of ours called Count Zaminder, where you can hide.'

Ahren and Ekan left Lord Plainsman, crossed the courtyard and saw Athlos leaving with his men, having finished their singing and acrobatic display. They told him what was going on. The next step was to get the officers, some of whom looked very ogrish, and the five hundred troops who were to go with them, out of the fort. Persheray's father called them and told them there was a serious uprising in a province north of Mattanga. They were being recalled and should leave immediately with their families. By late afternoon they all made their way down the track to the river and some time later Lord and Lady Plainsman also left. The Captain of the Watch and a few troops stayed behind. He ordered the monthly tally of the weapons: everyone except the guards on duty had to deposit their weapons in the weapon store, to be counted and inspected the following morning.

Later Persheray called the remaining officers, except the Captain of the Watch, to his father's apartment for supper. He said that a friend of his father's was expected, with an escort, and the gates were to be kept open until they arrived. After sunset when the light had faded, a farmer, dressed in his best and posing as Lord Plainsman's friend, and Rajay, dressed as an inconspicuous retainer and hiding in the crowd, arrived with about a hundred and fifty partisans. As soon as they were inside the gates were closed. Ahren was waiting in the yard and raised nine fingers to Rajay, to indicate how many officers were with Persheray. Athlos, also dressed as a retainer and heavily disguised with a cloak over his head and body, stayed with the partisans and guided them towards the weapons store, where they stood innocuously in front of its entrance. They did not know the Captain of the Guard had virtually disarmed the garrison for the night, but they did know that most of the arms would be stored there and any fighting would be less bloody if the defenders had fewer weapons. The supposed friend of Persheray's father, Rajay and his friends were escorted up to Persheray and the officers.

'Good evening,' Rajay began politely, 'I want my fort back. Lay down your arms and no one will get hurt.' The officers spun round.

'It's the Mouse!' yelled one, as Varg-Nack drew his sword to guard Rajay.

'This whole thing is a trap!' cried another, lunging at Persheray with a dagger, whether to hold him as a hostage or to kill him no one discovered, because Rajay was as quick as lightning and within seconds the officer was dead.

'Surrender or die,' Rajay demanded. 'I have a large number of armed partisans in the yard and what's left of your garrison will not support you.' The officer nearest the door made a run for it, but Namoh wounded him in the arm. He groaned in pain and the others begged for mercy.

'Thank you for saving my life,' Persheray stammered, kneeling at Rajay's feet.

'I'm very grateful to you, and don't kneel. What's happening in the yard?' he turned to Valya, who ran in at that moment.

'The Captain of the Guard has ordered his men to surrender,' Valya panted. 'The partisans dealt with the few who didn't want to.'

'Excellent! We'd hoped that captain would help,' Rajay glanced around the room. 'Namoh, see to that wounded officer, he needs medical help, and the ones who've surrendered can go in the dungeons for the moment.'

'There's a nurse in the housekeeper's rooms,' Persheray looked at Witten, who had also been slightly injured.

'Go, I don't need you here,' ordered Rajay, 'and send up some more partisans as guards.'

Rajay was not absolutely sure of everyone's loyalty and told the remainder of the people in the fort to assemble in the courtyard. He gave them the choice of joining him or leaving. Apart from the officers they were all Daish Shaktay people and keen to serve their rightful king. When he announced he was giving a month's pay in advance they nearly all signed on; job security was their main concern. He ordered Athlos to stay at Confluence Fort with Persheray and also gave an important position to the Captain of the Guard, who had made the job of retaking the fort so much easier. Danard raised the red standard, Luth's cloak, over the fort and it could be seen by the light of the two moons up that night.

CHAPTER 2

THE BATHING PARTY

The next day Rajay spent time with Persheray, Athlos and the Captain of the Guard. Witten put to rights the chaotic financial situation left by Lord Plainsman, who had been at the mercy of his overlords in Mattanga; Danard went through the garrison and appointed men to all the jobs needed to keep the fort running safely, securely and smoothly; Varg-Nack checked out the kitchen staff, stable hands and people on that level, to make sure they were all reliable and trustworthy, and the rest of Rajay's friends saw to a thousand jobs which had to be done to restore the fort to being an efficient part of the Daish Shaktay defences.

At midday everyone in the fort had to swear the oath of allegiance to Free Daish Shaktay with Rajay as its leader. He sat in the courtyard with the sacred sword on his knee and one by one people came up, saluted him and touched the sword, and that meant *everyone,* from Persheray, the temporary commander, down to the humblest cleaning woman. Varg-Nack and Lee stood each side of Rajay, swords drawn, in case of trouble.

'It gives me a chance to have a look at them and them me, and when they touch that sword they're touching something with powerful vibrations that will help them on a subtle level,' he explained.

In the evening there was a feast, and while everyone in the fort was enjoying themselves, Rajay, Lee and Ahren went into the quiet of the walled garden. They sat on the stone steps, still warm from the day's sun, in the soft moons' light, surrounded by fragrant herbs in neat flower beds, stone pots and urns. These gardens could be found in all the forts and the herbs were not only for cooking but were also the medicine chest. It was lit by lamps, as was the whole fort on this evening of celebration, and below they could hear voices, music and singing. A few armed partisans lurked nearby to guard Rajay, in case there were any disloyal people still around.

'So, one more is returned to us - and an important one at that. You did stupendously well,' Rajay congratulated them.

'Beginner's luck,' said Ahren, and Lee agreed.

'Maybe, but you did it. One small thing Ahren, don't be so generous with the jewels in future. A couple were enough - what you gave Persheray could equip a small army, but don't worry, they were stolen ones from the Chussan baggage train – easy come, easy go!' Rajay laughed, and at that moment Persheray appeared at the entrance of the garden, unwilling to intrude. 'Come and join us,' Rajay called out and he approached shyly.

'Um, I've been telling people about that inner awakening you did on me. Could you do it for them?' he asked Ahren.

'You've got your work cut out,' Rajay smiled. 'Persheray, collect anyone who's interested in the Great Hall tomorrow morning and these two will do the rest.' He went off and Rajay continued. 'You know your business. Let me show you some more of mine.' He laid a map on the steps and pointed to another fort beyond the hills to the south of them. 'We need that one back too - Midway Manor Fort. It dominates the road from here down to the centre of the country. It's critical we control that route, but every move we make against Mattanga, we risk our lives.'

'We were also in the temple when you made the vow,' Lee reminded him.

'All right,' Rajay paused as Varg-Nack approached, wanting a bit of peace and quiet after an exhausting day's work. 'How's it going?' Varg-Nack gave the thumbs up sign, indicating that all was fine. 'I was about to tell the boys about that appalling commander at Midway Manor.'

'I heard in the kitchens that someone finally did him in,' Varg-Nack sighed, sitting down, 'saves us the trouble.'

'True enough. That fort was under the command of an inhumanly cruel man who'd sold out to Karlvid of Mattanga. He was unfortunately a friend of my father's. His wife was always urging him to join me, and finally he killed her by throwing her off the battlements - said it was an accident, but there were witnesses who swore blind that it wasn't.'

'It sounds like he deserved to be murdered. Who's in charge now?' asked Lee.

'That's just it. Midway Manor has traditionally been commanded by that family and the three sons are squabbling as to which one gets the job. Luth told me the father had been killed, and had me send a letter to them, saying that as I'm the son of King Partap, their father's friend, perhaps I could visit the fort for the forthcoming Autumn Harvest Festival, act as mediator and solve their problem. Today, an invitation to the festival arrived, with one of Athlos's men. I've sent for Bart Charval and his friends, plus there are about four hundred local men secretly in my service in that area, and we'll also have Athlos's people. That should be enough.'

Lee and Ahren led the awakening programme the following morning and nearly everyone in Confluence Fort attended. They were seen as liberators and with Rajay encouraging them everything was easy. He suspected that the vibrations on the sword they had touched helped too. Over the next few days various groups of men arrived; first the leaders of the Midway Manor area partisans: farmers, tradesmen, schoolteachers and a doctor, all secretly trained in warfare, and later another of Luth's cells of fighting monks, from northern Daish Shaktay. Rajay met them in the castle yard.

'Friends,' he began, 'men of my kingdom, I need your help. The sooner we free the whole of Daish Shaktay from the Mattanga overlords, the better for all of us. This is our land, so let's make it that way once more! You are my hands, arms and legs, and nothing can be done without you. I lived on a farm as a child and know the ways of the country. At this time of year we bring in bundles of branches and other fuel for the winter fires and also dried grass for the animals. Is this done at Midway Manor?'

'Yes, sir,' said a thin, wiry man, his face wrinkled from a lifetime of tilling the ground in the hot sun. 'My cousins have the contract to supply it.'

'Please come here, Mr...'

'Sim, Your Honour, Sim Patter at your service,' Rajay took him aside.

'Mr Patter, I want your cousins to do a simple and important service for our country. Ask them if they'll allow my partisans to carry the bundles into the fort, with a few villagers to guide them. They'll get paid just the same. Can you manage that?'

'They'll be only too happy to help! You're our leader, not those stupid quarrelling boys at the fort right now.'

Midway Manor Fort was built on an outcrop of rock at the top of a valley. Its sides were heavily forested and a cooling river ran through it. Below was a plain with the all-important road, visible from the fort. On it were several villages and farms belonging to the family who commanded the fort. The local partisans loaded up with bundles of branches, dried grass and maize stalks, and began depositing them in a barn in the fort. This was done every year and the bundles stayed in the barn for a month or two until needed, but this year they concealed weapons. Rajay, his companions, Bart's contingent of twenty or so farmers turned partisans, and Luth's monks all hid in the nearby forests.

It was then Valya's turn to do his bit. He did a good job of looking aristocratic, because that was his upbringing, and went to Midway Manor to make sure the invitation was still open. He rode his black charger up to the fort with all the confidence of the ruling classes, put on the swaggering walk and slightly sarcastic tone of voice that went with the part and asked to see Nilad, the eldest brother. He knew Valya; they had met at social gatherings on the rare occasions Valya went to them. Valya was ushered in with no trouble and taken up to Nilad's private apartment.

'Greetings! If it isn't Valya Northwestern! How are you these days?' drawled Nilad.

'Well, thank you.'

'I hear you're with Rajay Ghiry. Exciting stuff, but your future might be a bit uncertain,' Nilad knew Valya had been disowned.

'He's a great patriot and a skilled diplomat.'

'We heard there's a price on his head, because King Karlvid has had enough of his tricks. However, I'll support the highest bidder, if you understand me. What's this I hear about his taking back Confluence Fort?'

'Yes, it's true. He does want to reunite the country and regain our full independence, but we nobles don't really care who runs the show, as long as we have our lands and wealth. You're in an excellent position, because whether Karlvid keeps control of this part of Daish Shaktay, or whether Rajay takes it back, you'll be fine. After all, your father and Rajay's father were good friends. My situation is not so easy.' Valya did not like telling lies, but the odd one was necessary to gain the trust of this collaborator with the enemy.

'I heard your family are being difficult. Mine are too - let's hope Rajay can make my brothers see sense. It's obvious I should be the next commander, because I'm the oldest, but try and get them to understand that simple fact? Impossible! They've written letters to Mattanga about me, saying I'm incompetent. You've no idea how much money they've wasted, sending bribes to get King Karlvid to make one of them the fort commander.'

'What a headache! What have you done about it?'

'I sent more letters to Mattanga, with bigger bribes.'

'Then what happened?'

'King Karlvid demanded the annual tribute, the taxes we've collected from the people who live in this area, but that was the money we'd used for the bribes!'

'I do see your problem. I'm sure Rajay will help you. By the way, does the invitation for the Harvest Festival still stand?'

'Yes, indeed, I've been waiting for him these past few days.'

'He's nearby, and he's got some retainers with him.'

'The more the merrier – oh, and he'll be quite safe. We won't give him away to Karlvid's men.'

A little while later Nilad called his brothers to him.

'Fortune is with us,' he began. 'Rajay Ghiry and his men are coming to visit. We'll welcome them, keep them here for a day or two until they get careless, then massacre them all and pick up the reward for their heads. That will solve the problem of the missing tribute money.'

Pilad and Sakrad, the younger brothers, discussed this when they were alone. They had a different plan, which did not involve their elder brother. Pilad was not intelligent and did not realise that Sakrad intended to use him too, then discard him. Sakrad had heard of Rajay's increasing power and felt it might be to his advantage to protect Rajay rather than kill him. Plus he realised it might not be that easy to kill the Mountain Mouse and his brave followers, and if he failed the repercussions would be terrible.

Valya returned to Rajay and the others with the news, both that the invitation was still open and that these people also knew Rajay was a wanted man.

'Let's check by asking on the vibrations, whether it's safe to go,' suggested Lee. Everyone felt cool on their hands, but with one or two tingles, indicating there might be some difficulties.

'They won't let us take our swords into the feast,' Rajay warned, 'but all of you must have daggers hidden on you and any other weapons you can conceal.' They made various plans, in case they were attacked during the feast. They also checked the vibrations of the three brothers. Nilad and Sakrad were hot on the right side, especially on the sixth centre, in the forehead, indicating they were both in their ego. The third brother, Pilad was not alright in his heart centre, indicating fear and insecurity.

Rajay and his men arrived and showed no sign of recognising Varg-Nack, dressed as a peasant and toiling with the porters, actually partisans, bringing in their bundles of branches. In the troopers' dining hall word was going round that the dispute about the command would soon be over. All the members of the garrison were natives of Daish Shaktay and firmly believed that Rajay could accomplish anything.

'Maybe we'll get our pay on time, at last,' said one man hopefully.

'I'd prefer some leave, I haven't seen my wife and kids for months,' complained another.

'It's about time someone with sense is running this place. I'm going back to being a highwayman in Mattan province if things don't look up pretty quick,' added a grim looking individual with a scar across his face, presumably from his time robbing travellers.

Rajay's contemporary was the youngest brother, Sakrad, and Rajay seemed to be supporting his claim to be fort commander. The Harvest Festival was traditionally a time for a scrumptious meal and heavy drinking, but Rajay insisted that none of his men touched a drop of alcohol, because the success of the operation depended on their being stone cold sober. Predictably, the two younger brothers were soon quarrelling with the oldest one, Nilad. Their voices rose at the High Table in the Great Hall and Rajay watched as they played into his hands. His men were seated where they could all see him and were alert and ready for trouble.

'I'll have you thrown out of the fort!' yelled Nilad to Sakrad.

'You'll be lucky, I've got the king on my side!' Sakrad slurred.

'He's no king, just an upstart whose father worked for Karlvid,' muttered Pilad.

'Get out of my fort, both of you!' repeated Nilad. Soon he sagged over the table and Pilad and Sakrad dragged him out of the hall trussed him up like a hunting trophy, and had him carried to a lockup at the top of a small tower.

'One down, two to go,' Rajay murmured to Valya, sitting next to him. 'Tell Sakrad that my men will guard Nilad, so his staff can enjoy the festival.' Rajay knew his plan was going well; Sakrad thought his was too.

The following morning most people at the fort had severe headaches and slept late. In the guest rooms, Rajay had been up since dawn, putting the finishing touches on his plans with his companions and partisan leaders.

'You all know what to do,' he began. 'We need this fort, and we need everyone in it, because they're all Daish Shaktay people.'

Rajay and Valya ate breakfast later with Pilad and Sakrad, whose heads were swathed in wet towels. They both felt appalling, as a result of the large amounts of potent mead they had drunk the night before.

'How about going for a swim? It will make us all feel fresher,' Valya suggested.

'Good idea,' agreed Pilad.

'We could have a picnic lunch there. Let's take your officers too,' added Rajay. 'I'd like to meet them.'

'Yes, and it will help them feel better,' groaned Sakrad, clutching his head. 'Where's brother Nilad?'

'Still in the lockup, and my men are keeping an eye on him. Let's leave him there for the time being,' replied Rajay helpfully.

'Definitely,' chuckled Sakrad.

'Oh, absolutely,' concluded Pilad.

The bathing place was delightful. Steps went down to the river where it had a clear and sandy bottom; on one side was thick greenery and behind was the cliff on top of which the fort was built. At its base were natural caves, and water dripped through the rocks making cooling streams which fed the river. Masses of red flowers grew on the banks of these streamlets and darting turquoise kingfishers completed the picture. Rajay, Valya, the two brothers and the officers bathed and then relaxed on the river bank. Valya and Rajay made convincing small talk and after some time Lee arrived with the lunch.

'Everything all right?' Rajay asked, as if referring to the picnic.

'Yes, sire, perfect,' replied Lee. He put his attention on Rajay's subtle self and felt his heart pounding with excitement and relief. It was a good thing the brothers did not share their subtle awareness. When everyone had tucked into the meal, Rajay walked over to Lee, standing discreetly under a tree.

'So?'

'It's yours! The garrison are yours too. I hope you don't mind, we gave them a month's pay in advance.'

'Wise move. We need to be sure of their loyalty - and the casualty list?'

'None. When the members of the garrison, suffering from shocking hangovers, were faced with four hundred armed, sober and alert partisans, who had retrieved their weapons from the bundles they brought in, the garrison was only too happy to surrender.'

'Well done. What about Nilad?'

'He hollered from the lockup window, but we told him no one was going to get hurt. I think he got the message.'

Rajay returned to the party. They all had a sleep after the meal and the sun was in the west when they finally moved. They began walking back and once round the bend could see the walls of the fort above them.

'What's that red flag on the flagpole?' asked Sakrad.

'That's the flag of free Daish Shaktay,' explained Rajay.

'What's it doing on our flagstaff?'

'Rajay has solved your problem,' said Valya.

'Is this some sort of a joke?' demanded Sakrad. Rajay clicked his fingers and Bart Charval's men, with Ekan, came out of the greenery, arrows aimed at the brothers and officers at point blank range.

'It's not possible,' moaned Pilad.

'It's perfectly possible,' replied Rajay. 'None of you deserve to command this fort. As king, I'm going to take it back myself, because I'm ultimately the owner of all the property in this land. This being so, I'll arrange for new title deeds to be made out so all three of you get a share of your family lands down the valley. Isn't that better than fighting one another for control of the fort?' The brothers had to agree, but Rajay hadn't finished. 'You must apologise to Nilad. Your behaviour last night was disgraceful. When I've reunited this land, if you can reform your ways, I'll reconsider making one of you the fort commander and the other two can come and work for me. But it's up to you to show that you've changed for the better. In my country people have to deserve their promotions, not just inherit them.' They realised they had been outmanoeuvred in every way.

'Ekan, Bart, escort these men back to my fort.'

CHAPTER 3

FORTUNE TELLERS

Rajay ordered the three brothers out of the fort that evening. The next morning he called Lee and Ahren to his apartment, formerly that of the brothers.

'I told a lie yesterday when I said all the land in this country is mine, as king,' he began. 'The land belongs to the people. I'm only an arbitrator, but when dealing with egotistical asses like those three, what else could I say?' Lee and Ahren were silent, not knowing how to answer. Rajay looked at the map in front of him on a low table. 'There's another fort we must try for, but it's going to be difficult. I'm concerned that you two are risking your lives and this isn't even your country.'

'This *is* our country,' went on Lee. 'We Teletsians worship the Mother Earth. This is her heart centre, and if her heart centre is not all right, ours isn't either. We've been to Sasrar, so we're aware that the primordial Tree of Life is reflected in her and also each one of us.'

'I feel the same,' agreed Ahren, 'but Lee puts things into words better.'

'All right,' Rajay showed them the map. 'We're here, and southwest is Santara, our old capital. That's where our Northern Regiment is stationed. South of here is another line of hills and in that pass, through which the road runs, is Gap Fort. It overlooks a small town and is the limit of Karlvid's area of influence. South of there is the part of Daish Shaktay that we administer,

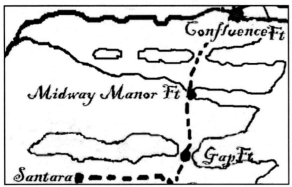

but the ogre peoples keep a strong garrison at Gap Fort. Athlos's informers have discovered that the commander has a weakness which we'll try and exploit. To take that fort, we need someone, or some people, inside to open the gates late at night, so we can get in and fight.'

'And that's us?' said Lee.

'Yes. You're from Teletsia, so presumably you know about fortune tellers?'

'Obviously! Most people there can't live without them.'

'Could you pretend to be fortune tellers, with as much mystery and magic as possible?'

'We've been all sorts of people recently,' laughed Ahren, 'One more disguise isn't going to make much difference.'

'The commander of Gap Fort is addicted to fortune tellers and everyone knows Teletsians are the best. Are you with me?'

'Oh yes,' added Lee, 'I'm not going to miss out on this one.'

Meanwhile Valya and Varg-Nack were in a corner of the Officers Mess eating breakfast. They had been friends from childhood, because when Valya ran away from his father's castle to be with Rajay, he often hid in Varg-Nack's parents' cottage, in a village near Santara. Namoh and Danard came in.

'We're going to try and take back Gap Fort,' Danard whispered.

'How?' Valya asked.

'Rajay's got a plan to get in using Lee and Ahren, posing as fortune tellers.'

'Whatever will he think of next?'

'No idea, and let's hope no one else does either. We've got to meet him with the Northern Regiment, nearby, in the forest. We have to bring them up secretly because the Mattanga people there will have heard of our success here and at Confluence and may be expecting trouble.'

'Being as the boundary between Northern Daish Shaktay and our own Central Daish Shaktay is only a little way south of Gap Fort, it shouldn't be too difficult.'

'We've got a lot of informers there. They'll spread plenty of misinformation about us to the Mattanga folk, who'll be told we're going home via the western road and are nowhere near.'

'When do we leave?'

'Right now. We've got to do this fast, before they find out what we're up to.'

'Talking of fortunes,' Valya hurriedly finished his breakfast, 'Lee and Ahren have brought us good luck, and Asha too.'

'It's because they've lived in Sasrar,' Namoh interrupted. 'We should all go there eventually.'

'Maybe Rajay will create a Sasrar here,' went on Valya, for whom there could never be anywhere to equal Daish Shaktay.

'That's the general idea,' added Danard.

'Come on – less talk, more action,' Varg-Nack made to leave. 'We've got work to do, like, half a country to win back.'

Later in the morning Rajay took Lee and Ahren to a courtyard at the back of the fort, where there was a well. He sat on the wall at the edge and invited the other two to join him. They looked at the water below.

'There's a well similar to this at Gap Fort,' he explained. 'When I was a child my mother and I lived there for some time. One day we were sitting on the side of that well and she told me there was a hidden passage under the water level which led to a tunnel - a secret way out of the fort. I thought she was joking, but dived in as she suggested, found the tunnel and came out in a cave on the hillside. This well is the same. Dive in and see if you can get out by the underwater passage. It's important you get it right, as the one in Gap Fort may be your escape route. I warn you, it's not that easy. You first, Ahren - take off your outer clothes - give them to me.'

Ahren was glad to cool off in the water and found the underwater passage immediately, but Lee came up once or twice, spluttering for air, before he got it right. They met Rajay in the cave outside the walls, where he gave them back their clothes.

The local partisans and the militia became the new garrison at Midway Manor, a new commander was appointed and Witten and Ekan arranged the changeover of command. The new steward, who had only taken service under Rajay that day, was sent to the nearest town to do some shopping. He was mighty puzzled by the shopping list, but since it was his first order under his new employer, he was eager to do as well as possible and didn't ask any questions. In the evening he returned loaded down with packages and deposited them on the floor of Rajay's room.

'I couldn't get the powder for making green smoke, sire,' he apologised.

'It isn't the season for fireworks.'

'It's all right, thank you for trying,' Rajay handed him a silver piece. Once alone, Lee and Ahren eagerly unpacked the parcels.

'Look! A crystal ball,' cried Lee.

'I can't see anyone's fortune in that,' said Ahren, 'only the carpet underneath.'

'Whatever are those small bones for?' asked Rajay, fascinated.

'Throwing the bones: you tell the future depending on how they fall - ancient Teletsian speciality,' Lee demonstrated.

'Do you know how to read them?'

'No idea, but no one else at Gap Fort will either. I'll make it up as I go along,' Lee assured Rajay confidently.

Two days later Lee and Ahren arrived at the town below Gap Fort to tell fortunes. Customers rolled in and gossip rolled out. Because Lee and Ahren could feel their customers' vibrations, their subtle inner natures, they could figure out quite a bit about them and offer useful advice, even if they had no idea about their futures.

Rajay met the regiment from Santara and they hid in the forests. The fort commander did not hear about the army but was thrilled when told about the genuine Teletsian soothsayers. Soon Lee and Ahren received an invitation to visit him, and accepted it. Lee's last client before the meeting was a well-built, veiled lady - Witten in disguise. Lee told him that everything was ready, and met the commander in the afternoon. He had a scaly skin, clawlike hands and little horns growing on the top of his head. Lee tried not to be alarmed. He knew about ogres.

'It's good to do a consultation at night,' he insisted. 'The magic is most potent if a larger number of people are present. Can we meet in the Great Hall after dinner?'

'I don't want everyone to know my fortune,' the commander objected.

'You can have your officers, or whoever eats with you, drugged or something. It doesn't matter if they're not fully conscious; it's their presence that's needed.'

'All right. Can you whisper my fortune in my ear?' He evidently had much to hide.

'Yes indeed, sir. We'll come after dinner. Before that we need to do some preparations.'

One of the 'preparations' consisted of drawing some water from the castle well to put in their 'magic' jug, because they needed to know where the well was. They had previously been shown where the tunnel came out on the hillside, by a local partisan.

In the late evening Ahren drew strange designs on the floor of the Great Hall, with the officers looking drowsily on. He laid the crystal ball in the centre, lit a censer full of incense and swung the billowing smoke around the hall. Lee played a monotonous tune on his flute. The officers were enjoying the after effects of the sleeping draught that had been put in the wine and some were already snoring on their chairs. Lee threw the bones and the commander was entranced. One officer did not sleep and watched carefully; his grandmother had come from Teletsia and he was not convinced by these fortune-tellers. He too was unknowingly under the influence of the sleeping draught but he wasn't as far gone as the rest. Lee and Ahren did not notice him.

Lee whispered some nonsense in the governor's ear, supposedly what the bones had foretold, and Ahren got to work with the crystal ball. He walked round it mumbling old Teletsian nursery rhymes under his breath and nearly everyone, but not the officer whose grandmother came from Teletsia, assumed they were magic chants. Then they looked into the crystal ball.

'I see something important,' said Ahren, 'my colleague will interpret it.'

'The crystal ball comes to life!' declared Lee. 'A far off land - a great palace - King Karlvid is talking about you.'

'Tell me more!' whispered the commander.

'Do not use your weapons for three days: no hunting or shooting practice and don't allow your men to get involved in violent activities. Then great wealth and blessings of peace may easily come to you, but if there is any aggression in the near future, accidents could occur.'

The Teletsian stiffened; he realised this advice could be dangerous, and coupled with the fact that this 'fortune teller' had been mumbling what sounded like nursery rhymes, made him very suspicious. Ahren suddenly felt afraid and wasn't sure why. Was it Lee? He felt Lee's vibrations and realised he was in his ego: the right fourth finger was throbbing when he put his attention on Lee, a sure sign he was out of balance. This was perilous. Ahren made a bandhan of request.

'Does the crystal ball tell you any more?' demanded the commander. Lee walked catlike round the ball on the floor, as if looking for more information.

'No, sir,' said Lee. Ahren was relieved – Lee would not say anything more which might spoil everything.

The session finished and the commander ordered most of the men to take a few days' leave. Only a small guard was to remain on duty. His mind was full of fantasies of the wealth which was going to come to him, for he had great faith in the fortune tellers, who went out into the yard and chatted for some time in the balmy night. The fort's gates were closed at sunset, so they were to stay in the guest quarters. Unnoticed, one man followed them and stood in the shadows; a half-drugged part Teletsian who half knew something was amiss.

There were two rings of walls around Gap Fort. The first gatehouse, in the outer wall, was on the side of the hill, at right angles to the one in the inner ring of walls. The inner ring followed the crest of the hill, so a person standing on the top of one gatehouse could not see the other. Rajay, Danard and Valya crept close to the outer gate with nine hundred men. It was easy to hide in the dark streets near the fort, because in recent years the townspeople had built houses closer and closer to the walls.

It was well after midnight and there were no moons up. Ahren's responsibility was the outer gate. He got out through a small drain in the inner wall, which Rajay told him about, because when he was a child he used it as a way of getting out of the fort secretly when he wanted to play with friends who lived in the town. This was when he stayed at Gap Fort with his mother. A slim adult could squeeze out through it, but it would have taken too long for nine hundred soldiers to get in that way.

The sentries on the top of the walls took some time to make a full turn and it was very dark. Ahren made sure Rajay and his men had as long as possible to get from the outer gate to the inner one without being seen. He made his way round the hillside to the outer gate and the guards there didn't spot him immediately, because they were playing cards on the ground inside the gate. As he approached they stood up.

'Whozat?' mumbled one.

'What're yer doin' out here?' muttered the other.

'I'm a fortune teller and I've just told the governor's fortune. It's not good, but there's nothing I can do about that, so please let me out; I'll give you each a gold coin if you will. The guards on the inner gate did.'

'Wot do yer say, Crum?' one ogrish guard asked.

'Let's do it - it'll be the quickest gold piece I've ever made!' replied his mate.

'All right, give us the gold, lad.'

At this moment Ahren heard the call of a certain night bird, which signalled that Danard was in the street outside and had heard him. Ahren handed over the gold and the guards opened the gate. Rajay, Danard and Valya rushed in and had killed them before they even realized their error.

'Ahren, you've done your bit,' said Rajay, 'go to where the well tunnel comes out.' Ahren went out of the open gate and walked innocuously up the street, while the soldiers filed swiftly and silently up to the inner gate in the darkness.

Lee, in the courtyard, heard the bird's call and knew Danard was nearby. Now it was his turn to get the guards to open up. He looked around and thought he saw a dark shape in the corner of the yard, but wasn't sure. He would have to risk it, because Rajay's soldiers were between the inner and outer walls, and the sentries patrolling the top of the inner wall might see them, because one of the moons was now rising. He walked towards the gate where a guard stood – the other had gone to the guardroom, up some stairs. Lee went through the same routine as Ahren - he took out two gold pieces and asked to be let out. This guard was not cooperative and needed more gold. Eventually he agreed, then realised he had left his keys upstairs in the guardroom, so went up to get them.

Lee waited nervously. Again he heard the bird's call. The guard came down with his keys, took out two iron bars which were slotted into the gate, laid them on the ground and agonisingly slowly began to unlock the door. Up above, the sentries noticed Rajay's soldiers. They shouted down to the gateman and Lee picked up one of the bars and hit him hard on the back of the head. He dropped like a stone and Lee hurriedly opened the gates. The other guard woke up and started down the stairs and the half Teletsian officer, who had been watching in the corner of the yard also came running towards Lee.

Lee could not escape out of the gate because Rajay's men were pouring through it. He ran across the courtyard pursued by the officer, in a fort full of enemies. He darted into a passage, the officer shouting at people to stop him, but no one heard in the pandemonium. Then Lee heard a shot and felt a searing pain in his shoulder. There was another shot and his ankle was on fire and barely able to support him. He ran on - he *had* to reach that well - but which way? He had memorised it in the daylight but the maze of corridors and courtyards were not easy in the darkness, added to which he was in great pain. *Where* was that well? He kept running and the noise of battle was loud in the yard behind. Finally Lee saw the well. Soldiers were rushing towards him, almost trampling on him in the darkness and he pressed himself against the side of the passage to let them past. His consciousness was slipping. He reached the side of the well and heard someone behind him. He took a deep breath and dived in, his strength waning.

Back in the courtyard the drugged officers could not fight much, but the men-at-arms put up a stiff resistance.

'It's the Mouse!' yelled the Captain of the Guard, who had not been at the fortune telling session. He rallied his men and ogres and made for Rajay, who was flanked by Varg-Nack. Two ogres went for Varg-Nack and more attacked Rajay. He could easily have been killed, as the odds were heavily against him. Rajay, who had fallen on the ground, was about to be spitted by an evil looking ogre when Valya jumped in front of him, giving him time to get up, and together they killed the ogres, but not before Valya had been wounded.

Soon the members of the garrison, taken completely by surprise, were either dead or begging for surrender. A combination of careful planning, luck and outrageous bravery won the night. The ogrous commander fought to the last and as Lee had predicted, entered a state of great peace: he died a warrior's death. Eventually Danard raised the red standard of Daish Shaktay on the fort's flagpole and the defeated Mattangan soldiers were locked in their own dungeons. Still out of breath from fighting, Rajay hurried to see Valya, who was lying on a stretcher moaning with pain and slipping in and out of consciousness, in the makeshift hospital. He held his friend's hand to give him faith and hope.

'Where's Lee?' Valya gasped.

'I don't know,' replied Varg-Nack, who was with him.

'Do you know where the tunnel from the well comes out?' Rajay asked Varg-Nack.

'No, I've never been here before.'

'He may be there. I'll have to go myself.' Rajay left Valya with the doctors and Varg-Nack, let himself out of a small postern gate at the rear of the fort and went to the mouth of the tunnel, hidden in some bushes. 'Lee, Ahren, are you there?' Ahren stood up. He had been sitting on the ground nearby, hugging his knees against the night chill. 'Are you all right?'

'Yes, rather cold. How about you?'

'I'll do - a few cuts and bruises – the usual. Is Lee with you?'

'No, isn't he with you?'

'No.'

'He must still be in the fort. It's ours, by the way.'

Ahren congratulated Rajay but picked up his apprehension. They returned to the fort and it was searched again, but there was no sign of Lee. Then Ahren noticed some blood on the wall at the side of the well. Dreading to do it, he looked in, half expecting to see Lee's body in the water, but nothing. He was exhausted and sat down. Rajay, who had been elsewhere, came up to him, noticed his worried expression and put a hand on his shoulder.

'Have you looked inside the tunnel?' Ahren shook his head. 'Don't give up hope.' Rajay pulled Ahren to his feet and they went round the back once more. There, catching the dawn sunlight as it shone into the long, cave-like tunnel, Ahren saw a Sasrar key lying on the ground, and Lee near it. They ran to him and he opened his eyes.

'Did we win?' he gasped.

'Do you seriously think I'd have left my men and come to look for you if we hadn't?' said Rajay. 'Through the grace of the Goddess of Daish Shaktay, we now have control of Gap Fort. We've routed the ogre peoples' strongest garrison, thanks to your help.'

'Just don't ask us to do any more fortune telling,' laughed Lee. 'Ouch!'

'Come, my friend,' smiled Rajay, and he and Ahren carried Lee outside and laid him on the ground in the morning sunlight. 'I must go - I've got a thousand things to see to. I'll send the doctor round.'

'What happened after you dived into the well?' Ahren asked Lee as they waited on the deserted hillside, the walls of the fort rising up high behind them. Below they could see farmlands in the valley and forests covering the high hills that stretched to the horizon. The town was the other side of the fort.

'I felt for the tunnel, swam up the underwater passage, pulled myself out of the water and collapsed. The tunnel led into that cave, lit by moonlight, and I heard someone splashing out of the water behind me. It came to me - my Sasrar key has the powers of all the keys! I remembered Prince Roarke's key with the sixteen petals, which killed our kidnappers, and put my index finger in the little indentation in the back. Suddenly my key grew, glowed like white fire, revolved around my finger and flew towards that man who looked like a

Teletsian coming at me with his dagger drawn. I saw my key behead him, but then I passed out. His body is round the corner of the tunnel.'

'What a night!'

Later in the morning Rajay held court in the Great Hall. First the captured officers were brought in, roped together. Some were local lords Rajay had known from childhood and he verbally blasted them for supporting Karlvid of Mattanga. After that the ogres, and people who were turning into ogres were dragged before him. They were scaly, their hands and feet clawlike, they had small horns on their heads and their voices had a sinister ghostly quality.

'I hear you eat human flesh,' began Rajay.

'Yes, it's necessary for us on occasions; our religion demands it,' replied the first arrogantly.

'But we only need common villagers, not quality folk,' added the other.

'Some of my quality folk live in the villages,' returned Rajay. 'Meet Varg-Nack. His father is a village blacksmith.' Varg-Nack bowed his head respectfully. He was tall, broad shouldered and powerfully built as befitted the family trade. One of the ogres licked his lips. 'Are you prepared to change your ways?'

'We would lose our powers without our quota of human flesh. We are a superior race and humans are our natural food,' insisted the ogre who had licked his lips at the sight of Varg-Nack.

'Are you willing to leave this continent?'

'How can we? It's our home. Our priests have assured us that humans who haven't transformed into us higher beings are there to serve us and be our food.'

'I give up. Varg-Nack, deal with them as you see fit.' Varg-Nack took the ogres outside, kicking and screaming, under a strong guard, and they were not seen again. Rajay turned to the other officers. 'What am I to do with you? Some of you are even my relations. Surely we must be united in our desire to be free of these demonic creatures? You'll stay in these dungeons until your families ransom you. What right do you have to enjoy the privileges of a fortunate birth if you behave like slaves?' He looked around the room and many of them hung their heads. Rajay was well aware that although most of the people of Daish Shaktay were behind him, some of the powerful families were jealous and bore him a deep grudge. Finally, Rajay forcefully proclaimed, 'Valya Northwestern is to be the new Commander of Gap Fort.'

As always, Rajay was chivalrous towards the ladies, who were mostly the wives of these collaborators. His soldiers would escort them and their children to their homes, but they did have to leave all their money and jewellery behind, because, as he tactfully put it, someone had to pay the reliable soldiers who were protecting them. He showed everyone in the hall his sword, including the local partisan leaders and the officers of the Northern Regiment. He read the inscription and one by one they came and swore allegiance to him and an independent Daish Shaktay. Afterwards the crowd dispersed and Rajay called

Ahren.

'How's Lee?'

'The doctor reckons he'll be fine, but Valya's not too good.'

'Is he conscious?'

'Intermittently, and he's still in a great deal of pain.'

'Go and tell him he's had a big promotion and he'd better get well quickly so he can take it up. Give him healing vibrations and ask the medics to try a dose of that herbal painkiller Melissa gave us on him. It'll probably knock him out, but that may be a good thing right now. I'll come and see him shortly.'

Rajay left some of his companions to arrange everything at Gap Fort, and also the Northern Regiment. He wanted Valya to go to Malak Citadel as soon as he could be moved. The best medical help was there and unfortunately there was a strong possibility that he might lose his leg or even his life.

CHAPTER 4

CROSSINGS FORT

Next morning Valya and Lee set off early in a horse litter, accompanied by the regimental doctor and a bodyguard. Rajay took another route and a large company of cavalrymen; even in Central Daish Shaktay he took no chances. With him were Namoh, Ekan and Ahren.

'I'll ride at the front with the officers, because I want to get to know them,' said Rajay. 'You three stay back and keep a look out for any Mattanga soldiers who've escaped from Gap Fort.'

It was a long way and Ahren got talking to his new friends.

'Tell me about this next fort we're going to,' he asked.

'You remember how Rajay forgave Valya after Crossings Fort fell to us?' said Namoh.

'And now Valya is to be a fort commander, assuming he recovers from his wounds,' mused Ekan.

'I'm sure he will. The vibrations were cool when I asked, and he's brave and strong,' went on Namoh. 'He was much better this morning when I went to see him. Most people at Gap Fort knew the saga of Crossings, and that's why Rajay made the announcement so publicly.

'Crossings is between here and Malak Citadel. It's on a hilltop overlooking the crossing of five main roads. A year ago, Rajay had already taken control of the forts around Santara and Malak Citadel, but Crossings was administered by the powerful Lord Chor Bardmarsh. Although not exactly in King Karlvid's service, he sympathised with him. Chor was cruel, lazy and addicted to opium and alcohol. He also had an over-inflated opinion of himself and a foul temper.

'Soon after Rajay took over the administration, he went to see Lord Bardmarsh. He humbly explained his intention to free Daish Shaktay, with him as its king. This being so, he asked Chor to join him and accept him as overlord. Chor treated Rajay as if he was an insolent schoolboy, saying if anyone was fit to rule Daish Shaktay it was him.'

'But surely Rajay is heir to the kingdom, isn't he?' said Ahren.

'It's not that simple,' Ekan took over. 'By the laws of hereditary, Chor also had a good claim, but he was a useless man, whereas Rajay has the ability to pull this country together and he's the people's hero. He's completely dedicated and selfless, whereas Chor only wanted power. Valya's father also has a claim - Valya is Rajay's second cousin - but Lord Northwestern's lands lie in the part of the country which is a province of Mattanga at the moment. He's happy if he can keep his lands and wealth by collaborating with Karlvid. In any event, next Rajay showed the lengths he was prepared to go to when he tried for a marriage alliance with Chor's daughter Esmeralda. We did our best to stop him - there's a limit to what we'd let him do for Daish Shaktay.'

'Is she that bad?' asked Ahren, knowing that Rajay's friends never argued with him beyond a certain point.

'You don't know Esmeralda!' Ekan laughed ruefully. 'Her nature is like her father's, but worse, if that's possible. I know one shouldn't be too biased by looks, but she's - she reminds me of a buffalo with a stomach ache.'

'Ekan is too complimentary. She's enormously fat and as spotty as a raisin bun,' added Namoh.

'Maybe she would have improved,' suggested Ahren charitably.

'Some hope! Anyway,' Ekan took over again, 'Rajay sent an official proposal, insisting it was worth it if it meant a peaceful and united country.'

'What happened next?' Ahren continued.

'We all breathed a sigh of relief when Chor said he wasn't having his daughter marrying some upstart mountain mouse. At this point Rajay went for a direct challenge,' continued Namoh. 'He sent old Chor a letter, saying "I'm the rightful heir to this kingdom, so you must submit to me."' To this Chor replied, '"You're a mere boy, come and fight me if you dare."'

'Where does Valya come in?' asked Ahren.

'Now. Valya met Rajay when they were children and he would frequently run away from home and ride his pony a long way across wild country, living like a gypsy, to find Rajay and the rest of us. Valya's family were at their wits' end and as he grew up he didn't change.

'Finally his father got him the job of junior steward to Chor Bardmarsh, and this was when Rajay was beginning to bring some of our forts back under his direct control. We were already a tight knit group and were disappointed, we thought we'd lost Valya but at that time he felt he couldn't break with his family. Rajay sent a message to Chor saying he would like to meet him once more and the reply, inviting Rajay to Crossings, was brought by Valya. Chor didn't realise Valya had been close to Rajay; in fact between the opium and the alcohol I don't think old Chor realised much. Valya warned Rajay that Chor planned to have his men ambush him and told him where. Rajay accepted the invitation to meet Chor, took a number of us with him and we ambushed the ambush. The meeting was not a success, because Chor was not expecting Rajay to arrive alive. When we trotted into the yard at Crossings Fort he was completely unprepared, but merely said that everything he had already told Rajay still held true.

'Two months later Valya arrived secretly at Malak Citadel and begged Rajay to take him back. By now he didn't care if his family disowned him, something his father had sworn to do if he so much as mentioned Rajay's name. Being as Valya's father had already had one heart attack and Valya would soon become Lord Northwestern if he was not disowned, this was quite a step. He was throwing away the certainty of inheriting the largest estates in the country for Rajay, whose position was very insecure at that time. Rajay told him to return to Chor and continue working for him as if nothing had changed.

'Rajay wanted to come to a compromise with Chor, and Danard and I delivered the proposal. Valya was Chor's bodyguard and we met in Chor's library at Crossings. He was drunk and all we got out of him were streams of abuse about Rajay and Queen Jansy. Soon Chor drew his sword and ordered Valya to help him kill us. He assumed we were unarmed, because we had been made to leave our swords at the gatehouse, but Valya stood at the door without moving and we drew daggers out of our boots. Danard threw his and caught Chor in the neck and I finished him off with mine.

'At that moment Chor's eldest son came in and drew his sword to slay us. We had our backs to him after dealing with Chor, but Valya cut him down as he entered and saved our lives. Valya stood back for us to escape. He closed the door, stood guard outside and said Chor was in conference and was not to be disturbed when some servants brought a meal.

'Meanwhile we left the fort and lit the bonfire we had prepared the night before on the hill behind Crossings. This was the signal for Rajay, hiding in the forest nearby, to attack. He was inside the fort with his men, pretending it was a friendly visit, before anyone raised the alarm, and he managed to take it, even though it was a tough struggle. This was the most violent act we've done against our own people, but there was no alternative. Valya rejoined us immediately after that.

'We've had as much trouble from jealous nobles as from Karlvid's men - hence the public proclamation of Valya as the new commander of Gap Fort, because he's an aristocrat who hasn't been consistently loyal. The appointment was a way of showing those officers at Gap Fort that Rajay will forgive past lapses.'

'And Valya's family disowned him after he rejoined you?' asked Ahren.

'Yes, but Rajay's going to try to get them to take him back. Valya's a hero now and his family realises that Rajay means it when he says he's going to be king of the whole country. He sent a letter to Valya's parents last week, asking them to come and see him at Malak Citadel.'

There was tremendous mutual respect between Rajay's companions. Neither Lee nor Ahren ever picked up anything approaching jealousy if Rajay gave any of them more attention. Their totally different backgrounds seemed to bond them even more, rather than drive them apart, as might have been expected.

The sun set and they had not reached Crossings Fort. The Daish Shaktay forts were run under a very strict code of discipline; no one was allowed to enter or leave them after sunset, so they stopped in the valley where the

Bardmarsh clan had tried to ambush Namoh and set up camp there.

The following morning Rajay met the Aydriss family, who were in charge of the fort. Sir Brin and Lady Aydriss were kindly, comfortable people who had known Rajay from childhood, and on more than one occasion when King Karlvid's men had been chasing him and Queen Jansy, he had stayed with them, hidden at their manor for safety. Lady Aydriss loved him like a son; she had four daughters but no boy of her own. The eldest and youngest girls were unmarried and living at home.

'It's good to see you again,' Rajay greeted Commander Aydriss.

'It's a pleasure, and what stories of success you bring with you!' replied the good-hearted man.

'Many of us older ones in the country are really proud of you,' added Lady Aydriss expansively, and they talked for some time.

'I remember there were one or two weaknesses in the defences here,' Rajay mentioned. 'I'd like your chief officer to take me round the fort.'

'I'll call him over. His name is Gram Odain,' said Commander Aydriss.

Here at Crossings, the curtain walls were not as high as in most forts because it was built on the side of a high cliff, nevertheless Rajay wanted to check them. He walked around the parapet on the inner side of the wall and looked out over the plain and the roads stretching away down the valleys. At the foot of the cliff, far below, was a village. At one point an extra sentry had been placed, and he saluted Rajay and Captain Odain as they passed.

'Why have you put that man there?' asked Rajay.

'It's like this, sire. Last week a milkmaid climbed over the wall there and went right down the cliff to the village, in the night.'

'You're not serious?' Odain nodded and Rajay went on, 'I'd like to speak to her.'

'She's in the fort now, delivering milk. I'll have her brought here.'

'Fine, but don't frighten her, or we might not get the information we need.'

He climbed down from the walls and the milkmaid was brought, her eyes wide with fear. She stood in front of Rajay, looking at the ground. She wore the strident, clashing colours of the country people: a long full skirt, a blouse and a length of material draped over her head and upper part of her body and carried a brass pot on her shoulder. He could see her trembling; she knew she had broken one of the most important rules of the fort.

'What is your name, sister?' Rajay asked gently.

'Heeram, My Lord,' she avoided his eyes.

'Your pot looks heavy. Why don't you put it down while we talk?'

'Yes, My Lord,' she did so, eyes firmly on the ground.

'Heeram, just tell me the truth. No one is going to hurt you.'

'Yes, Lord,' her eyes were still lowered but she had stopped shaking.

'It's all right, you can look at me.' She did so, very shyly, and Rajay smiled reassuringly.

'My Lord, I bring milk up to the fort every morning and evening, but last week we had the Harvest Festival dances in the village and I stopped to watch them on my way up. The sun was already low when I reached the fort and the head cook wanted to talk to me about some extra orders. When I left the kitchens the sun had set, so I ran to the gate, but was too late. The guards would not let me out, but showed me where I could stay for the night inside the fort. I had to get home, because my little son was alone there. My mother, who usually stays with us, was visiting my sister...'

'So you had to get back to him,' interrupted Rajay. 'Where's your husband?'

'With your Northern Regiment.'

'Go on.'

'I crept round the walls and found a part where I could try to get down. It was very hard and in one place I slipped and barely managed to grab a bush.'

'Heeram, I need you to climb down again, exactly the same way.'

'Yes, Lord, but...'

'But what?'

'When I saw the place in the daylight, I was so scared. It's so steep,' Heeram began to tremble again.

'You must, if you can. If you can get down, an enemy could get up. Please try, for the sake of your country. A man can come with you, with a rope for you to hold onto,' said Rajay. Heeram was silent for a few moments, then gathered her courage.

'My Lord, we hear so many stories of *your* bravery. Yes, I'll do it.'

So Heeram climbed down once more and the military engineer watched her carefully. She looked like a spider on the cliff face, but did follow an old path. After she had finished the scary descent, the path was destroyed. Rajay was impressed by Gram Odain's thoroughness and promoted him to Commander of Confluence Fort, with immediate effect.

'We'll be sorry to lose him,' Commander Aydriss commented. 'He's a good man.'

Rajay decided to spend that day at Crossings Fort and go on to Malak Citadel on the one after. Later in the morning he, Ahren, Namoh and Ekan went down to the village, to the open space in the middle of the cottages, sat on the wall around the edge of the well and met the women as they came to draw water. They talked with them and played with their bare footed children and Rajay subtly asked questions of the women which told him whether his new tax and administrative system was working out well. He knew that looted gold could pay armies, but plunder would never replace a stable peacetime economy. The sons, brothers and husbands of these women, and the women themselves, were a large part of Daish Shaktay's wealth, if they could be helped, by a just government, to ply their trades and work their lands profitably. Heeram heard they were there and came to offer them mugs of fresh milk from her cows. A soldier came up to Rajay.

'The gifts are ready, sire,' he said.

'Heeram, come back,' called Rajay. She returned, and round the corner came the soldier leading two sleek brown heifers with soft eyes and wet noses, their horns garlanded with flowers and brass bells hanging from their necks. 'You've done us all a favour today, because of your love for your son. These are for you. Nevertheless, I beg you not to do any more climbing like that.'

Heeram's hand went to her mouth in amazement.

CHAPTER 5

VALYA

In the afternoon Lee and Valya arrived. They had come by a different route, so Ahren had not seen them on the road. They were made comfortable in Lady Aydriss's airy and pleasant guest room, and Rajay and Ahren immediately went to find them.

'How are they?' Rajay asked the military doctor.

'Master Lee is making a remarkably quick recovery, sire, and seems to be doing some sort of spiritual healing on Lord Valya.'

'I'm sure he is, but how *is* Valya?'

'Not good. I doubt we can save his leg. The journey has taken a lot out of him. It's sad, because he was better before we left, but now he's gone down again.'

'I feared as much. Ahren, go and give Valya vibrations. They can even help with wounds, which is why Lee is healing so fast. Valya is very receptive, but he needs more than Lee can give at the moment.' Rajay called for Ekan.

'Ekan, ride on ahead. If you change horses, you'll easily reach Malak Citadel by morning. Alert the relay stations to have fresh horses ready throughout the night for Valya's litter. When you reach Malak Citadel warn Dr Belsanto - he's the only surgeon in the country who can safely put his patients in a coma, with sleeping drafts. Valya's leg and foot are badly damaged and he needs to be operated on, but he must be unconscious while it's happening or the shock and pain might kill him.'

Ahren went in, found Lee sleeping and Valya looking most unwell.

'Hey, don't give up, you're going to be fine!' said Ahren breezily. 'I've come to make you feel stronger.'

'Try anything you like,' whispered Valya weakly. Ahren gave him vibrations and Rajay joined him. He also put one hand towards the sun and the other towards Valya, and started moving his hands in the gestures which healed the inner subtle centres.

'I don't usually do this, but today is an exception,' said Rajay.

'Now we learn your secrets!' observed Lee, who had woken up and was watching from the other bed. Rajay said nothing because his attention was fully on his friend, and the degree of power flowing through him to Valya was formidable. Both Lee and Ahren felt a rush of cool wind, their hearts completely overflowed with the compassion that Rajay was radiating to Valya, and they, with their collective awareness, picked up.

'That's better,' affirmed Rajay after a short while.

'I feel less pain and my will is stronger,' Valya looked at him in wonder. 'Always something new when you're around, I guess.'

'We've got to get you to Dr Belsanto at Malak Citadel, and fast. Leave after you've eaten and Ahren will come with you. You must have faith though.'

'You know I always trust you,' Valya managed a smile.

'Now more than ever, you must. Once you get there, Asha will also help to give you vibrations.'

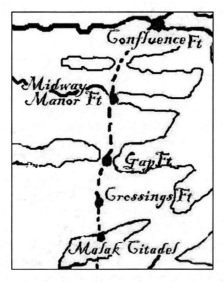

Ekan had already left, riding his fast warhorse for the first leg of the relay, and Valya and Ahren went a little later. Lee was planning to go with the rest of the party the next day and even Rajay was astounded at how well his wounds were healing. The doctor declared it to be impossible but had to believe what he saw and asked Lee to awaken his Tree of Life so he could also help his patients. Rajay swore Lee and Ahren to secrecy and told Valya to say it was only the two boys who had given him vibrations. He said sorting out Daish Shaktay as its king was a full time job and he had to leave the spiritual side to others, at least at this point in time. If everyone knew how strongly the vibrations flowed through him to heal people it would never end, and Rajay was far too considerate and caring to turn anyone away. Almost everyone at Crossings Fort and a fair crowd from the village wanted their inner awakening, so Rajay asked Lee to stay back for a few days when he and Namoh left the following morning.

'Did you ever think you'd be doing this when we made those vows in the temple?' asked Rajay as he said goodbye.

'After my journey to Sasrar,' replied Lee, 'I've learnt to expect absolutely anything. I'd much rather do this than fight.'

'I agree, but sometimes fighting is unavoidable.'

As soon as he reached Malak Citadel, in the early morning, Ahren was shown my room and banged on the door hard enough to wake a hibernating bear. I was just finishing my morning meditation. It was definitely finished after that.

'Asha, it's me. Can I come in?' he called, and I opened the door.

'Great to see you!'

'Valya's been wounded and you must come and give him vibrations. He's got to have an operation today. We've been riding through the night with him – he was on a litter and he's very tired.'

'Oh my God, no! Is he going to be OK?'

'I pray so.'

'I'll be with you shortly. I'll bring my new recruits along too.'

I quickly dressed in the first clothes that I could find, rounded up Amber and Deradan, and soon we three and Ahren were helping Valya to be inwardly strong for his operation by giving him vibrations. He looked much better by the time Dr Belsanto was ready to start some time later.

There was a man at Malak Citadel whose job description was Master of Ceremonies. When he heard that Rajay was arriving he was in his element, because there would be a special gala welcome to celebrate his triumphant homecoming. I said to Amber that if Rajay had been riding all day he would be very tired, and that might be what was least needed. However, she said it was traditional and he would expect it. I had much to learn about court protocol.

Rajay arrived earlier than hoped, shortly before sunset, and the reception was not quite ready, so he went to Dr Belsanto's clinic. The streets were empty because everyone was at the Citadel. Rajay asked anxiously about Valya and was told the operation was finished, but he was still unconscious. This was the dangerous time – patients sometimes never came round after these heavy sleeping drugs. Next Rajay went to the temple dedicated to the Goddess of Daish Shaktay, a beautiful but small building in a little garden at one side of a square. The old priest greeted him as he entered, because he had known Rajay for years. Rajay knelt and gave thanks that his mission to free his country was going so well and that few lives had been lost so far. He said a special prayer for Valya and then told the conscientious priest to come up to the Citadel and not to worry about leaving the temple for a short time.

Together they walked up the hill and Rajay sat under a tree with Deradan, and gave him the latest news while the arrangements were finalised. Soon a crowd of people collected. He greeted those he knew and smiled graciously at the rest. His trusty mare was replaced by a prancing white stallion wearing gold inlaid harness, and the Master of Ceremonies arrived with elegant clothes for Rajay - a red damask coat, thick gold chains for his neck, highly polished knee length boots, and a silken turban with an impressive crest jewel that transformed him from a guerrilla fighter into a king. A redundant groom tried to help him onto the horse but despite his heavy clothing he neatly vaulted into the saddle by himself.

The trumpets blared and the procession moved off. Four guards held a large red and gold umbrella over Rajay and the road had been sprinkled with fragrant coloured powders. People held flaming lanterns to light the way up to the Citadel, children showered rose petals over him and dancers and musicians went ahead. At the outer gate of the fort the officers' wives, led by Amber, asked him to dismount, then offered him garlands and waved lamps and sweet-smelling incense around him. A number of unmarried girls, including me, were at the second gate, offering more flowers and singing songs and at the last gate Queen Jansy welcomed him home. The cannons boomed from the walls of the fort and the gun salute was taken up in the distance, all around the country.

Having done my bit, I was about to find a place at the back of the Great Hall, with Ahren, but Deradan told us we were needed at the front. I was looking my best in a beautiful rose-pink silk gown, my dark hair was entwined with fragrant white flowers and I was wearing some spectacular jewellery that Queen Jansy had given me: gold earrings, bangles and a pearl necklace which framed my many jewelled, multi-coloured Sasrar key on its golden chain.

'You've become quite a lady of the court!' teased Ahren. 'Everyone is looking at you.' He didn't realise it was him, not me, that people were pointing at as we walked, because the gossip about him had already spread.

'What's it like, being a soldier and a partisan?' I asked.

'Sore muscles, exhausting, you never know when the next meal is going to appear and you get eaten alive by insects. Rather like our journey from Teletsia - but Rajay and his friends are great.'

'I've missed you all. I'm not much good at court life.'

'I'd say you've taken to it like a duck to water.'

I chuckled and we entered the Great Hall, transformed with tapestries on the walls, flowers and bright lamps everywhere, over a thousand people in their smartest clothes and at one end Rajay sat on the throne on a raised dais. Bonor, the guard who was part of my meditation group, came over and told us to follow him. Rajay, despite the fine clothes, gold and jewels, was still the same young man who had become an elder brother to me, but his aura of dignified royalty was overwhelming. He saw us and indicated for us to stand near him. There were various speeches, none too long, followed by a praise song, and then Rajay told everyone how three important forts had been brought under the direct control of the Malak Citadel government and how the ogre king's garrison had been turned out of Gap Fort. He thanked everyone who had helped to make this possible.

'We can and will gain our full political freedom by diplomacy and if necessary war,' he proclaimed in a forceful tone. 'I went to the Temple-in-the-Mountains to pray for guidance and more than one miracle was granted me. Firstly, I was given the sword of our freedom and it was exactly as the prophecy said: a maiden gave it to me and there was a statue of a tiger nearby. She insisted she had been given it by a living tiger, and the inscriptions on it are also as foretold.

'Secondly, she and her two friends, young though they are, have come from the fabled kingdom of Sasrar to help us awaken our own spiritual powers and give us that inner strength we'll need for the testing times which may lie ahead. The sword itself has great potency, so I would like you to swear allegiance to our cause and come up one by one and touch it. I promise that just touching it will change you for ever. This is your land and I am no more than your caretaker, but to win it back we must be strong and resolute, and this sword will help us to have those qualities. While we're on the subject of being changed forever I'd like all of you to take advantage of the wisdom these young people will share with you. Please come here, Ahren and Asha.'

I wished the ground would swallow me up but there was no escape. We climbed onto the dais and gave Rajay the salute of respect. We held our hands together as in prayer, gave a slight bow and then touched our foreheads three times, as was always done to the King of Daish Shaktay.

'Asha,' he said softly, 'take the sword when I give it to you and lay it on the dais.' I panicked at doing this in front of so many people and it showed in my face. He smiled, 'It's all right, you don't have to. Ahren, could you take it and touch it first, as an example?' To the Master of Ceremonies he ordered, 'Call for silence, I want to say something else,' because there was a buzz of conversation. Rajay stood up, drew his sword from its jewelled scabbard and held it up for all to see. He read the inscription, then gave it to Ahren.

'Go down to the town and see how Valya is,' Rajay continued quietly to Ahren and me. 'I've just noticed his mother walking in. Tell the guards to say to her that I want to meet her afterwards and she should stay here. I don't want her worrying if Valya's still unconscious, or disturbing him if he's come round – they don't get on very well at the best of times.'

I gave the message to the door guards, and Ahren and I walked to Dr Belsanto's hospital. He was in his office relaxing over a cup of herbal tea. He had given his staff time off for the gala and was keeping an eye on Valya himself.

'I've done all I can,' said the pleasant, grey haired doctor. 'I've had to remove the smallest toe on his right foot, but the leg's still there and we can only pray it heals. How did he do it?'

'He was defending Rajay, who reckons Valya definitely saved his life,' explained Ahren.

'Lord Valya, and all His Majesty's friends, will do anything to keep him safe. They're a great group - I know them well because when they get wounded they often come to me.'

'Can we see him?'

'Yes, he's come round, but he's very sleepy. Do some of your spiritual healing. Can't do any harm,' suggested the doctor sceptically. We went in to Valya's room and he was drugged and groggy.

'We've come to give you some vibrations,' I said encouragingly. 'It's great that the doctor has saved your leg.'

We stayed with him for some time. He responded well and smiled gratefully, despite his pain and muzziness, and soon went off to sleep. We gave him another prayer bandhan, because although he still had his leg, it would be some time before it healed, if it healed.

Ahren and I went to see Valya again the next day. He was still in pain but much more alert, and I felt he wanted to talk to me, but I had to go and see Mr and Mrs Ricemaize about our next awakening programme. Ahren stayed with Valya and I promised to spend longer the next time I came to see him. I went to their home, which was nearby, and after we had made our arrangements for the programme, Mrs Ricemaize gave me some spiced herb tea and refreshments, and during our inevitable chit chat I told them about Sasrar. We got on to the subject of the flying horses, and how they made what was good better, but exposed what was wrong or evil.

'Funny you say that,' she observed. 'Since you've been in town those two priests who complained about you to the queen have been in big trouble. Almost like, since so many of us here have had our inner awakening, it's had the same effect as the flying horses. We all feel much more confident to stand up for what is right now and it's not only that King Rajay is doing so well – something has changed within us, but those two priests have been exposed. One has been investing his temple's money in slave trading. He's been getting away with it for years. The other has been spying for King Karlvid and was caught last week.'

'I hope all the priests here aren't like that.'

'No, some are very devout, but they didn't complain about you, just the reverse. They'll come to the next programme, especially now His Majesty has done your advertising last night, in the Great Hall.'

The morning after this Rajay asked to see me in a lovely room called the Watch Tower Pavilion on the top of the palace. The watch room, from where the sentries could see far and wide over the valleys and plain beyond Malak Citadel, was above the pavilion where Rajay did most of his informal work. It had walls of filigree marble, a balcony at the front and a breeze always blew through it. I went up and Rajay was alone, sitting on a divan, eating breakfast and reading some papers. He was casually dressed in a pair of loose trousers and a long cotton top and was definitely 'off duty'.

'Come in and sit down,' he pointed at another divan. Initially I was a little apprehensive, but felt calm joy coming from him, so relaxed and did as he asked. 'Do you want some breakfast?'

'No, thank you, I ate already.'

'You did well at the gala. You and Ahren were a great asset.'

'Were we? It didn't occur to me.'

'Yes, in more ways than one.'

'Your mother gave me some of the jewellery I wore, and the dress. She's been so generous.'

'She lives simply, but is famous for giving gifts, and she so enjoys having intelligent young people around her. She'll treat you like a daughter. How are you doing with awakening Trees of Life?'

'Fine. We're using the Corn Exchange.'

'I'm so grateful.'

'It's a pleasure. I've already made friends with half the town.'

'I know my country though. Be honest, have you had any problems, like, people criticising you because you're a girl?'

'Not to my face. There was one incident but your mother dealt with it.'

'She doesn't put up with that sort of thing. So, do you like Daish Shaktay?'

'Yes, very much.'

'I don't quite know how to put this, but I need your help.' I looked worried. 'Don't look like that. It's nothing hard or dangerous. Let me start at the beginning. Until recently the nobles warred among themselves and played right into the hands of the Mattanga Empire. A number of them support Karlvid, openly or not so openly, but now I'm starting to free and unite our country, they aren't so sure. Many of them are arrogant and lazy, but I need their support. Danard and Namoh had to kill Chor Bardmarsh, but that approach doesn't solve anything in the long run. Dr Belsanto sent a message up early this morning to say Valya is definitely out of danger, and he could be my role model. I spoke to Valya's mother last night; the family will have him back as heir, on one condition.'

'What's that?'

'He must get married; they reckon that will anchor him.'

'His leg may have been crushed, but no one will ever crush Valya's free spirit. He's like a young eagle.'

'That's a great description of him! He's a brave, deep soul, who's devoting his life to our country. It's been hard on him these last few years, torn between honour to his family and allegiance to me. No superficial nobles' daughter for him, but when his mother talked to him it turned out her first choice for his bride was the only thing they'd agreed on in years.'

'Good, I'm glad,' I wondered where this conversation was going.

'Valya's mother saw you on the dais with me and she's an almighty snob. You're the talk of the country at present: favoured by the king and mysteriously foreign. Like all my friends, Valya admires you a great deal. Could you marry him?'

I stared at Rajay, temporarily dumbfounded. 'I tied the brotherhood band on him. Isn't that relationship absolutely sacred?'

'Yes, but you didn't give him one. He'd gone up to the Zaminder's that morning, when you tied them on us at Belar. Take some time and think about it. The only people who know are you, me, Valya and his mother.'

I put my hands out and there *was* a little coolness when I asked if Valya would be a good husband for me. For a moment I wavered. He was intelligent, kind and receptive to our Sasrar awareness. By anyone's standards he was very good looking and would soon become the wealthiest person in the country. I knew if we were married, I could come to love him as a wife should. Not only that, once Rajay had won his war, as I was sure he would, I'd be living in a beautiful country ruled by an honorary brother. Then I remembered our oath to Teletsia and felt so much coolness that I turned to see the source of the wind. I was confused.

'Don't let me get in your way,' Rajay helped himself to another cup of herbal tea. 'You've got some big questions to ask.'

Did I really want to become a nobleman's wife, tied to a life of respectable convention? In all honesty I didn't. Strangely enough, it was Valya's position as the first lord of the land, or soon to be so, that attracted me least to this whole idea. Also he was quite conservative in some ways and in Daish Shaktay noble women were expected to sit around and not do much, and definitely not have their own opinions. The fact that Rajay supported my giving awakening programmes was considered very radical. Again I thought of Teletsia and going back there to try and fulfil our vow - tremendous coolness on my hands. That might be the way out, as far as Valya was concerned. We got on well and if I turned him down without good reason he would think it was because of his disability.

'If you ask a question which involves you personally and emotionally, you don't always get an unbiased answer,' observed Rajay, as he buttered himself a crunchy oven-warm bun.

'You're the king and perhaps I shouldn't ask you anything so personal, but you're so accurate as far as vibrations are concerned. Could you possibly put your attention on what's in my mind at this moment?'

'Right now I'm your elder brother. Ask in your heart what's there anyway.' I thought of our vow.

'It's extremely cool, whatever you asked.'

'Could you help me once more?' I thought of becoming Lady Northwestern and spending the rest of my life on Valya's estates.

'There's nothing wrong, but not the blowing coolness of the first question.'

'I don't think I'm right for Valya.' I explained what I had been thinking when he felt the different degrees of coolness and he agreed. 'Maybe between us we can find someone though. There is someone and she got on well with him. The only problem is, she's a nobleman's daughter.'

'Who's that?' asked Rajay, because this was often the way marriages were arranged, some subtle go-betweens who nudged things along the way they were developing in any case.

'Melissa. They talked about herbs together endlessly, when we were at the Zaminders.'

'She'd be very suitable. Leave it to me. First I'll put it to Valya, and if he's happy to go ahead, I'll send a letter to her father. What shall I say to Valya about you?'

'Tell him I have a vow to fulfil, just like him. I hope he won't be too hurt.'

'He's bound to be disappointed. We'll explain that when we asked the vibrations, marrying him wasn't the coolest option. He'll respect that, as much as he respects you and me.' Rajay got up to leave, indicating the meeting was over, but then stopped, turned around and smiled. 'And when you do decide to get married, let me know if I can be of any help. After all, I'm your honorary brother now, aren't I?' I shyly smiled back, but he hadn't finished. 'And when my turn comes, give me a bandhan and say a prayer, because unlike you, I won't be able to marry whoever I like. For me, it'll have to be what's good for Daish Shaktay.'

I didn't visit Valya for a day or two and instead sent Ahren and Deradan to give healing vibrations, also Mr Ricemaize and Bonor the guard, who had powerful and awakened Trees of Life and by now knew how to help him. He was soon well on the road to recovery, but as Rajay predicted, was dejected that I had rejected his proposal. This made it difficult for him to consider Melissa, even though he had enjoyed her company when they were together. I finally plucked up the courage to go and talk to him and explained about my oath. When I told him what an incredibly kind hearted, generous and likeable girl Melissa was and I was sure she felt quite strongly for him, he became more open to the idea. Rajay, Valya and I tried the vibrations and it came out very cool that they were absolutely right for each other. He agreed Rajay should send a letter to Count Zaminder on his behalf, but unfortunately Valya's gossipy mother had already put it about that I was to marry him and it took some time to set the record straight.

In one way it was good. I now lived with Amber and was doing awakening programmes with music, so needed to practise. Many an evening Deradan would come over and after having supper with us would help me. If it had not been for the freedom struggle and the fact that Rajay needed him as his First Secretary, he would have become a professional minstrel like his father. However, he was sometimes lonely, as he had no family and was often by himself when his friends were off campaigning. As time passed, I realised he wasn't only coming over to Amber's to practise music. Sometimes he treated us to his own compositions and ecstatically beautiful they were too. His usually solemn face lit up when he sang and played with fluid joy, but I picked up that he was sending messages to me personally. Deradan was caring and considerate and enjoyed my unorthodox ways, but marriage was not an option at that point and that was what he was hinting at. When he came to know I had refused Valya because of my oath, the content of the songs changed.

Melissa was sitting on a bench in her herb garden in the warm sunlight with her dog, a large, lightly built hound with long legs, long ears and a long tail. The beds were neatly laid out, the herbs flourishing and all around were wooded hills. Below her was their house and fort and beyond the valley, dotted with the cottages and small holdings of their staff, stretched into the distance. She was thinking about the news that Rajay had taken back three important forts. How she had loved his visit! Those gallant young men, who were not only brave freedom fighters, but had the depth to enjoy spending time with the saint. She couldn't forget Valya, the tall, slightly shy one who was so handsome, the disowned aristocrat who knew so much about herbs. If only he hadn't been disowned, and if only Daish Shaktay was not in the middle of a guerrilla war… but no, it didn't bear thinking about, her father would never let her marry a destitute man who could be killed at any moment, she was sure of that. And he had not shown any inclination for her in that way. It was nothing more than a girl's dream, she told herself.

She also missed me, because I had given her the gift of inner peace and joy. Melissa was doing her morning meditation regularly, and felt her inner Tree of Life growing ever stronger. She had been sharing the experience with many people in the Belar area, with the help of Pulita the grocer's daughter, but she longed for our vibrant company.

Her father came towards her across the garden, looking serious and carrying a letter. He sat down beside her.

'Who's that from?' she looked at the letter.

'Rajay Ghiry, the rightful king of Daish Shaktay.'

'It isn't often we get letters from kings! Is it private, or can you tell me?'

'It's private and it concerns you.'

'Tell me,' she went on, nervously.

'Rajay is becoming powerful and we desperately need strong friends. He's asked something which involves you and I'm begging you to agree, because our little state is so fragile, caught between Chussan and Mattanga.' Melissa knew what was coming.

'Do you want me to get married?'

'Yes, if you could, dear. It might save all our lives if we have Rajay Ghiry behind us.' She hid her head in her hands; her pet hound licked her sandaled feet and her father tried to calm her by putting his hand on her arm.

'I'll do it. You know I will, but it's such a shock. To have to leave all of you, and my garden and the animals …. I can't see myself as a queen. I know Rajay's a great soul, but…..'

'It's not Rajay,' interrupted her father. 'He just wrote the letter.' Melissa looked even more dismayed and wondered desperately who was to be her fate. 'It's that tall one you kept talking to about herbs.'

'You mean Valya?' her face lit up.

'Yes. He's been wounded, and although he'll probably be all right he can't fight any more. He may have to go home to his family and they'll only take him back if he's married. He's asked Rajay to put in a good word. He thought if the proposal came via the king, you'd be more likely to accept.'

'Oh dad, this is too good to be true!'

She got up and hugged her father, patted the rather perplexed dog and ran off to tell her mother she was going to marry a wonderful man, and the wise young King of Daish Shaktay had suggested the match. On her way into the house she passed Persheray's parents, Lord and Lady Plainsman, who were hiding with them, coming out to the garden. They looked surprised as she ran past, very excited – Melissa was not usually a flighty sort of girl.

'I take it that's a yes,' Count Zaminder said to himself as he sat on the bench and patted the dog at his feet. He liked young Valya Northwestern; exactly the sort of match he would have encouraged, if times had been easier. The count was a kind man and would never have forced his daughter into a marriage unless she wanted it too, even if his little land's survival depended on it. He went to his study to write a letter of acceptance, while the courier from Daish Shaktay had some food in the kitchen. He had no idea what was in the sealed envelope, only that it was important to bring back an answer quickly, because His Highness would soon go off fighting again and this matter had to be concluded before he went, in case he didn't return.

CHAPTER 6

USEFUL INFORMATION

Rajay was in the Great Hall, sitting on a divan in front of the throne dais and Deradan was at his side with a list of petitioners. Flanking them were two guards, but Rajay's sword from the temple was behind them on the throne and he did not appear to be armed. A number of people were waiting at the other end of the hall, now bare and empty again, the decorations from the gala having been removed. One by one they were called forward and he did his best to solve their problems. Finally there were only two left; prisoners under guard. Ahren and I had received a message to be present. I entered the hall and recognised the two priests who had complained about me and subsequently got into worse trouble. The first one was led forward and looked at Rajay with disdain, then at me and Ahren. With his left thumb and forefinger, Rajay rubbed the fourth finger on his right hand. This finger was connected to the sixth subtle centre and was tingling, indicating that whoever Rajay had his attention on had an over-inflated ego. I felt the same on my fingers, and also a pressure in my head, when I looked at the man.

'What have you got to say for yourself?' Rajay began.

'I haven't done anything wrong. What a private individual does with his money isn't your business,' the priest replied defensively.

'Well, actually, it is,' Rajay rubbed the left side of his forehead, the seat of the ego. This man's vibrations were so bad he was giving us pain. 'Firstly, it's my job to protect my subjects from slavers. You invested your temple's money in a boat for capturing and selling slaves, taken from the villages on the south coast. Secondly, if you made a profit, which by all accounts you did, and a vast one, the government is entitled to ten per cent in tax.'

'I demand to see a lawyer.'

'Forget it. In a court of law you'd be convicted for your disgraceful business deals and also as an accomplice for kidnapping and murder, because some of the fisher folk your slaver friends captured died trying to defend themselves. Kidnapping and murder both carry the death penalty in the law books, so you're better off in front of me. I can't rewrite the ancient laws but I can soften them. Your property is forfeit to the state and you'll be sold to the slave traders who supply the Mattangan coal mines. I'm told they're short of slaves to work them. The proceeds from both you and your property will go to compensate those families you've destroyed. Guards, take him away. Deradan, see my orders are carried out to the letter.'

Rajay turned to us. 'I detest slavery, but at this point in time I can't do anything about it in the Mattanga territories, so it's a better fate for him than being executed for murder. When I'm fully in control of this country I'll take the death penalty off the law books.

'The other priest is at least sorry for what he's done and although he's been spying against us, I feel there might be some hope - his subtle self isn't so bad. Keep your attention on his inner side while I talk to him.'

The second prisoner was brought forward and today he was not wearing his red silken robe. I felt his vibrations and they weren't good, especially in the subtle centre at the neck, which registered as a tingling on my left index finger, indicating guilt. The central part of the heart centre was also totally constricted, because he was very afraid. Rajay was uncompromising and firm when dealing out justice and one couldn't go much lower than spying for the enemy.

'And you?' he demanded.

'My Lord, I've realised the folly of my ways. In my religion we emphasise the forgiveness of past misdeeds. What I've done is so wrong you probably won't even consider pardoning me, but can I speak to you in private?' The priest knelt and put his head on the floor and Rajay let him stay there while he spoke to Ahren and Deradan in an undertone.

'This one has a reputation for quietly knifing anyone who gives him trouble. I don't know whether it's true, but I'm not taking any chances. Are you armed?'

'Yes, I've got a dagger in my boot,' replied Deradan.

'No, but I'll keep an eye on him from behind,' added Ahren.

'I've also got a knife, so if he tries anything we can defend ourselves quite easily. Tell Asha to stand aside where she can hear, but not be in danger,' whispered Rajay, then in a normal voice told the guards to stand further away. They were surprised but did as instructed. 'Get up and don't cringe before me,' he said sharply to the quaking priest. 'You can speak out in front of these two; with their spiritual powers they know where you're coming from. My secretary, Deradan, also has this awareness, so there aren't many secrets from him either.'

'Your Highness, my sources tell me that King Karlvid is aware that you've taken back three more forts and have destroyed his garrison at Gap Fort,' began the man.

'That's going to get back to Mattanga very fast,' countered Rajay.

'Sire, I have much more information for you,' he went on nervously.

'Go on.'

'He's going to send a large army against you very soon.'

'That's scarcely surprising,' Rajay thawed slightly, 'but continue.'

'To begin with, none of his generals wanted to lead the troops, but then

Garno Comeni, always your father's bitter enemy, said boastfully, "Who is this Rajay Ghiry? I'll bring him here in an iron cage and throw him at King Karlvid's feet."'

'We'll see about that. And then?'

'In private he was less confident and his favourite wife, a very ogrous woman, persuaded him to try some treachery. She suggested that your power comes from the Temple-in-the-Mountains and if he sent his men there to destroy the image of the goddess, he could easily defeat you. Sire, you know our religion reveres that goddess and when my friends informed me of this, I sent a message to warn the local people to hide the statue. Only yesterday, I heard that Comeni's men did go to destroy it, but someone had hidden it. Also the Mattanga soldiers were attacked by some tigers near the temple.'

'That information redeems you somewhat.'

'When these men reported back to Comeni, he said he'll invade Daish Shaktay, but he may give you one more chance to surrender.' Rajay told the man to stand back and called us.

'What do you reckon? Should we forgive him?'

'Yes,' I begged. 'I asked the vibrations and it comes out that he's truly sorry for what he's done.' Rajay agreed and again called the man forward. It was interesting that Rajay consulted me, a mere girl, to help decide the fate of this man who had been so critical of me, partly because I was a girl.

'I'm told the head of your order has dismissed you from the priesthood, but if you want to stay in Daish Shaktay and do some honest job, you're free to go.'

'How can I thank you, Your Highness?'

'By reforming your ways. Try and help our country, your country, in future and don't create any more problems. If we can win our full independence it will be better for all of us, including you. Guards, let this man go free,' and he walked out of the Great Hall wiser and less scared. 'We'll watch him closely and if he does do any more spying, he'll reveal his accomplices to us. We're creating an efficient information service for precisely that sort of thing.

'So - that's it for today. Let's go and eat and then we've got to figure out how to save the country from Garno Comeni.'

I supposed Rajay was so used to living on the edge that this catastrophic news did not faze him as it would most people, but I found his sense of detachment amazing.

Deradan ate with us; he and Rajay's friends often did, but on that day Namoh and Ekan had gone to see their families and the others were busy elsewhere. The young men shared a comfortable and untidy apartment in the large central building. I went there one day and felt sorry for the maid who had to try and create order out of their relaxed attitude to their living space. When on campaign they were neat, trim and organised, but at home they were chaotic. I suspected Rajay had something to do with the contrast; he was not bothered how they lived off duty but kept them as safe as possible when they were fighting. After the meeting with the priests we went up to the Watch Tower Pavilion and soon lunch arrived.

'What are you going to do?' asked Ahren.

'Make a bandhan of request, to begin with,' Rajay said, and we did so.

'I *think* I had some significant dreams last night.'

'What do you mean, you *think*? Either you dream, or you don't,'

'It's just that I don't usually have important dreams.'

'Let's hear.'

'I saw you in a richly decorated tent on an open space below a fort and with you was a tall, fat, gross looking man. You had something hidden in your hand: a sort of knife with rings.'

'You saw the spring dagger. It's a deadly weapon – a knife which can be held in the hand by means of two rings which attach it to one's fingers and a spring releases the blade from the shaft. Assassins use it. Brilliant idea! The fat man you described has to be Comeni.'

'Later in the night I had another dream. In this one I was in a large wood, which covered both sides of the valley where we were and I was surrounded by lions and tigers, but they weren't interested in me. The centre of the valley was open with a road running through it up to a fort. It looked like Midway Manor, built on an outcrop of rock halfway up the valley. Lower down the valley were soldiers and tents - a military encampment. I could see that beyond the fort was a sheer rock face and the tigers were running around everywhere.'

'I always think of my soldiers as my lions and tigers.'

'Hidden in the woods at the sides of the valley?'

'You have it. Ahren, I'll make sure you're given some gold, and for you Asha, some jewels from Comeni's baggage train when we've captured it.'

'With respect, the best jewel for me would be to see you as crowned king of the whole country,' and I offered Rajay a tasty dish of roasted wild duck.

'One thing at a time, we're not home yet.'

After eating, Rajay asked me to order some coffee. I was about to go down the steep stairs to the lower levels of the tower, when we heard people coming up.

'His Majesty is with the visitors,' we heard the guard say, and who should walk in but Luth. We welcomed him respectfully.

'Good to see you again, Asha,' he greeted me. 'You're doing well,' Luth praised Rajay, 'but also introspect, to make sure you set the right example. Much is given to you, but much is expected. Many people are looking to you for their deliverance and you need the support of all your countrymen, rich and poor, to free Daish Shaktay.'

'Thank you for that advice. We've got a problem: Garno Comeni,' Rajay explained.

'I know, that's why I came.' Luth sat on a divan and I served him food.

'Ahren had a dream,' Rajay went on. 'He saw Midway Manor Fort. If we could get Garno Comeni there we could hide my men in the forests round about. That valley is a cul-de-sac and we might be able to trap and ambush him and his army.'

'First catch your fish and only then can you fry it.'

'Master, tell me what to do, because my country depends on my not making a mistake. Our armies are not strong enough for an open battle with Mattanga.'

'We'll play on that monstrous ego of his, and write him a letter to lure him into Daish Shaktay.'

'Deradan, bring your writing materials,' Rajay asked, and he went to fetch them, and to Luth, 'You heard about the incident at the Temple-in-the-Mountains?'

'Yes, very stupid on Comeni's part. His arrogance will be his downfall.'

Rajay's coffee arrived and I served him. When he had private meals, he preferred not to have the staff present more than was necessary, so I did the honours. How my life had changed since we had left Teletsia! There I had been a nervous schoolgirl, living in a small apartment with my brother and parents, who struggled to make ends meet. True, my ancestors had been wealthy and had held important positions in the country, but our material possessions had been confiscated by the Sorcerers years before. Deradan returned with ink, pens and paper.

'I've heard a lot of good things about you, Deradan. You can tidy this up, because you're the scholar, but I'll dictate the gist. Are you ready?' said Luth.

'Yes indeed, master. I'm so glad to have met you. I deeply regretted not having come to your hermitage.'

'Someone had to escort that baggage train home to Malak Citadel and you did that excellently. Wars are expensive and Rajay needed that booty to pay his soldiers.'

'Don't we know it!' laughed Deradan, and dipped his pen in the ink.

'Respected Lord Comeni,' Luth dictated,

'I have heard you are planning to visit my land. I do sincerely pray that you are not going to make war on me and will be coming in a spirit of peace and reconciliation. You are a valiant man and your brilliance is like fire; that you should come and visit me is an honour.

'I am flexible, humble and peaceful, and if you will come and meet me at one of my strongholds, I will explain all my actions to you. I will give up all my forts to you and after that I will no doubt be free from fear. Then the great ones at Mattanga will understand that I am only trying to help them, because I am a loyal vassal of my overlord King Karlvid.

'Please come to Midway Manor Fort. Your army can camp in the valley, which is very beautiful. It has a cooling river running through it and is surrounded by forests. You and your army can experience all the pleasures of the world there and we can have a discussion and overcome our differences. I will be waiting for you and you will be my honoured guest. I will immediately hand over the fort to you, once we

have talked things over and understand each other better. I would request you to enter Daish Shaktay via Confluence Fort and I will make sure that no one hinders your progress in any way.
I remain, etc.

'That should do the trick. How do you sign yourself these days?' Luth asked Rajay.

'Rajay Ghiry of Daish Shaktay, the same as I always have.'

'Do you have an efficient relay service, or do you want to use mine?'

'We have a good service, but not as far as Mattanga.'

'Between us we'll get this letter there fast. Whether Comeni falls for it or not, you must prepare for war. He'll bring an army to Daish Shaktay very soon.'

CHAPTER 7

LURING THE ENEMY

Rajay's departure two days later could not have been more different from his gala arrival. He, Ahren, Deradan and a small company of guards left in the early morning when it was still dark. First they went to the shrine dedicated to the Goddess of Daish Shaktay in the Citadel and knelt down in front of the simple but beautiful image of the goddess and her tiger. On behalf of all present, Rajay prayed that they would be strong, selfless and fearless instruments for the freedom of the country. After this Queen Jansy, Amber and I gave the traditional flame blessing, waving lamps in an arch around them, knowing they were going to risk their lives for the rest of us.

Grooms waited outside with swift horses - Rajay's mouse-brown mare stamped her foot and swished her tail as if she knew something important was about to happen. Rajay wore the sacred sword; its subtle power was its most important quality but it was also a fearsome weapon: superbly balanced, with a lethal cutting edge and wrought of the finest steel. In his saddlebag was the precious spring knife.

'This one needs a big bandhan of prayer,' he said before leaving, and together we made one. They galloped out into the darkness, their road faintly lit by the dim Moon of Compassion.

Rajay's company reached Crossings Fort just before sunset. As they approached the fort, Ahren felt joy and confidence in his heart, as if there was some great and subtle power there. He and Lee were sharing the same room as Lee and Valya had been in some days before. Lee was completely recovered and walked without a limp but that was not what Ahren noticed most - his face was shining and he radiated an almost palpable power.

'How's life?' Lee began. 'Hobnobbing with royalty at Malak Citadel?'

'Yes and no. Rajay's still the same underneath,' Ahren replied. 'And you're OK again?'

'Yes, and I've given almost everyone around here awakening of their Tree of Life. Earlier today we got together in the village and did a request bandhan for the freedom of the country and it felt amazing; there must have been five hundred of us, and the very trees rustled in the cool breeze as we did it.'

'Something's certainly happened to you. They told us in Sasrar that the more you give awakening, the more the power flows through you.'

Within a couple of days all Rajay's companions reached Crossings and then left again to gather troops and raise the local partisans. Luth's letter to Comeni reached him when he had already left Mattanga for Daish Shaktay, at the head of a large force. He replied, and as Luth had predicted, accepted Rajay's invitation to meet him at Midway Manor Fort. Then there was a rush on, because Rajay and his entourage had to reach the area first and secure themselves in the fort. The main part of Rajay's army, although much smaller than Comeni's, was to approach the valley over the wooded hills that flanked it and to hide unseen in them.

At Confluence Fort, Commander Gram Odain, along with Athlos, who was also there, were horrified when they saw the size of Comeni's army passing below, across the ford over the Shaktay River and up the steep road into Daish Shaktay. They had been told to let him go by, but their hearts sank nevertheless. Sim Patter, the man who had been so helpful to Rajay at Midway Manor, had come as a messenger.

'Sir,' he said to Gram Odain as they looked from the battlements of Confluence Fort at the lines of infantry, cavalry, elephants, cannon and baggage trains, 'I remember what His Highness said to me at Midway Manor: "Trust me Sim, and say a few prayers." I reckon that's all we can do.'

'You're right,' added Athlos. 'My master Luth set this up and I've never known him make an error of judgement.'

At Midway Manor worse reports about Comeni were coming in. Before he left Mattanga, he had a premonition that he might not return. For him, wives were easily replaced, but if he did not come back he did not want them marrying anyone else, so he called his fifteen wives to him and one by one murdered them.

Soon Comeni and his army were camped in the valley below Midway Manor. Rajay, some of his friends and a strong garrison were in the fort itself. Envoys went back and forth for a few days and meanwhile the Daish Shaktay soldiers were secretly collecting in the nearby forests. Rajay made sure the local people made a show of receiving the invaders politely and Luth wandered around Comeni's camp in his usual guise as a monk, gathering information.

After many messages had been sent to and fro, Rajay and Comeni finally agreed to meet in a pavilion in front of the fort, with a maximum of two guards each.

'Tomorrow will be the day,' Rajay told his companions, as they met in the fort the evening before. 'The envoy will soon come for the last time. Danard and Deradan, go out to the forces hidden in the forests, at first light. Danard, you lead the troops on one side of the valley and Deradan - you're to command those on the other side. Ekan, you're in charge of the cannon on the battlements. Varg-Nack, you've always been my bodyguard, and I want you to come with me tomorrow. Ahren and Lee, which of you is the better swordsman, and who is stronger at hand-to-hand fighting?'

'Lee, on both counts,' said Ahren, 'but I'm the more accurate marksman.'

'I'll go along with that,' agreed Lee.

'Then you, Lee are my other bodyguard. I want you to conceal my sword under your cloak. Can you manage that, along with your own, which you'll wear openly?'

'No problem.'

'Ahren and Namoh, lead the troops out of the fort, and you, Witten bring the local boys from down the valley, so if it goes as planned we'll have them on all four sides. We'll meet at dawn to meditate and do a collective prayer bandhan. Now go and rest. As long as we do our best, whatever happens, we live or die as true warriors of freedom.'

Everyone except Danard left. Rajay asked to see one of his officers, a man from Falton, a town in Daish Shaktay, and he was in the room when the envoy from Comeni arrived.

'I know this man!' Rajay said, and recognised the envoy when he entered. He had formerly worked for Rajay's father, but had been enticed into the service of King Karlvid. His family came from Falton. Rajay had been told by his spies in Comeni's camp that this particular man would come and had found someone who knew his family, hence the officer.

'Hartel, what a pleasant surprise! Please sit down,' Rajay smiled warmly.

'I have the final details here, sire,' said Hartel stiffly.

'Thank you. Put them on the table. How are your family - your father, the innovative farmer, and your brother, the famous professor at Falton University?' Rajay knew Hartel had not seen them for years, since defecting to the ogre king's court.

'I don't know.'

'Someone told me your lands are flourishing. It's good to hear about families that are doing so much for our country.' Hartel looked glum. He sorely missed his fields and fruit groves and the hills where he had hunted deer.

'Hartel, this man is from Falton. Maybe he can give you some news,' Rajay introduced him to the officer.

'Indeed I can, Mr Hartel,' he said. 'Your mother is very ill and, I'm sorry to say, will not last much longer. Is there anything you'd like me to tell her?'

Rajay read the proposal, but out of the corner of his eye watched Hartel, who gave some message to the officer about his mother. After a moment or two the officer said, 'Sire, I'll come back later, when you're not so busy.' Rajay nodded and the man left. Rajay, with his subtle awareness, felt Hartel's guilt and remorse.

'Hartel, you're a citizen of Daish Shaktay. Tell me honestly, what is Comeni planning to do tomorrow?' He looked at the envoy, and the depth, power and sincerity of his gaze was such that few could return it. Hartel was silent and Rajay went on. 'We have spies in Comeni's army. I know the rumours, but if you, my fellow countryman, will tell me what you've heard, I'll believe you.'

'He'll try and kill you.'

'I'd heard as much, but Comeni mustn't realise I know this. And Hartel, a free pardon awaits you if you want to come home. You've hurt your family deeply, but that can be put right.'

'Thank you for being so forgiving, sire. I pray you survive tomorrow.'

'I pray so too, for my country as well as myself.'

Hartel left and Rajay went out onto the balcony and looked over the valley, bathing in the golden light of the full Moon of Good Fortune. The Moon of Compassion was lower in the sky and the Moon of Wisdom had already set. Below, in the valley bottom, were the tents of his enemies and hidden in the forests were many of his own men. Danard came out behind him.

'You all right? Need anything?'

'Tomorrow, either I kill Comeni, or he kills me,' Rajay murmured.

'Did the envoy tell you that?'

'Yes,' Rajay looked up at the moons. 'The world where I came from had only one moon. Otherwise, it was similar to this one in many ways – the length of the day and the year were more or less the same, and the intelligent species, humans, were almost identical. Did Lee and Ahren explain all that to you?'

'That you, and quite a few others here, are souls from this other world, who have taken your birth here to help this one.'

'True. Did they tell you why we have to get these ogres out of Daish Shaktay and eventually off the face of the earth?'

'No, but it's obvious, isn't it? They're demonic and this is our land.'

'There's more to it than that. For the people on this world to evolve, which they have to, the way has to be open for more groups of people to go to Sasrar. You see how strong and in harmony with the flow of life these three young Teletsians are? That's because they've been there and have been transformed. If these ogres get any more powerful they'll stop people going through this part of the world, which many of them must do to get to Sasrar. There's good and there's evil. The evil wants to destroy the good, or it will itself be destroyed.'

'What happens if the evil isn't destroyed, or if the people don't transform?'

'On the world I came from, people went so far from the right path they created weapons that could have wiped out every living thing, if they'd been used in large numbers. Also, they destroyed many species, and damaged the climate and the lands themselves by living in a way which was out of balance with Mother Nature. You wouldn't believe some of the problems they caused by their arrogance, greed and foolishness.'

'Why are you telling me this?'

'Because if I get killed tomorrow, you must all go on fighting, not only for Daish Shaktay, but for the future of the world. My mother is also one of the souls from elsewhere, so she'll guide you. Ask Deradan to come back. He was playing some instrument he found here earlier, so let's ask him to entertain us for a while. I need to take my mind off Comeni before I sleep.'

In the morning the guards waited anxiously on the battlements, looking at Comeni's army, which outnumbered the hidden Daish Shaktay soldiers by six or seven to one. They could see the pavilion where the two leaders were to meet, below the fort and some way above the tents of Comeni's troops. It was lined with swathes of silk, ropes of semi-precious jewels hung between the supporting poles, rich cloth covered the divans, silver lamps hung from the roof and costly rugs covered the floor.

At the appointed time, Rajay and his two guards left the fort and simultaneously Comeni approached from the other direction. Rajay looked elegant, mild and innocuous. He wore a white silk overshirt and a knee length damask waistcoat, his loose brown trousers were tucked into leather boots and on his head was a bejewelled turban. He appeared to be unarmed. His two guards, Lee and Varg-Nack, wore swords and cloaks.

Comeni, walking from the other direction, was tall and heavy, and was flanked by two ogrous guards of the same build. He reckoned it wouldn't take very long to kill Rajay and his two attendants and then Daish Shaktay would be his. He had previously told his officers about the Teletsian sorceress he had heard about down at Malak Citadel and how he would send her back to Teletsia and pick up a handsome reward, after forcing her to teach him her magic powers. Comeni was about to enter the pavilion and as agreed his guards waited outside.

'A pavilion fit for a king,' he sneered as he looked inside, 'but too grand for a mere vassal.'

'When my master arrives, he will offer it all to you,' said Lee, who had come on ahead a few steps. He had Rajay's sword hidden under his cloak. Rajay entered the tent, and Lee went outside to join Varg-Nack and Comeni's guards. The arrangement was that neither Comeni nor Rajay should be armed, as this was to be a friendly meeting. Lee talked to one of Comeni's guards to distract him, but his ears were strained to hear Rajay, if he should call for help. Varg-Nack placed himself behind the other guard, so one slice of his sword would fell him if Rajay called.

Inside the pavilion Rajay stood in front of Comeni, who was at least a head taller and twice Rajay's weight. Comeni had the scaly skin of one who was turning into an ogre and small knobbly horns on his head.

'Come, Rajay Ghiry. Let me embrace you, for you are like a son to me,' Comeni did not wait for an answer put his left arm around Rajay. He held Rajay's head in a vice-like grip under his arm and tried to plunge a dagger into Rajay's back, but Rajay was prepared and was wearing a mail shirt under his clothes. The dagger glanced off harmlessly and he shouted for Lee and Varg-Nack.

Comeni had taken no such precautions. Rajay pressed the catch of the spring blade hidden in his hand, released it, plunged it deep into Comeni's stomach and turned the blade in his belly. Comeni screamed in pain and fell forward. As he did so, Rajay took a larger dagger out of his boot and plunged it deep into Comeni's back, where it stuck.

By this time Varg-Nack had killed one of Comeni's guards but the other one ran in to help his master. Before Lee could stop him, he brought a powerful blow down on Rajay's head with his sword, slitting the turban like a lettuce, but Rajay had a steel cap underneath the folds of silk, so again the weapon rattled off without hurting him. Unfortunately this guard parried another blow and caught Rajay on his cheek, which began bleeding profusely. Lee threw Rajay his sword, then helped Varg-Nack kill the remaining guard, while Rajay knelt by the groaning Comeni.

'Mercy,' he wailed.

'No!' cried Rajay, his blood dripping onto Comeni. 'You had my father murdered and you butchered your helpless wives,' and slashed off his head. He picked it up and took it outside, standing on the side of the tent facing the fort. Ekan, on the battlements above, saw him and fired one cannon, the signal for attack.

'Rajay, are you all right?' cried Lee.

'Just about! Better than that rascal, at any rate,' he pointed at Comeni's head, which was lying on the ground beside him.

'I'll take you to the surgeon,' Varg-Nack was adamant. 'That wound needs to be stitched, and fast. You've done enough for Daish Shaktay today.' Somewhat grudgingly Rajay allowed himself to be escorted back to the fort.

The Daish Shaktay soldiers readied themselves in the woods on both sides of the valley. Infiltrators, dressed as hawkers and tradesmen, who were wandering around the enemies' camp, ran to the horse and elephant lines, cut the animals' pickets and beat and goaded them to gallop madly through the camp, causing havoc. Then the infiltrators ran to the side of the camp and waved red flags, the signal that they were safely out of range.

Comeni's soldiers were completely unprepared, resting before the fun of despoiling Daish Shaktay began, and Ekan and his group fired the cannons on the battlements into the camp below. Some soldiers were trampled by the stampeding animals and some were killed by the cannon balls. Comeni's soldiers frantically fled, either into the woods, where they were cut down by the Daish Shaktay soldiers, or down the valley where the local militias, led by Witten, ambushed their escape. From all sides the Daish Shaktay soldiers converged on the Mattanga army; no mercy was shown to any who looked ogrish and to begin with even those who looked human were not allowed to surrender. Rajay's soldiers knew that Comeni had tried to kill their king at the supposedly peaceful meeting, so had little compassion. Eventually Danard, Deradan and the other commanders stopped the wholesale slaughter and allowed the survivors to give themselves up, but the valley floor was littered with corpses.

The prisoners included a large party of officers who, at the time of the battle, were swimming at the bathing place behind the fort. When they were captured some of the Daish Shaktay soldiers made off with their outer clothes, so when they were taken to Rajay, they had the added humiliation of being only clad in their underwear, that they had been swimming in. Rajay, whose cut had by now been seen to, ordered all the prisoners to be put in the dungeons, then received his friends and his chief officers in his apartment.

'You've no idea what we've captured today!' said Deradan, his left arm in a sling from a wound. 'More guns, military equipment and war animals than we know what to do with.'

'Comeni had enough gold in his baggage train to pay our armies for a year,' added Witten.

'Only you know how much we needed those cannons,' Deradan went on. 'We can't buy them, even if we had the money, because they're made in Luker, which is a province of Mattanga.'

'What about our people?' asked Rajay. 'I want a full list of our casualties.'

'It's not too bad, because the enemy were completely unready,' replied Danard.

'All our wounded men must be well cared for and the families of the dead compensated with some of Comeni's gold.' Rajay turned to Witten, 'There'll be plenty over for the treasury, and those officers who went swimming are going to pay us richly for their freedom. We're going to make this war pay so well that in the end we'll bankrupt Mattanga.'

Ahren had been on the battlefield organising the care of the Mattanga casualties. Keeping the officers alive was very profitable; the cost of giving them medical treatment was nothing compared to the ransoms they were going to have to part with for their freedom. The ordinary soldiers who had been wounded were mostly not of the ogre race. Many were originally from the conquered countries and forced into the military, so Rajay let Ahren have some of the captured gold to give to the villagers around Midway Manor, to take care of them. Namoh, who had met the envoy the night before, came in.

'Hartel died in my arms. His last words were, "Please ask King Rajay to forgive my disloyalty. Give this signet ring to my father and tell my family I missed them so much in Mattanga."'

'It may have been the best ending, because unless I'd forced them, they'd never have taken him back,' Rajay sighed. 'These split families are one of the cruellest aspects of this whole bad business.'

Finally Luth strolled in and Rajay immediately knelt before him.

'That was a resounding success!' Luth congratulated everyone. 'Nevertheless, it's only a start. Get up, Rajay. Have you given thanks to the Goddess of Daish Shaktay?'

'Yes, that was my first thought after Comeni failed to kill me.'

'You're very fortunate to still be alive.'

'I'm aware of that, and deeply grateful for all the help I've had, both human and divine.'

CHAPTER 8

HELP FROM THE TIGERS

Having utterly destroyed Comeni's army, Rajay collected his forces and went on a lightning campaign to some other forts under the ogres' control, in the mountainous north-eastern corner of the country. Ahren, Varg-Nack, Danard and Namoh went with Rajay while the others began collecting ransom money from the imprisoned officers. Rajay was eager to win these forts back because they guarded the rich ruby and sapphire mines and whoever controlled those forts had the wealth the mines brought. The present commanders were petty nobles from Daish Shaktay who had given their allegiance to the ogre king. Two of the three were prisoners in the dungeons at Midway Manor Fort and the third had been cremated on the battlefield, along with about three quarters of Comeni's soldiers.

Rajay moved his cavalry rapidly. Deradan forged a document saying that as Comeni had been defeated it was decided to abandon the other forts in the area - the most senior Mattangan officer in the dungeons at Midway Manor had been forced to sign it and the acting commander at the small Ruby Mine Fort fell for the ruse. At Sapphire River Fort, way up in the mountains, some Daish Shaktay men disguised themselves as a large pack train and loaded up their horses with foodstuffs, supplies and weapons wrapped up to look like replacements. They had captured some Mattanga equipment and animals, so the consignment looked genuine and the horses had the distinctive brand of the Mattanga army horses on their rumps. Led by Ahren, who was obviously not from Daish Shaktay, the pack train was allowed to enter the castle, which was half empty, because most of the soldiers had joined Comeni and were either dead, prisoners, or hiding in the woods around Midway Manor. It was a short fight and soon the fort was surrendered.

After this they recaptured one more fort which originally belonged to Daish Shaktay, High Plains Fort, in the mountains between Daish Shaktay and Mattanga. This time Rajay's men dressed themselves as Mattanga soldiers and also had a Mattanga standard – the bleeding skull on a black background - captured from another fort. Too late did the Mattangan garrison realise their mistake, for by that time the Daish Shaktay force was in the fort. It was another short, sharp struggle, but Rajay and Danard knew the layout of the fort and soon overcame the unprepared enemy. Varg-Nack was put in charge of this important frontier post. The campaign was a complete success and the garrisons in the captured forts were replaced by troops loyal to Free Daish Shaktay, coming along on foot some way behind the cavalry.

This soon got back to Malak Citadel and Queen Jansy summoned the Council of Elders. Deradan, who had brought the news, and I were invited to sit with them in the austere Hall of Charts, where a large map of Daish Shaktay was displayed on the wall.

'It's going well, although I hope Rajay hasn't been too ambitious on his present campaign,' cautioned Queen Jansy.

'The reports are excellent and it's time we had control of those mines again,' said Commander Aydriss, down from Crossings Fort.

'It'll make a big difference to the country's financial state,' added Deradan. 'Rajay is coming home now and he'll be here within a week.'

'I called you all,' explained the queen, 'because we have an ever worsening problem in the south. This is Commander Ratnarg from Rivers Mouth Port.' A stocky, bearded man stood up. 'We all know that in days gone by,' she continued, 'we had a number of forts on the coast. We were great traders and our navy was respected by many nations, but now we have only one port to speak of, a mere handful of boats with guns, the sea forts have been destroyed by our enemies and we have no way of protecting our long southern shoreline. Commander Ratnarg will speak about this.'

The commander bowed with a flourish, to conceal his nerves at speaking in front of the foremost people of the kingdom. He was a doer rather than a talker.

'Good sirs and Your Majesty,' he nodded respectfully to the queen, 'a great many ships from the naval base at Port Volcan have been sighted near Coconut Isle, our large island just off the south coast. The head of one of our fishing fleets, who often brings us information, says the ogres' men have claimed it for Mattanga. Also their slavers are raiding our coasts in great numbers and our people are being taken and sold in Port Volcan slave market. We can't stop them because we don't have a navy.'

'To build up the forts takes time, money and manpower,' said the queen, 'and a navy requires sailors and shipwrights as well.'

The fabulously rich Port Volcan, beyond the mountains which formed the south-eastern boundary of Daish Shaktay, had a large slave market, was a great centre for trade and was the Mattanga Empire's naval base in the Sea of Illusion. In addition it was the port of embarkation to a place of pilgrimage on an island in the sea. The ogres believed that if they went there and offered enough money, they would eventually go to paradise. Some of this money stayed in Port Volcan because the captain of any ship who would sail over the Sea of Illusion could ask an enormous price.

Commander Ratnarg suggested that the coastal people, mostly excellent sailors, could man a navy, but ships were lacking. After the meeting, Deradan and I sat with him while he had some food. He was more at ease with us and told us that two months before, most of his family had been taken by a slaver and his home village burnt. We were filled with disgust and pity.

In the afternoon, Amber and I walked to an orange grove outside the Citadel walls. The dark green leaves rustled overhead, the scent of the blossom was overpowering, and ripening fruit weighed down the branches. On the far side of the grove we could see a valley of farmlands and beyond was forest. We sat on a fallen tree trunk and talked about the meeting. As we did so, it became obvious to me what I should do, so I tore a page out of my diary that I had brought with me, and wrote a note.

Your Majesty,

If I am away for some days it will be because I have blown through the key and have taken the help of those who answer the call. They know me and will look after me well. I have an idea that might help solve the present problem.

Respectfully,

Asha.

'Amber, I'm going stay here for a bit. If I don't return for some time, don't worry about me, but be sure to give this note to Queen Jansy, it's very important. Here, take my journal too.'

She was confused at my request but didn't refuse. After she left, I took off my Sasrar key and blew gently through it. I didn't know how long the tigers would take to answer my call. I lay on the grass and had a short nap and did have to wait some time, which was nothing, considering they could have been anywhere in the country. I awoke when I saw a large tiger standing near me and another a little further away. They both wore gold collars and knelt at my feet. One nuzzled me, indicating that I should climb on its back. I knew enough of the classic language to say, 'Take me to Zafan if he's still at the Old Port, or wherever he is now.' They understood, I got on the back of the larger one, they loped off through the orange grove and then ran along the sides of the tall stands of sugar cane in the valley. Soon we disappeared into the forest, the tigers bearing me far away from Malak Citadel.

To begin with I enjoyed the ride, but as afternoon turned to evening I grew tired and lonesome. It was very different from when I had been with friends, two years before. These tigers went much faster; perhaps they knew I was a better rider by now and that we were in a hurry, so they took turns to carry me. Night came. The forest gave way to farmlands and I saw the lights of villages as we hurried on - the moons made shifting shadow patterns on the country lanes as the tigers padded on untiring. It was approaching midnight and I kept nearly slipping off from exhaustion, when they stopped near a farmhouse. The watchdogs barked, I slid to the ground and the tigers disappeared into a nearby wood.

A farmer came out with an ancient gun over his shoulder, carrying a lantern and in spite of my extreme tiredness I saw the amusing side: 'Don't shoot', I thought, 'that contraption looks so dangerous it could as well backfire and kill you as harm me.' He saw me and I walked towards him.

'Welcome, stranger!' he called. I felt his vibrations: cool and he had a kind heart. The tigers had chosen well. 'Well bless me, didn't I see you at – what did you call it? That awakening programme at Malak Citadel the other day?'

'Yes, that's me,' I replied cautiously.

'What are you doing here alone, so late?'

'I'm on an errand for the king. Can I stay the night?'

'Yes, it's an honour. Come in lass, can't have you standing out here. My missis will fix you up with some food and all.'

I was given bread and cheese to eat and a clean, soft bed to sleep on. In the morning I was shown the wash house in the back yard; it doubled as a wood shed, and one heated water over a log fire in the corner, a simple but effective arrangement. After breakfast I thanked the rather bewildered farmer and his wife and set off, walking in a south-westerly direction with no explanation of where I was going.

Once I was well away from the farmhouse I called the tigers, who came out of the long grass at the side of the track. I mounted one and we set off again at a fast pace. All that day we travelled on and I changed tiger periodically. Mostly we went through forested land; there weren't many paths or roads and at night I slept by their sides in a cave and ate some of the food the farmer's wife had given me that morning.

The next day the tigers ran on far into the night and would stop to smell the air then go on again, sometimes slightly altering direction. Eventually we came over the brow of an incline and there was the Shaktay River shimmering in the moons' light - the further bank was too far to swim; the water much too deep to wade. 'What now?' I thought, and noticed that down below was a boathouse at the water's edge. I dismounted and crept nearer. Beside it was a jetty with a small boat tied to it. I walked to the edge of the jetty and behind came the tigers. I peered inside the dinghy and saw a pair of oars. What luck! I slipped off my two heavy silver bangles inlaid with pink pearls and hung them over the pole where the boat was tied up. 'Rajay doesn't want thieves in his land, but I'm going to have to borrow this boat,' I thought, and stepped into it.

There was a violent rocking as the tigers jumped in behind me. I untied it and began rowing across the river with them, and they were extremely heavy. It wasn't easy, and I was not strong enough to row myself and the two tigers. We began to drift downstream, and try as I might I could not regain control of the boat. I became very scared, and after some time the river passed through a small gorge, where it was narrower, and the current was quicker. On one occasion we barely missed being dashed onto some rocks, but finally came out into a broad, calm stretch of water. Here at last I managed to explain the problem to the tigers, who promptly jumped into the water and swam to the further shore, which was not too far away. I rowed to an opening in the trees and found a break in the creepers and half rotten branches dipping down into the water. I tried not to think of the enormous snakes I'd heard lived in places like this and my worst enemy at this moment was my own fear, because the tigers would protect me. Dawn was breaking as I jumped out of the boat onto the sandy bank and pulled it well up and out of sight. 'Not that I'll ever find it again,' I thought.

Soon I was on a tiger again, but progress was slow as the tigers insisted on going straight inland through the thick vegetation. After some time they stopped and allowed me to rest. I slept until the afternoon, drank at a stream and felt desperately hungry, then noticed an old, moss covered temple. Inside the small domed building stood a weathered statue of a goddess with a tiger at her feet. Some forest dweller had recently left an offering of fruit, nuts and flowers, but the greater part of the donation had been abandoned at the entrance in a little basket.

'Please forgive me if I take what has not been offered,' I said, to ease my conscience. I ate and on we went. Just beyond the temple we reached the Old Forest Road and the tigers ran down it. I recognised some landmarks and as night fell knew we were nearing the Old Port. The tigers went slowly and carefully, peering from side to side. I saw the ruins silhouetted against the night sky and soon we were on the path to Zafan's hideout. My steed stopped for me to get off and melted into the forest.

'Who goes there?' A man's voice rang out.

'A friend. I come from Rajay Ghiry of Daish Shaktay.' Even as I said the words 'Daish Shaktay' the camp was waking up. My heart overflowed with relief as I recognised Zafan's foghorn voice.

'Good gracious, it's Asha! Whatever are you doing here?' Zafan pushed past the sentry and emerged from the darkness, hair tousled from sleep and without his usual seaman's boots. 'You've certainly grown up! Where are the others?'

'I'm alone this time.'

'Too much to take in too quickly,' he yawned. 'Let's get some rest. We'll talk in the morning.'

He showed me where I could sleep, and the next thing I knew it was day, and Zafeena, Zafan's sister, was bringing me a warm drink.

'What a fantastic surprise!' she began. 'I wanted to wake you ages ago but you looked worn out.' I told her that I'd come from Daish Shaktay and needed to talk to Zafan. 'You're lucky; he's off on a mission this evening. A company of men are coming down the Old Forest Road with a consignment of slaves. They'll meet the slave merchant's boat near here, so our people have to intercept the captives before they do.'

'I won't take much of his time.'

Zafeena gave me a change of clothes and showed me where to wash, so I was soon clean and tidy once more. I talked to Zafan, explaining how Daish Shaktay needed a navy and money to service it.

'I've heard about Rajay Ghiry,' he began.

'We must do our utmost to help,' said Zafeena, who was listening, one eye on the cooking as usual.

'If you could support Rajay with your ships, it would make your work much easier. He's trying so hard to build a strong country there and to drive out the ogres and...' I smiled weakly, trying to think of something persuasive to say.

'Before you go on,' Zafan interrupted, 'I received a message from Master Theon this morning, when you were still asleep. It came via the dolphins, our messenger service. It said, "Give all possible help to Rajay Ghiry."'

'So my whole journey has been a waste of time?'

'On the contrary, it may be that your journey was what prompted the message.'

'I don't understand. Theon is an enormous distance away.'

'Theon is one of the senior guardians of this world, meaning he's absolutely at one with the universal flow. When you, who have been to Sasrar, or one of the guardians desire something which is important, it is often felt by the guardians themselves. So Theon responded - all the more so if you made such a daring trip alone. By the way, how did you get here?'

'On a tiger, with another one to guard me.'

'I thought so. Can you take a message to Rajay Ghiry?'

'Yes, indeed.' Zafan gave me some instructions involving Port Volcan. 'It's a strange name,' I mused.

'There's an old volcano there. It's a terrible town. All dirty money, slaves, or money bled from the ogres' unfortunate subjects, or from people who are prepared to trade with those devils. It's also a large naval base.'

'A raid?'

'Possibly, but keep that to yourself. Tell Rajay Ghiry I'll meet him at River's Mouth Port. I don't like to let you go back alone but the tigers won't let us see them. They'll look after you and not let the slave traders see you. Before you leave I want you to talk to my men about the Tree of Life. You know all about that nowadays, don't you? Zafeena and I received our awakening some months ago from Theon and Mazdan, last autumn in fact. They said it was time we had it and began using its powers. We gave our men awakening, but you can tell them more.'

'That's incredible, because that's exactly when we started giving it to people!'

I soon had a large gang of 'pirates' sitting together on the ground, feeling cool vibrations and inner peace. I taught them the two bandhans and some techniques to clear problems – using the candle and soaking the feet in salty water.

After that I left. Once out of sight of the pirate's lair I called the tigers and we were soon lolloping up the Old Forest Road, because they were eager to take me home to Malak Citadel. They led me straight to the rowing boat with no trouble at all. We crossed the river at night, the tigers swimming beside the boat, and left it tied to the branch of a tree near where a tributary joined the larger Shaktay River, a long way downstream from where I had found it originally. There was a track up the waterside and eventually we reached a small village in a clearing above the bank. The settlements were always well back from the water, because of the frequent floods in the rainy season.

By now it was early morning and I did not know what to do. Was this where the boat owner lived? I got off the tiger, told them both to hide and walked into the village. Some dogs started barking and almost immediately a woman came out of her cottage.

'Who are you?' she asked, surprised.

'Um, I have a little problem. I had to borrow a boat – I left some bangles for it.'

'Oh, it was you! We heard about that. Very nice bangles, I'm sure, but what we need here are boats, not bangles,' she called for her husband, who also came out, looking very sleepy.

'Right, I'm the local policeman, and you'll stay here until we've straightened this out,' he ordered. Just my luck to have met exactly the wrong person.

'Please, I wanted to tell you I left the boat tied up near where a smaller river comes into the big one, some way down there,' I pointed downstream, 'and the owner can keep the bangles. I was on the king's business but ...'

At this moment the tigers, who must have felt my fear, came round the corner of the village street, and pandemonium resulted. Many other dogs started barking, the man and his wife ran back into their cottage, their dogs took cover, I jumped on the nearest tiger and we made a rapid retreat. I had done my best to explain my theft but it had been less than ideal.

My tigers delivered me at Malak Citadel two nights later. Although the gates of the Citadel were closed at midnight rather than sundown, I was too late to get in so decided to try my luck with the Ricemaize family, where I sometimes did awakening programmes. Sure enough, when I reached their house I could see a light burning in the window of Mr Ricemaize's study. I banged on the door and he opened it.

'Asha! Come in! The king's back and he's been looking all over for you. Well, his men have. Where on earth have you been?'

'I had to go to the country for a few days,' I answered evasively. 'Can I stay the night? I just got back and it's too late to get into the Citadel.'

'Please do. I was checking accounts. Since I've had this inner awakening, business has been excellent but that means more work. I'll send word up the hill at dawn about you.'

Early next morning Lee came down. I greeted him warmly, not having seen him for some time, but he didn't reciprocate my feelings.

'I can't tell you how anxious I've been. Where did you get to?'

'Umm...'

'I don't know if Rajay's been worried or angry or what, but I can't see how you're going to talk your way out of this one.'

'I'm sure he'll understand; I left a note for Queen Jansy. You had great success at Midway Manor, I hear.'

'Yes, but don't change the subject. Rajay wants to see you - now. Why can't you stay home and sew tapestries?'

'Not my style.' Lee knew me of old and we left it at that.

'He's waiting for you in the Watch Tower Pavilion. You'd better look respectable. It might help.'

A little later and much cleaner, I climbed the stairs to the airy room and could hear Rajay and Deradan working. I hovered in the doorway, nervous. Lee was behind me, also expecting trouble.

'Come in,' Rajay betrayed nothing. 'Sit down. I'm busy with Deradan for a while.'

We sat in the corner near the balcony. I'd done exactly what I'd promised Rajay I would *not* do: I'd gone off alone, and for days on end. I wondered what he was going to say. None of the options seemed pleasant and initially my heart was pounding. He took absolutely no notice of me so I went into a meditative mood and put my attention on him. It was better to know where he was. I felt peace and joy, which was surprising. I assumed it was because he was so detached that my arrival has not affected him at all and that he would finish whatever was making him feel so good, after which he'd change his mood when he spoke to me. After some time my apprehension subsided.

'Better now, Asha,' I heard him say, and opened my eyes. He was looking at me and smiling. 'Why were you so worried when you came in? I shouldn't have to settle your inner state!' Then I realised he had been calming me down, using his vibratory awareness on me with his attention, all the time he was working with Deradan. 'I promised to bring you something from Comeni's baggage train but I thought you might like this instead. I had it specially made for you.'

He picked up a small leather bag and took out a priceless gold ring with a large sapphire surrounded by many small rubies. The sapphire was spherical and a star with six rays played over its surface as the light caught it. There were tears in my eyes as I thanked him, as much because it was his way of saying he was not displeased, as because of the beauty of the gift.

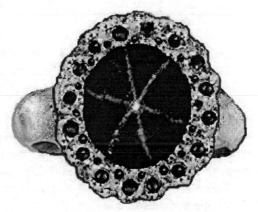

'My country owes you more than a ring, for giving awakening to so many people,' he said as I put it on. I didn't know how to react, because I'd arrived steeling myself for a major reprimand. 'My mother gave me your note. I knew you'd be all right.'

'Two tigers came to my call:

one to carry me and the other to guard me.'

'But why? Where did you go?'

'I've done my best to find you a navy. I went to see someone I know who works for the Emperor, disguised as a pirate. His name is Zafan and he told me to give you this message: "Tell Rajay Ghiry I might be able to help him. He should go immediately to River's Mouth Port and I'll be waiting there for him. Ask him to bring about a thousand of his swiftest cavalry and anyone who knows their way around Port Volcan."'

'Are you serious?'

'Dead serious.' Rajay looked at me, assessing the situation. I looked back and thought, 'Please, trust me as you've asked us to trust you.'

'So, what's this Zafan bringing to River's Mouth Port?'

'I don't know. He said something about men and boats. He and his fellow pirates won't disappoint you.'

'That's true! They've helped us before,' put in Lee.

'All right. The vibrations are very strong. So, next point: who knows Port Volcan?'

'I do slightly and Witten does, very well,' replied Deradan. 'He used to live there.'

'Where is Witten?' Rajay asked. 'I was expecting him yesterday.'

'He stopped off at Crossings,' Lee said, 'something personal, I gather.'

'He should meet us at Rivers Mouth as soon as possible. For cavalry we'll use some of the Southern Regiment, which is stationed at Falton, near there. When can the others get there?'

'Ekan and Namoh the same time as us, but Danard and Varg-Nack will need longer because they're up north,' Deradan explained.

'I'll need them all - not Varg-Nack though, he's too important at High Plains. Can you send messages to everyone?'

'Will do, but I'd like to come with you this time,' begged Deradan.

'Most definitely,' asserted Rajay, and to us, 'I hope your pirate friend is as good as his word.'

'He'll be as good, if not better, that I guarantee,' I promised.

'We'll leave tonight.'

Lee walked across the yard, over to Amber's house with me, silent.

'Why so quiet? I asked. 'That's not like you!'

'I'm sorry, I completely misjudged you, as usual.'

'You were right to be annoyed. I was lucky, because Rajay could have been really angry.'

'You did get off lightly, all things considered. He said only the other day, "If I had a real sister, I'd want one like Asha." But I do worry about you. Our parents would be utterly horrified if they knew what we get up to these days.'

'I think they'd be delighted, as long as they only knew afterwards.'

'I hope it comes to that.'

CHAPTER 9

THE KING AND THE PIRATE

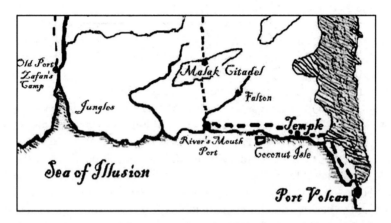

Deradan sent messages by the relay service and Rajay had his usual meeting with the Council of Elders before he left. He always settled affairs in this way, so the country would run without him if he didn't return. Just before he left the information service received a message from a village near the Shaktay River about a suspicious girl who had escaped from the local policeman by riding on a tiger. Rajay grinned when he was told about it, as he mounted his mouse-brown mare in the Citadel yard, and told the man who brought the message not to worry, the girl was on important state business, but commended the villagers for their thoroughness.

The expedition to Rivers Mouth Port left soon after sunset. Rajay moved fast and they travelled only at night, because there were spies in Daish Shaktay, men paid to report on troop movements, especially those involving the king, to Mattanga. For the first night the road led through the craggy hills to the south of Malak Citadel, then across farmlands, but on the second they rode down steep, torturous passes as the higher land gave way to the coastal plain. Rajay knew every twist of the narrow ravines even in the moons' light, and they reached the fort overlooking the port the next morning. It was a grim, high walled compound, similar to all the forts in Daish Shaktay, and inside were numerous buildings where a garrison was housed and the town was administered from.

Commander Ratnarg was amazed that his prayers had been answered, and so soon. Rajay and the rest of the company were welcomed with due protocol and the dignitaries of the area insisted on giving a lavish banquet in his honour. The feast took place in the Great Hall of the fort at lunchtime. Before it began Rajay took Commander Ratnarg aside and asked him if a navy had arrived, possibly manned by men who looked like pirates. The commander assumed His Highness was making a joke and that it would be polite to laugh at it, which he did. Rajay was puzzled; Commander Ratnarg realised his error and apologised. He said if there were any pirates wandering around the town he would have arrested them and lamentably a navy was one thing he didn't have. Ahren and Lee overheard the conversation.

'Zafan's words were "boats and men," not a navy and sailors,' said Lee.

'We'll be wasting our time at this feast. Let's go and look for Zafan. You know him - he won't march up to the fort and present himself openly,' Ahren suggested

'You're right. I'll tell Rajay where we're going and why.'

They excused themselves, left for the town and made their way through the narrow alleys into the port area. They strolled aimlessly around the docks for a while, not knowing where to look for Zafan.

'If I remember rightly he likes his food. Let's check out a few restaurants,' was Ahren's idea. Delicious smells of fresh fish being fried told them where to go. They tried seventeen eating houses, some dark pokey caverns, some elegant and expensive and others with tables outside on the squares and streets, all full of noisy sailors and other visitors such as hard bitten traders, but with no success.

'Perhaps he's restocking. Let's try some ships' chandlers,' Lee, the sailor, took over. They visited seven, that sold everything anyone could ever need for sailing and ships. No luck, even when they tentatively asked about sailors who looked like pirates. The owners of these businesses didn't much care who their customers were, as long as they paid their bills, but couldn't help the boys at all. In the eighth the proprietor invited them into his office for a cup of coffee. Ahren and Lee assumed it was because they were foreigners and maybe had good tales to tell.

'Any unexpected ships come in here recently?' asked Lee

'Young sir, this is the only free port for a great distance. A lot of shipping comes here all the time.'

'Any fleets?'

'Well now you're on to something,' said their host, pouring them black, syrupy coffee and offering them sticky, honey-covered cakes. 'A strange fishing fleet turned up this morning. Didn't have any fish to sell though; they looked more like small gunboats to me.' Lee changed the subject and pretended to lose interest. The crusty ex-sailor, a bright-eyed old man with a bald head and a long beard, was not deceived. 'Lad, those sailors are right religious. They have to be, what with them weird goings on in the Sea of Illusion and these slave ships scouring the coasts. You'll find them as came in recently at the temple dedicated to Father Ocean. It's on the waterfront: tall golden spires and lots of green flags. You can't miss it. They all go there when they come back safe and sound.'

Lee and Ahren thanked him and left when they had finished their coffee. Outside in the hot sunlight a few men sat on bollards on the quayside, gossiping, and some stray dogs snored in patches of shade under cranes and gantries. The harbour was full of ships of all types, the smell of the sea permeated the area and sea birds fought noisily over some scraps of food lying on the ground. The boys found the temple and went into the cool, dark shrine where they watched brawny, tattooed, pigtailed sailors offering flower garlands and rose petals to the statues of Father Ocean and his consort. Then they sat on the steps outside, watching the worshippers come and go. Soon a shifty looking sailor approached.

'Are you King Rajay's men from Sasrar and known to Cap'n Zafan?' he enquired.

'Why do you ask?' replied Lee.

'The Cap'n is waiting behind the temple for you. Could you follow me?' He stood up and walked off.

'You reckon he's all right?' asked Ahren.

'Yes, the vibrations are cool,' Lee had his hands out.

'I felt that too, so let's go.'

'Behind the temple' was an oversimplification. They followed the sailor up narrow, crowded and smelly lanes, avoiding dead rats in gutters and piles of fetid rubbish, then through a decaying, but beautifully tiled doorway into a courtyard. On the veranda at the further side sat Zafan. He stood up and

welcomed them both with a bone-cracking bear hug. They sat down, cool sherbet drinks were brought, they gave each other the main news of the previous two years and got down to business.

'Where's the navy?' asked Lee cautiously.

'We have to go and fetch it,' Zafan tossed off these words as if he was discussing buying food for a party. 'I want you to bring King Rajay here so we can go over plans. He'd better come in the evening, with no more than one or two bodyguards.'

They went back to the fort and Rajay was in one of the state rooms. The banquet was over and he was having a much-needed rest, and the boys were also very tired as they had been riding all night. Deradan, standing guard outside Rajay's room, told them to lie down in the reception room and have some sleep, which they did. Later Witten arrived. He had come straight from Crossings Fort and was also exhausted, having ridden by relay, changing horses as they flagged, while he rode on and on. Rajay heard his voice and came out of his room.

'Thanks for coming so quickly, Witten.'

'No problem, I gather there's something afoot concerning a navy.'

'Yes, as you well know, we desperately need one, and although it sounds unbelievable, someone known to Asha and the boys might be able to get hold of some warships for us. Whatever, we'll give it a try. I've had enough of these slavers taking our people away like cattle.'

That evening Rajay, Deradan and Witten, hooded and cloaked, along with Lee and Ahren, left the fort and threaded their way through the maze of dim allies near the docks. After a few wrong turnings they found the tiled doorway, banged on the now closed door and were let in. Lee introduced Rajay and the others to Zafan.

'So, you need a navy and money to service it?' he began.

'Yes. Can you really manage it?' asked Rajay

'I'll try for the navy and you concentrate on the money. Port Volcan is very rich. With luck and maybe some 'supernatural' help I'll capture the fleet, leaving you free to plunder the town.'

'How *on earth* do you plan to help yourself to an entire navy?' Rajay continued. Even his schemes didn't extend quite that far.

'I'll explain. Let me show you the layout of the place.' Zafan took out a map of the town and environs of Port Volcan, on the Sea of Illusion just beyond the south-eastern border of Daish Shaktay. 'Port Volcan is in two parts: Port Volcan Naval and Port Volcan Mercantile. In the middle, on the headland, is a fort.'

'What's that?' Rajay pointed to a shape behind it.

'It's a dormant volcano. It might come in very handy.' Zafan outlined his plan.

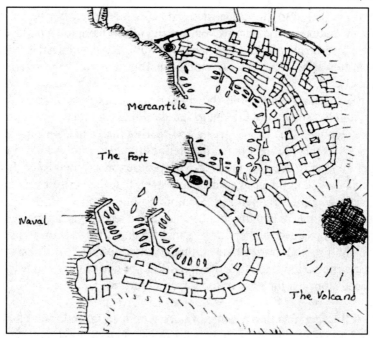

A man galloped east along the coastal road. He was carrying a large purse of gold coins and he frequently exchanged them for fresh horses. Many said he was a criminal on the run because he was armed and hid his face, but no matter, he was wealthy. Some way before the mountains that formed the border of Daish Shaktay he stopped at a village by the sea and requested hospitality. This was customary in Daish Shaktay, and as he was courteous and spoke like a nobleman the headman invited him in to eat supper with his family. He listened as the food was served.

'That good brindled cow went off again this morning. I couldn't find her anywhere, as usual,' said the headman, a farmer.

'She used to be the best milker of all, however now she gives good milk in the morning but is dry in the evening. I can't understand it,' added his wife. Then a boy from one of the neighbouring houses came in.

'I found her! She was on the hilltop, overlooking the sea. Her udders were streaming with milk and it was falling onto a rock in the shape of an elephant's head. I've seen her up there before, but to-day I made sure. It was as if she was giving milk to the rock.'

The stranger, Rajay in disguise, was intrigued and asked the boy to take him to the hilltop. They soon found the place and Rajay noticed that round the rock in the shape of an elephant's head were some other stones, shaped like the four petalled flower on my ring. He felt the vibrations of the rocks to be powerful and peaceful, returned to the headman's house to sleep, and dreamed that a boy was talking to him.

'The elephant's head represents the principle of innocence and wisdom and the hilltop is sacred to those qualities. The cow has been offering worship in the way she understands and now you, as king of this land, must build a temple there. See that the people who live here pay homage to it and what it represents, and then they'll be blessed with another quality, the ability to overcome all obstacles.'

In the morning Rajay told the farmer about his dream, apart from his identity, and left some gold for him to start building a temple above and around the stone elephant. The farmer was a god-fearing man and didn't question the instructions of this pleasant but authoritative stranger, who promised to come back before long to see how the work was progressing. When Rajay had gone the farmer looked at the gold coins and noticed that the portrait head on them was exactly like the stranger. He said nothing but got to work on the temple immediately, thankful that his country had such a saintly young man as a king.

Rajay soon reached the borders of Daish Shaktay. He rode on and spent the night in a half ruined tower in the mountains overlooking Port Volcan, having let his latest horse loose to graze. He hid his sword and clothes carefully, under some loose stones at the base of the tower's inner wall.

The following morning a ragged figure with a bandaged foot, cloak, stick and begging bowl hobbled down from the mountain pass into Luker, a province of the Mattanga Empire, the capital of which was Port Volcan. Soon this pathetic specimen of humanity was sitting in the market place, begging for alms and listening to the talk of the merchants and traders.

The Teletsian warehouse was doing a brisk trade, selling guns to replace those lost to the upstart Mountain Mouse, Rajay Ghiry. King Karlvid's cousin, a ruthless murderer, was about to embark on the pilgrimage to that island in the Sea of Illusion where he might with luck obtain eternal salvation. He was offering a shipload of gold, silver and jewels. One man had actually seen the treasure in the Guildhall of the Sapphire Merchants. The Governor of Port Volcan was becoming even more lax and the soldiers at the fort spent most of their time lazing around, partying and gambling. The beggar listened carefully for a couple of days then staggered out of town and back to the mountains.

No one had seen Rajay at Rivers Mouth Port for some days and word got around that he had gone back to Malak Citadel on urgent business. Danard also left River's Mouth Port for the north with the cavalry, which had been on manoeuvres. In the evening he called a halt. It was the usual simple camp: the men slept next to their horses and everyone carried his own belongings and rations. At midnight the bugle blew and the soldiers were told to go eastwards. For three nights they journeyed like this, and rested, hidden, by day. Finally they reached and camped in the valley with the old ruined tower.

Meanwhile Zafan's 'fishing fleet' crept along the shore, putting in now and again at villages in the creeks that indented the coast of Daish Shaktay. Once a warship from Port Volcan intercepted them and the captain demanded:

'Where are your fish?' Zafan told them he was transporting rare medicinal fish oil to Port Volcan for sale. The oil was tested on a slave, who went into a deep coma after drinking a spoonful from a bucket of water with one drop diluted in it.

'It's powerful stuff, sir,' said Zafan. 'Don't worry, he'll come round in a day or so.'

The ogrous captain merely threw the unfortunate slave overboard.

That evening Lee walked over to the ruined tower, now the home of many seabirds. A flurry of wings met him as he entered and saw a beggar sitting in a corner; he had walked through the camp shortly before. Some of the soldiers had charitably offered him food but he declined, and no one took much notice of him.

'How's Port Volcan?' asked Lee, recognising Rajay.

'Obscenely rich and largely unguarded – perfect! Have you got some clean clothes for me, and my horse?'

'Of course.'

The Governor of Port Volcan Mercantile was attending an official banquet at the fort. The Admiral of the Fleet was there and the general in charge of the fort was giving an excellent evening's entertainment. The governor had a third helping of the delicious dessert and yet more wine. He felt he could, because there was no pressing business the following morning, so he would sleep late and go to work at lunchtime.

'I heard that chap Rajay Ghiry was at Rivers Mouth Port last week, with his cavalry,' slurped the admiral between mouthfuls of crème caramel.

'Better mop up that place one day,' yawned the general, in no hurry to go anywhere that didn't offer non-stop parties.

'The Mouse won't bother us here, not with our navy and garrison and your militia to defend the town,' went on the admiral, to the governor.

'Another goblet of wine?' asked the general, and promptly fell asleep over his own gem-studded golden tankard, which crashed to the floor.

The garrison were, in fact, not defending Port Volcan, but were also sleeping off a night's partying, very satisfied with the non-existent discipline of their army life. The following day the governor had such a headache that he couldn't concentrate on the Weekly Council Meeting in the Guildhall.

'A strange fishing fleet has come in, flying a neutral flag,' said a merchant.

'They have a miraculous fish oil for sale; it's a sleeping draft and anaesthetic,' added another.

Zafan put in at Port Volcan Naval Base to the south of Port Volcan Mercantile, around the headland from the city. He began selling his fish oil to ship's surgeons and civil doctors. He and Zafeena had concocted the drug and an extremely small dose went a very long way. It had nothing to do with the fish oil; that just disguised and diluted it. The secret ingredient which put everyone to sleep was being given out free, in its concentrated form and without the fish oil, to trusted friends of Zafan working as cooks, cleaners and water carriers for the army and navy.

Some peasants built a large bonfire at the lip of the volcano crater, which having been dormant for many years was now grass covered. It was a primitive rite to the volcano god and none of the educated people of Port Volcan took much notice. At midnight, the bonfire was lit. Zafan's friends had been told to watch for this bonfire and when they saw it to put the sleep inducing drug into all the water supplies. Zafan went on doing a brisk trade with his fish oil and the profits went to his friends, to make them even keener to do their secret work for him perfectly.

That same evening the governor had attended another banquet and the gossip was that Rajay Ghiry and his band of ragamuffins were approaching. They were in the hills near the Daish Shaktay border, only a day's march away. 'Nonsense!' was the well-informed reply, 'No one can travel through those mountains in such a short time.'

The following morning the governor woke up with another brain-searing headache. His secretary was standing over him.

'Black coffee,' he groaned, pulling the sheet over his head. The secretary delicately uncovered it. The governor covered his head once more and repeated the order for black coffee, more angrily.

'Sir,' insisted the unfortunate secretary, 'Rajay Ghiry is outside the city with a large number of armed men. He's demanding an enormous tribute, the price of Coconut Isle, which we have recently taken over. Also he says we must return all the slaves from Daish Shaktay still in the city and give financial compensation for those who've been sold on. If we don't, he's going to sack the city and take the wealthy people hostage. Sir, can you hear me?'

'Tell him we'll have a Council Meeting at lunch time and let him know our terms this afternoon. Now go away, my head is splitting,' came an irritated voice from under the bedclothes.

'He's going to attack shortly after dawn. That's some time ago, because it's taken so long to wake Your Excellency.'

'Go away. He wouldn't dare sack Port Volcan.'

Outside the city Rajay was giving final instructions.

'First, the looting parties with soldiers to guard you are under Witten, who'll lead you to the richest houses and the wealthiest places. Only fill your sacks with gold, jewels and valuables. If you can, steal horses and load them up with your booty. Capture prosperous looking merchants as hostages but on no account touch any religious institutions or priests. Don't harm the poor, don't kill unless it's absolutely unavoidable and above all respect the women and children. Namoh and Deradan, go to the slave market with at least two hundred soldiers and free the slaves. The burning parties under Danard, follow. This town is rich because of slaves, tribute from us and many other immoral reasons. We want to destroy this town as a port, so once we've plundered, burn the municipal buildings, the slave market and any other places like that. Try not to burn people in their houses. The fourth group, under Lee and Ahren, bombard the fort by way of a diversion and withdraw if they offer any real opposition. I have a strong feeling they won't, especially as the day wears on.

'Right, go for it. We need money to free our country from these devils.'

CHAPTER 10

PORT VOLCAN

Rajay's soldiers poured into Port Volcan Mercantile and apart from the din they made it was deathly quiet. Word had gone around that the governor was not going to help in any way at all. Most of the richest merchants had already fled to the fort, while others either hid with their belongings behind barred doors or had gone to the hills above the city, where many of them had villas.

The Governor of Port Volcan Mercantile finally woke up. He called for his family and servants but they had left; only the retired doorkeeper had stayed behind and he hobbled in with his walking stick when his master shouted for his valet.

'Sir,' ventured the timid old man, 'Rajay Ghiry and his men are raiding the town. Already they've looted many of the richest mansions. You can't believe how much they've taken! Is there anything you need?'

'Give me my cloak. I have some business at the fort,' replied the governor. 'This raid is a matter for the army. Peace loving citizens like myself cannot deal with this sort of anarchy.'

At that moment a chaotic din was heard.

'This is the governor's mansion…' shouted Witten from below, his voice lost in the tumult. The governor took his cloak and put on the first shoes at hand, his bedroom slippers, then went swiftly down the back stairs and out of the servants' door, while Witten's party broke into the front of the house.

'I've found the gold plate!' shouted one trooper.

'Do we take silver?' asked a man struggling with some gold inlaid silver trays from the store room.

'Yes, but no copper or clothes, not worth the bother,' cried Witten. 'Tell any servants to help themselves to whatever is left and then to leave quickly, because this place is going to be burnt.'

'Hurry along there,' ordered another voice. 'We've got to meet His Majesty at the Goldsmiths' Market.'

At the market some of the gold merchants were begging to be let off. They all looked like ogres and some had completely transformed into these despicable creatures because of their inner natures.

'Pay up!' was Rajay's reply. When the portly gold dealers tried to get out of making contributions he merely said, 'For years you have taxed, ruined, enslaved and even eaten our people. Where was your sense of justice then?'

Some traders from foreign lands had warehouses that they were prepared to defend very courageously. Rajay left these untouched, because so much wealth had been abandoned by the cowardly merchants who had fled, there was no need to waste time and effort fighting for their riches. He also warned these people to get out of town. Only the Teletsian warehouse was attacked because it was rumoured to be full of guns for Mattanga. It was not, but there was a great store of gold and this Rajay took. He also took the treasure from the ogre king's cousin. This devil, at that time in the fort, was sorely vexed when he heard this, because now he had nothing with which to buy his eternal salvation at the island shrine.

'It'll take more than gold to save his soul,' commented Witten, as he hoisted it onto two heavy horses they had found in an abandoned brewery. Throughout the day the men of Daish Shaktay plundered without much opposition.

Namoh and Deradan took their force to the slave market and arrived just before the daily auction began. The slaves were locked in cages and Namoh made sure the people who had the keys didn't escape. The owners, guards and auctioneers were very cowardly and gave up without a struggle. Namoh promised not to kill any of the slave dealers who helped free their merchandise, but once free, the slaves themselves weren't so forgiving and lynched a few of their captors before anything could be done to stop them. All the men and boys who had been liberated wanted to join the raiding parties, but the women and smaller children were sent to the base camp outside the town with the booty. Some of the loot was later given to the freed slaves, so they were not left destitute.

Wherever the burning parties went, day became night as the smoke blotted out the sun. When the merchants reached the fort they blamed the general for not driving out the invaders. He muttered excuses and said it was the fault of the governor of the city.

'Where are your five hundred men at arms?' the general asked the governor when he arrived. 'Why aren't they defending the city?'

'What five hundred men at arms?' demanded the governor angrily. Everything was going wrong that morning.

'The Town Militia - I've been sending you money for the salaries of five hundred soldiers for years.'

'How do you think I paid for our parties? The Town Militia only existed on paper.'

By now no one was going to enter or leave the fort for some time, because Lee, Ahren and their men were bombarding the gate from hidden vantage points on a nearby hill, an elegant suburb, with some small cannon. Next everyone tried blaming the navy, while reports were sent down to the great hall from watchmen on the fort's battlements.

'The governor's palace is in flames.'

'Trading ships are all sailing away.'

'A string of packhorses are leaving the Silversmiths Street, heavily laden.'

Soon a strange thing started happening. As people took food and drink, they began to fall asleep and those still awake realised it was not sleep but a coma. Some suspected the water from the well, because even though it looked and tasted all right, anyone who drank it became unconscious.

'Bring water from outside,' yawned the general as he too fell asleep. However, because of Lee's bombardment, the gates of the fort were closed, so this was impossible.

The navy personnel did what any self-respecting sailors would do when threatened from the land. They took to their ships and lay a little offshore to await developments. It was a warm day and soon everyone was asking for water as they watched the smoke billowing up from the town. One by one they too fell asleep. Zafan waited until sunset. He was in a warehouse in the docks, winding up his final business deal. The news from Port Volcan Mercantile over the hill was appalling. He advised his customers to leave town for a few days in case things got worse. The wealthy of Port Volcan Mercantile who refused to pay a tribute were either taken prisoner for ransom, or in a few cases, killed. Rajay's spies discovered that these were men who had frequently tortured and murdered people in order to extract money out of them or their families, or were the cruellest slave dealers. The naval port was almost deserted because everyone had taken refuge in some ship or the fort. Dan, Zafan's first mate, came to find him.

'Sir, the ships lying offshore are drifting about quite aimlessly and I can't see any sailors on them,' Dan said. 'There were one or two ships with crews behaving in the usual fashion, but when they saw all the others seemingly bewitched, they sailed out to sea.'

'Time for us to move, but let me look through the spyglass first to make sure,' said Zafan. He checked around the harbour and everything as was as he had planned – except for the two ships that had sailed away. He suspected they would make for Mattanga to give word of the attack, but he, Rajay and their men would be far away by then. Zafan's sailors approached the naval galleons in their fishing smacks.

'Boarding parties ready!' shouted Zafan through his loud hailer. 'Watch out for anyone not asleep!' The small boats came up to the superb ships flying the flag of Mattanga. They were boarded by the fishermen and pirates, without any defence being shown. These pirates were the trusted servants of the Emperor of the Ocean and the fishermen were from the coast of Daish Shaktay and had all lost relations or friends to the slavers. 'Tip the sleeping officers into their life dinghies and cast them adrift. Throw any ogrous ones into the water. Whistle for the whales and dolphins when you're ready.'

Some time later a fleet of warships could be seen sailing westwards. Each ship was towed by some whales or a school of dolphins, with ropes in their mouths. How the foam sparkled in the moons' light as they sped away to Daish Shaktay! On each ship were a few pirates or fishermen. There were also a large number of snoring galley slaves and other sailor slaves. In three days time they would wake up free men, with a well-paid career in the offing in the newly acquired navy.

Zafan fervently hoped the whales could avoid and outdistance any other ships they might come across, but he need not have worried, because the whales and dolphins were in contact with each other and would warn of any approaching shipping. They were the sentries of the Sea of Illusion and knew the whereabouts of everything that floated on it. Zafan dispatched sixty ships in this manner for Daish Shaktay, but by midnight he had run out of pirates, fishermen and the whales and dolphins to accompany them. The remaining few naval craft he dealt with differently. The slaves in them were freed from their chains and hauled into his fishing boats in their comatose state and the rest of the crews were cast adrift in their dinghies and left to bob around the port. The boats themselves were set alight.

Most of Zafan's fishing fleet melted into the network of creeks in south-eastern Daish Shaktay, but a few boats stayed behind with Zafan. The following morning saw Lee, Ahren and some soldiers still bombarding the fort, although virtually everyone was asleep there by now, so by midday they gave up.

In the early afternoon, one young man, with an expression of scared fanaticism, came down from the hills carrying a white flag. He and some fellow merchants had been hiding in a villa above the town and had conceived a plan. He was stopped by a group of Daish Shaktay soldiers and brought to Lee.

'I want to see Rajay Ghiry and we'll offer generous terms,' he said. His father had recently received a large shipment of emeralds and lapis lazuli, intended for the court of Mattanga and these jewels were now safely at the booty camp in the hills. Lee tried to be chivalrous and took him to Rajay, who was checking loot with Witten in the former Gold Exchange, where the amount of gold bricks lying around made the place look like a builders' yard. Ahren went with Lee and the young Port Volcan merchant, noticed the mad glint in his eyes, so stood near Rajay with a drawn sword. The merchant's terms were ridiculous given that ninety-five per cent of Rajay's opponents had either fled or were asleep. Nevertheless he listened patiently, while Witten came and went and he gave occasional instructions. Finally the merchant finished speaking.

'Your governor is cooped up in the fort, like a lazy woman in her boudoir,' observed Rajay. 'Do you seriously imagine I'll accept terms like these?'

'I'm not a feeble woman and here's something else for you,' he cried, and drew out a dagger. He rushed headlong towards Rajay, pointing it at his heart. Fortunately Ahren was faster. He whipped up his sword and sliced off the would-be assassin's hand, which held the dagger. So great was the young man's impetus that the stump of his arm drove straight into Rajay, as Ahren gave him another, mortal blow. They all fell down in a bloody tangle and some guards standing by thought Rajay had been killed.

'Kill the hostages in retaliation!' cried one.

'No one to be killed unless I say so!' shouted Rajay, getting up unharmed but bloodstained.

The last pack train left the city, but before the Daish Shaktay soldiers did, they chalked this message all over the town:

The volcano may erupt soon. When you wake up, get out of town for at least a month.

CHAPTER 11

THE AFTERMATH

Deradan was guarding the camp outside the town, as load after load of plunder was deposited there. He arranged for the whole force, plus a large number of stolen mules, donkeys and horses, to carry the treasure out of Luker Province into Daish Shaktay. That evening everyone camped on the mountain pass and the next night they reached a flower strewn valley well into Daish Shaktay. Crickets chirped and all was peaceful; only the dirty coats of the soldiers indicated where they had been. The troops had some food and gave the tired animals balls made of beans to ease their exhaustion, because they had been heavily loaded and it was a long trek. Except for the guards everybody went to sleep. After resting for a short time Rajay woke up Lee, Ahren and his other friends.

'If you aren't too tired, come with me.' They followed Rajay to the brow of the hill from where they could see the sea, and beyond that Port Volcan, still burning from a hundred unchecked fires. Rajay told everyone to sleep and he would wake them at the right moment. Lee was wide awake so he and Rajay sat out the rest of the night together, Lee listening to tales of freedom fighting and in return relating sagas of far off lands. They went on speaking as the constellations wheeled overhead and the moons circled the sky. Later on it was still dark but a streak of light on the horizon warned of the coming dawn.

'Now wake the others,' said Rajay. Lee did so and his friends came and joined him. 'Look over there!' he cried and pointed towards Port Volcan. As the sun rose there was a vast explosion. 'That was Zafan blowing up the Port Volcan arsenal,' he explained. 'It may easily set off a volcanic eruption. That's why I had the men chalk up those warnings.'

The next day Rajay sent out scouts to discover whether there were any signs of pursuit, but there were none. He began a tally of what treasure was to be sent to Malak Citadel and what was to be retained at Rivers Mouth Port. Each captain of a hundred men had to give his account of what he had brought away, under the exacting eyes of Witten and Deradan. Rajay warned that although the wealth looked endless, it was needed, because without a full treasury he could not go to war or maintain the navy. Exceptionally precious items were brought to Rajay's tent, which was being used as an office. A magnificent ruby and diamond diadem was presented to him.

'This is for Queen Jansy,' said Rajay without hesitation. Then an exquisite pendant was brought, a large golden locket engraved in high relief with a picture of the Goddess of Daish Shaktay, complete with her tiger and all studded with precious stones. Rajay passed it round for everyone in the tent to see. 'Do you think Asha would like this? After all, she did more or less instigate this operation.'

'I think she'd want you to have it,' advised Lee, knowing I already had more jewellery at Malak Citadel than I dreamt of owning in a lifetime. He left to bring in more treasure and a newly appointed officer entered, a ferocious looking man, immensely strong, from a mountain tribe on the eastern borders of Daish Shaktay.

'Yes, Gar Warl?' asked Rajay brightly.

'When we were on our way out of Port Volcan we came across a band of armed retainers with a carriage full of rich baggage and there was also a most attractive young lady. She's betrothed to a nobleman in Mattanga and was on her way to her wedding, but her beauty is such that when I saw her...'

'I sincerely hope you didn't trouble her,' interrupted Rajay.

'Oh no, sire. I brought her for you.'

Gar Warl indicated for his men to bring her in and they pushed her towards Rajay, rather roughly. Her head was bowed, she was veiled and one could see nothing of her face or figure. Women captured like this were spoils of war, but the girl was brave enough not to fall at his feet and beg for mercy, even though she was shaking with fear. In Port Volcan Rajay had the reputation of being a wild brigand who murdered people on sight, or enchanted them before torturing them to death. He did look scary, with his sword and dagger, three days stubble on his cheeks and clothes which could have been cleaner.

'Madam,' he began politely, 'If you'd uncover your face we'd see each other better.'

She did not attempt to obey him. Rajay gently picked up the corner of her veil and saw she was strikingly good looking. She assumed that like many of the great lords of Mattanga, he would have a harem of women, slaves who were no better than prisoners and this would be her lifelong fate – or would he kill her, because she was the daughter of his enemy? Or sell her into slavery? Nevertheless, the longer Rajay looked at her, with an expression of innocent kindness on his face, the more her fear melted away. He was healing her subtle heart centre and dissolving her fear with his attention. He was also wondering whether it would be safer to keep her with his people for some time, or let her go free. He foresaw trouble in Mattanga, possibly war. As he cleared her subtle self, he picked up that she had a good feeling coming from her.

'I am glad we've been able to meet, even if the circumstances are not ideal. Please accept me as your brother,' he said courteously, to her astonishment. He smiled, wondered whether to complement her on her obvious beauty, but decided against it and let her veil drop. 'It's most unfortunate that you've been frightened. What is your name?'

'Sagara Samudra, Your Majesty. My father was the Admiral of the Port Volcan Fleet....'

'Lady Sagara, I need a navy to protect my coasts against slave traders, but I have nothing against you personally. I long ago took a vow to look after any girl or woman who crosses my path, so you'll be sent on your way safe and sound. Tell your new family in Mattanga that I want to set people free and protect them, not enslave them.' At this point she did finally fall at Rajay's feet and clutched them in gratitude.

'Thank you for respecting my honour!'

'Stand up. I'm your brother now, so you mustn't behave like that. Before you go, I'd like you to talk to two of my friends. It might be of advantage to all of us eventually.' Rajay turned to Gar Warl, cringing in the corner of the tent. 'You, do something useful for a change. Find Lee and Ahren, and tell them to come here immediately.' Gar Warl was only too keen to make amends for his grievous error and ran off to do as asked. 'The rest of you can also leave - and send some refreshments for our guest.' When they were alone Rajay invited Sagara to sit on one of the folding stools. 'In my country women are respected, so they don't need to wear a veil.' Sagara took the point and threw back hers, smiling shyly.

'They're not true, all the bad things they say about you.'

'I've heard the stories. They're incredible, aren't they?' Rajay sat on another stool. 'I was putting my attention on your inner nature just now, what you'd call the soul. You have a strong sense of honour and morality, but you need to become conscious of your connection with the all pervading power. I'm going to leave you with two young men who've been to the legendary country of Sasrar and they'll give you a very beautiful experience. I want you to tell people in Mattanga about this. No more fearsome crocodile gods!' At this juncture Lee and Ahren walked in.

'Oh, hello Rajay, Gar Warl said you wanted us,' said Ahren breezily.

'This is Lady Sagara from Port Volcan. Could you to awaken her Tree of Life?'

'Pleasure to meet you, Madam,' Lee greeted Sagara courteously.

Some time later a much happier and more confident Sagara was sent on her way with dignity. From that moment she secretly supported Free Daish Shaktay and told all her friends how gallant the dreaded Mouse had been. Gar Warl did not need to be reprimanded; it took him days to live down the shame of having so misjudged Rajay.

Rajay told Deradan to go to Rivers Mouth Port as quickly as he could with enough gold to arrange everything concerning the navy that the whales and dolphins were bringing. Witten, who knew Rivers Mouth, was to find a competent architect to oversee the rebuilding of the coastal forts and the construction of new ones as fast as possible. Namoh was to find people to man their garrisons. He was excellent at this: a farmer's son himself, he always managed to get the country people enthusiastic about becoming soldiers. Lee and Ahren wondered at these somewhat elaborate instructions.

'Rajay will probably take off somewhere,' commented Danard. 'He often disappears after a big engagement. Those instructions are a give-away.' The following morning Rajay woke Lee and Ahren before dawn, while the rest of the camp was still sleeping.

'I need you two,' he whispered. 'Will you come with me for a few days?'

Soon after, they set off. They put in at one or two villages by the sea. Rajay wanted to find out how much they had suffered from the slave raiders: a great deal. He assured them that this would not happen any more. He did not say who he was, but had an extraordinary way of inspiring people even when incognito. They also gave awakening to many of the villagers. They could see the volcano above Port Volcan across the sea from the cliffs overlooking the coast and Rajay frequently looked in that direction. That evening, they were resting after an evening picnic on a cliff top and Lee was entertaining the others with his flute. Suddenly Rajay pointed towards the port.

'I have a feeling this is the moment,' he interrupted - unlike him, as he had great respect for Lee's music. 'Now watch!' They did so and for a short while nothing happened. Then a vast explosion occurred and the whole side of the volcano disappeared in smoke and rocks. Red fire belched out and that part of the sky was blotted out by the rising canopy of smoke. A red river poured over the volcano's rim and fell down the mountainside to where Port Volcan lay in ruins. Clouds of steam arose as the molten rock reached the sea and then dust, ashes and smoke, along with more steam obscured the whole scene.

'That's the end of Port Volcan,' observed Rajay. 'Theon warned Zafan that if he blew up the arsenal on the side of the volcano, it would erupt. It does so every hundred years or so and was recently becoming very unstable. The

explosion set off what was coming anyway. I hope everyone left the town.'

Rajay wanted to see how the elephant head temple was progressing and the next morning they reached that village. It was obvious from their clothes, weapons and fine horses that they were well-to-do warriors. The same family Rajay had stayed with before welcomed them into the farmhouse, a beautiful building made of wood with a high-pitched roof to keep it cool and surrounded by a garden shaded by coconut palms. They were offered food, then visited the site of the temple and Rajay was impressed at how much had been done; a wood and thatch roof had been built over the natural stone elephant. He was taken to see a man who was designing a more permanent sanctuary and a contractor who would provide the stone and stonemasons.

Meanwhile, Lee and Ahren entertained the family with songs and music: Lee on his flute and Ahren singing and playing a drum. These were the Sasrar songs, able to awaken the Inner Tree of Life, and soon Lee worked round to that. He told them how they came from a wonderful land where all the people, especially the country folk, were awake to their inner spirit and how he and his friend could pass on this experience. Soon the whole family and most of the villagers, who had collected in the yard outside the farmhouse, were feeling peace, joy and coolness. At this point Rajay came back and asked the villagers to meet him at the stone elephant's head the following day. This was done and Rajay asked them to put their hands towards the rock image in the ground. To their amazement they all felt a cooling wind coming from it.

'That's why I wanted you to build a temple,' he said. 'That coolness is the wind of the divine power and in certain places it flows very strongly. If people come and pay their respects to this image, they'll feel good and may get what you'd call miracle cures and blessings.'

'Do we have to have priests here and all?' asked Mr Marlgond, their host. He didn't sound too keen.

'It's a good idea if someone can make sure the vibrations, as we call the coolness, coming from the elephant image are in good order. If people who are not alright come here to worship they may leave their inner dirt behind and dull the healing power, and beneficial vibrations. But if you can feel the vibrations well and know how to clear the subtle dirt then it can again give out a powerful coolness and blessings. He or she should keep the statue or image spiritually clean so worshippers can get the best from whatever they're worshipping. It doesn't have to be a full time job, in fact it shouldn't be, and whoever does it shouldn't be paid. The best thing would be if one of you from the village could go with my two friends for some time, to learn how to do it.'

At this a well-grown lad, younger than Lee and Ahren, stood forward. He was the brother of the boy who had taken Rajay to see the elephant's head in the first place.

'I would like to, sir. My name is Jaggo Jaigat. I've finished my schooling, but don't have any commitments.' Rajay looked at him then turned to Lee and Ahren.

'What do you reckon?' he said, as they checked the boy's vibrations.

'Fine,' said Ahren, and Lee agreed.

'You can leave with my friends tomorrow, Jaggo. I want to stay here a bit longer, so you can take my horse. I want my vet to look at her when she gets home; she's not quite herself.'

The next morning Lee and Ahren left with Jaggo. They soon got talking.

'She's a nice horse,' Jaggo commented, as he rode her with the sensitive confidence of one brought up with animals.

'She should be,' said Ahren. 'You know who her master is?'

'I heard you call him Rajay.'

'That's right, Rajay Ghiry, your king,' added Lee.

'I thought as much. Don't worry, I didn't tell the Marlgond family. Wow! Are we going to Malak Citadel?'

'Yes, via Rivers Mouth Port,' explained Lee. 'I think the Marlgonds also figured out who Rajay is. They understood, as you did, that he doesn't want to advertise his presence. He prefers to spend his time with the down-to-earth, hardworking folk of his land; they matter much more to him than people who think they're superior for some stupid reason or other.'

Rajay sat in meditation and watched the temple go up, constantly aware of the power of the sacred rock. It occurred to him that the local people had already received a great blessing – the navy would keep the slavers away and they would no longer have that fear hanging over their heads. Maybe fate had guided him there on his way to Port Volcan and the fact that he had started the temple before his raid was one reason why it had been such a success.

One morning, very early, he was alone near it and felt an inner tension, as if something was calling him. He often had the desire to wander around his country in the guise of a mendicant for some time, so he could enjoy his land and help transform it spiritually. More than once he asked himself why he went on trying to free and unite Daish Shaktay and why he didn't just advise his friends how to defeat the Mattanga Empire, and then abdicate as an autocratic ruler in favour of a democracy. He was not averse to fighting when it was the only way of resolving problems, enjoyed the excitement of guerrilla operations and treated his ongoing conflict with Karlvid of Mattanga as a necessary political game, but he had absolutely no lust for power, and most of all wanted to encourage other people to grow, mature and gain the ability to run their country themselves.

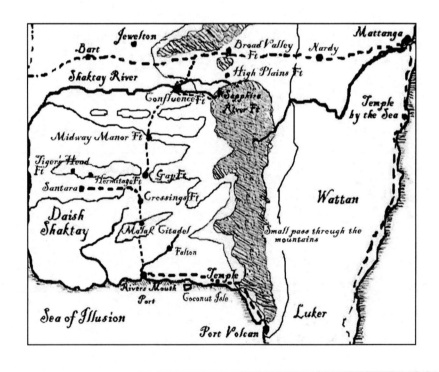

PART THREE

THE WHEEL OF FORTUNE

Daish Shaktay and part of the Mattanga Empire

CHAPTER 1

LIFE AT COURT

As soon as the young men left Malak Citadel the atmosphere completely changed. Rajay's dramatic lifestyle was replaced by a more utilitarian feeling, and Queen Jansy went quietly on running the country and giving people wise and compassionate advice. I continued awakening Trees of Life and the girls from the kitchens arranged programmes in their villages. I spent some pleasant days going out into the countryside with them and also gave programmes at various schools, where the children became masters of the new, higher level of awareness and often brought along their parents, which filled my heart with joy as the same feeling radiated back to me from everyone I met. Once this was established and people began to feel a deep inner strength, they trusted the warm and cool vibrations as a guide, became much more self-confident and less bound by outworn superstitions, fears and conventions.

My only problem was Valya. He had moved to the comfortable home of Amber and Saber Rizen, the Captain of the Guard, in the Citadel compound, where I lived. Valya had been lonely in the young men's apartment, especially when the others went off with Rajay. He was healing, but his leg was still in a splint. We did our best to keep him cheerful, but he had moments of being morose and I wasn't the one to cheer him up. Queen Jansy suggested that we should try to get Melissa to come to Malak Citadel. The acceptance of the proposal had reached Valya, but no date had been fixed for the marriage, partly because he was still laid up and partly because Rajay was away, and wanted to give Valya a wedding worthy of one of his friends. Consequently a messenger was sent to Melissa - this was somewhat unorthodox, but as Amber pointed out, 'The sooner Valya is well, the sooner they can get married'.

Deradan returned from Port Volcan with the treasure and deposited it safely in the vaults of Malak Citadel. Early that evening I was in the Rizen's living room with him, the Rizens and Valya, who was hobbling around on crutches. Deradan was telling us his story.

'When I arrived back at Rivers Mouth Port,' he began, 'Commander Ratnarg called me. You know how he tries to do everything absolutely correctly and meticulously?'

161

'An uphill struggle with you lot!' I commented.

'I asked him if any ships had arrived from Port Volcan recently. He replied that strangely enough, the day before, an entire navy had sailed into the port, flying the red banners of Daish Shaktay. He thought he'd gone mad or was dreaming, but the ships were very real. Then a responsible young man named Hampen, a mariner from the land of Tong, where Witten's family comes from, arrived to see him. He was a freed galley slave and said the captain of his ship, a pirate who had now left, had told him to ask for some gold for all the sailors. Commander Ratnarg told Hampen that he knew nothing about this but asked him and the ships to wait in the harbour for a few days. Ratnarg asked him

how he'd got there and Hampen said he didn't know because he'd been asleep for three days, but something to do with whales. Ratnarg gave up at that point. Then I turned up and gave him a fair amount of gold from Port Volcan.'

'I think Rajay and Zafan's inspired spontaneity is more than Commander Ratnarg can handle,' I smiled.

'Possibly, but he's getting used to us now. I told him to make up crews from these freed slaves if they wanted to work for us and to fill out the navy with local men. Those ships are to defend our shores against slave traders.'

I happened to look out of the window and noticed some riders on the road from the north, approaching fast. They disappeared into the town, but some time later came through the main gate of the Citadel. It was Melissa, her brother, three bodyguards and Luth. Apart from Valya, we all went out to the courtyard to welcome them.

'I must see Rajay, quickly,' Luth began anxiously, as he dismounted.

'He's somewhere on the south coast,' Deradan told him.

'There's an army from Mattanga about to enter Daish Shaktay. How soon can we reach him?'

'I don't know, because we don't know quite where he is.'

'We've got to find him as soon as possible.'

Luth had met up with Melissa's party, who as they had neared the east-west road to cross it going south had seen a large army travelling west. They had hidden as it passed but it filled them with horror. We went to Amber's house but in the panic forgot that for Melissa and Valya it was a very important meeting. It was for the best, because while we were all talking and trying to decide how to help, I noticed them happily sitting together in the corner of the living room.

Late that night a tired messenger arrived with worse news. The army, with their general Coroso Raspatto, had crossed the Shaktay River on rafts further west than Confluence Fort and were making for the old capital of Santara. The Daish Shaktay forces were all in the east of the country and the few militias had not been able to stop them. By great good fortune Lee, Ahren and Jaggo arrived in the early morning, just as Luth and some messengers were about to leave for the south.

'Rajay's on the south coast, near Coconut Isle,' said Lee.

'Draw me a map,' demanded Luth, relieved.

'Will do. That village is easy to find.'

'Asha, come here a moment,' Luth wanted to borrow my key to call the tigers. It always surprised me that he didn't have one, but he said he didn't need one. He decided to wait until midday and if they hadn't arrived by then he would use the relay service horses, but the tigers were quicker and never got tired. Later I took Luth down to the fruit grove and there were the two tigers who had taken me to Zafan. Luth climbed on one and they made off - very fast.

Rajay sat near the stone elephant's head in deep meditation and felt the warmth of the morning sun coming up over the hills. He turned to acknowledge Father Sun and saw Luth sitting beside him.

'What are you doing here?' asked his master.

'I'm overseeing the construction of a new temple,' smiled Rajay, his heart at peace. He looked at the ocean and the tranquil village below.

'You must leave for Malak Citadel immediately. Your country has been invaded by another Mattangan army. I came on a tiger and he'll take you back. In fact there are two and they'll take it in turns to carry you.'

Rajay jumped up, meditation forgotten. 'Why did the information service not tell me sooner?'

'Because no one knew where you were. That's the disadvantage of being a king – you can't just take off and not tell anyone of your whereabouts.'

'I've had many roles in my past lifetimes, and of course we do remember them. I've not been a king before - a partisan, yes, and a lawgiver, a doctor and a farmer, but never anything like this. Sometimes I get so fed up with killing people, telling them what to do and solving their problems, I need a break. But there's no escape - can you finish the job here?'

'Naturally – this is also important. And Rajay – you've got some great friends helping you, but they need you to be there, all the time. You're their leader.'

'I prefer to encourage others to take responsibility.'

'Later. This is no time for philosophical discussion.'

Rajay bowed to Luth and hurried back to Malak Citadel on the tigers, via out-of-the-way paths.

Two days later he slipped into the fort - only one guard saw him enter when the gates opened at dawn. Rajay forbade him to tell anyone of his return and went straight to Lee and Ahren's room.

'What's this about an invasion?' he asked, and Lee told him that Raspatto, a nephew of King Karlvid and very ogrish, had moved himself and his extended family into the New Palace in Santara. With him was his army, nearly eight thousand strong.

'It could be worse,' said Rajay. 'An army at Santara isn't as bad as an enemy garrison in one of the bigger forts, like Gap or Tiger's Head. I know every nook and cranny of that palace; it was my home. I wanted to get the picture from you two first, because you're more detached than the others.'

'I'm not sure about that,' Ahren disagreed, but Rajay took no notice.

'Tell my mother and the Council of Elders I'll see them at lunchtime. Otherwise I don't want anyone except my friends to know I'm home. I'll bath and rest in your room so as not to advertise my presence, if you don't mind. Have some breakfast sent up, but don't say it's for me.'

'Will do,' said Lee.

'I haven't slept for two nights or days. Those tigers don't give up, do they?' Rajay chuckled and relaxed on a divan with his head back and his eyes closed. He slept until midday, then met the Elders, a sure sign he was going on another dangerous mission. In the evening the rest of us had an informal supper party with Amber and me. We had invited Rajay, but didn't know whether he would come. The front door was standing open, but he knocked before entering.

'Come in, we're honoured,' Amber greeted him and we stood up respectfully. 'We were talking about your successes at Port Volcan.'

'Sit down, you're my friends and we don't have to be so formal. Yes, the raid went perfectly, thanks to everyone playing their part so well. Daish Shaktay won't have any money problems in the foreseeable future, that's for sure! And now we have a sizeable navy.' He didn't mention the present troubles and we had a delicious supper, after which Rajay wanted to talk about something - we all guessed what. Amber put their best chair in the middle of the room for him and we sat on the floor.

'I need your help,' he began. 'First, let's meditate together.' He sat on the floor with us, saying it was better that way, because the earth element could draw out our imperfections more easily. We put our hands on our knees, palms upwards, allowed our attention to float to the top of our heads and felt thoughtless joy and coolness flowing over us. Lastly we reawakened our Trees of Life and did the bandhan of protection so we could maintain that glorious feeling. 'I need your collective desire to inspire me to free the country,' he went on.

We were now behind him, directing the vibrations towards him. Although he was in general peaceful confidence, there was a slight problem in the heart centre on the right side, the place of the father, husband, ruler or king. This registered as a tingling on my right small finger. Rajay's sense of responsibility towards his country was absolute, but the constriction had to be cleared for the all-pervading power to flow through him more easily. Soon the tingling went away and coolness flowed over my hands as I put my attention on him.

'That's better,' said Ahren, who felt the same thing.

'It's come to me, how to deal with this Raspatto,' declared Rajay. 'We'll leave tonight. It's going to be risky and none of you need come unless you want to.' All the men wanted to go but Rajay asked Deradan to stay back with Queen Jansy. He wasn't happy at having to miss the action yet again but Rajay was insistent. 'I especially need Ahren and Ekan, because you're both very accurate marksmen. Danard – and Namoh, do you both remember your way around the New Palace?'

'Obviously!' grinned Danard. 'All those games of hide and seek there when we were kids. How could we forget?'

After this, Rajay took me into Saber's, Amber's husband's - study, a cosy little room full of books and illuminated manuscripts from the Citadel library, because Saber was a great reader.

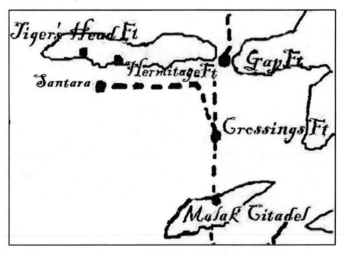

'I've got another present for you.' Rajay showed me a magnificent engraved gold pendant, inlaid with diamonds and rubies, of the Goddess of Daish Shaktay on her tiger.

'With respect, you can't. This should go to your mother,' I objected.

'She wants me to give it to *you*. It's the Lionheart's family talisman. They're a powerful family from Mattanga province who sold out to the ogre peoples.

It's part of our haul from Port Volcan. What it was doing there, I've no idea. Without you the raid wouldn't have happened, and this navy we've captured is going to save many lives, so take the pendant and don't argue. I don't have time to spend ages convincing you that you deserve it.'

He put it on the desk in front of us, bowed his head, made the gesture of respectful greeting and left the room. I felt tremendous gratitude radiating from his heart.

CHAPTER 2

DEALING WITH COROSO RASPATTO

Only Queen Jansy, Deradan, Amber and I were there to see the young men off later in the night. The queen stopped them as they went to the courtyard, to bless them with the traditional parting offerings of flame, incense and garlands. When she came to Rajay, he bowed, drew his sword and laid it at her feet. The gold and jewelled inlay on the hilt reflected the lamp flames as she made an arc with them over his head.

'My son, pray that just as you were able to kill Comeni, you'll be able to defeat this devil too.'

The gates of the fort were opened and they galloped out into the night. Few knew their king had come and gone, least of all the spies paid to inform Coroso

Raspatto of his movements.

Santara lay in a broad, fertile valley. To the north were craggy hills, and winding roads led down from them to the valley. The partisans made for Tiger's Head Fort, to the northwest of Santara and perched on a clifflike scarp shaped like a tiger's head. Rajay had not brought any troops, so Danard and Namoh left the others who had come from Malak Citadel, because their farm was on the hills nearby and many people knew them personally. In village after village, the Hillfarmer brothers received a warm welcome from the headmen as they gave instructions and immediately local men of all walks of life left their jobs to serve their king.

Coroso Raspatto was expecting trouble. He was not as foolhardy as his predecessor Comeni and believed the reports from his fellow countrymen that Rajay Ghiry was as slippery as an eel and as cunning as a fox. He posted guards on the roads into Santara and forbade anyone bearing arms from entering the town. His army was camped in a park across the road from Rajay's childhood home, the New Palace, which he had commandeered for himself and his large entourage. The gates were well guarded and Raspatto felt fairly safe.

Most people who lived in Santara sent their families to the hills, where they could take refuge in the Daish Shaktay held forts if there was any violence; shops were boarded up and the standing crops around Santara had been burnt. The fields were black and bare to prevent the invading army from having the chance to gain anything from them. When Rajay heard this he sent messages telling the farmers he would compensate them for their patriotism.

On the road, Rajay had met some of Luth's men who were staying in a monastery in Santara. He asked them to discover exactly how Raspatto spent his time: where he slept, how he had his food prepared, where the guards were and where the court musicians stayed, et cetera. They went on their way and reappeared two evenings later at the Tiger's Head Fort with the requested information and by the next morning a group of perhaps eight hundred men from the nearby villages had collected at the fort. He called them together in the courtyard.

'Will you help me punish Raspatto? I need some of you to come to Santara with me and the rest of you will be needed up here. If anyone is afraid, go home now. Success and failure lie solely in the hands of the Goddess of our land and we are mere instruments.' They talked among themselves and a village schoolteacher stood forward.

'Sire, we're all with you. Some of us have already sworn on your sword to rid our lands of these ogres' men. With you to lead us, we'll go anywhere.'

Ahren, Ekan and a large body of partisans stayed back, on a hill between Tiger's Head and Hermitage Forts. They spent the afternoon tying oil lamps to trees and setting wood for nearly a hundred campfires on an area of flattish ground above the pass up from the plain.

The schoolmaster had relations in Santara and one was a girl of marriageable age. He went to the authorities and claimed they had found a suitable young man and requested permission for the wedding party to enter the town that evening. He was given a special permit from the Mattanga guards, because wedding parties such as this were common in Daish Shaktay and the groom would ride a horse or elephant, accompanied by his friends and relations, to the venue of the marriage. The schoolmaster returned to the hills with the precious permit and in the evening the marriage procession came down a farm track near Tiger's Head. The bridegroom was on an elephant and as was the custom, his face was concealed behind a fringe of flowers. The others rode horses or walked. Near Santara a band joined them and made raucous music while they danced in front of the elephant.

After nightfall Namoh, Lee and a hundred or so men trickled into a mango grove on the outskirts of the town. They had come over the burnt fields to avoid the checkpoints; some sat round a lantern at the entrance to the grove as if they were night watchmen and started playing cards. Others formed a company and marched towards Raspatto's army camp in the Pleasure Gardens across the road from the New Palace. The camp sentries challenged them but they knew the passwords perfectly, having been taught them by local partisans, who had made it their business to learn them. The new soldiers explained they were reinforcements from the north of the country, apologised for being so late and melted into the camp.

The marriage procession could be heard in the distance. The guards at the town gates cheered and waved them past, because everyone enjoyed a celebration. No one noticed that one of the cavorting guests wore a sword under his cloak inscribed 'King and guardian of Daish Shaktay'. Once in the vicinity of the New Palace the marriage party dissolved into its component parts: Rajay, Danard, who had been posing as the bridegroom and twenty of the bravest local men.

A Santara citizen strolled down the street outside the New Palace and glanced at the front door where the sleepy sentries, leaning against the wall, gazed back with heavy eyelids. The citizen reported to Namoh's contingent, by now in a side street near the kitchen entrance to the palace. There were no guards here, only a couple of cats.

'Guards on the front as usual, Cap'n Namoh,' the stroller whispered.

Namoh's group made their way to the front of the palace, leaving Rajay, Danard and his men in the back alley. Rajay indicated for them to do a bandhan of protection and put his finger on his lips for silence. He knew the way in; many times as a child he had begged titbits from the cook there. Rajay and Danard crept in first.

Two cooks, ogres, were warming their clawlike hands over a fire in the kitchen, because in the spring here the nights were chilly. They were discussing how they had kidnapped and cooked some local children - these creatures were cannibals. Rajay made a sign with his hand indicating the cutting of the throat,

Danard nodded and with lightning fast efficiency they dispatched both of them. The door from the kitchen into the front of the house had recently been bricked up, because Coroso Raspatto liked his privacy.

The intruders had been warned of this and some began removing the bricks with picks they had brought with them. The noise disturbed a nervous serving girl, who happened to be nearby, inside the palace. She was hunchbacked and stuttered and lurched up to the chief ogre guard to tell him of the noise, but what with her shyness and her speech impediment, she had only half delivered the message when he told her to stop annoying him or he would eat her at his next orgy. She shambled off to her mother's attic room and was told not to get involved with what did not concern her. Soon the hole in the wall was large enough for the uninvited guests to crawl through into the main courtyard and they found, as had been reported, that it had been converted into a hotel of tents for Raspatto's relations and minor wives. Rajay had been told that Raspatto was sleeping in the master bedroom, a room he knew well because he had often used it.

Danard and some of his men crept up to where the musicians were housed, in a room above the main entrance.

Rajay led a few others stealthily up to Raspatto's sleeping quarters. He had them hide round the corner of the passage, because he had been told there would be a guard outside the master bedroom, but there was not, so he indicated for them to follow him up the passage - very quietly. They waited outside the door and Rajay entered. In the bedroom was a lamp and Rajay's sword glittered in its light. Raspatto's first wife was with him; she woke up as Rajay entered, jumped out of bed and stood between him and her husband, asleep in the bed.

'Lady, get out of the way! This sword is not for you,' he whispered. She knelt down, her head on his feet.

'My life is nothing but please don't kill my husband. I'll die in his place rather than be made a widow.'

'I hear you, but keep quiet and get out of this room immediately.'

Two partisans took her firmly away. Raspatto had none of his wife's courage. He opened one eye, recognised the dreaded Mountain Mouse, knew about his noble attitude to women and prayed to the Crocodile God of Mattanga that Rajay would be swayed by his wife's appeal.

At this moment the palace band began playing dance music very loudly, as if for a party. Danard and his men were forcing them to do this, at dagger-point.

'Is this the way you guard the palace?' taunted Namoh as he cut down the sentries on the front door with the help of Lee and the partisans from the mango grove, while Rajay's men opened it from inside. Namoh and his men entered then barred the massively strong doors behind them, so none of the soldiers from the camp across the road could get in to help. The partisans inside the palace slew any ogres and guards they found. There was a tremendous din in the palace courtyard: people shouting and utter pandemonium, but absolutely no response from the eight thousand troops so nearby.

The band played on.

A sentry challenged Lee, who was an excellent swordsman and thought he could handle him easily. Lee stepped backwards in a corner of the courtyard during the brief fight and just as he delivered the fatal sword thrust fell into a deep cistern. He tried to find a handhold to pull himself out but there was none and he was in trouble. If he cried for help he'd be killed; if he didn't he'd drown. Then he felt a hand grab his.

'Don't worry, I'll pull you,' someone whispered. Moments later Lee was safely out, and he saw a hunch-backed girl disappear into the shadows.

Upstairs in the master bedroom, Rajay noticed Raspatto's sword lying by his bed.

'Defend yourself!' he pointed at it. He stood still to give Raspatto time to get out of bed and unsheathe it. Raspatto, however, had no intention of fighting and made a jump towards the open window. He was nearly out when he delayed a moment too long, unsure of what was below, so Rajay slashed off most of his fingers as he hung onto the windowsill and he fell, screaming with pain, into a prickly rose bed in the courtyard.

'Get out of my palace or I'll be back to kill you!' Rajay shouted from above. 'Leave my country and take your army with you or we'll kill them too!' Raspatto picked himself up and ran into the tents in the courtyard. Namoh, below, saw him and followed, while Rajay watched from the window.

'Don't chase him!' he shouted. Namoh pretended not to hear and disappeared after Raspatto; soon screaming was heard and some of his surviving guards ran to help. Namoh couldn't find Raspatto in the semi-darkness, hiding with his women.

'Enough, let's leave!' Rajay ordered as he ran downstairs to help Namoh. Danard, also in the yard by now, blew a whistle, the signal for retreat. In the unlit disorder Rajay found Namoh tangled up in a curtain surrounding some woman's boudoir-tent, about to be run through by a guard. He had already been wounded on the arm and was bleeding profusely. Rajay dealt with the guard, freed Namoh and they fought off more guards, then all of the intruders managed to get out of a small side door. They melted into the alleys they had known from childhood.

'How's your arm?' whispered Rajay to Namoh as they ran

'Not as bad as it looks - more blood than pain. It's not deep.'

'You're a complete idiot - for heaven's sake listen to me in future!' They stopped to catch their breath and discovered everyone was accounted for, but some more were wounded, including Danard. 'You were all great – but come on, time to get out of here!' Rajay congratulated them, hiding the stab wound he had received in his shoulder when saving Namoh.

They ran through more narrow streets, with short cuts through gardens, until they reached the mango grove, one badly wounded man carried by the others. He stayed back with the local partisans and unfortunately later died. The partisans had horses ready and the others left town at a gallop through the blackened fields and concealing fruit groves and took the pass that led up to Hermitage Fort. Back in the mango grove bugles were blown and almost out of earshot another took up the call, until by a relay system Ahren, Ekan and the rest, waiting on the pass below the supposed campsite on the hills between Hermitage and Tiger's Head Forts, heard the signal. Ahren and Ekan had been watching throughout the night.

'He's done it!' Ahren shouted, to wake the others. The men further up lit the fires which had been laid on the ground, pouring oil on them to make them burn brightly. Others lit the lamps they had tied to trees. All the fires and lamps had been placed where anyone looking from Santara would assume they were the campfires of the raiders. False information about this had been spread around the town and Raspatto's army camp.

At the New Palace, the band was finally persuaded to stop playing. Lamps were lit and the mayhem became only too obvious – over twenty guards and ogres dead, and more wounded, including Raspatto. He nervously emerged from the harem; his severed fingers were dressed and the rose thorns removed from his body. The fingers had been cleanly cut off but no one could find the missing bits because one of the partisans had taken them from the bedroom windowsill and dropped them in a drain. Raspatto was in agony and his fury knew no bounds. He would never hold a sword again.

He cast around for someone to blame and was told that the Mountain Mouse and his men had escaped without a single sign of pursuit from the army across the road. Consequently, late in the night the commander, General Eiyer, was summoned. He was originally from Daish Shaktay but had defected to Mattanga and the more he saw of the ogre people's ways the less enthusiastic he felt about fighting their battles. In the evening rumours had been going round the camp that Raspatto was going to throw a wild party at midnight. Eiyer's reaction was to let them get on with it. When he heard the noise across the road at the stated time he went back to sleep and only later discovered that King Karlvid's Viceroy to Daish Shaktay had been attacked by the Ghiry upstart. The rumours about the party were traced back to some soldiers, reinforcements, who had arrived late that same evening and later disappeared into the night.

A number of fires were seen on the nearby hills, a sure indication that the partisans were camping up there. General Eiyer decided that his army of sleepy foreign conscripts was simply no match for the Mountain Mouse and his dreaded freedom fighters so did not send a force after them. As he stood before Viceroy Raspatto he regretted all the decisions he had made recently and prayed for a miracle to save him.

'When the enemy attacked, I assumed you'd already died defending me!' roared Raspatto.

'We were told you were having a party, sire,' replied Eiyer.

'Some party! I think you're in league with this Ghiry fellow.'

'Sire, I am told that the rebels are camping on the hills nearby.'

'Well then, unless you want to visit the torture chambers of King Karlvid, you'd better get after them right now, but leave me a strong bodyguard.' Raspatto was mortally afraid that Rajay would return as promised.

Almost immediately Eiyer left town with a force of five thousand mounted troops, in a last desperate attempt to save face. He led them across the Santara valley at a gallop and soon neared the hills - he assumed he would be attacking a tired band of rebels who had been up all night. Rajay, Danard, Namoh and Lee were at that time approaching Hermitage Fort, and when Rajay reached there he almost fell off his horse and only then admitted to having been hurt. However, a doctor was waiting and soon everyone was attended to – a few days rest would see them right. The partisans who had accompanied them to the town were also on their way home: innocent villagers returning from a wedding party.

The partisans waiting on the pass now numbered over twelve hundred. It was nearly dawn, the sky was lightening and Ahren and Ekan both lay on a flat rock overlooking the valley. Ahren could see the road below, with the approaching enemy cavalry.

'About time too!' he sighed, looking through a spyglass.

'I thought they were too chicken-hearted to come,' commented Ekan. 'Let me look and I'll make a guess as to how many they are.'

Every partisan had already decided on his spot behind a bush or rock and now they climbed the steep cliffs on either side of the pass. Their guns were loaded, their arrows ready and they waited in silence. General Eiyer's troops were now nearing the top of a narrow ravine, the lower part of the pass. Above was a flatter area where the fires had been simulating the camp, and where Eiyer assumed that Rajay Ghiry and his men were sleeping after a night of causing chaos in Santara. Lower down the path was narrow and precipitous and full of twists and turns.

It was a massacre, as the red glow of dawn lit the sky. Ahren and Ekan picked off the horsemen in the lead and then hundreds of arrows and bullets came from unseen marksmen high above. Others blocked the retreat with a rain of arrows lower down. Consequently there was no escape either up or down and Eiyer and most of his men were killed or wounded. None reached the top of the pass.

When the survivors struggled back to Santara, this made Coroso Raspatto even more eager to get out of Daish Shaktay. He, his household and the remainder of the army were harried by Rajay's guerrillas back to where he had crossed the Shaktay River on rafts, only to find they had disappeared and they had to swim across hanging on to branches, or row in the few boats they managed to steal. Not many made it back to Mattanga and Raspatto was lucky not to have been killed somewhere along the way.

CHAPTER 3

THE CALM AND THE STORM

R ajay's reputation was awesome at the court of Mattanga, where Coroso Raspatto did his best to evade criticism by magnifying the power of his enemy. Rajay himself continued to give all credit to the Goddess of Daish Shaktay, whom he insisted both inspired and protected him. For three months no one from Mattanga dared step inside the borders of Daish Shaktay: the borders as defined by Rajay, the uncrowned king. He knew, however, that this was only a breathing space. If one of Karlvid's provinces gained independence, others might follow. Rajay strengthened his forts and enlarged the army and meanwhile there was a great deal of administrative work to be done at Malak Citadel, being as Witten had arrived from the south with good news. Some foreign merchants who had previously had their warehouses at Port Volcan wanted to change to Rivers Mouth Port, because Port Volcan had virtually ceased to exist. They were invited to Malak Citadel, which was simple and utilitarian; the Great Hall was large but plain and even Queen Jansy lived in a modestly furnished suite of rooms.

When the foreign merchants arrived all this temporarily changed. Silken carpets of many colours were laid on the flagstone floors and tapestries depicting ancient victories of Daish Shaktay were hung on walls; Rajay's dais was converted into a regal stage and a gorgeous red satin canopy covered the throne. The sentries wore brightly coloured uniforms and outside the hall tame leopards were held on leashes, ready to be set on undesirable characters. All these things had been borrowed from wealthy nobles and businessmen. Rajay, up on the dais, caught our eyes and smiled as the first ambassadors arrived: tall, blue-black skinned men of great dignity from the Melitsian Islands in the far south. Five other delegations came and soon impressive trade agreements were being drawn up.

We all helped to arrange Valya's wedding. His father was very ill on their estates further north, so his mother was not able to get involved as she was looking after him. Rajay wanted to invite all the nobles in the country, as these were the social circle of Valya's family. This wedding was a political statement, just as Valya's appointment to the command of Gap Fort had been. His health improved by leaps and bounds once Melissa arrived and soon her feelings for him were being returned. She was entirely unmoved by the fact that even now, no one knew whether he would be able to lead a normal life again. I breathed a sigh of relief. After some weeks the splint was removed and to everyone's delight Valya could walk.

Witten was gloomy and I couldn't understand why. I asked him what the matter was and he told me he also wanted to get married, to Amber's elder sister Pearl Aydriss, but Rajay was not in favour, because he had lived with the Aydriss family for some time and knew Pearl frequently created discord between the sisters and then made it look as if someone else was the cause of a problem, when it was her.

'He said what I did with my life in that way was up to me,' explained Witten, 'but begged me to be careful, for my own sake. So now I'm not sure what to do.' I could see he slightly resented Rajay's advice, but in Daish Shaktay once people married they stayed married, even if the relationship was not happy, so it was better to make the right choice before jumping headlong in. I suggested he did nothing for the time being, hoping that in time everything would work out one way or the other.

I went on doing programmes to awaken the Trees of Life and the groups got bigger and bigger - by now all my first recruits from Malak Citadel were themselves running groups. The mood of the ordinary people had become optimistic and defiant, especially in areas where we had awakened large numbers. Two evenings before the wedding we had a programme in the Covered Market and Lee and Ahren joined our music group. Many of the aristocratic guests had already arrived and the market was full. The fact that some of the young heroes were performing, and with Deradan leading the music it would be well worth listening to, meant that some of the people came who were not initially interested in the spiritual side.

However, after some songs the majority of those present entered into the vibrant atmosphere. I noticed Rajay and Queen Jansy, along with Valya and Melissa come in at the back while we were singing. After the programme I felt a distinct change in the guests; there was less arrogance, ego and criticism and more gratitude towards the young men who were risking all to make the country free for everyone.

The day of the wedding dawned and in the morning we had the traditional cleansing ceremony, where Melissa, the bride, was smeared with a paste of fragrant herbs on her arms, hands, feet and face, after which it was washed off and she was symbolically as pure as a baby. We spent the day painting hennaed designs on her feet and hands and dressing her unruly hair. She wore a beautiful robe of red silk and a veil of real golden gauze. Her jewellery was made of gold from the mountains and pearls from the coasts of Daish Shaktay, her wedding gift from Queen Jansy. Melissa had been blooming in beauty as her relationship with Valya had modestly and cautiously developed and on this day she looked truly lovely.

Valya was taken some way out of the town and an elephant was brought for him to ride on. This time, unlike the one at Santara, the procession actually *would* finish up with the bridegroom arriving at the place of the wedding: the Great Hall of Malak Citadel. Rajay, his friends, and Lee and Ahren were part of the procession.

Near the throne dais a cloth had been stretched across the hall and Melissa and those of us who were her maids of honour were with her on one side. She held a garland of red roses, at the appropriate moment the cloth was dropped and on the other side was Valya with his men friends. He looked more nervous than when confronted by the hoards of Mattanga, Danard insisted. I suppressed a smile. Valya also had a garland and he and Melissa put them on each other while we applauded.

They were an impressive couple: Valya was very handsome and Melissa was neatly built, with a mass of curly, reddish-brown hair. Her eyes were green and sparkling and she had the lighter, rusty skin of the peoples of the north-eastern lands, where her mother had come from. A small fire was made on the floor in the centre of the hall and they sat by its side and made offerings together, after which Valya's scarf was tied to Melissa's veil and they made vows. Each time they did so they walked around the fire and the vows reflected the qualities of the seven subtle centres, as pertaining to marriage.

First they promised to be completely faithful to one another; for the second centre they vowed to bring up their children to be loved, cherished and spiritually aware. The vow of the third centre was to do with material well-being; Valya promised to share his wealth with Melissa and she promised to use it unselfishly. At the level for the heart they promised to always place their love for each other on a high pedestal and never to let petty differences mar this precious gift. Melissa looked shyly at Valya from under her veil, because they had not had a single harsh word since they had met. At the level of the fifth subtle centre, placed in the throat, they vowed to put the collective good before their private interests. The fact that Valya walked lamely round the fire, wounded in the service of his country, was evidence of that. Melissa was also, because she had agreed to marry to help her father gain the support of Rajay Ghiry before she knew her husband was to be the man she already held in her heart. The sixth vow, like the sixth subtle centre, concerned forgiveness, and they promised to always forgive one another, if any mistakes were made. Finally, for the seventh subtle centre, they promised to always help each other remain at one with the source of the deepest bliss and joy: the Tree of Life.

Now came the political aspect of the marriage. Rajay had asked Melissa and Valya permission to include this and they agreed wholeheartedly. The nobles present knew that Valya was one of Rajay's companions and had frequently risked his life for him. They also knew that Valya had vacillated, been forgiven, and now stood high in Rajay's esteem. Valya and Melissa walked up to the dais and in front of the throne was the sacred sword. The first thing they did in their married life was to kneel and touch it with their right hands. Rajay gave a short speech about Valya's bravery, begged all the guests for their support and asked them to also swear the oath of allegiance on the sword. Rajay and his supporters had twice defeated armies sent to invade the country and had captured a vast amount of wealth, and an entire navy, from Port Volcan. The exorbitant tribute which had been draining Daish Shaktay would not be sent to Karlvid any more so they would all benefit from reduced taxes.

Rajay knew some of the nobles and rich people were jealous of him, and that they sympathised with Mattanga. He was asking them, on this public occasion, to show their support for what he had achieved with the help of young men like Valya. Most were happy to do this; some mumbled under their breaths and one or two quietly absented themselves – Rajay noted which.

After this he went to Valya and Melissa, surrounded by well-wishers, and presented Valya with a thick gold chain and a fine signet ring engraved with the arms of Daish Shaktay, while to Melissa he gave a stunning necklace of diamonds, sapphires and rubies.

There was dancing and feasting, and the next day Melissa and Valya left for their herb farm so he could further recuperate, after which he would take up the command of Gap Fort. The farm was Lord Northwestern's wedding present to his estranged son, his way of patching up their relationship, when he discovered Valya's bride was very knowledgeable about herbs. Any girl who could stop his son gadding around with the Ghiry rebel deserved a farm, a mere trifle for a man who owned more than three hundred. Lord Northwestern was too ill to attend the wedding and no one dared tell him Valya was soon to become commander of one of the most important forts.

When the couple had left we discussed the events of the last few days and Rajay felt the fact we gave awakening to so many nobles and their families before the wedding, and that almost all of them were prepared to take the oath of allegiance, were definitely connected.

These halcyon days were not to last. In Mattanga King Karlvid found someone he could trust to carry out his instructions. Vittorio Lionheart was a brilliant general, sadly for Daish Shaktay, and he wished it had not been him; he had always admired the Ghiry family. Luth arrived at Malak Citadel with this serious news one wiltingly hot day just before the summer rains began. He entered the Watch Tower Pavilion where some of us were sitting with Rajay, who stood up and offered Luth his own seat, and refreshment. Luth took the refreshment but refused the seat and sat on one of the side divans.

'This time we're in big trouble,' Luth warned Rajay.

'It's very serious,' Rajay agreed. 'I know Lionheart; he's bold, intelligent and subtle. We won't be able to hoodwink him as we have the others.'

'And worse, he has a faithless rascal as his second-in-command, one Duratman Offlen, a favourite of the ogre king. Lionheart is well named. He's essentially an honourable man and this may be in our favour. In former times his family wanted independence at any price. I don't know what can have possessed him to serve Karlvid.'

I remembered the pendant Rajay had given me and realised there could not be two noble Lionheart families, so I left the room and fetched it.

'Forgive me Rajay. I don't mean to be ungrateful for such a magnificent gift, but I feel very strongly we should get this back to its rightful owner, presumably General Lionheart. Then he'll see, on his own family jewel, the very goddess who protects the country he's been ordered to destroy.'

'You're right, and I won't argue with you, if you really do want to give it back.' Even at this uncertain time, Rajay smiled. I hadn't exactly argued with him when he had insisted on giving me the pendant, but near enough. We heard footsteps on the stairs and it was one of Luth's monks who had arrived by the relay service. He bowed to Rajay with due respect and Rajay nodded to him in recognition of his homage.

'Cheyla,' began Luth, 'for you to come all the way from Mattanga, the situation must be dire.'

'It is, master. We've heard that Lionheart and Offlen are going to enter Daish Shaktay via High Plains, to retake the sapphire and ruby mines.'

'I had one of my dreams last night,' I added, 'I heard a voice saying, "Rajay has received his kingdom as a boon and it is destined to be free and strong, provided he has absolute faith."'

'Thank you for that,' he replied quietly. Lee gave me a piercing stare; he still wasn't too sure about my dreams. When we were alone I told him the rest of it, which was that not all of Rajay's friends would come back this time, but it wasn't clear who would be lost.

'I can't help it,' he said. 'We were there when they made their vow. If it's our time to go, then that's it. I won't abandon Rajay now.' Ahren agreed.

Later in the day Rajay prepared to depart with the Malak Citadel guard. He told Danard to mobilise as many troops as possible from elsewhere, and to follow him, while he would go straight to High Plains. Danard was to wait at Sapphire River Fort until he received a message to join him.

CHAPTER 4

THE BLACKSMITH'S PASS

Iigh Plains Fort was on a rise in the centre of a wide valley, in the mountain chain that ran down the eastern side of the Northern Continent. It lay some way south of the east-west road between Mattan Province and Daish Shaktay. Varg-Nack was commanding it, with a strong and well supplied

garrison, but he was going to need all the help he could get. Lionheart planned his invasion carefully. He had contacted anybody in Daish Shaktay who had a grudge against the Ghiry family. This meant Rajay had to travel cautiously, at night. At each fort they picked up more mounted troops, but it was never going to be enough and he knew this.

They stopped briefly at Sapphire River Fort and had expected to see Ekan, who was overseeing the strongholds which guarded the mines, but Rajay was told by the second-in-command of this fort that Ekan had taken a number of soldiers to High Plains when he heard that Lionheart was approaching. Rajay went on to High Plains and left most of the cavalry at Sapphire River Fort, with instructions to follow when they received a message. They slipped in the back gate, because the enemy's troops were at the front, but Ekan was not among the officers who greeted him, and Varg-Nack took Rajay into his private rooms.

'Please sit and have food and drink,' began Varg-Nack. He appeared to be uneasy about something.

'Where's Ekan?' asked Rajay.

'Our spies told us Lionheart was a good four days march behind Offlen, who had come on ahead against Lionheart's orders. Yesterday Offlen stormed the lower fort's walls, being as High Plains is a fort within a fort, on an elongated hilltop. Ekan took out a force to meet him, with under a thousand men against Offlen's five thousand, who were trying to climb the wall. Ekan fought like a tiger until he was within sight of the hated Offlen. Sixty of our men had already fallen and some asked Ekan to draw back.

'Men who love Rajay are already dead, so I'm going straight for Offlen!' he shouted and ran headlong at him, sword in hand, but before Ekan could reach him Offlen's personal bodyguard had clubbed him down. All the Daish Shaktay soldiers fought on. '"What if Ekan has fallen?" they cried. "There are lots more of us and we'll avenge him!" Indeed, they fought so well that Offlen and his men had to retreat, but we lost a hundred and seventy-nine soldiers – too many - and another two hundred wounded, some seriously. We couldn't reach Ekan's body then and when our men did get there it was gone. We fear the enemy took it for cremation with their own dead.'

Rajay bent his head downwards so no one could see his anguish. Ekan had been a childhood friend and had taught Rajay almost everything he knew about animals. 'Let me be alone for some time,' he lamented.

The next day Vittorio Lionheart and his endless army completely surrounded the fort.

The Wheel of Fortune was to turn even lower. Lionheart wanted to starve the Daish Shaktay garrison into submission, whereas Offlen preferred to attack recklessly. Lionheart had a healthy respect for his enemy but Offlen took this as a sign of sympathy towards Rajay. Offlen sent a report to Karlvid accusing Lionheart of treachery. Meanwhile the siege continued. Water was no problem and the Daish Shaktay strongholds were always well stocked with provisions.

High Plains Fort had a secret exit. An underground stream flowed through limestone caverns some way below it, one could walk through them, and the caverns, and stream, came out on a hillside well away from the fort. The next day a messenger was sent out this way to Sapphire River Fort, telling Danard to bring as many troops as possible to fight Lionheart. After a week another messenger was sent, and then another, but after a month still no help came. Offlen made frequent attacks on the outer ring of walls and towers until they eventually fell. The defenders withdrew to the inner fort.

Since being at High Plains Varg-Nack had done a great deal of tunnelling and now the path at the side of the underground stream was large enough for horses as well as men, and only a very narrow wall of rock lay between the end of the tunnel and the hillside. This had been left on purpose. There was only a small cleft there at present, where the stream gushed out, but this could be enlarged in no time. The entrance to the tunnel was behind the hay store in the fort.

Lionheart had to go back to Mattanga because of Offlen's letter of complaint. As soon as Offlen was alone he began attacking the upper fortifications, throwing away many of his men's lives and wasting much ammunition, but sooner or later he would breach the walls and take the fort. Still no reinforcements appeared. It was the season of rains now and on these high lands the storms were sudden and heavy. One morning Rajay called his officers to him.

'This evening we will have to surrender, but we will not open the gates to the enemy until tomorrow morning.'

High Plains Fort was surrendered at sundown but Rajay's envoy explained to Offlen that the gates of the Daish Shaktay forts were never opened between sunset and sunrise. That night there were many parties and little guarding done in Offlen's camp, and he was drunk with alcohol and pride.

'Who says Rajay Ghiry is a tricky character?' he boasted. 'I've defeated him in one month and tomorrow he'll be my prisoner!' He drank mulled wine in his tent with his officers, wearing a wool cloak against the mountain chill and hunched over a brazier. Outside the wind moaned and the rain fell out of a thundery sky.

No one heard Rajay and his entire garrison evacuate the fort via the underground tunnel, leaving only a few straw-stuffed images of sentries on the walls, tied to their posts in case the gale blew them away. The last man to leave carefully piled hay near the door into the tunnel and locked it behind him. The invaders would eventually find it but by then Rajay and his men would be far away. No one in Offlen's camp thought anything strange about an especially powerful thunderclap, in fact the last few rocks of the tunnel being blasted away, so the horses and men could come out onto the dark hillside.

At dawn Offlen prepared to enter the fort. His men had earlier noticed it was very quiet and there were some straw images of men on the walls. They suspected something, knowing Rajay had a reputation for working miracles, but did not dare say anything to Offlen. His officers climbed the walls with ladders and opened the main gate from the inside. The fort was deserted: no troops, and worst of all no Rajay Ghiry. Then someone reported that the Daish Shaktay force was galloping towards the Narrow Pass, the short cut to Sapphire River Fort. How they had got out of the fort along with their horses no one had a clue, but that was typical Rajay Ghiry.

'After them at once!' shouted Offlen. 'Take three thousand of our swiftest cavalry. We'll soon outdistance their unfit horses that have been cooped up for weeks.'

Unfortunately this was true. The Daish Shaktay foot soldiers and other retainers from the fort escaped into the surrounding mountains or hid in the many caverns in the area. Those of the High Plains garrison who were mounted, including Rajay, reached the Narrow Pass well after midnight, having only rested briefly at mid-day. Lee and Ahren went aside during this rest and with their Sasrar keys called for the guardian tigers to come and help them, if by chance they were anywhere nearby.

By the moons' light Varg-Nack saw through his spyglass that Offlen's cavalry were catching up fast, and the Daish Shaktay horses were all but spent. At one place on the pass it was necessary to dismount and lead the horses round the many boulders. If anywhere, this was where to hold it against their pursuers.

'Rajay,' Varg-Nack begged, 'your safety is vital to Daish Shaktay. Without you our land will never be free. I'll stay here with most of our men and block the way, and you and a few bodyguards must go on. When you reach Sapphire River Fort fire the cannon and we'll follow. We'll easily hear because the storm is over now.'

'I'm not going to leave you here to be butchered,' cried Rajay vehemently.

'Then Daish-Shaktay is finished,' declared Varg-Nack. 'You must go, for the sake of our country. If you don't believe me, try the vibrations you trust so much. Leave Lee and Ahren here because they bring good fortune.'

'You've got to go, Rajay,' urged Ahren. Reluctantly Rajay clattered on through the rocky pass with the remainder of his tired men and spent horses.

Varg-Nack took his position in the front and told Ahren and Lee to stay back, and come forward when needed.

'Do we use our keys in fiery discus mode?' Ahren asked Lee.

'If we do, they'll only kill the soldiers who are attacking us directly. Plus we may lose our keys, because they'll fall on the ground after doing their work, then we'll have no protection against the next wave of soldiers coming along behind. No, better keep them round our necks unless there's no other hope.'

Soon they were all fighting, hard pressed in the narrow ravine against many times their number. Wave after wave of ogres and traitors in their pay attacked the brave and determined few. Some of the enemy tried to ride their horses through the narrowest part, but they stumbled and fell. Many ogres were shot by the Daish Shaktay soldiers and their bodies littered the narrow defile, making it even more difficult for the others to get through. Try as they might the Mattanga troops could not make much headway. Lee and Ahren fought side by side in the moons' light and more and more fell on both sides. The boys had both been slightly wounded and were getting very tired. Then they saw a large tiger standing in the deep shade of the ravine's side, waving its tail angrily. It wore a golden collar and three others appeared, roared and ran in front of the Daish Shaktay soldiers.

'Don't be afraid!' shouted Lee to the soldiers as they bounded past. 'These are the guardian tigers of Daish Shaktay, come to help us!'

'We've got magic keys to control them! Fight by their sides!' cried Ahren. At that moment a bloodstained trooper came up, his eyes white with terror and panting with exhaustion.

'Good sirs,' he stammered, 'take command. Varg-Nack is beheaded but - but ...' Ahren caught the man in his arms as he stumbled, 'he fights on, with no head.' They laid him on the ground behind a rock and pushed their way forwards to where the fighting was fiercest. There they saw the miracle, a headless body wielding a sword in the eerie moons' light. The elusive tigers and what was left of Varg-Nack dominated the narrowest part of the ravine. Any Mattanga soldiers who approached them were destroyed; both the tigers and the headless body were lightning fast and everywhere at once. The horses of the Mattanga cavalry were terrified and stampeded back down the pass, trampling some of the soldiers who had already dismounted. It was chaos.

Whenever Mattanga soldiers approached the living corpse and they were slain by the hand holding the sword, stained red from the blood of countless victims. The tigers snarled and pounced from the shadows and were invulnerable, as if from another dimension. Most of the remaining Mattanga troops stood transfixed and the tigers picked them off like flies. Shortly before dawn the Daish Shaktay men heard the boom of a cannon and knew their king was safe. The enemy had either fled or been killed and as the morning sunlight shone on the headless body it crumpled onto the ground and became a normal corpse. The tigers disappeared and all was quiet in the pass once more.

The surviving Daish Shaktay men limped in to Sapphire River Fort the next day and Rajay ran into the yard to meet them.

'By the Grace of the Goddess, you're alright!' he cried.

Lee and Ahren dismounted and took Rajay to the corner of the yard. 'Varg-Nack fell on the pass,' said Lee simply, knowing there was no way to soften this catastrophic news.

Rajay groaned. Lee and Ahren gently put their right hands on his back, at his heart centre, in an effort to help him bear the bitter shock. At that moment another violent thunderstorm broke overhead, as if the skies themselves were sharing his grief.

The pass where Varg-Nack gave his life for his friend was renamed the Blacksmith's Pass.

CHAPTER 5

ADVICE FROM LIONHEART

Namoh, stunned by the news, demanded to see the acting commander of Sapphire River Fort, Captain Gurra-Burrow.

'Why didn't you send reinforcements?' he shouted. 'We've lost a vital fort and a large number of our brave soldiers.'

'Sir, I was told to wait for a message, but none came,' the frightened man replied.

'Where's Danard? He would never have left the king in a lone fort with only a small garrison against a large army.'

'He had to return to Confluence Fort because we heard another army was approaching Daish Shaktay there. He said he would give orders when he returned so I just waited.'

'So you just waited,' repeated Namoh cynically. 'Get out of this fort and leave the army, and don't make trouble for your king or country again, that is if we still have a king and country a month from now. Be gone before His Majesty calls for you - he's lost two of his oldest friends and may not be as forgiving as me.'

Deradan, also veering between fury and grief, came in and knew Namoh was way out of line saying this but fully supported him. They needn't have worried. Athlos, with his ring of spies, soon discovered that Gurra-Burrow had been bought by Offlen. Gurra-Burrow was responsible for the murder of the messengers from Rajay requesting reinforcements and for forbidding the troops to go to his aid. He was executed for treason.

In Mattanga, King Karlvid was satisfied that Lionheart was still loyal to him but cautioned him strongly. When Lionheart returned he was pleased to find the flag of his overlords, the bleeding skull, flying over High Plains Fort. Later he and Offlen discussed the victory.

'It's the Ghiry boy we wanted, more than the fort,' Lionheart complained.

'I'm sorry sir, he slipped out by night, during a heavy storm.'

'I hear your men failed to catch him due to a headless swordsman and some tigers?'

'Yes, there were eyewitness reports.'

'Is no one free of this magician's tricks? Every story involving Rajay Ghiry has miracles and magic in it. It's just an excuse for our own incompetence!' Lionheart's hand crashed down on the table, making the silver samovar shudder.

Alone in his room at High Plains Vittorio Lionheart was unable to sleep. Memories and doubts assailed him. His great-grandfather had been the ogres' first commander, tricked into joining them when they had mysteriously appeared in their ships from beyond the seas. Vittorio himself had been orphaned at the age of eight and had risen high in their service. His ancestral lands were near Mattanga, but the very thought of rebellion seemed hopeless. His family had also worshipped the Goddess of Daish Shaktay and deep in his heart was a desire to be free again: free to rule his own lands and free to worship the Goddess, whose qualities were love, compassion and defence of the oppressed. His overlords worshipped a fearsome crocodile headed god who had to be placated with human sacrifices.

Lionheart had been brave to the point of recklessness in his youth, but now in later life his subtlety won him as many victories as force of arms. Nevertheless, however much he raged outwardly he could neither hate nor despise Rajay Ghiry. When he began this campaign, with the might of Mattanga behind him, he was sure Rajay would soon be defeated. But over a month for one fort? And then young Ghiry had got clean away with all his men! Would he, the great Vittorio Lionheart, really find it so easy to reconquer Daish Shaktay? It was tricky terrain, full of crags and forests, with strong forts and a highly trained guerrilla force all over the land, second to none in cunning and bravery. Worst of all, kill one commander and another equally as effective would spring up in his place. Lionheart admitted none of these misgivings to Offlen.

Rajay immediately took the reinforcements that had been waiting at Sapphire River Fort back to Confluence Fort, downriver. They destroyed the soldiers from Mattanga who were besieging it and then the same troops under Danard went back up to the mines area to stand against Lionheart. Rajay stayed at Confluence Fort for a few days. Persheray was still there, and Rajay spoke to him in the castle garden one evening, ordering him to join his parents at the Zaminder's. Persheray's admiration for Rajay helped lessen his grief, at least in public, but when Persheray left Rajay was again disconsolate.

'For me death is nothing, just a change of clothes. Why couldn't I have been killed instead?' he lamented.

'Because you're the king and you've got to lead Daish Shaktay to freedom,' replied Ahren stoically, although he also felt utterly dejected. 'Varg-Nack was having problems at High Plains.'

'What do you mean? He never said anything to me.'

'Many of the officers there wouldn't obey him because his father was a blacksmith. He'd struggled with that ever since you put him in positions of responsibility, but was too honourable to complain to you.'

'Yet another reason why I wonder why I bother to go on. Is there any point in trying to free this country for these useless people?'

'You told us that once enough people have had their Trees of Life wakened, they'll change,' Lee took over.

'Maybe I was too optimistic.'

'Look at your sword: you're the king and guardian of Daish Shaktay. Please, lead your people.'

'Yes, I will. I won't give up, but my friends and I grew up with an almost impossible dream. Just as that dream started to become a reality, one is crippled and two are killed. And another was killed earlier, shortly before you met us.'

They were silent, and far below the Shaktay River flowed on by. A servant brought one of Luth's men to the walled garden. He sensed something was amiss. One could have cut the atmosphere with a knife.

'Please join us,' Rajay put on a good face.

'Sire, I bring a note from Master Luth.'

Rajay,

I was grieved to hear of the passing of Ekan and Varg-Nack but when the stars are destined to set, it is best they do so in all their glory. Two bright stars have set thus, but the kingdom remains, and stars always rise again. Lionheart is not completely lost to our cause. Send Lee and Ahren to him with the pendant that Asha gave back to you.

Luth

Later Lee and Ahren went up to Rajay's room. He was alone, and assumed they had come to get the pendant, as it was decided they should leave for High Plains as soon as possible.

'The Lionheart family jewel is here,' began Rajay.

'That's not what we came about,' said Lee. 'You're a guardian and the burden on you is desperately heavy.'

'You don't have to tell me.' Rajay's head was bowed in sadness and his hand was on his forehead.

'We felt your grief,' Ahren went on. 'We came to share our vibrations with you and perhaps give you a little inner joy. Is that all right?'

'Very much so!'

Rajay sat cross-legged on the floor, his back to Lee and Ahren so they could direct the healing vibrations towards his Tree of Life. They asked in their hearts that the all-pervading power would allow the vibrations to flow though them, then they reawakened Rajay's Tree of Life by raising their hands behind his back, gave him the bandhan of protection and took a lighted candle. They moved it up behind the left side of his back a number of times and directed their left hands to the log fire in the room, with their right hands towards his left side to fill it up with vibrations. Soon the cool vibrations started flowing strongly. They felt Rajay's still, strong and compassionate heart centre. The sadness and heaviness left, and Rajay was his normal self once more - confident, positive and surrendered to whatever fate had in store.

'Rajay's fine again. What happened?' asked Namoh the next morning.

'We gave him vibrations; even he needs them sometimes. You can do the same when we're gone,' suggested Ahren.

'I thought we'd lost him this time. Rajay's so detached; you never know when he'll take off to the hills and completely give up being the king. This royal persona is nothing more than a mask for him, to be cast off when he's fed up with it.'

'You're wrong there,' said Lee intensely. 'He knows what he's got to do, and by all the heavens he'll do it. If he's depressed it's because he cares so much. He's a spiritual guardian of one of the heart centre countries, remember.'

Lee and Ahren wore the brown clothing of Luth's monks. They shaved their heads - Ahren tried to hide his archery scars and Lee endeavoured to look lowly and modest. They reached High Plains Fort a few days later and amnesty was granted as was customary, because they were monks. They asked to see Supreme Commander Lionheart. Lionheart was in conference with his officers so the two boys waited outside his room with a guard. They overheard some of the conversation.

'.......I'm telling you, we must storm the forts, one by one, regardless of how many men it takes,' insisted Offlen. 'Our soldiers are there to be killed, so why not make use of them? The main purpose of this campaign is to bring Daish Shaktay under our direct control again and to destroy this upstart.'

'And what if we should fail?' replied Lionheart. 'We would look perfect idiots, and this Ghiry is very wily.'

'He's superhuman,' murmured one of the officers who had been rendered witless when he saw Varg-Nack fighting without his head. He was on indefinite sick leave. 'His generals can fight without their heads, so who knows what he himself might do?' Lionheart took no notice; he was sure his men had suffered a mass hallucination that night.

'We should proceed cautiously, first capturing the towns and villages,' Lionheart proposed 'Then the demoralized soldiers in the forts, whose homes will have been taken and whose families will be begging for peace, won't be so hard to overcome, by either bribery or brute force.' The officers left and Lionheart was alone in the room with Offlen, and his misgivings.

'Sir, there are two holy men who would like an audience,' said the guard. 'They say you prayed for help and they are here for you.' Lionheart looked startled. It was true that since entering High Plains Fort he had more than once called on his family goddess, something that had not seemed necessary for many a long year.

'All right, send them in. Make sure they are unarmed, and stay outside the door, in case I need you,' cautioned Lionheart. He knew some of these monks were sympathetic towards the rebels and were possibly spies. Lee and Ahren entered with a pang of tragedy in their hearts, because the last time they had been in this room was with Varg-Nack. Offlen showed no sign of leaving and after a few moments of strained silence Lionheart opened the conversation.

'I hope you will tell everyone you meet on your wandering how powerful our army is.'

'Sir, forgive me,' replied Lee, 'but we are neither impressed nor intimidated by earthly might. It is the power of the divine which moves us.' At this moment Ahren began chanting softly. Offlen, with a scaly skin and horns poking through his hair, was listening eagerly. His vibrations were burning when Ahren put his attention on his inner nature, which meant he was completely out of harmony with his true self and the divine power. The chant Ahren used was one he had learnt in Sasrar to neutralise the effects of such people and sure enough after he had repeated it eleven times, Offlen looked ill at ease and left the room. They heard him running down the stairs. As soon as they were alone, Lionheart relaxed.

'Do you really think Rajay Ghiry is inspired by the goddess of these lands?' he asked. The chant had done something wondrous; a cloud had lifted from his head and his heart was lighter than it had been for a long time.

'Oh absolutely,' answered Lee, trying to sound unworldly. 'It is even written on his sword, which came to him in miraculous circumstances.'

'You know a lot about this enemy of mine. Have you met him?'

'Yes, indeed,' smiled Ahren openly. 'We bring a gift from him.' He took the locket from its box and placed it in front of Lionheart. Something reacted inside the Mattanga general. For years he had lived among beings for whom the worship of a woman was blasphemy and nonsense, but in front of him lay one of the greatest heirlooms of his house. It was a treasure that had been handed down from father to son and the legend was that originally it had been a gift from the Goddess herself, who had appeared to one of his forefathers after an inspired victory. It had been lost at his father's death forty-five years ago, but he had seen it many times as a child.

'How did Rajay Ghiry get hold of this?' wondered Lionheart.

'I don't know,' Lee replied. 'His message is, "You and I are both descendants of the same family who, in the name of the Goddess of Daish Shaktay, swore centuries ago to defend these lands against any who prevented people from living in a free and dignified fashion.'" Lionheart said nothing but clutched the jewel close to his chest. He looked at Lee and Ahren as if they had him at dagger point.

'Who are you?' he asked nervously, no longer the commander of thousands but an upright man defeated by his conscience.

'We are from the sacred kingdom of Sasrar and have come here to see that the way there is not closed by your overlords. You can kill us if you want but it would not be honourable and you put honour above everything,' declared Ahren bravely.

'You have opened my heart,' admitted Lionheart, 'and revealed to me something I didn't know was still there.'

In Sasrar Lee and Ahren had learnt to direct the divine vibrations of love and truth with their attention alone, to whatever part of a person's character, or inner subtle centres, were weak or vulnerable to evil. They did this now. They were not forcing their will on him; merely focusing divine, compassionate attention on Lionheart and he could respond as he wanted. Offlen, being thoroughly rotten, had run away, but Lionheart was basically sound, albeit influenced by adverse circumstances. A fifty year old cobweb was gone from his mind; as if he had been hypnotised since childhood and was now free.

'King Karlvid is very powerful. Rajay Ghiry can't defeat our armies, because we are too strong. He must eventually come and offer me terms. If he does, I'll arrange an interview between him and my king. My son Sarn lives in Mattanga and if Rajay goes there under our protection, he'll be treated like one of our family.'

Lee and Ahren left. They had been more successful than they had ever hoped. Offlen was suspicious, especially when he caught a glimpse of the locket, which Lionheart kept with him at all times, but he could not make any definite accusations.

CHAPTER 6

NOBILITY IN DEFEAT

The weather was hot and humid. Regiments of white-topped thunderclouds rolled across the hills and valleys, forming and reforming into storms. Lionheart waited for reinforcements from Mattanga and then entered Daish Shaktay. After fierce fighting at Sapphire River Fort, by sheer weight of numbers the fort fell. Danard and most of his troops escaped, melting into the mountains. He met up with Rajay at Gap Fort, the centre of operations.

Lionheart forged slowly forward. Despite losing men all along, he forced his way through ambushes, night attacks, guerrilla harassments and all manner of other tricks. Lionheart occupied the north-eastern part of the country and meanwhile Offlen entered the valley over which stood Midway Manor Fort. He had tried to take the fort but after five attempts and losing many men to both strong opposition from inside the fort and the partisans in the forests on each side of the valley, he finally gave up, as he was supposed to meet Lionheart. At Gap Fort, Rajay knew the noose was drawing tight. Witten was sent back to Malak Citadel to make sure the treasure and wealth were well hidden and to make contingent plans if the northern half of the country was lost to Mattanga once more. One evening Rajay spoke to Valya, now commander of Gap Fort, and Melissa.

'I gather your father finally died,' he began.

'Yes,' Valya replied, 'but we made up before he went.'

'So you are now Lord Northwestern and overlord of vast estates.'

'Yes, but possibly not for long. Offlen is laying waste the area around Midway Manor and our lands and villagers may be the next to suffer.'

'I pray not. In any event, I want you, Melissa, out of here. Go to Crossings Fort for the time being.'

'I'm not going anywhere without Valya,' she retorted. 'If he stays, I stay. I can fight, if I have to. I can use a bow and arrow, a gun and if needs be a sword. My brothers taught me.'

Valya looked horrified and opened his mouth to say something, but Rajay interrupted before he had a chance: 'Please do what I say. I'm your king these days and I'm under oath to protect you.' Melissa looked at Rajay in silent confusion. He softened, realising her attitude was not arrogant disobedience but a desire to stand bravely by Valya. 'The vibrations indicate you should both leave for somewhere safer. Try to understand that when I ask you something, that's where my authority comes from. We're not going to let this fort go without a fight and Valya can't help in that way any more, so leave while you still can. You would be a major liability because my soldiers would just try to protect you in an armed struggle. It's the way we are in this country.'

'We'll go tomorrow morning. I wish I could be with you, even if it's hopeless,' said Valya sadly.

'If they catch you they won't kill you,' Rajay went on. 'They'd take Melissa to Mattanga and probably do dreadful things to her, but you they'd ransom and you wouldn't come cheap. Lionheart knows I'll never desert you, however much it costs. He knows we're very rich now: you personally, and I hold the purse strings of a well-run country, dripping with the wealth of Port Volcan. So that's another reason to have you out of the front line.'

'Come, my dear,' Valya called Melissa and prepared to leave.

Offlen did terrorise Valya's people, and many other villages and farms as well. He burnt, looted and murdered the villagers and captured any of the women, children and animals who had not fled into the forts or hills. However, reports filtered in from Luth's men who roamed the countryside and penetrated the enemy's camps that there was a marked difference of opinion between Offlen and Lionheart. Two or three of Lionheart's officers had been reprimanded by Offlen for refusing to lay waste the villages, saying they were deeply impressed by the just and happy way of life in Daish Shaktay and they had no wish to destroy it. Offlen, completely transformed into an ogre, was suspicious of anyone who showed the slightest mercy.

Rajay went on fighting a guerrilla war. He did not want to surrender until it was absolutely necessary and still had some small hope that he could defeat the Mattanga army. For a month or so, he was constantly on the move, leading raids from the forts against the baffled invaders. He usually travelled speedily, by night, and led his elusive and deadly companies of soldiers where the attack was least expected. Often when pursued by the Mattanga troops he would hide with the farmers and villagers, who were all totally loyal to him and although Rajay rarely had time to sleep or eat, he looked as fit and bright-eyed as ever, despite the fact that the enemy was gaining ground every day.

Then the blow fell. Spies reported that Lionheart was ready to attack Gap Fort. Lee and Ahren were out on a raid when, on the horizon, they saw a great army, accompanied by heavy guns and siege equipment. They hastened back to the fort with the news and soon it was surrounded. After some days the aggressors managed to dig a tunnel under a watch tower of the lower fort and blew it up. Many men were lost on both sides and then the attack intensified. The next day the whole of the outer defence works fell to Lionheart's forces and Deradan was captured. He had been in command and had refused to leave his post even though wounded by the explosion. In Lionheart's tent that evening a conference was in progress.

'Let's send him to Mattanga in chains,' urged Offlen, knowing this would please King Karlvid. 'He'll be thrown to the crocodiles as an offering to our god.'

'And what would be the reaction throughout Daish Shaktay?' demanded Lionheart. 'No, this province has always been virtually ungovernable. I want to make it docile and profitable, not a graveyard for our armies in the face of ceaseless partisan attacks. These people will fight to the last man if provoked. My way we'll get these forts back with less bloodshed and trouble.'

'You worshippers of the goddess are all the same. You'll unite against our king sooner or later,' retorted Offlen angrily. He had again caught a glimpse of Lionheart's pendant.

'I'm the king's most trusted general,' Lionheart suppressed his fury. 'Guards, bring in the Daish Shaktay commander.' Deradan was brought in, his legs shackled and hands tied, his head held high despite being in great pain from wounds and burns. Lionheart ordered him freed.

'You're a brave and valiant man,' began Lionheart.

'I've heard and seen the same of you, sire,' replied Deradan. 'If I'm brave it's because my king is my inspiration.' He was thinking, 'Your problem is you serve the wrong side.'

'You could rise high in the service of King Karlvid. Here's gold, if that will encourage you.' Lionheart pointed to a large bag of coins at his feet. Deradan recognised them: Daish Shaktay crowns. Rajay had ordered them minted recently with gold from Port Volcan and on each coin was engraved: 'Rajay Ghiry, King, by the grace of the Goddess.' On the bag was an inscription composed by Deradan himself: 'Shining like gold Rajay Ghiry reflects the light of freedom for the good of all,' and this gave him courage. His life hung by a thread, and most likely before him lay the torture chambers of Mattanga and death in the jaws of a crocodile.

'I serve Rajay Ghiry. No amount of money will change that,' he replied. As First Secretary of Daish Shaktay he earned a generous salary, although he had little chance of surviving to enjoy it.

'I admire your loyalty,' again Lionheart praised Deradan. 'In fact I admire it so much that you are at liberty to go free, as an example of my clemency.'

'May the Goddess of Daish Shaktay shower blessings on you,' Deradan dared to say. He could hardly believe what he had heard. After he left Lionheart spoke to Offlen.

'If we continue to fight, we'll take months to capture every fort and we'll lose many more men. You see, we'll get these northern forts back very soon.' Offlen gnashed his ogrish teeth but could not argue with his superior.

Deradan returned to Gap Fort, pulled up onto the walls in a basket as the gates were well and truly closed. He went immediately to Rajay, who took one look at him and called the doctor to dress his wounds and burns. After this was done Rajay asked Lee and Ahren to help him give Deradan vibrations and only after he assured them he was feeling much better did Rajay allow him to give his report and talk strategy. The fort commander was also summoned.

'Danard and his men are harrying the enemy forces from the rear, sire,' the commander began, 'then they're melting into the mountains before anyone can catch them, but it's not having much effect. The enemy's numbers are too great. Our country groans under the burden. Not only that, we're running out of food and have already had to slaughter some of the horses for something to eat.'

'Daish Shaktay has groaned ever since the ogres first overran it,' lamented Rajay.

'Let's ask the vibrations what we should do,' suggested Lee. He was praying that Rajay would take this moment to go to Lionheart. It was his way of saying this to him, without speaking out.

'Yes, it's obvious,' Rajay picked up his hint.

'It's cool. It's time,' stated Ahren.

'You're right,' conceded Rajay. 'We can't win against Lionheart and Offlen. I'll offer terms to Lionheart before this Offlen does anything to his credit, or I'll have to deal with that wretch instead.'

A signal was sent to Danard in the forests: a code of flags, visible to him with his spyglass. He was to harass Offlen's side of the army to distract his attention for some time.

'Lee, Ahren,' Rajay asked, 'go to Lionheart and tell him I'll meet him.' They made bandhans of request and protection and then slipped out with a white flag. Offlen was away from the camp, looking after Danard's diversion: an ambush of some reinforcements who arrived at an opportune moment.

'So, you've come, as I hoped you would,' began Lionheart. 'It gives me pain to destroy this land which Rajay Ghiry is rebuilding so successfully. If I crush him completely I'll mutilate something of great value.'

'He wants to offer you a peaceful settlement but doesn't want Offlen to be involved.' Ahren explained. His approach to diplomacy involved simply telling the truth; Rajay would never send him on a mission needing hypocrisy. Lionheart liked this young man's forthright style because it was so unlike anything he was accustomed to.

'I'll do my best.'

'Will you see Rajay alone, now?' Ahren went on. The fact that this young man, little more than a boy, called the king by his first name meant they were close. It also meant the Rajay Ghiry trusted his enemy to respect diplomatic immunity, because envoys were sometimes killed.

'Yes, I will see him.'

'You swear by your Goddess, who is also the protector of Daish Shaktay, that you will not harm him?' added Lee.

'I promise on her image,' and he took the pendant from under his clothing and put his hand on it, 'that I will treat him like my own son.'

Lee and Ahren returned to the fort and reported back to Rajay.

'I'll go tomorrow,' he replied.

'What if he kills you?' objected Deradan. 'He may not be as honourable towards you as he was to me.'

'The vibrations are cool to go. If he does kill me, or takes me as a prisoner to Mattanga, then it's better I'm finished than all of us. If we go on as we are that's what will happen. You know the contingent plans.'

Many of the Mattanga officers could not believe their eyes when they saw Rajay approaching alone and on foot. Some thought he must be an impostor, others were sure there would be some surprise attack and all of them wanted a close look at the legendary Mountain Mouse. Lionheart came to meet him, they walked to his tent and once inside Rajay was invited to sit comfortably and informally.

'Thank you for sparing my commander,' began Rajay.

'Your men are each as brave as the last. Never have I met such dedicated soldiers and I'm certain you're their inspiration,' replied Lionheart cordially.

'I'm honoured to have such people in Daish Shaktay. This is one reason why I've come to sue for peace. In return you may raise your standard over this and the other northern forts.' Rajay listed them, starting with High Plains and ending with Tiger's Head, above Santara.

'That will have to be done. The only way you can help your country is to offer your allegiance and subservience to Karlvid.'

'Let me think this over until noon tomorrow.'

Rajay felt intuitively that he should play for time, and sure enough, in the afternoon news arrived which changed things considerably. The two brothers of Chussan, Shaitan and Kaitan, hearing that Lionheart and the bulk of the Mattanga troops were tied up in Daish Shaktay, were sending their army across the desert. Spies had seen it preparing to leave Chussan City and had sent messages to Mattanga. The army was to invade some outlying provinces of the Mattanga Empire and some small allied states. Karlvid was furious when the brothers, whom he considered friends, decided to do this just when he was short of manpower to oppose them.

The war against Daish Shaktay was exorbitantly expensive and Port Volcan, the source of much of Mattanga's wealth, had ceased to exist, so although King Karlvid was overjoyed that the offensive was going well, he was worried. His treasury was empty, with little coming in and enormous amounts going out. He had a passion for building palaces, and statues of himself all over his empire and these were also a great drain on his finances. Mattanga was an overripe pumpkin: plump and colourful outside but rotten within. Lionheart knew this.

As promised, Rajay went to see him again the following day. This time

196

some partisans had bribed menials in the Mattanga camp to drug numerous animals there so they became wild and unmanageable. Elephants, horses and mules careered around the camp causing trouble. Offlen had to go and sort things out.

'I have another proposal to make, as a result of yesterday's news,' Rajay suggested.

'Tell me, if it would help us both,' replied Lionheart.

'Instead of going straight to Mattanga, I'll join you and secure for your king the areas the Chussan brothers want to conquer. Together we'll manage this very quickly and it will give King Karlvid some idea of my promise of good faith to him.' Rajay reasoned that if he helped Lionheart now he could retake the same provinces, originally part of Daish Shaktay, later on. Lionheart thought this over from his point of view.

'That seems an excellent idea,' he agreed. Karlvid was short of troops, because so many had been killed in Daish Shaktay.

'I'll have my secretary draw up the treaty immediately and then we can start for the north.' Rajay said, but thought, 'then my poor country can recover somewhat, until we're ready to fight back.'

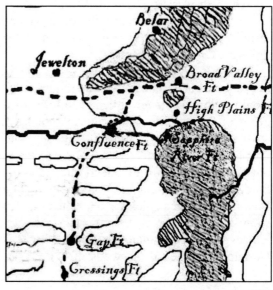

CHAPTER 7

ALLIANCE WITH THE ENEMY

Shaitan and Kaitan of Chussan wanted to capture the land north of Daish Shaktay. Some of this was desert, but it was a rich desert full of diamonds. Then there was the Belar area, ruled by Count Zaminder, who had to give tribute money to the Mattanga Empire, and further south again were farmlands and the east-west road. Near the road were some forts, nominally under the control of noblemen tributary to the ogres, such as Lord Chandan of Jewelton. This was where Bart Charval lived, and Rajay called for him and his men. Count Zaminder's men were also sent for, with his son Bukku to lead them, because that little country was desperately vulnerable.

Rajay had Deradan as his commander, and Lee and Ahren went too. Deradan said the thought of serving alongside ogres was one of the worst challenges of his life, but Rajay was adamant. Danard, Namoh and Witten stayed behind with Queen Jansy and the Council of Elders. Valya, now Lord Northwestern, was at Crossings Fort and would soon go to his homeland to see the occupying ogre troops respected the terms of the treaty and did not ravage north-western Daish Shaktay.

'At the moment we have the ogres actually in our land,' Rajay said to Danard. 'I want you all to protect the heart from these vermin, even if the outer limbs are temporarily paralysed.'

To see Rajay marching to war alongside the Mattanga forces was a shock to everyone but he had chosen five thousand loyal soldiers to go with him, who would follow wherever he led. The lords of the forts to be captured had all heard of Rajay Ghiry and Vittorio Lionheart. The combination of the two terrified them and they were mostly men who preferred to buy peace rather than fight. At first virtually no blood was shed and two of the forts simply sent out an envoy inviting Lionheart and Rajay to enter and make terms. At the third, Rajay's brilliant ideas and well-disciplined troops enabled him and Lionheart to gain a quick victory. The despatches to Mattanga were written to show how Rajay was an important asset to the Mattanga fighting force. However, Lord Chandan, who ruled from Jewelton, was not so faint hearted. He had strengthened the walls of his city and posted large guns on them.

Lionheart knew that taking this town would be no easy matter, so he withdrew to a safe distance while deciding on his next move.

Offlen lost no time in starting rumours: 'Ghiry is making Lionheart too cautious', or 'Rajay Ghiry is finding excuses not to fight.' Offlen wrote frequently to Mattanga, where his associate was the bitter and fingerless Coroso Raspatto. They wanted to discredit Rajay and then get King Karlvid's permission to assassinate him. Rajay was aware of this and suggested to Lionheart that the Daish Shaktay contingent should take a small mud-brick fort in a valley approaching the city, in order to allay Offlen's suspicions.

The Daish Shaktay troops were to attack in two groups: the first at dawn under Rajay and the second some time later under Deradan, with Ahren, who would come up after the element of surprise was no longer relevant. However Duratman Offlen, wanting the expedition to abort, managed to detain Deradan so he arrived late and by that time Rajay had been forced to retreat. Rajay lambasted Deradan in front of the entire Daish Shaktay force. Ahren was amazed - it was completely out of character. Deradan asked to talk to Rajay in private.

'I've had enough,' complained Deradan when alone with Rajay and Ahren. 'You can't expect us to risk our lives for these ogres and have to deal with two-faced rascals like Offlen. It wasn't in the vow.'

'In that case you'd better find us an ally powerful enough to help defeat Mattanga,' replied Rajay calmly.

'I'd be only too happy to,' Deradan retorted, incensed by Rajay's detachment.

'Go fast and take some of the men with you. And you too, Ahren.'

They were surprised, but did as he said, taking with them two thousand stalwart soldiers. It had all happened to suddenly and the next day, when they were nearing the main east-west road, Deradan called a halt and spoke to Ahren in private.

'We're crazy,' groaned Ahren. 'We've walked out on Rajay when he needed us most.'

'No, I don't think so,' replied Deradan. 'I've known Rajay a long time. He rarely loses it with us and absolutely never in front of the men. If he wants to criticise us, he'll do it in private. He wanted us to go off; that's why he pushed me over the edge.'

'You're right, it's cool on vibrations when you say that - so, now where?'

'We'll send a message to Luth and ask his advice, and meanwhile make for Crossings Fort by the byways, so no one will find us, with luck.'

It was an open rumour that Deradan had deserted, to find an ally to help Daish Shaktay oppose Mattanga, possibly the Chussan army, which was approaching from the north. Deradan was brave and popular - not the type of leader the Mattanga forces would want attacking them. Lee asked Rajay why he had been so critical.

'Deradan is bright, so he'll figure it out and Ahren will work everything out using the vibrations. I knew I could goad Deradan into deserting and I want to finish this charade of fighting alongside the Mattanga forces. This defection will bother Lionheart. Who knows? It might be me next.'

Lionheart was indeed worried and decided not to try to take Jewelton. Offlen continued to make problems for the Daish Shaktay soldiers and everything was becoming very complicated. Lionheart took Rajay out riding alone one morning. They soon left the few irrigated fields and were in the dry semi-desert round Jewelton, empty apart from the odd herd of goats picking at the few bushes growing in the parched earth. Lionheart told his bodyguards to stay back, well out of earshot.

'My son,' he began, 'you've proved your worth. I'm writing to King Karlvid to recommend that you become the Viceroy of Northern Daish Shaktay and vassal king of the central part, as before. If you go to Mattanga now, no one will be able to say anything against you. I'll stay here until you return with your appointment confirmed, so I can make sure the Mattanga troops don't harm your people. If as much as one hair on your head is touched in Mattanga, I swear, by the honour of the Lionhearts, to kill myself. My son Sarn, our guards and our palace will be at your disposal.

'And by the way, I've just received messages saying the Chussan army will not be coming this way after all.'

Rajay was dubious, but the vibrations were mostly cool to go. He sent for Danard and Namoh, his noblest elephant, his finest horses and other trappings of royalty to make a good impression at Mattanga. He also asked for a large amount of money and jewels as presents. The rest of the Daish Shaktay troops were sent home. Bukku Zaminder also went home, grateful that Rajay, by judiciously changing sides and calling him to help, had saved his little land so far. Deradan and Ahren met Luth on their way to Athlos's temple and he told them they were right to make for Crossings Fort.

Some days after this Rajay's entourage met Sarn Lionheart at Broad Valley Fort, administered one of Karlvid's vassals. Sarn had gifts for Rajay from the ogre king, a pearl-embroidered robe and a diamond-encrusted dagger. Namoh, with his characteristic black humour, wondered if it was to replace the one Rajay had left in Garno Comeni's back some time before. Rajay wondered what to do with them, because their vibrations were painful. Karlvid also sent a letter.

'Most Esteemed King of Daish-Shaktay,
Come to Our court at Mattanga without delay. Please have full
confidence in my sincere feelings towards you. When you come to
see me I will give you honour and royal favours. After that you will

be able to return home.
I remain etc, yours,
Karlvid, Supreme Protector of the Mattanga Empire.'

'It's lies; the vibrations of this letter are worse than the gifts, but we have to go,' commented Rajay. As they were about to set out, the priest from the nearby village came to give a farewell blessing.

'Rajay Ghiry should be king round here,' he insisted, and because he was so old and doddery, Sarn didn't try to correct him. For Rajay he whispered a different piece of advice. 'Young man, Luth warns that you're going into the crocodile's jaws.'

'Tell him I can only follow my destiny,' he whispered back.

Rajay set out for the capital of his arch-enemy with Danard, Namoh, Lee and some retainers, including Bart Charval. Sarn was their guide and host. He had heard the gossip about Rajay - the magician, the ruthless partisan, the slippery eel, but took to him immediately and within days it was obvious that his loyalty did not lie with Karlvid.

Sarn was about Rajay's age but had been brought up in the fetid environment of Mattanga, full of intrigue and in-fighting. Consequently he found Rajay and his followers a welcome change, like a fresh wind from the mountains on a hot day. The Daish Shaktay group were close knit, alert and witty, and Rajay was not only good company, but very profound, a quality completely lacking in most people in Mattanga.

Sarn was fascinated by the way Rajay and his friends would meditate peacefully every morning and evening, and would wave their hands around in strange ways, but having done so were even more full of life. Also they could know a considerable amount about people and situations by putting their hands out and saying, 'It's cool, OK', or, 'Not so good, it's warm and tingling.' He realised this was what his fiancée's friend Sagara Samudra had been trying to teach him and within days he had learnt how to do it too.

The contrast of these partisans to Karlvid's courtiers was absolute. Since coming to the throne Karlvid had murdered his three brothers, their wives and even their children. Danard told Sarn how Rajay protected everyone in Daish Shaktay, from the poorest to the richest and women in particular.

The party made their way through the mountain passes, then down the gently sloping hills to the province of Mattan. Here everything was lush and green; the rivers had been dammed, canals built and the bountiful land yielded crop after crop. In every town were tax collectors and soldiers, a symbiotic relationship of violence and extortion, and on nearly all the crossroads were statues of King Karlvid or his father, reminding everyone who was in charge. Sarn became increasingly impressed by Rajay as the days passed and Rajay listened carefully to everything Sarn told him; the court of Mattanga was even more corrupt and decadent than when he was last there.

CHAPTER 8

SUBTLE FORCES

Now I must go back a bit, to when Rajay was fighting alongside Vittorio Lionheart. I was then at Malak Citadel, as usual staying with my friend Amber and her husband Saber, the Captain of the Citadel Guard, and I wondered if there was anything that could be done to help using subtle power. That very morning the answer came.

'Asha, don't bother about doing lunch for us today. Queen Jansy wants you to go and see her,' said Amber.

Although as a senior officer's wife Amber had a soldier servant, the young chap assigned to her wasn't much good at cooking, and that's something I've always enjoyed. I dressed myself smartly and modestly, and went to the queen.

'Come, my dear. What have you been doing lately?' said Queen Jansy, sitting at a stone table under a shady tree in the garden outside her apartment.

'I've been busy, Your Majesty. I'm doing awakening programmes in other villages and towns, as well as Malak Citadel.' She indicated for me to sit with her.

'You must be careful.'

'With respect, I only go where Saber Rizen says I can.'

'Take a bodyguard when you leave the fort. Not everyone is behind us even in this area. You're doing well though; I can feel the people are more confident, more honest with themselves and more joyful, even though our country is in dire trouble. It would help a great deal if the collective vibrations were stronger in the part of the country nearer the conflict. Lee did very well awakening people at Crossings Fort. Could you go and see what you can do there?'

'Yes. I'd like to.'

'You should be all right for the time being. I'll send you with an armed escort and that nice boy from the village on the coast can go too - what's his name?'

'Jaggo.'

'That's him. Try to awaken as many people as possible and you could also do some fire ceremonies to destroy negativity and ask for help. Do you know how to do that?'

'Yes, but I'd need a book with the names of the different aspects of the divine to be called upon, in the classic language. I didn't learn them by heart when I was in Sasrar.' Queen Jansy gave me a small leather-bound volume which was lying on the stone table in front of her. It was a treasure. There were lists of names, describing in detail the qualities of each subtle centre - but this was no printed book. Each page was a handwritten and illustrated manuscript, decorated with flowers, scrollwork designs and even animals, all in rich colours and gold leaf.

'Take it, a gift from Rajay and me. It might help to save Daish Shaktay.'

Jaggo and I went to Crossings and Valya was there.

'What's going on?' I began.

'Rajay's last words were, "Trust me as always; we aren't beaten yet," but it's very bad.'

'We mustn't give up hope. When you go back to your estates, you and Melissa must give awakening to as many people as you can and teach them the two bandhans, at the very least.'

'Don't worry, we will. At least I still have my estates. Rajay managed to wrangle that in the peace treaty, but I've got to pay a vast tribute and I don't know how my tenants and I are going to manage it.'

'With a lot of bandhans and maybe some Port Volcan gold - I'm sure Deradan and Witten will think of something. There's another thing you can do, the fire ceremony. We'll do one here and I'll show you how.'

'We'll help any way we can.' Valya paused, looked self-conscious and then continued, 'Thank you for arranging things between Melissa and me. We're perfect for each other.'

'I'd have been useless as an aristocrat's wife.'

'You may be right there. I'm not sure my people would have taken to a Lady Northwestern who rode around on tigers!' we both laughed. 'What I saw in you was what I wanted to see – never a good basis for a relationship - whereas you saw my true self.'

'It wasn't that.' I was impressed by his candour. 'I have to honour a previous vow.' So that was cleared up between us for good and all.

Many of the people who had been given their awakening at Crossings would make bandhans, often sitting in groups and reverently asking the same thing: 'Give us peace, give us freedom, protect our king.' After some days we decided to do the fire ceremony. A fire was prepared in the yard of the fort where we would worship the divine power in the form of the fire and ask it to take away any negativity which stopped our requests working out. Word got around that Queen Jansy had asked us to do this and there must have been five hundred people in the yard in the early evening. First we all reawakened our Trees of Life and then we praised the power of the first centre, the customary way to start. Jaggo was in charge of the fire; he lit it, offered melted butter to it and kept it going.

Valya, who had the book Queen Jansy had given me, read out one hundred and eight qualities of the fourth subtle centre, in us at the level of the heart, and on the planet in this area of Daish Shaktay. He had evidently managed to get some education between his months of playing truant with Rajay as a child and read the names in the classic language well. After each name was said, dried herbs were offered to the fire. We took a few in our right hands and raised them up the left side of our bodies. When we had raised our hands we rotated them three times above our heads and offered the herbs to the fire. After this was finished, anyone who wanted could ask the fire to absorb any problems they could think of. We did a big collective prayer for the deliverance of the country and as we did so a flash of lightning lit the darkening sky, followed by a clap of thunder. It was still the season for rain and we had been lucky to get a dry evening. I was sure the lightning was Mother Nature blessing our efforts.

Nothing came of our fire ritual for a few days but then it all made sense. Deradan, Ahren and no less than two thousand strapping men-at-arms arrived, saying they had decided not to fight for the enemy any more. Commander Aydriss pulled his moustache more than I had ever seen him do as he didn't know how to handle this. I asked Ahren when this had happened and it had been the day after we had done the fire ceremony. The next day messages came from Rajay. Deradan and Ahren were forgiven, the men-at-arms were to be paid off and given leave until next called for and Deradan was to go to Malak Citadel and take up his usual duties. His message to Ahren was, 'Use your Sasrar powers to help us.'

That evening, Ahren and I were sitting together on the ramparts of the fort, looking out over the fields, fruit groves and villages in the valley far below, as the sun set on this insecure and war torn country.

'What do you think he meant?' I asked.

'Don't know. Rajay often says things spontaneously, but very accurately,' Ahren replied.

'What we've often done, ever since we left Teletsia and those earthquakes took place, is to set events in motion, sometimes of a destructive nature, like when those two priests complained about me at Malak Citadel. They were exposed and things they'd got away with for years came out into the open. We had a lesson on that at school in Kedar. It's called the power of positive destruction.'

'The what?' said Ahren absently, not much into long words.

'The power of positive destruction. It destroys evil when, beyond any reasonable limits, evil threatens to destroy goodness. It works out when a number of people have had their awakening in an area and are therefore in touch with the all-pervading power.'

'I remember now. What we need is something to finish off all the ogres, not just the odd army here and there.'

'The flying horses! They *are* the power of positive destruction. Wherever they put their feet, the good gets better and the bad gets exposed and destroyed. But how can we get them down here?'

'I'm going back to Sasrar to fetch them. We've got to use those flying horses.'

'Who would ride them?'

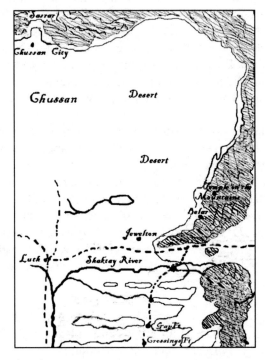

'Robin can, and I could if he came too, but he didn't want to leave Chussan.'

'Maybe you could persuade him.' Then I had another idea. 'A circus! You and Robin could take it to Mattanga. It might work, especially if you took the tigers.'

'And Athlos's mates as an acrobatic troupe!'

We occasionally felt Robin's vibrations to see how he was, and usually he was fine. Sometimes warm on the right, presumably because he was doing too much. Once or twice his heart centre was constricted, indicating insecurity, but he was a partisan and often in extremely dangerous situations, so that was to be expected. I looked at my golden ring. Much depended on how Robin reacted to it. He had always helped us Teletsians and maybe he would do us one more big favour. I thought of Valya, wounded, and Ekan and Varg-Nack killed, along with so many others from Daish Shaktay, and how Rajay was again and again risking his life.

206

'Ahren, I want you to give you this ring to Robin. He knows it, with its design of a four petalled flower, and knows what it symbolises - the ability to overcome all obstacles. I'm also going to give you this other one for him. The rubies and sapphire represent Rajay's gratitude to me and are symbolic of this country. Tell Robin.'

'I'll do my best. That's assuming I myself can get back up there.'

Valya and Melissa left for their home to do what they could. Then another of my bandhans of request came to fruition. Sir Brin and Lady Aydriss were traditional Daish Shaktay nobles but nevertheless, when Rajay made it clear that girls should also give awakening, they encouraged their daughters Pearl and Coral, who still lived with them, to do this. Coral was enthusiastic and within a week or two we were going round the villages together. Occasionally Pearl would come but she could sometimes be quite abrasive. One day I was sitting in my room and she knocked on the door.

'Come in, please,' I said. 'I'm writing my diary.'

'You have such a wonderful life. It must be worth writing about,' said Pearl morosely. 'I'm stuck here, getting older, unmarried, with nothing much to do.' She stood looking out of the window for some moments and then went on, 'Asha, I need your help. If I tell you my problem will you promise not to tell anyone?'

'Of course not.'

'You know Witten?'

'Yes, indeed.'

'I'm fairly certain he wanted to marry me, but when he told Rajay he lost interest.'

'Do you know why?'

'Rajay's known me for years,' she said sadly. 'Sometimes I was so rough and bossy when he stayed with us. I was the oldest, and wasn't very nice to either him or my sisters in those days, and even now I have such a sharp tongue. I'm not surprised if he didn't want Witten to marry me. Witten's a great man, and I don't deserve him. How can I become gentler?'

I felt her vibrations. My index fingers were tingling, and the whole of my right hand.

'Don't worry, I'll show you some treatments that will clear the subtle centre in the neck and then you'll start to speak more sweetly. Especially if you get involved with the awakening programmes, you'll probably change naturally when you give people peace and joy.'

'I'll do anything. I so want to become a nicer person.'

I gave her some treatments to clear the problem in the throat centre: regular meditation, the chanting of certain names and inhaling the smoke of a certain seed when it was parched, and within a few days Pearl began to soften. No one could believe how she had changed, but she had, and became one of my most useful helpers. After a few weeks she and her sister, and also Heeram the milk lady, were so competent I wondered if I should move on. I sent word to Queen Jansy asking her advice, because Valya and Melissa wanted my help. The following note came back.

> *My dear Asha*
>> *Go to Valya's with an armed escort but get a written guarantee from Lionheart that you won't be harmed. Beware of Offlen and his men. They are not to be trusted.*
> *With my love and blessings,*
> *Jansy Ghiry*

I sent a letter to Lionheart, who had moved into Gap Fort with a large garrison. Duratman Offlen was at Tiger's Head Fort above Santara, where he started to gather around him the Daish Shaktay nobles who collaborated with Mattanga.

CHAPTER 9

IN SEARCH OF ROBIN

When Jaggo discovered that Ahren was going north he was determined to go too. Ahren had a fine horse from the Chussan baggage train but Jaggo didn't have one of his own. Commander Aydriss came up with a simple solution.

'This is official Daish Shaktay business, so take some horses from here. I'll sort it out with Witten next time I see him. Has Rajay been paying you for your services?' he said to Ahren.

'Yes, very generously, but the gold is at Malak Citadel. I haven't got much on me.'

'I'll also give you both some money. The bill will be on the state.'

Jaggo and Ahren set off with letters from me for the folks in Sasrar. I prayed the two boys would make it because they were going through a war zone and then across a dangerous desert. Nevertheless, Ahren was a seasoned traveller and Jaggo was learning fast, and after quite some days of cautious travel they reached Belar. Bukku Zaminder and his troop had returned to Belar the day before, with the news that Rajay had left for Broad Valley Fort, en route to Mattanga. Count Zaminder feared the worst for Rajay; he knew his daughter's safety also hung in the balance and Melissa was very near to her father's heart. Ahren and Jaggo stopped for one night at the Zaminder's and pressed on.

Two days later they reached the village where they had met the old headman, Pahari, and after asking around managed to find his farm. He was delighted to see Ahren, because many stories had grown up about the three from Sasrar, and Rajay and his friends.

'So, you want to go back to the northern mountains?' asked Pahari, as his wife brought in the supper.

'Yes, and we need to find that young man who came with us, who was buying mules,' said Ahren.

'You mean Robin? My son is on a mission for him right now.'

'Is Robin near here?'

'No, the Chussan brothers decided to invade some lands to the south and sent their army across the desert. Robin got wind of this and planned an operation which has been a great success, but it does mean it's going to be difficult to get across it for the foreseeable future.'

'Why is that?'

'As you know, there's a string of wells all the way across the desert. What

Robin's lads did his end and my boy and his partisans did from this side was to make them temporarily unusable. They waited until the entire Chussan force was far into the desert, then our boys either poisoned the wells or filled them with sand and covered them up so no one could find them. Some they blew up and destroyed completely. Robin's men did the same on the other side. Consequently the army was stuck in the middle with no access to water.'

'Then what?' said Jaggo.

'Most of them died. A few who had camels made it across, but it was the end of the invasion idea.'

'So that's what happened! Robin saved us a great deal of trouble! But we're going to have to cross that desert,' Ahren took over again.

'There you've got a big problem,' replied Pahari. 'If you wait a month or two it will all be sorted out, because we'll clear the wells and the poison will wear off naturally, but right now it's difficult. If you go round the edge, on the foothills of the mountains, it's just as bad because those mountains are also very dry at this time of year. Plus it would take you ages.'

The first thing was to give Pahari and his family awakening of their Trees of Life, which Ahren and Jaggo did. Then Ahren explained how this opened the way to many powers which could be used to help put wrongs right. The vibrations affected Pahari and he became more eager to help.

'You mentioned something about camels,' went on Ahren.

'Camels are gold at the moment,' replied Pahari, 'and even if I could get hold of a couple for you, you'd still need to know the way.'

They went to bed, and Ahren and Jaggo did bandhans of request. As fate, or perhaps the bandhans, would have it, the next day Pahari's son Ferg arrived. Ahren told him that he had a fair amount of gold on him, and after hunting around for a few days not only did Ferg manage to buy camels but also agreed to guide them across the desert. Ahren found camels hard to get used to but Jaggo took to them immediately. It was a long and gruelling journey on account of the lack of waterholes but finally they made it to the foothills of the northern mountains, changed their camels for ponies and bid Ferg a grateful farewell.

They took to the valleys and passes that Ahren remembered so clearly from the year before. He had a good sense of direction and a brilliant memory and eventually he and Jaggo reached the astrologer's house in Upper Dean.

'My goodness gracious me!' said Mrs Pea-Arge, as Ahren walked into her kitchen with Jaggo. 'Whatever are you doing here? Who's your friend? Where are the others?'

'I've come to find Robin. This is Jaggo from Daish Shaktay, and the others are still there. Can we have something to eat?'

'Of course,' she gave him a floury embrace, because she was in the middle of making bread. 'Give me a moment to put these loaves in the oven, and then I'm all yours.' She told them that Robin and Lord Albion were away, but were expected in a day or two. After the boys had eaten a message was sent to the astrologers, and in the evening Ahren was summoned. He made his way up to the Great Hall, and cautiously entered. Only the youngest one was there.

'I'd hardly have recognised you,' he welcomed Ahren. 'Inwardly, I mean. You've grown so. I hear you and your friends are doing a lot to help Rajay Ghiry.'

'We've done our best, but the situation is very difficult.' Ahren explained how he had come to see if they could use the flying horses.

'It's you that's so good with animals, isn't it?'

'I feel very at home with them, apart from camels.'

'I know what you mean! Now, about the flying horses, we must be absolutely sure that all those who could possibly see the right course of action

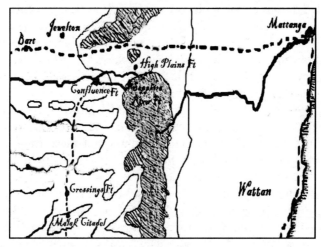

have had a chance and have turned it down.'

'I don't understand.'

'The flying horses set off destruction, and if the problem could be resolved without them then we shouldn't use them.'

'It's gone beyond that. Rajay has already lost three of his trusted companions, many good soldiers and the land has been partly overrun and ravaged.'

'Let's talk to Robin when he gets back.'

The next day Ahren and Jaggo were in the staff hall and they heard the voices of Lord Albion and Robin. There were warm greetings all round and Lord Albion left to see the astrologers.

'Robin, we need your help,' said Ahren.

'What can I do?'

'It's so bad. Rajay Ghiry may not even be alive still. These Mattanga ogres are horribly strong. Asha felt the only way to get the better of them is to use the flying horses to activate the power of positive destruction.'

'He's alive, but he's having a hard time,' replied Robin. 'Feel his vibrations, Ahren. You know how to do that as well as I do.'

'You know what I'm trying to say.'

'Yes, of course. Forgive me for being short with you.'

Since we had left, Robin had not thought much about us, as he had been very busy, but one day he was with Mrs. Pea-Arge. She had heard, from a party of travelling merchants, that I was betrothed to Valya. When he had received this news he had been disturbed, even shocked; it felt so wrong, so out of character. Since we had met, like Lee, he had kept a caring eye on me and had watched me grow up, often guiding me and trying his best to stop me doing what he defined as irresponsible and unexpected things.

'These are for you,' Ahren took my rings out of his pocket. 'Asha said you'd understand the significance of this one,' he put the ring with the four-petalled design on the table in front of Robin. 'It represents the ability to overcome all obstacles. She was given this sapphire and ruby one by the King of Daish Shaktay, Rajay Ghiry, for the work she's doing there. It represents Daish Shaktay and she prays you'll help, because as far as she can see, no one else can. They're very precious gifts and the fact she's sent them to you means she's absolutely begging you to come.'

Robin took the two rings in his hands and turned them over and over, especially the one with the four-petalled design. He knew its significance. He didn't want to get involved in Daish Shaktay but these rings were saying, 'Daish Shaktay desperately needs you – we're doing all we can; can't you come too?' He stared at them, perplexed.

'I heard Asha was betrothed to the First Lord of Daish Shaktay. She moves in very different circles these days. She must be married by now.' He put the rings on the table. Robin understood my message as, 'I'm a grand lady now, used to asking and receiving favours. These rings are mere trinkets to me. Can you come and do a bit of fighting for us?'

'Oh no, it didn't work out, although there was some gossip,' said Ahren lightly. 'Rajay wanted her to marry a friend of his - he's called Valya Northwestern, but she refused because of her vow to Teletsia.' Suddenly it all made sense to Robin. I was still the same Asha, committed to our continent-wide quest to free our countries, sincerely asking for his help. Overwhelming relief flooded him, so much so that he was surprised at himself.

'So what do you want?' he asked.

'Could you take the flying horses to Mattanga as part of a circus?'

'I'll give it my best. I'll do what I can for Rajay Ghiry. He sounds tremendous.'

'He is. You're going to get on famously.'

'I'll put these with my key, for safekeeping.' Robin was still staring at the rings. He took off his two-petalled key, which gave him the powers of the sixth centre, and put the rings on the chain with it. Then he hid all three precious jewels under his simple clothing.

The next day Ahren spoke to Lord Albion about getting Jaggo to Sasrar.

'No problem! Now Conwenna has opened the door, when you first went to Sasrar, it's easy for everyone else. He can walk through and a flying horse can bring him back later. I'll show him the way, because I'm going up there in a couple of days. The usual story: sheep!' Albion grinned. 'Robin has already gone to Sasrar to get some flying horses for the Daish Shaktay freedom struggle.'

'How's *your* freedom struggle going?'

'Not bad. We're making the country impossible to run and Robin's partisans virtually destroyed the Chussan army last month. They were coming down your way.'

'We heard. He did us a great service.'

'We've been on the plains in disguise, awakening the people's Trees of Life. It began to feel right to do so soon after you left last year, as if something opened in the cosmic Tree of Life. As a result people in Chussan are no longer afraid of the priests when they tell them they'll burn in hell if they don't give their wealth to the temples. Also when people are awakened, their body starts to reject poisons, so they give up their craving for strong alcohol and now the priests are going bankrupt as well. These so called holy men have the monopoly on distilling the spirits which are the national addiction. The present rulers have always been puppets of the priests, so when the priests lose their money and power, Shaitan and Kaitan will be in big trouble.'

Two days later Robin reappeared with four white flying horses out of a brilliant blue sky; their vast golden wings shining in the sunlight as they landed in the yard in front of the astrologer's mansion. Ahren's horse Zamba recognised him and demanded affection. The other two, new trainees, were shy, but soon made friends after being offered carrots. Robin had letters from our friends in Sasrar and the big news was that Tandi was the mother of twin girls. Robin knew this, but had wanted it to come from her. Conwenna and Derwin were also living with the family and sent their best wishes.

'I went to see the Grandmother and she's delighted you're awakening the Trees of Life in Daish Shaktay. She can feel the change in the vibrations of the world as a whole and she's sure it's the right moment to use the flying horses. Look, she gave me this.' From under his clothing Robin brought out a key to Sasrar. 'As I'll be operating in more than one area from now on, she gave me a key which has the powers of other areas, not just the sixth centre.'

CHAPTER 10

THE CROCODILE'S LAIR

Now we must again go back in time. Sarn Lionheart was sorry the journey to Mattanga was coming to an end. The few days spent with Rajay and his followers had been a delightful holiday, but eventually the domes and towers of the great city were visible on the horizon. Everyone saw seagulls in the fields where the earth was being ploughed and knew the Eastern Ocean was close. Sarn told Rajay to expect a reception when they reached the city; he assured him that a delegation would meet him some way from the town and a band would play dignified music in front of him as he rode in state through the streets.

That morning everyone in Rajay's entourage wore rich clothing, the horses' manes and tails were braided and everything was clean, shining and neat. Rajay, dressed in satin and jewels, was riding his elephant, resplendent with trappings of red leather inlaid with silver. They came closer to the city and Sarn looked worried. Where was the welcoming delegation? The more important the guest, the further out it came. The Daish Shaktay party was near enough for rich businessmen and the place where foreign ambassadors were usually met was long past.

Still there was no welcoming party and they reached the outskirts of Mattanga, where there were suburbs of luxurious mansions, and beyond them a brown and sluggish river wound its way to the port. They had nearly reached Lionheart Mansion. Finally, as they entered the gates, a small and flustered group of men appeared to receive the King of Daish Shaktay, but there was no sign of the band because there had been conflicting orders from the King's Palace so no one knew what to do. Danard murmured angrily and the others muttered under their breaths. Something was wrong; there should have been a royal prince to meet them, not a group of petty officials. Rajay said nothing.

Sarn invited his guests into his gracious home: cool marble floors, comfortable carpet covered divans, refreshing iced sherbet to drink, fans being slowly moved backwards and forwards by unobtrusive servants, and outside fountains played in the gardens, where tall trees gave shade and rustled their leaves in the sea breeze. Soon Sarn had to disturb his visitors' ease.

'Sorry folks, but we've got to go to the King's Palace right now. It's the anniversary of his coronation today and we're supposed to be there.'

Sarn took Rajay aside and mentioned that if all went well, King Karlvid might want him to become one of his senior generals and that a marriage alliance between him and Karlvid's youngest daughter was being considered. Sarn could see from the expression on Rajay's face that this last suggestion was not welcome so did not give any details about her. Rajay tried to be detached. He had often told his friends that he would have to marry in the interests of the country, but at this moment he couldn't help praying for deliverance. Even Chor Bardmarsh's buffalo-like girl would have been preferable to an ogre's daughter, complete with scales and horns, no doubt. Rajay wondered which would be worse – fighting the ogre king's battles or

marrying one of his offspring.

'Whatever will help Daish Shaktay and Mattanga overcome their differences will be welcome to me,' he replied, in his most diplomatic manner.

The cavalcade set off once again. Mattanga was a large city and the King's Palace was some distance from Lionheart Mansion. The retainers from Daish Shaktay were entranced by the outer beauty of the capital, but Lee was in pain as the harsh, discordant vibrations of Mattanga registered on his subtle system. Two years in Sasrar and a year in Daish Shaktay, surrounded by people in tune with Mother Earth and their own inner selves had made him very sensitive. He wondered how he had survived all that time in Teletsia.

Rajay also saw behind the superficial splendour. Some of the slaves who underpinned the society and economy had originally come from Daish Shaktay, as had much of the wealth which fuelled the luxury, and again he prayed for eventual victory over these seemingly invincible devils. When they reached the outer gates of the King's Palace the visitors were asked to dismount; only the royal family were allowed to ride beyond this point. The twenty or so retainers which Rajay had brought with him were requested to wait in the outer court, while Lee, Namoh, Danard and Bart Charval accompanied him into the king's presence. They had to leave their weapons behind and Rajay's retainers kept an eye on them.

Inside was a large courtyard, surrounded by buildings and arcades. Flowerbeds and lawns covered the left hand side. Guards were everywhere and they stood to attention and watched carefully when the King of Daish Shaktay was announced. They had been warned about the Mountain Mouse.

The ogre king's anniversary celebration was taking place at the side of the inner court in a great hall, covered over, but open to the cooling breezes of the garden and backing onto the king's private living quarters. Sarn led his guests to the part reserved for foreign diplomats and ambassadors. They sat down on velvet-covered stools and waited. The back wall was painted red, with floral designs inlaid with semi-precious stones; half way up, in the centre, was a balcony and behind this a door led into the ogre king's rooms, Sarn explained. On the balcony was a throne made of silver, black mother-of-pearl and gold, and behind was a crocodile's head of the same material, with great rubies for the eyes and real crocodile teeth inserted in the gaping mouth. Behind the throne were filigree marble grills.

Rajay and his friends did not know it, but behind the grills sat the princesses, queens and their companions, including King Karlvid's youngest daughter Princess Zulani. Although she was still only in her late teens, she was renowned in court circles for her beauty, artistic talents and caring nature. She had never stooped to any of the ogres' baser practices and took after her mother, whose people were cultured and civilized, from some islands northeast of Mattanga. They had been taken over by the Mattanga Empire and Zulani's mother had been forced to marry Karlvid before he transformed into an ogre and was merely a cruel man. She was his seventeenth wife and had died young. Zulani had never developed any of her father's ogrish traits, either physically or psychologically. She had deep, reddish golden hair, blue eyes and a light honey complexion. With her were her closest friends: Clary, Sarn Lionheart's fiancée and Sagara, the daughter of the former Admiral of the Port Volcan Fleet.

The Admiral had escaped from Port Volcan only to be executed for losing his entire navy, but his daughter was now married and lived in Mattanga. Sagara had told her friends how gallantly Rajay Ghiry treated her when she was captured near Port Volcan. Zulani had been instrumental in saving Sagara, because as the daughter of a disgraced admiral, she was nearly sold into slavery. Sagara had shared with Zulani and Clary a very special experience she was given when Rajay's prisoner: the awakening of the Tree of Life. The three friends waited eagerly for a glimpse of the heroic young king.

The Daish Shaktay visitors arrived just in time and soon the skinny, scaly figure of King Karlvid took his seat on the throne. He glanced at Rajay, then pretended not to be aware of him, but Karlvid was very aware of him and very scared. He had heard the excuses and exaggerations of the survivors of the Garno Comeni disaster and the tale of woe from Coroso Raspatto.

'He's superhuman,' Raspatto maintained. 'The only way he could have entered the New Palace was if he'd jumped the height of a house to get past my guards. Either that or he can make himself invisible.'

On this day of peaceful celebration King Karlvid had taken the unusual measure of wearing a coat of chain mail under his gold embroidered shirt, he also wore a sword, and was flanked by his most deadly bodyguards. In front of the balcony where he sat, mingling with the crowd, were a hundred of his ablest fighters dressed as peaceful courtiers, but still the ogre king's teeth chattered in fear when he saw Rajay, sitting at one side with his retainers.

The court ritual began. First the chief torturers came forward with some instruments of their trade, to remind everyone how order was kept in Mattanga. Then fifty elephants were presented and each one knelt cumbrously at the back of the gathering.

Rajay was tired, though he did not show it. They had ridden all the morning in the burning sunlight, dressed in constricting clothes and covered in jewels, to demonstrate that Daish Shaktay was a land of wealth and importance. Bart was finding it all very tedious and after the twenty-third elephant dosed off, but Lee, sitting next to him, prodded him with his elbow and woke him up. He then looked on, glum and impassive, and in his boredom wondered if the farm hands had remembered to water the onion and melon fields back home. Lee amused himself by studying the architecture and the gold tracery patterns on the ceiling and columns, which looked very effective against a background of blue lapis lazuli. Danard and Namoh were alert and watching the gifts but their expressions gave away their feelings about the great Court of Mattanga: a false and hypocritical place.

The nobles, vassals and courtiers were announced along with their flamboyant titles, and offered their gifts to the king - an odd assortment, including one small dragon, a unicorn, numerous rare jewels and the inevitable sorrowful looking slave boys and girls from all over the world. In return, the ogre king gave the men who paid homage to him robes of honour and coronets.

Sarn was eventually asked to present Rajay. The Daish Shaktay party collected their scattered attention, picked up their gifts and walked to the front, Rajay in the lead. Sarn had hinted that he would definitely be given a robe of honour and possibly a princely crown. He would obviously receive congratulations for having successfully helped recapture the disputed forts for Mattanga and would most likely be confirmed as Viceroy of Daish Shaktay.

Before the party reached the front of the hall, Sarn told Rajay that he should kneel and touch the floor with his forehead before the king. Rajay had no intention of doing this and stood defiantly before the Crocodile Throne. He touched his forehead with his right hand, first for the Creator and the benevolent Mother of Creation and secondly for his own parents. This was how he expected his subjects to greet him, as a king.

Princess Zulani, sitting behind the grill, became alert, because her father had informed her that if the upstart from Daish Shaktay showed enough servility she would be married to him, to force him into the fold of Mattanga. Karlvid ordered her to remain hidden; he did not want his daughter to be so much as seen by these rebels. Rajay looked up at King Karlvid and Zulani could see him well. Her heart missed a beat as she saw a young man whose smile expressed joy, wisdom, innocence and trust, such as one sees in people who have grown up with love all around them. Princess Zulani knew that from then on she would do whatever she could to help further his cause, even if they never met. She had found her hero.

Down below, things were not going well, Sarn was extremely worried; Rajay had not knelt before the king and men had been executed for less. Karlvid glared at Sarn.

'He is a tiger newly come from the jungle and does not know our ways,' Sarn explained. Karlvid stared impassively in front of him, then raised his eyebrows slightly and looked at Sarn, who tried again. 'I had no time to coach him in our ritual.'

Karlvid was terrified. He whispered to his nearest bodyguard, 'If the Mouse is going to murder me, he might try now.' Rajay indicated to Danard and Namoh - feeling incredibly uncomfortable in red velvet trousers, satin cummerbunds and silk turbans - to bring the silver plates of jewels. They placed them before the king, who nodded, indicating he had accepted them. Now, thought everyone, he will speak to Rajay Ghiry, who has served Mattanga so well in the recent fighting. He was the uncrowned King of Central Daish Shaktay - would he now be made Viceroy of the Northern Sector too?

There was no word of greeting, no congratulation for his recent bravery - nothing. The king said something to the aide at his side. The aide repeated it to Sarn, who took Rajay away from the throne, back past the Royal Princes, the Viceroys of the Provinces, the Generals of the Army and the Admirals of the Navy. Sarn took Rajay, a king, to where the minor guests were standing at the edge of the Hall of Audience. He recognised the two men directly in front of him. One was an officer who had been brought before him after the battle at Midway Manor and the other was the commander of one of the first forts he had retaken in Daish Shaktay, three years before. This man had fled with his garrison.

'Why am I put back like this?' shouted Rajay angrily, breaking the hushed quiet. 'Why are these lowly men in front of me? This is an insult to my country!'

'Shh!' demanded twenty voices. Rajay took not a scrap of notice and went on loudly, so everyone could hear.

'I recognise the back of this one! He's run away from me in battle, and that one went swimming rather than face a fair fight. He was brought before me to be ransomed in his bathing trunks!' Sarn tried to draw Rajay aside but he was not to be humiliated and went on stridently, 'These Mattangans have no principles. They know only how to break their promises.' Rajay became the centre of attention, far more than the grovelling nobleman then receiving a reward. He stormed out of the Hall of Audience, followed by the eyes of hundreds of courtiers. 'I was invited here with promises of honour and recognition. What sort of a creature is this Karlvid?' continued Rajay in a loud voice as Sarn diplomatically guided him out of earshot.

'Perhaps the king didn't know who you were,' whispered Sarn.

'Nonsense! You announced me plainly enough,' roared Rajay.

'I'll try and arrange a private interview tomorrow.' By now they were in the gardens behind the gathering.

'I'll never go near that creature again as long as I live.'

Which might not be very long, thought Sarn desperately. No one could understand why Rajay had spoken so rashly. It seemed suicidal. The Daish Shaktay group returned to Lionheart Palace and soon three noblemen arrived.

'His Majesty begs you to return. He wants to give you a robe of honour and apologises for the way you were treated,' said one.

'I have enough clothes,' replied Rajay curtly.

'Please return to the Hall of Audience. It doesn't look good,' urged the next. Sarn pacified the nobles by explaining that Rajay was suffering from a touch of sunstroke. The nobles left, Sarn with them.

'Why on earth did you behave like that?' asked Danard frantically.

'I wanted to give everyone there a chance to see sense. We might still be able to defeat Karlvid.'

'You really walked near the edge of the cliff today.'

'I'm always doing that. At least I won't have to marry the reptile's daughter and be tied to a wife with scales and horns.'

'Don't be too sure,' said Namoh gloomily.

'I heard she's beautiful, and has a delightful nature,' added Lee.

'I doubt it, but in any case I'll never have to meet her and find out,' concluded Rajay.

After the ceremony was finished Karlvid learnt that Rajay Ghiry had refused to return to the royal presence. He was about to throw the Mouse into his deepest dungeon, but Princess Zulani, the only one who could come anywhere near her father's icy heart, pleaded with him and knew how cool his anger, saying Rajay Ghiry might calm down, and a brave man like that would be an excellent general if he could be persuaded to fight for Mattanga. Consequently a less extreme course was taken. The next morning Rajay and his companions were woken to the sound of marching feet. They found to their dismay that the Lionheart's palace was surrounded by members of the Security Force, in the garden and guarding all the doors.

'How dare you trespass on private property?' shouted Sarn at the captain. 'You look as if you're preparing for a siege. You can't invade our grounds like this!'

'Go and tell that to our Chief of Staff,' he smirked. 'He had the order direct from His Scalyness.' This was King Karlvid's nickname.

'I'll go straight to the king,' Sarn pulled rank over this minion with a small job and a big ego. 'This is no way to host a visiting head of state on a diplomatic mission.'

Sarn was able to use his influence to see Karlvid. 'Your Majesty, this behaviour towards Rajay Ghiry is against all codes of honour. You've made him a prisoner in our mansion, even after guaranteeing he'd be well looked after,' Sarn was risking his life speaking thus.

'I've changed my mind about this Mountain Mouse. We can't have every upstart who comes into our august presence disturbing court protocol as he did yesterday. Soon there will be no respect left for our great dynasty.'

'Sire, my father and I have both sworn with our lives to protect him.'

'In that case, I'll hold you personally responsible that he doesn't escape, until I've decided what to do with him. My men will shoot to kill if he tries to flee.'

'Sire, with deepest respect, the people will lose confidence in you if you do not honour your word.'

'Boy, you tire me. You don't understand anything. I'll have to speak to your father about you,' concluded King Karlvid, and went back to his pipe of opium.

The main gossip the next day in Mattanga, in the ladies' boudoirs of the Royal Palace, the city streets or the simple homes of the ordinary people, was not the anniversary of King Karlvid's coronation. Everyone was talking about the young King Rajay of Daish Shaktay who had stood up to their overlord. For the boys and girls he was a hero and many older ladies felt a desire to mother and protect him from Karlvid as they would their own sons. His forthright courage was a shining example to all the men, from young lads still at school to great grandpas. Many people in Mattanga saw things very differently as a result of the way Rajay had reacted to Karlvid. His words and actions had done as much for them as touching his sacred sword had for his fellow countrymen.

Sarn broke the news to Rajay that he was under house arrest, and for the first time in his life Rajay appeared to give way to despair. Even his brave followers felt utterly despondent. All except Lee, who put his hands in front of him and asked some questions on the vibrations. 'It's cool on my hands. It's going to work out, somehow,' he assured the others.

'We must sit in meditation and then make a bandhan of request such as we've never done before,' said Rajay.

Sarn watched with interest; he was also learning this way of solving problems. A number of the young courtiers who now knew about the Tree of Life secretly despised everything Karlvid stood for and held Rajay as their example, and this included Sarn, Princess Zulani and her brother Moozand. They became the leaders of a faction who sought to protect him. Zulani pleaded with her father for him to be allowed to go home and become the Viceroy, as Sarn's father had suggested, or be given a further chance to prove his loyalty to Mattanga by commanding a regiment in some far-off province.

There was also a group who wanted Rajay dead, headed by Coroso Raspatto, who had lost his fingers to Rajay's sword at Santara, and his sister, who had lost a fortune when her investment in a cargo of ivory had been taken by Rajay from Port Volcan. Firstly Raspatto's group were in the ascendant. His plan was to persuade King Karlvid to order Rajay to help quell a rebellion in a province north of Mattanga. On the way there, while going along the coast road, Rajay would be murdered and his body could be thrown into the sea. Sarn heard about this and told Rajay, who gave Sarn a large bag of gold to bribe some members of Raspatto's party to get this idea quashed. Also, Princess

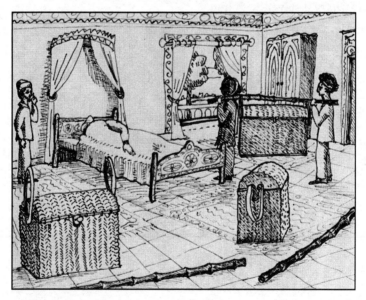

Zulani begged King Karlvid not to adopt such a crude plan.

Meanwhile Rajay discovered that Karlvid was in dire financial straits - the army and navy were on the point or mutiny; many people in the administration were fed up; the whole framework of government was splitting at the seams and the partisan king from rural Daish Shaktay was leader of a far more healthy state than all the opulence of Mattanga. Most of the noblemen at the court who were not ogres felt Karlvid had behaved shamefully towards Rajay. Sarn ordered his own guards to ensure that the Security Force in the garden did not murder his guest.

Rajay tried to buy his way out. He offered the ogre king vast sums of money and an even larger yearly tribute if he could go home. The Chief Treasurer was all in favour of this, because however he juggled the figures, Mattanga was bankrupt, but regrettably King Karlvid could not bear the loss of face that would result from accepting Rajay's offer. Karlvid knew he was already unpopular as an oath breaker and didn't want to become the laughing stock of the city as well. Rajay remained a prisoner and Mattanga sunk deeper into debt. He pretended to be enjoying his stay, telling everyone he preferred it to the endless hard work of governing a country. Matters stood for a couple of weeks and then he made another request to the ogre king: he begged to go to an island in the Eastern Ocean where only monks lived. He promised to become a monk and renounce all claim on his kingdom. King Karlvid merely sneered.

'He can become a recluse on Death Island, in our prison there. No one ever comes out of that place alive.'

The outlook seemed hopeless and Rajay called his retainers. 'You must all go home. Karlvid and his men may kill me and I don't want you murdered too.' They sadly left for Daish Shaktay and only Danard, Namoh, Lee, Athlos and Bart Charval stayed with him.

CHAPTER 11

THE LAUNDRY BASKET

Although Rajay was under house arrest, Sarn brought a number of man friends to visit him and they often had meditation and healing sessions. Sagara Samudra, Princess Zulani and Sarn Lionheart's fiancée Clary had also begun a group, although they were forbidden to visit Rajay. They made bandhans that he might survive and get back to Daish Shaktay. Rajay asked his cook, Bart Charval, to make tasty Daish Shaktay dishes, which Rajay would give vibrations to and send to the palaces of his new friends in large hampers, which were supported on poles and carried by porters. Initially the guards searched every hamper, but soon became bored of prodding and poking the mounds of rice and cauldrons of stew and thereafter only made the occasional spot check.

Danard and Namoh realised something was afoot. Although Rajay enjoyed a good feast now and again, he usually ate very simple food. By the second month of his captivity he was becoming a quite a gourmand, but this change of habits did not agree with him and he appeared to develop a serious liver complaint. He woke up one day moaning in pain and numerous doctors were called. He groaned when they touched his stomach so they prescribed various medicines and fomentations. His health became worse and it was whispered that he had been poisoned. Zulani and Sarn's faction were outraged; they complained that it was a shocking breach of faith and his visit had been shoddily handled from the start. Rajay lay on his bed contorted in pain and it looked as if the end was near. He called Sarn to his bedside and told him he was released from his promise of protection, and a few other matters were discussed. Sarn informed King Karlvid that he was removing his personal bodyguards from Rajay's part of the palace and made it clear that he was no longer responsible for his guest.

'The Mouse is not only in the trap but also defenceless!' gloated Raspatto.

'Soon we'll be able to persuade the king to arrange an accident, if nature doesn't solve the problem first,' said his friends.

Rajay had a massage every morning and the masseur was Cheyla, Luth's man.

'His Highness is very unwell,' Cheyla explained that morning to King Karlvid's guards on duty at Lionheart Palace. 'Please don't allow anyone to disturb him more than is necessary.'

'We'll do our best,' they said, because apart from the commander, who was very ogrous, Rajay was on excellent terms with all of them.

He decided to send one more load of Daish Shaktay cooking to his friends and that evening had two large hampers full of delicious dishes brought to his room so he could imbue the food with vibrations before it was delivered. Also in the room was another, similar hamper, as it was the day when the bedcovers and towels were changed. The clean ones were brought in this hamper and the dirty ones taken to the riverside in the evening, stored overnight in the laundry there and washed early the next morning. When the porters brought the hampers in, Rajay was hidden under a sheet and only the top of his head, covered by his turban, and his right hand with the gold bangle he always wore, were showing. The porters left the room, as they always did, and when they returned some time later the food hampers were taken out along with the laundry hamper.

The porters with the hampers made for the guard post at the mansion gatehouse and a guard looked inside the first one, containing the usual meat and fish dishes in large tureens. He glanced in the second, full of sweetmeats and cakes. The third hamper contained laundry and the guard opened the lid to see the usual jumble of towels, sheets and clothes, and at first did not search it, because who wants to poke around in someone else's dirty laundry? Dirty clothes were taboo in Mattanga and only the lowest class touched them. He decided to have a quick look, just in case, and was about to prod with his long staff when Sarn Lionheart shouted from across the courtyard. He was dressed up to go out and on his run-around chariot.

'Move those hampers!' he demanded angrily. 'I'm late, and they're blocking the way. Move them, *now!*'

The guard obeyed meekly and the hampers were waved on and out into the street. Once out of sight of the palace gates, two hampers went in one direction and the third, full of laundry, turned southwards. Soon the porters carrying the laundry basket were replaced. One who took over was a Teletsian, and Teletsian slaves were occasionally seen in Mattanga, and the other was strong and well muscled. They made for the washing place by the river, some distance away.

They passed a large townhouse where a celebration was starting and noticed Sarn Lionheart's fiancée Clary alight from a gilt coach and enter the porch, festooned with garlands and lights. It would be an all night do and many entertainments had been laid on to amuse the guests at the birthday party of Princess Zulani, and everybody who was anybody in court circles was there. In the shadows, unseen by the glittering guests, the hamper swayed as the barefoot porters ran on towards the river with it. What the leisured classes did with their time did not concern these outcastes of Mattanga society.

By the river was a broad flight of steps where the laundry of Mattanga was slapped, battered and soaped into cleanliness. There was a hut at the side and behind this was a rowing boat. The porters put the hamper in the boat and rowed across the river. On the other side they again set off at a brisk jog with the hamper slung between them. Soon they reached a barren plot of land with the ruins of a burnt-out mansion on it. The former garden was a jungle of shrubs, creepers and trees, and the porters set the hamper down in a tangle of bushes. Out climbed Rajay, helped by Lee and Athlos, the two porters, and up came Danard and Namoh, leading sleek horses. Namoh handed them respectable clothes because they would pretend to be prosperous merchants returning home after a business trip to Mattanga.

'You all right?' Lee asked Rajay, who had a roguish smile on his face. He was in his element, playing cat and mouse with his enemies once again. He had shaved off his beard and put white streaks in his hair.

'Never better!' he replied. 'But it was close when that guard searched the hampers.'

'Sarn played his part perfectly,' grinned Athlos.

'Bart looked perfect in your bed - really convincing with your turban and bangle,' added Lee.

'I hope he gets away safely,' Rajay said.

'Luth's men have changes of horses for a good way south,' Namoh explained. 'That will get you a long way from here, with a bit of luck before your escape has been noticed. The first change is behind the temple at Furzam, three towns down the road. You should be there by midnight.'

'How do we find it?' asked Lee.

'It's got a tall white tower - on the right as you enter the town,' said Namoh. 'We're not coming with you. Danard and I'll go west towards High Plains. We'll lay a false trail and draw off the pursuit. I have your signet ring.' Namoh was now on his horse, holding up the seal of the Ghiry family.

'And I have your sword, the greatest heirloom of Daish Shaktay, but not nearly as important as you,' added Danard, who had mounted his horse. 'I'll give it back when we meet up at Malak Citadel.'

'Give me that sword!' commanded Rajay.

'No way,' retorted Danard, preparing to leave.

'I beg you to, for your own sake!'

'If we're caught the ogre's men will think I'm you,' Danard shouted, and he and Namoh galloped away into the night.

The other horses were not ready, because Athlos was adjusting the saddles, so Rajay could not pursue them. A chill feeling crept over him as he stood helplessly wondering what to do. Written on the sword were the following words: 'Anyone who takes this sword without the owner's permission must die before a year has passed.' In his heart Rajay said, 'I do give him

225

permission,' but that wasn't his first order. Danard knew about this warning.

'We've got to get out of here, I can hear voices in the street,' urged Lee. Rajay swung into the saddle and the three of them pounded off southwards. His heart was heavy with foreboding, not for himself, but for his scattered companions.

At the party Sarn Lionheart hardly seemed to notice his fiancée Clary, daughter of the overlord of Wattan, the province south of Mattanga. Their marriage had been put off until Vittorio Lionheart should return from Daish Shaktay. She assumed Sarn's distracted attitude was because Rajay was so ill, and asked what the matter was.

'My dear, I've got some heavy responsibilities these days. When we're married I'll share them with you, but not now,' and he made some light-hearted joke to change the subject.

After returning home at dawn, Sarn crept over to Rajay's wing in Lionheart Palace. He saw a sleeping figure in the bed which looked like Rajay, even though the snores were completely different; Sarn was aware of this because they had shared a tent on their journey to Mattanga. 'No matter,' thought Sarn, 'no one else will know.' Sarn changed into some elegant but sober clothes. He absolutely had to get an audience with Karlvid, who was an early riser. He was having breakfast and his aides were in his room, discussing the arrangements for the day.

'Yes, my boy?' he inquired when he saw Sarn at the door.

'Sire, I have to go to my father's country estate for some weeks. As the safe conduct bond between Rajay Ghiry and the Lionhearts has been revoked, I can no longer be responsible for him,' Sarn bowed formally.

'He's no longer any concern of yours - go.' Sarn backed out with due humility. King Karlvid returned to the current business.

'Have we finally agreed to assassinate the Mouse tonight?'

'Yes, Your Majesty, our men will smother him in his bed. It will look as if he's died naturally from his illness.'

'If Sarn isn't involved it will be all the easier.'

Sarn left, but not for his country estate. He changed his clothes again, this time into the distinctive garb of a jewel merchant - a long robe and skullcap. With him was a heavyweight bodyguard slave. Sarn cut off his fashionable moustache, darkened his skin so it was almost black, and gold-rimmed spectacles completed the transformation into Mr Dart, dealer in rubies and sapphires. Rajay had supplied the jewels. Sarn slipped aboard the south bound mail ship just as she sailed on the morning tide.

Bart Charval woke up early after a poor night's sleep of impersonating Rajay. He had been disturbed throughout the night by every bird, mouse and whisper of wind. The few remaining kitchen staff were loyal members of Luth's order and as on any normal morning, they sang and chattered in the kitchen but tiptoed quietly as they brought 'Rajay' his breakfast. Later, Bart heard footsteps approaching and hid under the covers, pretending to be asleep. One of the Secret Police looked in and saw 'Rajay' sleeping peacefully.

At midday Cheyla arrived to give his daily massage.

'Everything all right?' whispered Bart.

'Yes, so far. Here are your clothes.' He tossed Bart a bundle and he went into the bathroom to change. Meanwhile Cheyla arranged Rajay's turban and a bolster in the bed to look like a man, and covered it with a sheet. Bart reappeared in his own clothes, his cloth shopping bag over his shoulder.

'Rajay left some gold for you,' said Bart, and gave Cheyla a fat bag of coins.

'I'll take it to Luth. He needs money.'

'It's for you personally.'

'When King Rajay has won back Daish Shaktay I'll accept his money, but this is for the freedom struggle.'

'As you please. In any event it's high time we left.'

They walked jauntily past the guards on the front gate and Bart stopped to have a friendly word with them. 'I'm going to get some medicines. The king is sleeping, so see he isn't disturbed.'

Once out of sight of the palace, Bart hurried to the Rice Exchange. Good rice was grown in the Mattan hinterland and as he was a farmer it was easy for him to attach himself to a home going mule train. Some rice farmers were lay followers of Luth and therefore sympathisers of Rajay, and Bart left Mattanga with a party of them.

At almost the same time as Bart and Cheyla left Sarn's palace, Rajay, Lee and Athlos were urging on their foam-flecked horses, their fifth change, down the road to the south. Danard and Namoh also rode all night, towards the hills west of Mattanga on the main road to Daish Shaktay.

Now it was evening. The wing of Lionheart Palace where Rajay Ghiry had been under house arrest for nearly six weeks was unusually quiet. No one had lit the lamps and the evening staff had not arrived. Bart had paid them off handsomely and warned them to leave town immediately. Finally, the Captain of the Security Force went indoors to see what was going on. The silence was uncanny. The captain knew of the assassination plans. 'Have they already finished him off?' he wondered. He crept into Rajay's bedroom and a stray cat jumped past him onto a balcony. He approached the figure sleeping in the bed. It was as still as death and the guard with him looked more closely. He pulled back the covers.

'He's gone, sir,' he said in a hushed tone. 'That's a bolster.' The two men looked at each other in mortal terror.

'By the Crocodile God of Mattanga!' swore the Captain. 'We'll be fed to the crocs in the harbour if we get the blame.'

'You'd best go straight to His Scalyness, sir,' said the guard, with the emphasis on 'you' rather than 'we'.

His Scalyness was watching a performance of tame dolphins, but nevertheless the Captain was admitted to Karlvid's august presence. He stood in front of the king, hands folded and head bowed.

'Move over, I can't see that dolphin,' grumbled the king. 'Why are you blocking my view?' The Captain just looked, his eyes fearful, his body trembling. He opened his mouth but no words came. 'Why aren't you guarding that rebel from Daish Shaktay?'

'Er...' he stammered.

'He's gone, sire. He's escaped,' said one of the king's aides.

King Karlvid put his clawed hand to his head and groaned. The dolphin show was stopped and the king and his whole court maintained a stunned silence. If only he had ordered Rajay's assassination one day earlier! If only he had not listened to Princess Zulani, who had begged him not to kill the dratted Mouse the day before, on her birthday, as had originally been the idea. (It wasn't her birthday but Karlvid had so many children he didn't remember this. She had pretended it was so as to give Rajay one more day.)

'Speak up! Or the torture will be even worse,' commanded the king.

'Sire,' lied the Captain, 'we paid repeated visits to his room, but then suddenly he disappeared. Whether he melted into the earth, or flew into the sky, we don't know – but it was definitely a case of witchcraft. He simply vanished.'

'I don't believe you,' roared the king. 'Take him away.' Thus ended the career of the cruellest of King Karlvid's henchmen.

Princess Zulani smiled, alone in her boudoir with her little image of the Goddess of Daish Shaktay. She placed a sweet scented gardenia in front of it because her fervent prayers had been answered. At the bestial court of the ogres, Rajay had become a beacon of light for her even though she would never meet him. Her father would soon marry her off to whoever he deemed most advantageous politically, and from then on her fate would be sealed, but her heart was joyful, her life had some meaning and until she became the prisoner of some unknown husband she would use her influence over her father in every way she could to help Rajay and his country of Daish Shaktay, whatever the final outcome of such a dangerous course of action.

Fifty thousand men and a few women: ogres, soldiers, spies, Secret Police and others were now alerted to recapture Rajay Ghiry and his party. The roads out of the city were blocked and boats were forbidden from leaving the port until further notice. All travellers were to be checked and questioned, but the birds had flown and had almost a day's start.

CHAPTER 12

FUGITIVES

It was early evening and Rajay, Lee and Athlos changed horses for the eighth time – or was it the ninth? They were collapsing with fatigue and although they were a long distance from Mattanga, it was not enough. Although they went more slowly when riding through the towns and villages many people had seen them hurrying southwards. They finally left their last change of horses with Luth's men and staggered to the docks of a small fishing port, where they bought a sailing boat for a handful of gold, set off towards some islands on the horizon - and a number of people saw them go. First Athlos sailed and Lee slept, but later, when only the dim Moon of Compassion was in the sky, Lee took the tiller and turned about, heading diagonally towards the mainland again, further south. Rajay and Athlos were sleeping peacefully.

The night was cool, with a fresh breeze. Yesterday was exhausting, tomorrow might bring capture or death, but tonight was perfect. Lee had a beautiful voice and sang the song in praise of Father Ocean that the mermen had sung to him on the Sea of Illusion two years before, after they had escaped from Tootle Dumpattick's island, and went in time to the slapping waves. After some time, having sailed further round the headland, he spied the dark outlines of another small coastal town, dominated by the towers of the Temple-by-the-Sea, where Rajay had first seen Luth years before. Lee woke the others. Athlos knew this coastline and took the tiller, because there were rocks near the shore; the large black masses rose out of the water and Lee and Rajay rowed slowly towards a little patch of sand between the high cliffs, directed by Athlos. As they beached the boat, a man stood up from the shadows and walked across the sand towards them.

'Sire, this way. We received a message about you from the fishing village. Please follow me.' The man, one of Luth's followers, led the fugitives into a cave well hidden from the shore and only approachable at low tide from the beach at the base of the bare cliff. They had to wade in the water because the tide was coming up, and arrived safe but soaking wet. Inside the cave were three more members of Luth's order.

'Athlos, good to see you!' one recognised him. 'Where's the king?'

'That's me,' Rajay replied. His youthful face contrasted strongly with his whitened hair.

'We're honoured! We knew you'd manage to escape,' said another. The third went up to him and knelt at his feet. Rajay smiled and indicated for him to get up.

'There's still hope for Daish Shaktay!' the leader cried with joy.

'With help from all of you. We wouldn't have got far without Luth's men,' Rajay thanked them.

'Sit down and get dry by the fire, Your Majesty. We've heard so many rumours these last weeks, and not all pleasant either,' continued the first monk, making up the fire and taking Rajay's wet cloak. 'We even heard you'd been murdered by Karlvid's men.'

'More likely Karlvid has killed his own men in his fury,' joked Lee darkly, also sitting by the fire.

The monks prepared a meal and the three travellers cleaned themselves up. The white dye was washed out of Rajay's hair and he looked more normal again. All Luth's men knew how to cook and the meal was delicious: a spicy shellfish soup, followed by fried fish with fragrant rice. Rajay teased them, saying they were in the wrong business and should open an eating-house.

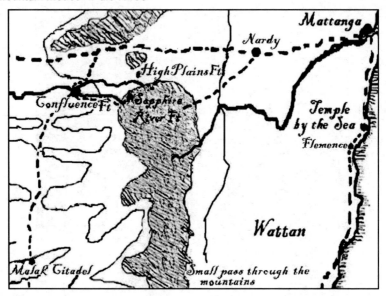

'Time for that later, sire, when you're safely on your throne,' the leader corrected him respectfully. 'Then we'll renounce our vows, find ourselves wives who cook as well as we do and start a first class establishment in Malak Citadel town - and you'll be our most honoured customer.' After that he became serious. 'I'd like to make a suggestion and as you're my king it can be no more than that.' Rajay laughed. Lee had not heard him laugh like that for a long time: a relaxed, infectious sound.

'I don't feel like a king right now. Let's put it this way, as of tonight I'm a free man and not a prisoner.' It was hardly the Great Hall at Malak Citadel, where Rajay usually held court. He sat on one rock in the cave and his companions on others, lit only by the flickering firelight and a couple of oil lamps. 'What's your idea?'

'Many people saw you come south. They won't all believe you've sailed to the islands, even though we've hidden the boat. You can't cross into Daish Shaktay here, because there are no passes and the mountains are too high to climb. Go further south, with me as your companion - I know the area. Lee and Athlos can hide here for some time.'

'That's sensible,' agreed Rajay, 'but first I want to go through the purification ceremony on the steps by the sea, behind the temple. Mattanga was very negative spiritually and I want to give thanks to Father Ocean, who rules this eastern coastal land.'

'It's extremely risky,' objected Lee.

'It's also very important, because to receive divine blessings I must be inwardly clean.'

'Can't I give you vibrations here?'

'No, that's not enough. My life and the future of my country are in great jeopardy at the moment. To get home I'm going to need all possible help on every level of creation.'

'Can we anyway give you vibrations, now, to make it quicker in the morning?'

'Yes indeed, and these men had better have their inner awakening.'

Lee did this and then showed the monks how to help clear and cleanse Rajay's already strong subtle self. Lee was astonished at his complete lack of arrogance when he said, 'My heart centre is weak, because I was very unsure of how things would work out in Lionheart's mansion,' or, 'I shouldn't have shouted at Danard. My throat centre is constricted. As usual, he and Namoh were trying to save me by risking their own lives.'

In the early morning, Rajay had the monks cut his hair very short, Athlos covered his forehead with ashes from the fire and also put them on his body, because he wore only a loincloth and a tattered cloak. The ashes on the body were as much to hide his fighting scars as anything else. Athlos gave Rajay a hollowed out staff, which he stuffed full of gold and jewels. A begging bowl around the waist and a little bundle of spare clothing completed the belongings of Rajay the mendicant.

'Do you want any shoes?' asked Athlos.

'Yes, I'll take a pair of those wooden sandals you wear.'

One of the monks brought a pair he had just finished carving. They also gave him a string of sacred shells to wear around his neck, the sign that he had completed the pilgrimage to this shrine. Shortly before dawn, a disguised Rajay prepared to leave the cave and told the leader of the monks to meet him at the temple later.

'Stay here until I send for you, or if I get caught, stay here until the fuss has died down,' he ordered Lee and Athlos.

He was rowed to the shore, landed on a beach north of the town and made his way towards the temple steps, by the sea. Those who were trained in the rites would wait there for pilgrims, and a young man sat modestly in the fading moons' light.

'Can you please lead me through the purification ceremony?' Rajay asked him politely.

'Yes, that's what I do here.'

'Can you do it now so I can leave here in the cool of the early morning?'

'We'll start immediately.'

The youthful priest had been praying for some way out of his predicament. His father had forced him to become an assistant to an older priest in order to gain a good education, but the old priest's wife treated him like a slave and he had received neither enough food nor enough education. However, he had managed to study hard on his own and was looking for an opportunity to get out of his apprenticeship.

They went to the water's edge and began the ceremony. The apprentice priest noticed the mendicant's muscular arms and shoulders, and the scars on his arms indicating he knew archery. He said nothing. It was not proper to inquire about a recluse's past, because he had renounced the world. First the apprentice priest carried out the symbolic cleansing with sea water, then anointed him with red and yellow powder. Finally, as the sun rose over the Eastern Ocean and the gold leaf on the towers of the temple behind them seemed to burst into flame, he asked Rajay to repeat the prayers after him.

'Father Ocean, You dissolve our mistakes in your vastness, so we worship you,' prayed Rajay, and put the flowers he had bought outside the temple on the water, in a little boat made of entwined leaves. The apprentice priest had taken many pilgrims through this ritual but was impressed by the reverence of this worshipper.

'Please, say this after me, and as you do so take up some water in your hands and scatter it, so the rays of the sun shine through it,' he instructed. 'Put your hands high above your head and say, 'Glory and praise to the morning sun, source of light and symbol of enlightenment.' Rajay repeated the words and they both heard marching feet and the clattering of horses' hooves in the street to the landward side of the temple. Aggressive voices were shouting at the doorkeepers, but the young priest disregarded the disturbance and continued. 'Finally we pray to the primal power, the Mother of Creation,' he explained. They did so and Rajay stepped out of the water.

'Thank you. Before I leave, put your hands out towards the ocean and the rising sun, and ask, "Please awaken that primal energy, that enlightenment, within me, so I may feel Her power flowing through me."' He did as asked and Rajay raised his right hand up behind the young man's back. 'Do you feel the cool wind of the spirit on your hands and above your head? And an inner stillness and joy?'

'Yes, whatever did you do? I know the rituals, but you've given me an extraordinary experience.' Rajay just smiled. Behind them they could hear loud voices.

'Have you seen the escaped King of Daish Shaktay, or his Teletsian sorcerer friend?' shouted the soldiers.

'We don't allow sorcerers in here - this is a holy place,' was the reply, 'and we've certainly not seen any kings.'

'Go to Daish Shaktay and you'll understand,' murmured Rajay. He picked up his staff and put on his cloak and sandals. His bundle of belongings was already tied on his staff. 'I have to leave at once. Please take this gift as a token of my gratitude. Don't open it until I've gone and especially not where anyone can see you.' He pressed a small bag into the apprentice's hand and made off in a southerly direction, away from the temple and the shouting police. He could not risk waiting for the other monk.

The apprentice priest opened the bag after the stranger had gone. In it were five flawless Daish Shaktay sapphires. Being a methodical young man he returned to his lodgings, where he packed his few belongings and books: classical language texts, medical treatises and textbooks of science and mathematics; he was well read in most branches of learning and hoped eventually to set up a school. He bought a mule for his luggage and told his master that he had to go home for a few days on urgent family business. This was not the case; he set off for Daish Shaktay. The next day he was stopped by a patrol and produced his credentials, explaining that having finished his training at the Temple-by-the-Sea, he was going to take up a job. When asked whether he had any information about the rebel, Rajay Ghiry, he looked mystified.

'Who's he?'

'The self-styled King of Daish Shaktay, said to be on the run in these parts.'

'I've been a novice priest for the last four years and I only see pilgrims who come for purification. Neither royalty nor rebels are part of my life.' In his heart he thanked Rajay Ghiry, because he knew perfectly well who the saintly mendicant was, for offering him a new life in the form of the jewels. Rajay had also, in a few seconds, given him the most powerful spiritual experience of his life. No way was he going to help these agents of evil find the Mountain Mouse.

Namoh and Danard were stopped three days after leaving Mattanga at a tollgate on a bridge, near the little town of Nardy in the evening. The police recognised their Daish Shaktay accents and they were taken into separate rooms for questioning.

'Do you know Rajay Ghiry?'

'Yes, most of us leading citizens have met him,' said Danard.

'Do you know him well?'

'I'm a landowner and I've spoken to him occasionally. I've been rewarded for my services to the community, like many of us.'

'When did you last see him?'

'Last year, at Malak Citadel.'

'Where is he now?'

'I'm told he's in Mattanga.' It was inconclusive, but a search revealed the signet ring and sword and then the questioning became threatening – they were both beaten, to try and get some useful information out of them. Finally Danard said, 'Yes, I'm Rajay Ghiry. I can't hide it from you.'

'I'll have to admit it sooner or later. I'm Rajay Ghiry,' claimed Namoh, in the next room. Then they were put in the same room and said that neither of them was Rajay Ghiry, but that they were travelling with him and he had gone on ahead, having avoided the toll bridge by swimming the river with his horse. The police were by now very tired and decided to leave it until the next day. Meanwhile most of the other local police constables were sent up the road to catch Rajay, but as no one at the checkpoints further on had seen anyone remotely like him they soon gave up. The brothers were put in a cell and left for the night. They were in a great deal of pain and barely conscious, and lay on the floor and tried to sleep.

Later someone took them out of the cell, handed them back Rajay's sword and ring, and put them on their horses. It was Cheyla, Rajay's masseuse, and he led them to a cowshed on the edge of the town. Here he helped them to change into monk's robes, they were pushed onto fresh horses, given by a cell of Luth's monks, and they rode through the night along lanes and paths to avoid the checkpoints. By midday they were in the high land between Mattan and Daish Shaktay. Danard and Namoh nearly fell off their horses in exhaustion and pain, and Cheyla realised he had to allow them to rest. He found a valley off the country road he had led them up, to the south of the main east-west highway, and they lay on the ground and slept. It was deserted – the bottom of the valley was a green and flower filled meadow and the hills were covered in tall deciduous trees. When they awoke Cheyla was roasting some rabbits over a campfire. He had picked a scarf full of nuts and some bunches of small purple grapes, and had laid them on the ground next to the brothers. The tethered horses cropped the grass nearby.

'That cooking smells good. What happened to us and how are we here?' asked Namoh groggily.

'You were captured, beaten up and questioned, but fortunately I was coming along behind you. I heard Rajay was with you,' said Cheyla.

'Is that what the police thought?' said Danard, nursing his badly bruised arm.

'They didn't know what was going on.'

'How did you get us out?'

'A combination of luck and money - by great good fortune my uncle lives in that town and I've sometimes spent holidays with his family. When the police stopped me, I heard you being questioned. They let me go, and then I went to the Chief of Police, who's a distant cousin of mine. I told him I recognised your voices, that you were my friends and I would vouch that you were loyal citizens of Daish Shaktay, yes, but nothing directly to do with the rebel. Something prompted me to say that like so many of your countrymen, you would tell any amount of lies to protect your king, but I knew you were both innocent. We went back to the checkpoint where you were being questioned, but you two had been put in another room by then, locked up for the night.'

'What about the sword and ring?'

'I told my cousin that Rajay often gave out replicas of his sword and ring to prominent citizens as favours, when the guard showed them to me. He said he'd have to discuss it with his colleagues in the morning before letting you free and my heart sank. I pretended to leave, but hung around and hid in the shadows. After a time my cousin went home, as it was midnight. I saw your horses hitched outside - evidently they'd been forgotten - and waited until everything was quiet. I crept closer, and noticed that the ogrish looking guard on duty was sound asleep and had left the keys on the table in the little guardroom. I know a thing or two about the body and hit him so as to knock him out. Then I picked up the sword and ring, and rescued you both.'

'May the Goddess be praised - but what about you? The truth is bound to come out sooner or later.'

'King Rajay gave me a letter of recommendation about my ability to adjust bones and muscles, and I'll start a practise in your land.'

'Seems like you can adjust more than bones and muscles! Thank you a million times.'

'No problem. I've heard about how much you've done for His Majesty. So many people are openly supporting him now; they're shocked at the way Karlvid lured him to Mattanga and then broke his oath. Ordinary folk aren't going to put up with these types much longer, you see.'

A large number of Karlvid's men were sent up the road to the west, because they were fairly certain Rajay Ghiry was somewhere in that direction. It was well known that he always kept his magic sword with him.

CHAPTER 13

THE HOLY BROTHER

Rajay had fallen in with a party of monks walking south to the next shrine, further down the coast. His plan was to turn inland and cross over the mountains north of Port Volcan. The monks gossiped about trivia and Rajay made signs that he had taken a vow of silence. After three days he found their pace too slow and forged on ahead, and two days later a patrol stopped the loitering monks.

'We're looking for Rajay Ghiry, a Teletsian youth with supernatural powers, and a heavyweight monk.'

'Haven't seen any Teletsians,' one said.

'Have you seen a youngish man, mid brown skin, medium to tall, straight nose, strong chin and maybe a beard?' demanded the leader of the patrol.

'A number of people would fit that description,' observed a monk. 'We had a fellow with us the other day like that. No beard though.'

Soon the patrol was detaining every wandering monk they came across. There were many pilgrims on this road, which led from the Temple-by-the-Sea to two more shrines - businessmen appeasing their consciences after a lifetime of shady deals; overweight dowagers with little else to do; families with a member near death come to plead for a miraculous cure; childless couples praying for children and many others.

On the edge of a town named Flemence a monk with a straight nose and a strong chin sat in meditation under a tree. The patrol saw him and without any respect for his prayers took him off to the police post. The village policeman was a devout man and was shocked to see this rough treatment of a pilgrim, and a monk at that. Rajay was thrown in the lockup with thirteen others the patrol had picked up almost at random. Three were pilgrims of various ages, two were businessmen and five were monks of different shapes and sizes: three had straight noses. There was also a bandit, by his looks and manner, with a straight nose and sharp chin, and a well-dressed traveller with a straight nose and a beard, out of place and standing uncomfortably in a corner. There was an old beggar with a mid brown skin and a strong chin, dressed in rags and covered in lice. The last was Rajay himself, interested as to who was being mistaken for him.

One by one they were questioned in the guardroom; Rajay was the last. One of the Special Police had a whip with nails in the thongs to encourage sluggish responders. Rajay replied to their questions eagerly and appeared to want to help; his story was coherent and convincing, even if rather far from the truth. The police were satisfied, Rajay was returned to the lockup and the leader of the patrol spoke to all the suspects.

'You'll stay here without food and water until the true Rajay Ghiry confesses.' He glared at the well-dressed traveller. 'We are fairly sure who he is,' he continued, still looking at the unfortunate man, 'and when he's come clean the rest of you can go.'

Rajay considered the situation: fourteen innocent men, one so guilty in the eyes of an unjust government that many had to suffer. They looked at each other without speaking, because the guards had ordered silence.

'There's a man coming tomorrow who'll be able to recognise Rajay Ghiry; a good thing too, because we don't want fourteen rotting corpses on our hands,' said the leader, outside the door.

Rajay waited. The other prisoners dropped off to sleep. He made a bandhan of request on his hand, praying that he would somehow escape. It was surprisingly cool and he felt peaceful and confident. Only the bandit was still sitting on his haunches, staring in front of him and fingering his dagger. He crooked his finger, indicating for Rajay to come closer.

'The Special Police have gone now and the local man is on duty until morning,' he whispered. 'He's sympathetic to your cause, and if you have money you can bribe your way out. Sire, pardon me, but you'd look like a king anywhere. Try to be more cringing and frightened. Your dignity shines out of you like the midday sun.'

'I'll try, and thanks for the advice,' Rajay, who also recognised the bandit for what he was, whispered back. 'If you want a regular job, on the right side of the law, come and join my army if and when I get home.'

'Good luck, Your Highness. I'll take you up on that.'

Rajay stood up and knocked at the door. Soon he was alone in the guardroom with the local policeman, apart from a few moths committing suicide in the oil lamp.

'I'm Rajay Ghiry. If you hand me over to the Special Police in the morning you'll get nothing for your pains except quite probably a knife in your back from one of my many supporters. I tell them this sort of behaviour is not right and they should be more forgiving, but if I'm not there to stop them, their vengeance is terrible. They love me like a father and have no absolutely no pity on anyone who tries to harm me.'

'Well, Your Royal Highness, what do you suggest I do?' The local man was tired and cynical, and could not believe he had the elusive Mountain

Mouse, the King of Daish Shaktay, in front of him. Rajay had previously taken a perfectly round pearl of considerable size out of his hollow staff. He placed it on the table.

'There is another alternative,' he continued, as his jailor looked in amazement at the jewel. 'If you will allow me and the other prisoners to escape I will reward you even more richly than this.'

The policeman was beaming all over his plump face. He looked at the ash-covered recluse, then at the pearl. With it he could buy that island in the creek and start a salt refinery. He had wanted to do it for years but never had the capital. He had always been an admirer of the young rebel and most of all

did not want a dagger in his back. Rajay smiled at him. No one had ever been able to resist his smile, the policeman had heard, and nor could he.

'That pearl will make you and your family comfortable for life,' promised Rajay, 'It's priceless.'

'All right, I'll do it. I'm proud to meet you and I wish you every success. You'll have to give me some more gems or gold, sir, if you have them, for my assistant who's guarding the door of the lockup.' Rajay had some gold pieces concealed in his other hand, in case he needed them. He handed one over and they walked out into the yard.

'Sorry to have bothered you, holy brother, there's been some mistake,' said the policeman loudly as they passed the lockup. He told the guard, 'Let 'em go, there's been a change of plan,' and to the prisoners he said, 'Don't let me see any of you tomorrow or you're dead.'

After they had all hurriedly left the policeman gave his assistant the gold piece from Rajay. Together the upholders of the law concocted a story of how the prisoners, led by the bandit, had broken out in the night. Rajay made off through the fields and early next morning bought and changed into some countryman's clothes, after which he buried his begging bowl and shell necklace. Later he walked into a farmyard and asked the farmer if he could buy a riding horse. The man was agreeable and saddled one for him to try, but unbeknown to Rajay horses were very cheap in this area as they were available in a semi-wild state on the nearby hills for nothing. He looked in his purse, found he only had some large gold coins from Mattanga and offered one to the farmer. It was generous for a horse even in Daish Shaktay, but here it was outrageous. The farmer was no fool.

'This is far too much! You've no idea of the value of a horse in these parts. You must be the escaped King of Daish Shaktay.' He was about to shout for his sons when Rajay pressed the whole purse into his hands.

'Sir,' he said, 'with that you can buy a hundred horses. Please let me take one!' and he galloped off, riding his expensive acquisition. He was not pursued and rode south for the rest of the day. The next day he turned inland but unfortunately the horse hurt its leg while fording a swiftly flowing stream so he had to abandon it. He made many bandhans of request for the tigers to help him, but they did not respond and he knew they would rarely go far outside their area, the fourth or heart centre on our world, except to the Temple in the Mountains, and Luker was part of the third centre, or ocean area. So again Rajay became a wandering holy man. He walked inland over the plains and made his way through the forested foothills, always heading southwest towards the mountain passes. He no longer had any money or jewels and ironically as he neared his own land he was reduced to begging for food, even though he had cellars full of treasure at Malak Citadel.

Bart Charval and his rice farmers were stopped and searched a few times. Their mules were laden with presents and other shopping for their families, from Mattanga. No one suspected Bart. He stayed with the farmers for a couple of weeks and lent a hand with the ploughing. Then, with some of the gold Rajay had given him, he bought a young bull and some cows. His hosts had a good strain of cattle and he took the opportunity to improve his own herd's bloodlines. He left in his own time, driving his cattle along the road, and took with him a slave boy he bought and then freed, to help look after them.

Sarn Lionheart, alias Mr Dart, kept to his cabin and at the third group of islands at which the mail boat put in, some days later, he left it, changed his name and disguise and became a young traveller, Bajast from the far land of Grote. He had plenty of gold and jewels, and knew there would be a place for him in Daish Shaktay. He had a letter of introduction to Queen Jansy if Rajay did not manage to return. He hoped Clary would wait for him, because although the match had been an arranged one, he loved and respected her, and knew the less she was aware of what was actually going on the safer she would be.

At this time I, Asha, had a dream that Rajay desperately needed the help of the tigers. I knew he did not have a key to call them and in the dream saw Rajay struggling through a mountain valley, and over a glacier and a snow covered pass. The next day I went into the woods and called the tigers. I went out again in the evening and there were two of them waiting for me. With my imperfect command of the classic language I explained the problem and described my dream. I had no idea if they understood me, and even if they did what they would do about it. I only knew I felt Rajay calling for help and as his honorary sister did what little I could to give it.

Rajay trekked on through the high mountains. He knew there were some passes into Daish Shaktay in this area and after asking the locals, walked up a valley which ended in a glacier. He was told if he could manage to get over the snowfield behind it, he would be in a valley which led into his homeland. He edged his way around the glacier, knowing it was dangerous to walk on one, because of crevasses, collapsed a number of times in the snow above it, but struggled on, ill clad for mountaineering and exhausted, and reached the valley on the further side. He spent the night in a cave and staggered on the next freezing, foggy morning before the sun showed above the snow-covered peaks around the valley. A light frost was crunchy underfoot, his chest was wheezing, he was chilled through and through and after walking all day down a valley, the next morning he decided to risk knocking on the door of a farmhouse. An elderly lady invited him in. For the pious, to entertain a holy man was an honour and she showed him to the fireside where she was making breakfast. Soon she set her best before him, but it was very plain fare.

'I'm sorry it's not better, holy brother. The troopers of that Rajay Ghiry came and took everything we had. They went off with our ducks, chickens, most of our cows and I don't know what else. They even took our precious brass cooking pots. I'd be after that Mountain Mouse with my rolling pin if he ever came this way.' Rajay looked at her arms, strong from a lifetime of hard work, and at the large rolling pin. He agreed that it was a sorry business, but the woman had not finished. 'Protector of Daish Shaktay indeed! How dare he call himself that! We're in Daish Shaktay now, and he hasn't done much protecting around here. I'd give him a bit of my mind if I ever set eyes on him, magic sword and white warhorse or whatever.'

Rajay was about to correct her. He never rode that white stallion to war or when his life was in danger; it might look flashy, but it was a coward and an idiot. Then he remembered where and who he was. As she continued to rant and rage he hoped that not too many of his subjects were being treated in this way and realised he would have to do something about this raiding. Between her lashing criticisms of him she told him the name of the nearby village, which he carefully memorised.

After breakfast her husband came in from his early morning chores and

Rajay thanked them, gave the expected blessing and prepared to leave, even though he was desperately weak, coughing horribly and breathing in gasps. However, the farmer's wife had other ideas and refused to let him go. He thought she had recognised him and would turn him over to the agents of Mattanga, who were everywhere, but no, she was merely being motherly. She made him stay in their hayloft, where he was warm, well fed and clean. She gave him some thick clothes belonging to her husband and said it was no good being a wandering recluse if the weather killed him.

Three days later, smiling gratefully, he set off feeling slightly better. She again made it clear she held Rajay Ghiry directly responsible for all her woes and although she was full of rage for him he was determined to repay her for her kindness.

At last he was back in his own land, but he was emaciated and very sick from sleeping out in the cold, damp mountains. Also there was still a great price on his head and many people seeking him, even in Daish Shaktay. At the top of a rise he turned off the track to rest in a wood and collapsed, delirious.

Some time later he opened his eyes and above him saw a golden key with a twelve petalled flower design, set with rubies, swinging on a chain in front of his face. It was almost identical to the one his mother wore and was being held in the teeth of a large tiger, who stood over him, wearing a gold collar. Rajay took his key and knew he had passed all the tests necessary to be the king and guardian of his country. The tiger lay down beside him to keep him warm and Rajay slept the whole day. In the evening it urged him to get on it and together they set off at a fast pace towards Malak Citadel.

PART FOUR

ENDS AND
BEGINNINGS

CHAPTER 1

FLYING HORSES

After Ahren and Jaggo had left for the north, I sent a message to Luth about taking the tigers to Mattanga and getting help from Athlos's acrobatic troupe, to fill out our circus. Luth replied saying he had talked to some of the tigers and they had agreed to the idea. Usually they would not go out their own area, but if the flying horses would, they would too. The tigers were fed up with the ogres of Mattanga, and Athlos's men would also help. If and when Ahren arrived back from Chussan with the flying horses, he had only to summon the tigers and Luth would send Athlos's men as acrobats too, because Luth was sensitive to the call of the key.

A couple of weeks after this a letter arrived from Vittorio Lionheart, telling me how delighted he was that I was proposing to do such important work in the north of Daish Shaktay. I couldn't believe he was our enemy. Along with the letter was an impressive document, signed with his seal, giving me freedom to travel anywhere in the north of the country to awaken the Trees of Life of people living there. I set off with an armed guard for Valya and Melissa's farm, some way to the west of Midway Manor Fort. Within a few days I was visiting the nearby villages to show people how to find inner peace and subtle power.

Danard, Namoh and Cheyla arrived at Valya's farm very early one morning dressed as monks, on worn out horses, saying Rajay was last seen going south of Mattanga, down the coast road. Valya gave them fresh horses and they set off that night towards Crossings Fort.

There were rumours about Rajay and everyone tried not to worry, especially when it became clear that Lionheart was losing his grip on Offlen and was not managing to protect the north of the country from this devil. Valya, whose lands lay in the part of Daish Shaktay presently being administered by Mattanga, was worried not only for his family's safety, but for his thousands of tenants. He sent letters to Lionheart assuring him of his loyalty and paid his enormous tribute money a couple of months in advance – it wasn't worth provoking the forces of Mattanga at this point.

I should have become more cautious, because although I had my pass of safe conduct I was technically in enemy territory in Northern Daish Shaktay. I went on going to villages and farms, often with only one or two of Valya's staff to guard me. He sometimes came with me, but not on this occasion. Melissa never did – she was expecting a baby and Valya insisted she took it easy. One day I was going to a village south of their farm, and it was some way so I told them not to worry if I didn't get back that night. We were trotting along a country road in some woodland, heard the sound of horses and didn't think anything of it until it was too late. Round the corner came a small troop of soldiers wearing the Mattanga uniform. Within moments it was over. They attacked my bodyguards, captured me, and I could not make any use of my key because my captors bound my hands.

One mounted soldier led my horse and on my other side was another rider. There was no hope of escape. Offlen had heard that 'the Teletsian sorceress', in other words me, was fomenting rebellion and giving powers to the people which would enable them to shake off the rule of Mattanga. Not everyone who got their inner awakening was totally loyal to our cause so this had got back to him. He had also discovered that there was still a large reward offered for me by the Teletsian Sorcerers.

I was to be taken to Tiger's Head Fort. My pass of safe conduct was not worth the parchment it was written on. Tiger's Head was about a day's journey and if I didn't escape before I got there, the outlook was grim. After some time the soldiers stopped for a rest and although I did not have a chance to escape I did manage to make a bandhan of request over my Sasrar key. Unfortunately, as I was making the bandhan, the soldiers noticed, although fortunately did not see my key, and again bound my arms behind my back. I couldn't do any more to help myself.

The day wore on and I was desperate. Banks of white clouds were scudding across the sky not far above, because we were in the hills near Tiger's Head Fort. The soldiers were strung out along a narrow valley and I looked up and saw the most unexpected and welcome sight of my whole life. There, hiding in the clouds, were some flying horses. I could see Ahren on one and Robin on another. We were at a bend in the road and most of Offlen's men were round the corner ahead of us.

Suddenly one of the horses swooped down, aimed a kick at the man on my left and he fell hard on the ground. The man on my right drew his sword but then an arrow from Ahren pierced him and he toppled from his horse. Another flying horse kicked the man behind us and he too fell to the ground. At almost the same moment Robin swooped down and pulled me onto his horse's shoulders. It flew up again, its enormous wings beating the air. I was absolutely terrified I was going to slip off.

'It's all right, I'm holding you. You won't fall,' Robin reassured me, feeling my fear. 'Close your eyes and you won't see the ground.' Offlen's other horsemen noticed us and realised angrily I had been rescued in the most unbelievable way. They took their guns off their backs, but by the time they had them loaded we were too far away. Robin held me firmly with one hand and I heard him draw a dagger with the other.

'Great to see you, but *what* a way to say hello!' he said as he cut the ropes binding my hands. 'I'm going to ask Yamun to land for a moment.' He did so, and called one of the horses without a rider. Robin put me on it and we were off again. When we were at least three valleys to the north of the soldiers, we landed in the craggy hills. Ahren helped me off my horse and had me sit on the ground. I was in complete shock and he and Robin tried to calm me.

'*Whatever* have you been up to while I've been away?' grinned Ahren. 'Robin is right, you need at least one of us to keep an eye on you at all times.'

Robin was behind me, giving me a bandhan of protection and putting his hand on the centre of my back at the level of my heart to settle my panic. 'We're here to look after you. Take it easy,' he went on soothingly. 'You're quite safe now.'

'You're magnificent, both of you. I knew you'd come back to help, but not like this,' I smiled with relief. We sat on the grass and relaxed, and the horses stood with their heads down and their wings folded, also resting.

'Somehow you were able to call the horses. They wouldn't obey us the whole of today and went their own way.'

'I made a bandhan on my key. I was praying for the tigers but couldn't get it to my mouth to blow through it for them.'

'A bandhan on the Sasrar key! That's the way to call the horses!'

'What would you have done if we hadn't turned up?' asked Ahren.

'I dread to think. Those men were from Duratman Offlen - he's taken over Tiger's Head Fort. Once they had me inside that place I don't think even the tigers could have rescued me.'

Robin stood up and patted the animals. 'Now these horses put their feet on this land, something will happen. They're instruments of pure power: the power of positive destruction, or salvation, depending on circumstances. Meanwhile, we need to get you somewhere safer.'

'Could they make it to Crossings by this evening?' I asked Ahren.

'Yes, I think so - the wind is behind us,' he replied.

Robin called the mare that had carried me. She trotted up and put her nose in his hand. 'Asha, this is Tama. I've trained her for you. She understands human speech and has agreed to help Rajay Ghiry and Daish Shaktay. Say hello.' I felt instant love for this white horse with her big dark eyes, soft nose and enormous golden wings.

'How can I thank you?' I said with feeling, because training a flying horse took a long time and much effort.

'My pleasure. I've also trained one for Lee,' and he called the other riderless horse. 'This is Misippa.'

'Let's get going,' urged Ahren. 'The flying horses don't like saddles or bridles, but you're quite a good rider these days and won't fall off – let's hope!'

He helped me to get on while Robin spoke to Tama; he knew I was nervous of riding her. We set off, trying to hide behind the clouds when we could. The horses' rhythmic wings ate up the distance and Daish Shaktay passed below us. Evening came, night fell, eventually we saw Crossings Fort by the light of a moon and below was the village.

'We'll land in those woods behind the fort,' shouted Ahren. We did so, and dismounted. 'The horses will be fine for the night. They can eat grass and hide in the trees, but what about us? We can't get into the fort - it's too late.'

'We'll go and see a friend of mine,' I replied. 'She helps me do awakening programmes around here. She's got a house at the end of the village.'

'Do I know her?' Ahren wondered.

'Yes, of course you do - Heeram the milk lady!' We walked down to the village while Ahren told Robin about Heeram's bravery and how Rajay had reacted.

'I can't wait to meet him,' said Robin.

'You're not the only one! We know he's escaped from Mattanga, but he hasn't been seen for ages.' I added.

'Have you checked his vibrations?'

'Yes. Try for yourself. He's alright, but his heart centre isn't very strong; I hope he's not ill.'

'There may be something wrong with his chest. We should give him healing vibrations from a distance; it might help him.'

'We've been doing just that.'

'You know Rajay, he'll most probably turn up in a way no one expects,' said Ahren.

We knocked on Heeram's door and she welcomed us in. Her husband was home, as the Northern Regiment was temporarily disbanded. The family had finished supper, but she told us she would cook us something nice if we didn't mind waiting. I was very dirty so she took me to the bathhouse in the yard.

'If you don't mind dressing as a countrywoman, I'll lend you something to wear,' Heeram offered. Some time later I reappeared in one of her brightly coloured costumes.

'That looks so right,' Ahren commented. 'Partisans should dress like the people they're fighting for.'

The next morning we went up to the fort to see the Aydriss family. We told Commander Aydriss about my rescue, the flying horses and that Queen Jansy knew about the plan to take them to Mattanga. He had received a message a couple of days before from the queen for me to return to Malak Citadel as soon as conveniently possible. He proudly told me he was going to become a grandfather, as Amber was pregnant and not feeling too well, and the queen wanted me to take over some of her lady-in-waiting duties. Daish Shaktay had an efficient information service, so I suspected that was not the only reason she wanted me back at Malak Citadel. Commander Aydriss wrote a strongly worded complaint to General Lionheart at Gap Fort, explaining how Duratman

Offlen had tried to capture me, and if it hadn't been for 'a cavalry force' arriving to save me, I would be in the dungeons of Tiger's Head by now. He had this dispatched immediately.

Ahren and Robin took the horses to a farm some distance away, where they would be out of sight. They returned at lunchtime and we had a leisurely meal, exchanging stories. Pearl and Coral, the two daughters still at home, asked about Sasrar, as did the parents. Word had got around that Ahren had brought a brave partisan from the north and all the fort's officers came to meet him. It was late afternoon before they left. Ahren, Robin and I went out into the garden at the back of the main building and sat on a bench among the many flowers.

'I can't believe you're here, in Daish Shaktay,' I began, to Robin. 'When I think of you I see mountains and the astrologers' house.'

'That was last year,' he replied. 'It looks as if I'm going to be operating in a number of areas from now on.'

'I'm glad. You can help get rid of these ogres. I don't know how, but I'm sure it's going to work out. It's so cool on vibrations.'

'Yes, it is. I'm not looking forward to going to Mattanga, but if we have to get those flying horses there to activate the power of positive destruction, I'll do it. Tell me honestly, why did you send those rings to me?'

'Firstly because I knew you'd come and help Rajay if I did, and secondly because there was some misplaced gossip about me, and I had a feeling it might have even got up to Chussan. I wanted you to know I'm still the same as I was, and not some Daish Shaktay aristocrat's wife. Valya's a great person, but not for me.'

'I did understand, and I had heard certain things about you. Do you want the rings back?' He had them on a chain around his neck, with his Sasrar key.

'No, they might bring you good fortune when you go to Mattanga. Actually, give me back my plain gold one, and Ahren, you keep it to remind you of Teletsia, because it has the four petalled design on it. Robin, take the Daish Shaktay one. When you get back you can return them.'

'*If* we get back,' said Ahren.

'You'll be fine,' I encouraged them.

'I've got some letters for you. I forgot last night,' Robin gave me letters from Derwin, Conwenna, Tandi and Raynor. I read them eagerly and he filled out some parts, especially about Tandi's twins.

Robin had changed; he now saw our involvement with Rajay as part of a larger bid for freedom which extended over the whole continent, perhaps further, and he was prepared to help us in that and not focus solely on Chussan. By lending my other ring to Ahren, he knew I had great faith he would succeed in Mattanga. When we returned to the house Commander Aydriss told Ahren that a message had arrived from Luth saying he should meet the rest of the circus at Bart Charval's farm, so he and Robin left the next day.

CHAPTER 2

BACK TO WORK

I returned to Malak Citadel immediately and went to pay my respects to Queen Jansy. While I was telling her my story, a guard entered.

'Your Majesty, there's a wandering monk in the yard. He has news of the king.'

'Show him in at once,' she ordered. These were nerve-racking days and it reflected in her expression. Nevertheless she now put on an enthusiastic smile and welcomed the wild, ascetic man, who was almost completely covered in a ragged cloak that also hid most of his face. He fell at the queen's feet and I could hear his rattling breathing. I wondered if he was too far gone to sit up.

'I have returned,' he said in a weak, rasping voice, but we instantly recognised it.

'My son!' She took Rajay in her arms, tears falling down her cheeks. We laid him on the divan and I helped, because he was in a bad state. The guards on the door whispered to each other and Rajay noticed them.

'You two,' he called weakly, 'don't tell anyone I'm back.'

'As you say, sire,' answered one, and the other nodded modestly.

'Asha, get Dr. Belsanto, quickly,' said Queen Jansy.

'No,' wheezed Rajay, struggling to breathe. 'I have to talk to you first, Asha.' I knelt in front of him and felt his forehead. He had a high fever.

'Now you're back we can all hope again, but you need the doctor. Please let me go for him,' I pleaded, and took his hand to feel his pulse, which was racing. 'Here, hold my Sasrar key. It will give you strength.'

'It's all right. I finally got my own key.' Rajay showed me the one the tiger had given him. I recognised it at once, because it had lost most of its leaves.

'It's the same key as Lee had, on our great journey!' It came to me: why wasn't Lee with him? 'Where is he?' I blurted out, and at this moment Saber Rizen, some other senior officers and Deradan came in.

'Asha, be strong and discriminating, as your Sasrar training has made you. You can know the truth of any statement,' he whispered to me, then went on in a louder voice, 'Lee was drowned; he sacrificed himself for me when our boat overturned. We hit a submerged rock at night.' I became very still. I didn't cry and displayed no emotion. I froze.

'I'll go and find Dr. Belsanto.' I stood up and left the room, clutching my Sasrar key.

'Don't tell anyone except the doctor that I'm back,' gasped Rajay.

'I'm sorry, Miss Asha,' said one of the guards as he saw my shocked face. 'Mister Lee was an excellent young man. We'll all miss him.'

I went outside, across the courtyard and down the hill to the town. I fought back the tears and then it came to me: what were Rajay's words? 'As strong and discriminating as Sasrar has made you,' and what was the greatest strength of Sasrar? The strength of the vibrations. 'You can know the truth of any statement'. That was a give-away. I sat down on a rock and asked the question on the vibrations: 'Is Lee really dead?' The cool vibrations did not flow at all and my palms felt hot and tingling. Then I asked, 'Is he alive, but Rajay is pretending he isn't?' A cool and unmistakeable breeze flowed over my hands even in the warm sunlight. Instead of fighting grief, I smiled and ran on to find the doctor.

Dr Belsanto was having breakfast with his wife and four children. I told him there was a crisis with Amber, who everyone knew was having a difficult pregnancy, and could he come immediately. Once we were out of the house I told him the truth. Back at the Citadel, I went over to Amber, explained what was going on, and she took to her bed, moaning convincingly. The doctor looked at Rajay and said it was serious, but that a few weeks rest should put him right.

'You can spread the news that I'm back, now it looks as if I'll survive,' he smiled wanly. 'Asha, let me have another word with you. I'm so sorry about Lee.' He indicated for everyone to leave.

'The strength of Sasrar; the vibrations,' I said to Rajay when they had all, except his mother, gone.

'That's it; I knew you'd understand. Sometimes it's necessary to tell a few white lies. He's fine, but in hiding until everyone has learnt of his death and stops hunting him. Then we'll send for him.'

I told to Rajay about my dream and how I had tried to tell the tigers what I wanted them to do.

'You saved my life. I wouldn't have made it back without that tiger. There are no words with which I can thank you enough - you are truly my sister.' A little later he was lying on the divan and people were welcoming him. 'Please tell everyone how bravely he died to save me,' he replied sadly when asked about Lee.

Within a day everyone in the district knew that Rajay was back and the whole of Daish Shaktay heard the guns booming from fort to fort and echoing from hilltop to crag to mountain. Spontaneous parties sprang up in every street and village, in the towns endless official functions were held and the temples of every religion were full of flowers of gratitude. The news about Lee spread, also to the ears of the Mattangan spies who were supposed to hear it.

The soldiers in the Mattanga army's garrisons shook in their shoes in the occupied forts to the north. The Mouse was home and had eluded his captors yet again. A number of the soldiers in these forts fled at this news, because there was a widely spread rumour that he would forgive any soldiers who abandoned their posts, but would be merciless towards those who continued to support Mattanga. So many men deserted from Midway Manor Fort, the scene of Rajay's victory over Comeni, that it was abandoned, especially as Witten arranged for monumental bribes to be given to the commander and officers. Confluence Fort was in a similar situation, and when Lionheart sent to Mattanga for reinforcements, he was told none were available because there was no money to pay them. Men from Daish Shaktay could not be lured either, because they weren't going to join the enemy out of charity and certainly would not oppose their beloved leader, Rajay.

Lionheart regrouped his remaining forces from Midway Manor and Confluence Forts to guard the ruby and sapphire mines, because that wealth was supposed to be going to Mattanga. Hardly any did, because partisans bribed the miners to steal as many jewels as they could, and send them to Malak Citadel. There were also some gangs of wily bandits in the area who raided the baggage trains; they were also on the payroll of the Free Daish Shaktay government.

When the news of Rajay's return was broken to King Karlvid he was doubly angry. Firstly, he had let the Mouse slip through his scaly fingers, and all the other fingers of Mattanga too. The caged tiger who had been so very wronged was home and was an even greater hero than before, and Rajay's subjects were all too ready and able to wreak revenge now they had their leader at their head once more. Secondly, one of the seven Teletsian rebels had been living under Karlvid's nose and he had only discovered this after he too had escaped. The Teletsian rulers were still offering a huge reward for them, but regrettably he was reported to have been drowned while helping Rajay Ghiry. Everyone in the Mattanga Empire soon knew about this, including Lee, still living in the cave near the Temple-by-the-Sea, with Luth's monks and Athlos. Rajay sent a message, and Lee and Athlos, with shaven heads and shell rosaries, set out for Daish Shaktay.

Rajay's health had held up just long enough for him to get back to Malak Citadel but he was very weak. Dr Belsanto's first diagnosis had been too optimistic and when he came again he decided Rajay had developed pneumonia. He was not too ill to see his friends, and soon Danard and Namoh arrived from their farm on the hills near Hermitage Fort. They returned his sword and signet ring.

Rajay was relieved that Danard was all right; maybe the doom prophesied on the sword had been avoided. When Rajay gazed deeply at him, wondering whether to say anything about the curse, Danard assumed it was Rajay's joy

at seeing him and his brother still alive after their harrowing escape. They exchanged stories, laughed about how they had eluded the forces of Mattanga and Rajay gave them a large bag of gold coins in gratitude. Danard immediately bought a manor house with good farm land some way north west of Crossings Fort; he was eager to settle their affairs, because the family struggled to make a living on some poor hill land and it had been hard, especially since his father had died some years before. He never mentioned these problems to Rajay, who nevertheless knew. If and when he was crowned king, Danard would become his First Minister and Rajay didn't want him to have to worry about his penniless relations any more.

What Rajay didn't know was that Danard's mother, a scheming woman, had arranged a marriage between his sister and the heir to one of the noble families who were collaborating with Offlen. The wedding was to be soon and Danard had not been able to dissuade her. Coming as she did from a simple farming family, and not being very deep, her head had been completely turned at the thought of joining the nobility. The fact that her sons were closer to the king than anyone did not impress her, because they were so humble. She wanted a title, wealth and lands for her daughter. If Danard had a fault, it was to keep bad news from Rajay, and Namoh would never override his brother.

I was often with Queen Jansy and consequently saw Rajay all the time, because he was staying in her apartment. Some days later, I was serving them lunch and she asked me if I had heard from Ahren and whether the circus was actually happening.

'Yes, I had a message today. They're at Bart Charval's farm, practising their acts. The tigers are there, along with some of Luth's monkey friends and his men, who make up the acrobatic troupe, and the flying horses. They're getting quite a show together.'

'Those horses are going to set something in motion but it's important they

253

don't get hurt or killed, or the reaction might be too great,' added Rajay, lying on the divan.

'Robin and Ahren are the best riders I've ever seen. If anyone can keep the horses safe, they will,' I replied. Queen Jansy left for yet another administrative meeting and I was alone with Rajay. He asked for more coffee.

'You're not wearing the ring I gave you,' he said as I handed him the cup. When Rajay was with me, Lee or Ahren, there was a brotherly informality about him. I tried, not always successfully, to remember he was nevertheless a king.

'That ring is one of the things which got those flying horses down here.'

'Tell me.' I did, and he agreed it was good that I'd lent it to Robin. 'I wish I had him working for me permanently. Still, it's in the interest of all of us that Chussan is sorted out.'

'Yes, and another thing, while I was up at Crossings, I became quite friendly with Pearl Aydriss. I wonder if I could put in a good word for her.'

'She's got a desperately sharp tongue and can be an absolute viper. Witten was very taken by her and I must admit I did warn him. After I'd done so, I wondered if I should have – after all, it's his life and he's not stupid, although we men can lose our heads when it comes to young ladies. I admire you if you've managed to get through to her.'

'She's totally transformed. Her family can't believe it.'

'How so?'

'Feel her vibrations.'

'Vastly improved,' he was pleasantly surprised. Rajay didn't have to use his hands. He could feel people's vibrations just by putting his attention on them. 'What happened?'

'She asked me if I could help her become a nicer person, so she started doing treatments on herself to clear the subtle problems from her Tree of Life, and she's helping me awaken people. After some time she got much better. Give her a few months, and then, please, ask Witten to give her another chance.'

'Let's leave it for the time being, because the political situation here is far from resolved.' Nevertheless, I knew I had touched his heart and he would try to rekindle things between Witten and Pearl when the right time came. Rajay could slaughter an enemy without any qualms, but with his extended family, which included most of Daish Shaktay, he was as compassionate as a mother with her new born baby. By chance, at that moment Witten himself came in with some documents.

'Can you check these projects?' he asked, then, seeing us both look at him with some surprise, went on, 'Am I interrupting?'

'No, we'd finished talking,' Rajay reassured him. 'The vibrations of those documents are very cool, meaning what's in them is fine. Tell me anyway, because it's good to hear what you're up to.'

Witten had a brilliant mind behind his twinkling eyes and broad grin. He sat down and they began discussing various schemes; he had evolved a system of taxation whereby the farmers were only taxed on the crops of that season: no crops, no tax, good crops, a larger tax. He also saw that new fruit groves were subsidised, new lands were brought under cultivation and the forests were well maintained and replanted, with financial incentives to do so. Many other projects were afoot. Corruption was heavily punished and the tax farmers put in place by the Mattanga government were removed, tax being collected by people who were directly answerable to Witten and Deradan. Rajay's childhood friends, chosen seemingly at random, were turning out to be the perfect nerves and muscles of the kingdom.

Gar Warl, the officer from the hill tribe who had so misunderstood Rajay's attitude to women after the Port Volcan expedition, was commanded to the king's presence. Rajay told him to find out exactly who had been raiding in the mountains of Daish Shaktay and to put an immediate stop to it. Gar Warl was to take some soldiers and resolve the problem. He was to personally deliver a purse of gold coins to an elderly farmer's wife in a certain village and take her crates of ducks and chickens, and six healthy young cows.

'Be careful she doesn't chase you with her rolling pin,' Rajay warned. 'She's a forceful dame.'

Having done this, Gar Warl was to go secretly through the pass, find the police chief who had allowed Rajay to escape and also give him a bag of gold. The Mountain Mouse kept his promises. Gar Warl left and next Rajay ordered a chest of gold coins put aside for war veterans. I was on the balcony outside his room at the time, so inadvertently overheard him.

'And if it's emptied?' asked Deradan.

'Then refill it, again and again,' demanded Rajay.

'People might abuse your generosity,' objected Witten.

'Our store of gold isn't endless,' added Deradan.

'Without the sacrifice of so many of our countrymen, we wouldn't be sitting here today,' went on Rajay.

'It's all very well to say that, but Witten and I have to balance the books of this country.'

'Forget the books. Money is to make people's lives easier and give joy - it has no other value.'

'Many kings have lost their kingdoms because their treasury was empty,' Witten persisted.

'I'm not denying it, but if you're worried people will take advantage of our offer send some reliable clerks round the country to find out exactly which families are suffering. We can't bring back their loved ones, but if they've lost family members or have permanently disabled people living with them, we must look after them. If we get short of money we'll sell off some state owned land.

'You should feel the vibrations when you make decisions. When you speak so basely your third subtle centre becomes constricted and that's the one from which material prosperity flows. If you, my ministers, think and act like this the country won't be blessed with wealth. Go and soak your feet in the stream by the orange grove and ask the water element to take out your meanness. Then sit on the Mother Earth in meditation for some time.' Deradan and Witten apologised and went off to do as he asked, and I revealed myself. 'I didn't realise you were there,' Rajay looked displeased, 'you know I never correct my friends unless we're alone.'

'I'm sorry, but it might have been worse if they'd known I was listening.'

'That's true. I'm blessed to have them, and let's face it, we've all got our weak points.'

Some days later Lee and Athlos reached Malak Citadel dressed as monks and everybody, especially me, was overjoyed.

'What a relief to see you both,' Rajay welcomed them warmly.

'I'm not cut out for the mendicant life,' complained a shaven headed Lee, 'I like a decent meal at least once a day and I don't like going around half naked. It's too cold, even in this warm country.'

King Karlvid sent a letter to Vittorio Lionheart, Viceroy of Northern Daish Shaktay.

> *Lionheart,*
> *You are relieved of your command. Please come to our presence to account for your and your vanished son's part in Rajay Ghiry's escape. I am sending my son Prince Moozand to look after the civil business in Northern Daish Shaktay and Duratman Offlen can continue to command the troops.*
> *Your king,*
> *Karlvid.*

The ogre king was certain he could never persuade Lionheart to fight another battle *against* Rajay Ghiry, and if Lionheart stayed in Daish Shaktay it was all too likely he and Rajay would soon be fighting against Karlvid. Prince Moozand was a pleasure-loving layabout and the full brother to Princess Zulani. He and Duratman Offlen despised one another. It was all too much for the gallant Vittorio Lionheart, who took to his bed and died. Some said he died of a fever, others of a broken heart and still others claimed he had been poisoned, but all the reports agreed on one point: he was holding the locket of the Goddess of Daish Shaktay to his breast when his servants found the body. Nevertheless, when it was to be cremated, the locket had disappeared.

Many a morning, Deradan and Lee were called to take down letters. Prince Moozand entrenched himself at Gap Fort in place of Lionheart and Rajay tried to establish good relations with him, as they had met in Mattanga. Moozand had no ogrish characteristics and disliked politics intensely, but at least he was unlikely to start a civil war against his father, as another of Karlvid's sons was trying to do, and a major part of the Mattanga army had been sent to deal with it. Rajay wrote to Moozand.

Most esteemed Prince Moozand,
Although I had to flee from Mattanga to save my life, I am still King Karlvid's vassal. I know that he is short of soldiers and as we are at peace we will send you two thousand of the best Daish Shaktay cavalry. They will be under your command, in case you should need them against the Chussan forces or your rebellious brother.
I would also ask if I might be confirmed as the Vassal of Central Daish Shaktay and hopefully also the northern part, and could take back at least some of the forts in that area to administer myself. Of course the tax from this part of the country would be sent to you. Please put this proposal to your father.
I remain,
Your friend and brother
Rajay Ghiry of Daish Shaktay

'Who pays for the upkeep of our troops?' asked Witten.

'They do!' replied Rajay cynically. 'The Northern Regiment is on indefinite leave at the moment. We don't need a large standing army right now, but it's a pity to let them slack off.'

Duratman Offlen, at Tiger's Head Fort above Santara, was not told of the letters going between Rajay, Moozand and King Karlvid; Moozand so disliked Offlen that he rarely told him anything. To everyone's surprise the following letter came back from Karlvid.

Respected Rajay Ghiry
'We received a letter from our son Prince Moozand recommending that you continue in your good work as vassal of Southern Daish Shaktay. However, we will keep Tiger's Head Fort where my commander Duratman Offlen is stationed; Gap Fort, where my son and the administrative officers are staying, and High Plains Fort. We are grateful for your offer of the cavalrymen and can no doubt find some use for them.'
Your overlord
Karlvid

Deradan discovered from the intelligence service that Karlvid had given up trying to get any wealth from the ruby and sapphire mines, because Rajay's 'bandits' had made them completely unprofitable. Consequently the Sapphire River Fort had been abandoned. Moozand explained to Offlen that due to his diplomacy, Rajay Ghiry had become a docile vassal like all the others of his father's empire, Mattanga still had direct control over the three key forts and a fat tribute was coming in regularly. Offlen, scheming and jealous, wrote to Karlvid.

My Lord,
Rajay Ghiry and Prince Moozand have formed a conspiracy. They
will be fighting you next. Beware, or this son may dethrone you.
Your servant
Offlen

Karlvid then wrote to Moozand.

Moozand,
I hear rumours that you are playing me false. As proof of your good faith
you must lure Rajay Ghiry to your fort, then entrap him and send him here.
He will not escape a second time. I am told you are friendly with him so it
should not be hard.
Your father
Karlvid

Moozand accused Offlen of slandering him and warned Rajay, suggesting that he recall his cavalrymen. Rajay did so; now he had Moozand's friendship there wasn't much point in leaving them at Gap Fort, being as Daish Shaktay was going to have to pay their salaries, because Mattanga was bankrupt. While this was going on Rajay was slowly recovering, although he was still very weak.

CHAPTER 3

PROVOCATION

Queen Jansy decided to go and stay at Hermitage Fort above Santara, east of Tiger's Head Fort. It was deserted at that time, for want of military personnel. She said she could keep an eye on Offlen if she was up there and as her lady-in-waiting I went too. By the terms of the treaty made before Rajay went to Mattanga, Tiger's Head, Hermitage and Gap Forts still belonged to Mattanga, although the actual situation was much more fluid.

Rajay had an enormous amount of support in the northern section of Daish Shaktay and even though the inhabitants did, grudgingly, pay large taxes to Mattanga, Moozand and Offlen knew their position was far from secure, especially since Rajay had returned. Queen Jansy's excuse for moving into a fort nominally under the control of Mattanga was so she could persuade the locals to comply with the wishes of their Mattangan overseers. She said she needed a garrison to guard her because she was a woman. The curtain walls of Hermitage were largely broken down and it was not a strong refuge, which supported her excuse. Somehow she managed to persuade Moozand and Offlen to believe this unlikely story.

As soon as we arrived, the majority of the garrison and a large number of supportive villagers were put onto the job of rebuilding the walls. Within a few days of arriving, complaints about Offlen began to pour in and the village schoolmaster who had been so helpful during the attack on Coroso Raspatto bought a petition. He explained that Offlen's men would make off with the male villagers, women and children were not safe and people who went out alone would disappear where Offlen's ogres had been seen.

One day a merchant came puffing up the steep path to Hermitage Fort and poured out his story, that Offlen's men were no better than bandits; they were attacking his mule trains and making off with his goods. He was not the only trader who had had this problem and the local militia had retaliated as best they could. They had captured one soldier and, as the merchant put it, 'We questioned him, M'Lady, 'til he saw fit to answer.' Under this not-so-gentle persuasion he had eventually admitted that Offlen had not paid his men once since they had arrived in the area, so the soldiers had decided to pay themselves and had gone raiding on their off days. The officers turned a blind eye and wished they could do the same; they had not received their salaries for months either. Queen Jansy listened to the merchant sympathetically, and promised that something would soon be done.

Like a man who decides to travel on the one day of the year that his horoscope warns of an accident, King Karlvid's next move was extremely stupid. He discovered his youngest daughter was an ardent worshipper of the Goddess of Daish Shaktay and she and her friends refused to have anything to do with the cruel practices of the king's religion, the worship of the Crocodile God, and that his son Moozand had been influenced in the same way. In retaliation Karlvid destroyed the temples dedicated to the Goddess of Daish Shaktay in Mattanga, killed many of the priests and levied a stiff tax on anyone who did not worship the Crocodile God.

Rajay on the contrary respected and protected all the religions in Daish Shaktay, provided they did not indulge in human sacrifice. When Rajay heard what Karlvid was doing he had Lee write this letter:

King Karlvid,

> *Your favours have been most bountiful to me, your humble servant, and although I was led by unkind fate to depart from your presence in Mattanga without formally taking your leave, I will perform any duty which is expected of a faithful vassal. It has recently come to my attention that your treasury is utterly depleted and to make up the deficit you have imposed a tax upon the pious worshippers of many religions.*

> *Not only that, you have ordered the pillage and destruction of many sacred temples and your men have killed their priests. If you look at any holy books you will find that the supreme form of God is the Lord and protector of all men, and you claim to worship the supreme. The different religions are only different colours of one rainbow, which is white light split up through a prism. To be bigoted against any style of devotion is therefore to go against your own scriptures.*

> *May the sun of royalty continue to shine on your face, but I fear it may not if you do your best to disturb the forces which rule all our lives.*

> *Yours,*
> *Rajay Ghiry of Daish Shaktay*

'I like the bit about departing without taking formal leave,' Lee chuckled. 'If you don't mind my saying, you were quite a weight in that basket, when Athlos and I carried you.' Rajay laughed too and Lee added, 'His sun of royalty is becoming a bit tarnished, wouldn't you say?'

'Yes, his every action shows him up for what he is, a fiend through and through, and his people are beginning to see that, at last. This is a final warning.'

When Duratman Offlen heard that Karlvid had been plundering the shrines in Mattanga he decided to do the same thing in Daish Shaktay. He burst out of Tiger's Head Fort accompanied by a large body of men and raided temples in and around Santara. That same evening some priests went to Queen Jansy and told her of the attacks, and she promised to do her best to resolve the problem.

The next morning she was combing her hair as she sat on her balcony at Hermitage Fort. To the southwest she could see the dark green of the fruit groves surrounding Santara, and smoke still rose from the burnt out temples of the previous day's violence. I came in with a tray of food for her; we lived simply here.

'Madam, your breakfast.'

'Thank you - put it on the table. Come and look at the valley.' I gazed at the stupendous view. At this moment the sun's rays were beginning to shine over the hills and plains in the distance and I noticed the smoke from Santara. 'Yes,' the queen observed, 'he's gone too far this time.' She looked at the gold tipped hills to the north and west and we could see Tiger's Head Fort in the distance. 'That's our strongest fort and at present the scorpion's nest, the billet of Duratman Offlen.' She sighed, turned away and I served her breakfast. Usually Queen Jansy was talkative at this time, but today she did not speak another word. After breakfast she had me send up her courier.

'Tell my son I need him here as soon as possible. If he's too weak to ride he must come on a litter,' she ordered him when he arrived.

'Yes, Your Majesty. I'll leave at once and take the fast relay service.'

'I will eat nothing until I see him.'

The courier ran down the stony pathway to the stables, because no large animal could get up to the keep, took a swift horse and galloped to the first town on the plains, where he changed horses, thundered through village after village and changed horses again before he reached Crossings Fort. There he rested awhile and had a meal, after which he forced his aching body onto another fast horse, and another, and another, as he sped southwards. That evening he reached Malak Citadel and was directed to the Finance Chamber. Dr Belsanto was leaving and had told Rajay not to do anything strenuous yet or his lungs might be permanently damaged. Rajay returned to the bundles of paper and parchment strewn around the various desks, and went on working with Witten, Deradan and Lee. He was signing a heap of documents and noticed the messenger, surprised he had walked in unannounced. It had to be important or the door guard would have stopped him.

'You're my mother's courier, aren't you?' he began.

'Yes, Sire.'

'Why have you come?'

'Her Majesty has called for you - urgently. She has sworn not to eat anything until you are by her side.'

'Saddle me my best horse,' ordered Rajay, standing up at once.

'But Rajay,' objected Witten, 'the doctor said...' He glared at Witten and staggered out of the room. No one, but no one, told Rajay what to do. He considered calling a tiger, now he had a key, but decided against it because he would have to take at least one bodyguard with him, because of his poor health.

On the first night of his journey he didn't change horses and kept to one whose paces he knew, an evil looking grey stallion with a tremendous turn of speed and great staying power. As his chest was so painful he rested at Crossings Fort the following morning for some time. Commander and Lady Aydriss begged him to take it easy, because they could see he was still not well, and Pearl and Coral, and Heeram Milkfarmer gave him healing vibrations. After that he rode all day, rested again at an inn for the night, ordering the innkeeper to hide his identity, and reached the outer walls of Hermitage Fort the next evening. He blew his horn; the queen heard it and sent down a litter, well aware that he would be too tired to walk up the path to the keep. He was carried into her presence, completely spent, half expecting her to also be ill. She was waiting patiently.

'Welcome, Rajay. First, have some food, so you can recover some strength.' I served him and stood back while he ate. When the king and the queen mother were together my relationship with them changed: gone was the friendly but respectful informality I enjoyed with both of them when alone with either of them. I was outside their intimacy as mother and son, and furthermore they were royalty and spiritual guardians of the fourth subtle centre on Mother Earth.

'My son, I want to challenge you to a wager,' said the queen, almost by the way. 'Asha, fetch some dice and the chess board.' Queen Jansy was brilliant at chess and had been patiently trying to teach me. I was embarrassingly bad. She was the supreme strategist in the real world whereas I wandered through life almost completely spontaneously - and that is no way to win at this game. To begin with she wanted to play dice, and Rajay did as she asked. He thought it odd that he had been summoned so far across his country at the peril of his frail health for this, but he agreed and they played.

'We'll play for high stakes,' she insisted. 'If I win, you must give me whatever I ask for. If you win the same applies.' I stood back, by the door, watched closely and something told me Queen Jansy was praying hard to all the powers she could command, which were considerable.

The queen threw double

fives; Rajay a one and a three. The queen won. Again they threw.

The queen threw double sixes; Rajay a two and a five. The queen won. Again they threw.

The queen threw a five and a six; Rajay a one and a four. The queen won. Again they threw.

Nine times they threw. Nine times the queen won. It was uncanny. I knew these dice were not loaded, so it was a fair match.

'Can we play chess?' asked Rajay belatedly. 'Luck may be with you, but chess is a game of skill such as we both play in the world of politics every day of our lives and I'm your match there.'

'As you wish.'

I set out the chessboard. The queen won five games running. Rajay didn't stand a chance. He might have been able to outplay and outmanoeuvre Karlvid and anyone else who dared oppose him in the real world, but on this board Queen Jansy defeated him utterly.

'That's enough. What do you want, mother?'

'Tiger's Head Fort.'

'You can have any other fort in the kingdom, even the two others still held by the ogre peoples, or the new sea forts on the coast, designed to protect our people from the slave traders.'

'You agreed on the wager. It's not like you to evade a challenge,' she replied implacably. I knew the calibre of both the people in front of me: finely tempered steel.

'Why do you think Offlen has chosen that particular fort? You can't storm it, it's large and it has its own well. In it he has most of the nobles who still oppose us as his officers, and he also has a strong garrison there. It's untakeable. Everyone knows that.'

'There has to be a way. Offlen is a devil. At the moment he has *all* the nobles who are still opposed to you there; the rumour is they are hatching a coup against us.'

'Give me some time to think about this.' Rajay stood up painfully and unsteadily, and then left the room.

'He'll do it.' The queen's eyes flashed in the way I had sometimes seen Rajay's do.

I found him on the roof of the keep. He tried to hide the fact he was in pain, but I felt his inner self and he knew it. Even his wheezing breathing gave him away.

'Ah, Asha, come, I need your help. Who will risk his life for me?' he murmured. 'Who has the necessary combination of bravery, initiative and skill?'

'You know your men.'

'Yes, I know my men. I know my officers, my commanders, my friends, but I also know that in all its thousand years as a place of refuge no one has ever successfully assaulted that fort. Two years ago we had to use guile and trickery.'

Rajay sat on the stone bench around the inner side of the battlements and looked towards Tiger's Head Fort on the distant crest. I heard Queen Jansy calling from below.

'Let me go. You're not well. Stay here and I'll see what your mother wants.' I went down into the living room.

'Do you know what this is?' asked the queen, holding up a plaited bracelet of silken threads.

'Yes, it's a brotherhood bracelet. If a lady gives it to a man she's asking him to become like her brother and to protect her at all times.'

'It's from a cousin of Danard's, for Rajay. It arrived just now and there's a letter as well.' I took both the letter and the bracelet up to him. He read the letter by the light of the moons. I felt a sad heaviness in his heart and he gave it to me to read.

> *Respected brother Rajay,*
> *You are my king and, I hope, my salvation. I heard you will be at Hermitage Fort today. I send this letter and bracelet with my trusted maid, who was allowed to bring me clothes after I had been captured by Offlen's men.*
> *My first cousin Danard told me you have been ill and he did not want to bother you with a difficult problem which has come up in our family. Danard's mother has arranged a marriage between his sister and the youngest son of Chor Bardmarsh. As you know, this family have always wanted the kingship. Duratman Offlen is gathering all the nobles who still bear you a grudge in an effort to start a civil war against you. I tried to warn Danard's sister to cancel the wedding but their mother found out. She wants status for her daughter at any price and betrayed me to Offlen. His men captured me and I am to be sent to Mattanga next week as a sacrifice to the Crocodile God. Meanwhile I am a prisoner at Tiger's Head Fort. Please help me.*
> *Your loyal subject and sister,*
> *Ariani Hillfarmer.*

I was devastated. I had met this girl. She was courageous and outspoken, as would be expected of one of Danard's relations. She had received her inner awakening at the programme we did the day before Valya's wedding

'Send up a courier,' Rajay ordered and soon one arrived. 'Go to Danard Hillfarmer, at his new manor in the valley near Crossings Fort. Tell Danard that his king needs him immediately, here. Remember to use the words 'his king'. His brother Namoh should also come, with at least two thousand of our bravest fighters, if possible. Then the courier must go speedily to Malak Citadel for Lee, because those boys from Sasrar often bring success with them.'

CHAPTER 4

DANARD FULFILS HIS VOW

The messenger left a trail of dust and gasping horses, and soon reached the leafy lanes between the fruit groves and fields of the fine, newly acquired manor of the Hillfarmer family. He entered the yard in front of the strong stone house to find preparations in progress for a large celebration. Tents were being put up, wagons of food unloaded and people were coming and going in all directions. No one took much notice of the tired stranger. He asked for Danard, various people pointed in different directions and he eventually found him in the Great Hall directing operations. By this time the messenger had gathered that Danard's sister was to be married a week later and a large number of guests had already arrived from all over the country and even further off. Some of them were being housed in tents.

'Please be seated,' said Danard courteously. 'Have something to drink and eat. I'll be with you shortly. Excuse me, but we're very busy today.' He went off on an errand and later returned. 'How can I help you?' he asked.

'I have a message from His Majesty. His words were: "Tell Danard that his king needs him immediately at Hermitage Fort." It's extremely important that you go straight away.'

' "His king?" That means it's official business of Daish Shaktay, not a personal errand, or he would have said Rajay, or I.' Danard looked around at the bustle and confusion. He called Namoh and introduced him to the messenger, who told Namoh about bringing the men-at-arms. Danard called his mother, sister and cousins. 'We'll have to postpone the wedding.' He was relieved at this chance to do so. 'First we must see to some work for the king and will need to take most of our men with us.' The family were

dismayed, but no one could say anything. They knew how high Danard and Namoh stood in the king's estimation and were proud to be related to the heroes. Only Danard's mother was distraught.

'What shall we say to the bridegroom? Such a noble family! The young man may not be prepared to wait,' she moaned.

'Tell him that when the Shaktay River flows uphill to its source and when the moons fail to rise for a year, then only will Namoh and I put our king's orders second and a family wedding first.'

The brothers bid their relations goodbye, took their weapons and mounted their horses, which the groom hurriedly saddled and brought to the front yard. Namoh would gather the rest of the soldiers and Danard would go straight to Rajay. Danard told his more trustworthy kinsmen and almost all of his male staff to follow him to Hermitage Fort immediately. Together the brothers rode under the arch between the two parts of the gatehouse at the bottom of the driveway and a dazed owl flew out from a rafter and flopped against Danard's arm. His horse was startled, and plunged and reared. To be hit by an owl was an appalling omen; even to see one in daytime was bad enough. Danard looked at the rolling lands they had bought with Rajay's generous reward for their bravery.

'The family will manage all right if I don't return,' he said to Namoh.

'Don't even think like that.'

Outwardly Namoh made jokes about the befuddled owl, but his heart was heavy. A little later he took one road and Danard another, and once alone Danard rode faster. He changed horses at a relay post and soon reached Hermitage Fort, where he immediately went to the queen and Rajay. She welcomed him formally, by waving the traditional lamps around his body in an arch. He acknowledged this gracious gesture and then turned to Rajay.

'You called me as my king, not as my friend. Why?'

'My mother wants something and only you can lead our men, being as I'm so weak at present.'

'The time has come for that devil Duratman Offlen to be driven out of Tiger's Head Fort. Will you try?' asked the queen. Danard bowed low, drew his sword and laid it at her feet.

'My Lady, you will have your fort.' Danard had known Queen Jansy since he was a boy and had deep love and admiration for her.

'You will be a part of our family for ever if you can win it back from that accursed man,' she promised.

'If the Goddess of Daish Shaktay guides me and both of you bless me, I have nothing to fear.'

When Rajay told Danard about the capture of his cousin Ariani, he frowned angrily and clenched his fists, because Ariani was an old, childhood friend and he knew of her determination to stand up for what she believed was right, even if it meant speaking out of turn.

Later, on the roof of the fort, Rajay and Danard talked further. Many a time

Danard had stood in awe before the sheer black basalt cliffs below Tiger's Head Fort and looked up at the forward Watch Tower, from where the sentries guarded the winding path up to the gate. As he spoke to Rajay he remembered that at the base of the cliff was a deep lake which reflected the cliffs and rarely saw the sun. It was like death itself, unclear and unfathomable. They realised the only possible way to take the stronghold and soon came up with a plan.

That afternoon Danard went down to Santara to find what he needed. Rajay could not even manage the climb onto the plain, so there was no possibility of his coming to assault the fort. Namoh arrived with his men two days later and Lee slipped into Hermitage Fort just before its gates were closed at sundown. The attempt was to be the night after and the nights on these hills were cold and clear, because it was winter. The next day the men were tense and excited, and Rajay gave them words of encouragement. I felt uneasy and reminded Lee to put the bandhan of protection on himself, and to remind Danard and Namoh, but they were so busy, I hoped he managed to tell them.

In the night Namoh, Danard and about two thousand men crept through the forest covered hills until they were near Tiger's Head Fort. They hid in the whispering pine woods on the flatter area around the base of the cliff at the lake side and the sighing trees reminded Lee of the ghosts of soldiers who had failed to take the fort in times gone by. They all waited and above the Moon of Compassion rolled overhead, reflecting its wan face in the black lake.

Danard had found and bought a tame cliffpad. This was a giant, tameable lizard that could be trained to scale cliffs with a rope around its neck. Cliffpads were so large and the suckers on their feet so strong that they could support the weight of a man on the end of a rope. They were sometimes used by shepherds to rescue sheep caught in craggy mountains. Danard had bought the most famous one in the district; it was big and powerful and known as 'The Mountaineer'.

He took it to the base of the precipice, tied the rope around its neck and sent it up. It scuttled up the almost vertical rock face, with nowhere for a man to put his hands or feet, but half way up it stopped, shuddered and looked back. Danard heard a man behind him gasp, because this was the worst possible portend. It was the village schoolmaster who had helped so much when they had attacked Coroso Raspatto in Santara.

'The cliffpad has seen the God of Death coming for you. Let's give up, because lizards are never wrong. The rope around its neck will lead us to our doom as surely as if it were a hangman's noose.'

'Are you a warrior? You speak like an old woman,' Danard hissed quietly, so as not to embarrass him in front of the others. Then Danard said as loudly as he dared to the cliffpad; 'Get up there, you wretch, or I'll give you to the dogs for their breakfast.' He threatened it with his drawn sword and it turned and fled up the rest of the cliff, its claws and suckers finding footholds in the glassy rock. Soon it reached the ledge on which the Guard Tower stood, but no guards bothered to look this way. They all faced the path much further along and around the corner. The tower was on a bastion out from the main fort. Danard looked up and hesitated.

'Can this lizard really bear my weight?' he said to the man next to him, who was a farmer.

'Oh yes, sir. I've seen this one in action. You needn't worry about him.'

'Sir, have a mouthful of this. It will give you courage,' offered another man.

'I'm all right for courage, but I'm very thirsty, so give me some,' he said, his attention on the cliffpad.

He took the leather bottle and gulped some mouthfuls. Danard had grown up with Rajay, who never touched any intoxicants. Because of this Danard never drank alcohol, so did not realise he had taken a large amount of almost pure spirit when he least needed his senses dulled.

'That stuff is horrible,' he said handing back the flask, and the cliffpad on the ledge braced itself as Danard climbed the rope attached to its neck, his heart beating fast with excitement. On his back were more lengths of rope and also his bow and arrows. He also wore a loaded pistol and his sword, the death knell of many enemies of Daish Shaktay. Soon he was up on the ledge.

Danard edged his way forward to the Watch Tower. Silently he put an arrow in his bow, because in front of him was a sentry with his back to him. He aimed carefully and the man dropped over the edge of the abyss like a stone, an arrow through his back at the level of the heart. Danard freed the cliffpad and secured all the ropes he had brought with him to trees and rocks, and three hundred of his men, along with Lee, swarmed up the cliff. Lee, who had climbed up last, threw the ropes back down the cliff, so the only way out was through the front gate. The rest of the men saw this and said nothing; each one had been chosen for his exceptional bravery.

Danard crept towards the Watch Tower, silently garrotted the ogre guard at the door and they all tiptoed inside. This was where the ogrous sentries slept, all fifty of them, mostly in a drunken sleep and swiftly, one by one, they were killed. In every room they lay dead, but one escaped - he was wounded, but fled before anyone knew he had gone. Danard and his men entered the yard of the fort but the escaped guard was banging on the door of Duratman Offlen's apartment.

'Sir, come out! Arm yourself! The Mouse's men are here! They've already killed all the sentries in the Watch Tower except me. If you don't come now you'll lose the fort,' cried the man, then he too coughed blood and fell to the floor.

Offlen had no intention of going out to risk his life against a few intruders, but to be on the safe side he sent his door guard to his elephant keeper with a message: 'Send our elephant Mandoom, who has been trained to kill, and he will trample these peasants under his feet.' Before being sent out the elephant was drugged with a potion to make him even fiercer and his eyes were red with fury when they took him from his stall. Danard was leading the fight against the men of the garrison, who had woken up and come out to see what all the noise was about. They were armed and were guarding the main gate, because someone had noticed a large force coming up the path outside. Some of Danard's soldiers in the courtyard quailed when they saw the ferocious elephant bearing down on them.

'There's no way out save heaven or victory! The ropes have gone!' Lee yelled as they began to retreat, so they all returned to fight and left a trail of bloody corpses where they cut down the sleepy defenders. Lee ran ahead and they regained their courage. Then Mandoom charged Danard.

'Now see what happens to country bandits who come in here!' shouted the elephant's ogrous rider. Danard jumped deftly aside onto a wall and nimbly vaulted onto the back of the vast animal. He sat astride its huge neck and the driver leapt off and fled, giving Danard the chance to plunge his newly sharpened sword into the elephant's brain. He jumped clear as the monster sank dead beneath him. Another soldier ran up to Duratman Offlen, and this one was not so courteous.

'Get up and fight! Your elephant is a gory lump of flesh!' he shouted through the door. 'He's dead and so will you be if you don't come soon.'

'Send the visiting nobles and let's see whose side they're really on,' bellowed Offlen, because they were all in the fort to plot a coup against Rajay. 'They can drive these village vermin over the cliff face and back the way they came.'

Next the nobles, including the surviving son of Chor Bardmarsh, who was to marry Danard's sister, were roused and ran into the yard. They looked for the attackers' leader, but it was difficult to find him in the night. Danard's sword flashed and struck home again and again, but his reactions were not as quick as they might have been, because the alcohol was coursing through his veins. Nonetheless one by one sleepy nobles went down before the partisans: farmers, tradesmen and villagers, led by their brave leader Danard. The nobles' bejewelled necks were cut, their scornful, arrogant faces were pounded in the dust, their shoulders shrugged at working men no longer. They were spattered with blood and lying on the ground. Lee recognised a young man lying slain at his feet as one of the nobles who had refused to swear allegiance on Rajay's sword at Valya's wedding. The same man who had warned Offlen before, watching from an arrow slit in the keep, ran back to Duratman Offlen and this time burst into his room.

'Now your nobles are all slain too,' he cried rudely. 'What will you say at the court of Mattanga when they ask you, "Where were you when the Daish Shaktay peasants killed those who supported you?" The courtiers will laugh in scorn and your ladies will be hiding in shame.' Up jumped Offlen, furious at this insult, hurriedly put on his metal breastplate and grabbed his sword. He ran down the stairs and saw that Danard's men were pressed on all sides, even though many of his own also lay dead in the forecourt. Nevertheless the intruders were starting to unbolt the main gate and he heard the cries of the main Daish Shaktay force, under Namoh, outside.

'By the Crocodile God! Am I too late?' Offlen cried wrathfully.

Danard was tired and his head was reeling; he had fought unceasingly for a long time and he turned and saw Duratman Offlen, large, strong and fresh, bearing down on him. Danard bounded towards his foe, wounding him grievously on the head, but Offlen's counter blow as he staggered was fatal. His heavy blade came down on the shoulder of Danard's sword arm and the most valiant warrior of Daish Shaktay fell dead, killed instantly. The remaining soldiers of the gallant three hundred tried to run out of the now open front gate, but Namoh, at the head of the incoming force, had seen his brother die.

'Will you leave Danard's body?' he shouted. 'Avenge his death to the last man!' and led his men in through the gates, at the same moment as Lee, who had been alongside Danard when he fell, turned on Offlen. Offlen, also wounded, was dazed with pride at having killed the most feared man in Daish Shaktay after Rajay Ghiry, but met his end at the hands of the youth from Sasrar, because Lee was a lethal swordsman.

The garrison fought on but gradually Namoh's men prevailed. When Offlen's troops saw there was no hope and no mercy was being shown to the ogrish soldiers, some even threw themselves over the cliff into the black pool far below. Lee ordered the last few survivors of the Mattanga garrison into the dungeons, where they found and released Ariani, Danard and Namoh's cousin. They did not tell her about Danard's death as yet.

'Go on, Lee,' said Namoh, tears for his brother streaking his blackened cheeks. 'There's the hay store. Let Rajay know the good part of the news.' Lee tried to suppress his own tears, went over to the hay and set it alight. Soon the flames leapt high into the night sky.

On the far hill, at Hermitage Fort, Rajay, Queen Jansy and I saw the fire as we stood anxiously waiting on the keep roof. This was to be the signal of victory.

'They've done it!' I cried.

'Danard is truly a tiger!' declared Rajay joyfully. He coughed and wheezed, pulled his blanket around him and wished he were there to see the two brothers' dirt covered, smiling faces.

Namoh returned to the mangled body of his brother. Some soldiers made a crude litter and placed the fallen hero on it, and on this simple bier Danard's body looked as noble as it had ever done in life, with his sword placed at his side. Namoh felt no elation, no triumph of success, only a dark vacuum where his heart had been. He could not force himself to leave the remains of his brother. It did not occur to him that Daish Shaktay was now free of its most dangerous foes, both those of Mattanga and the disloyal nobles within the country, because they were all dead in the yard of the fort. Rajay would rule the whole kingdom again, because there was no one else the ogre king could send against him now Offlen had been killed.

The vow was fulfilled. Namoh looked again at his brother's serene face, the lips slightly parted, as if he was about to tell some amusing tale which would bring yet another smile to the face of his friend, his king. As the soldiers made their way down from Tiger's Head Fort, the guns, manned by the men of Daish Shaktay once again, boomed out the victory and the drums rattled mournfully by the litter of the dead conqueror.

CHAPTER 5

POSITIVE DESTRUCTION

Lee rode on ahead to break the news to Rajay. It was past sunrise and he went straight into his room without even knocking. Rajay was sitting in meditation and turned to see who had come in. As soon as he saw Lee's face, he knew.

'Who?' he demanded.

'Danard. He was as brave as you'd have expected. It was instantaneous. I was fighting next to him and I'm sure there was no pain.'

Lee felt deep sorrow pouring out of Rajay's heart as he groaned in anguish and threw himself on his bed. As he did so, there was a clap of thunder, even though the sky was clear, and the ground shook.

Up at Gap Fort, where Moozand had his garrison of ogres and men of Mattanga, something equally traumatic happened. The town had been almost completely destroyed in the fighting some time earlier and all the inhabitants had gone elsewhere. These loyal Daish Shaktay citizens had no desire to be anywhere near the ogre's men, or to do business with them. Since Rajay had come back they were sure he would turn the Mattangans out again, so they were hiding in the villages. Gap Fort was built on the top of a hill and at the same moment that Lee broke the news to Rajay about Danard's death, the top of the hill exploded. This whole area of our world was volcanic, but no one suspected Gap Fort had been built on a dormant volcano. There was a violent explosion and the whole keep dissolved as ash, smoke and molten rock belched out and onto the surrounding countryside. The Mattanga garrison and everyone in the fort were killed. Moozand was not there, so he escaped. He was strongly opposed to Duratman Offlen's plans to foment a counter attack against Rajay and had taken to the hills for a week with his hunting hounds.

At High Plains Fort, the only other one still in the hands of the ogre peoples, a major earthquake rocked the region and the epicentre was exactly under the fort. As there were hollow limestone caverns underneath the whole fort collapsed into the ground and again many people were killed. Those who survived left for Mattanga; they had had enough of Daish Shaktay.

When Danard's body was brought to Hermitage Fort to be cremated with full military honours, Queen Jansy was deeply distressed. I had never seen her like this. For her, Danard had almost been a second son and her grief was, if possible, even greater than his real mother's. For seven days Rajay neither spoke nor smiled. He was taken back to Malak Citadel on a litter and his chest was again seriously weak. Everyone in the country mourned the passing of his oldest friend. Now four of Rajay's childhood companions had been lost: first Kalan, early in the guerrilla struggle, then Ekan, Varg-Nack and Danard - plus Valya had been wounded. Danard was gone, just as the full glory of victory was beginning to illuminate his beloved land.

On the seventh night of Rajay's mourning, Lee and I saw a light in his room, because we had all returned to Malak Citadel. Our hearts went out to him so we went up to his apartment. His door was open and he saw us hanging back in the passage outside.

'May we come in?' Lee asked. He nodded blankly. We sat respectfully on the floor and none of us said anything. Perhaps we had been too presumptuous to disturb him and I got up to leave.

'Any news from Ahren and Robin?' Rajay stopped me.

'A message came by the relay service this afternoon. The circus is ready and they're nearing Mattanga. They've put on one or two shows in smaller towns and their fame is spreading. The monkeys and the tigers are wonderfully cooperative, and Athlos's men have a brilliant acrobatic act, but the horses are the star attraction. Robin has got them doing some incredible turns.' Rajay brightened a little.

'I'm glad it's going so well. How long before the power of the horses manifests, do you think?'

'I don't know, but it will. We were told, many times, in Sasrar that their power is absolutely bound to work things out somehow,' asserted Lee.

'I wish it could have done so here, without Danard having had to be lost,' said Rajay sadly.

'I think that when they came here, their influence somehow forced Offlen to show his true and terrible self. Then, something had to be done, and forgive me for saying this,' Lee hesitated, 'but your grief over Danard's death is most probably what caused the volcanic eruption and that earthquake.'

'You've understood what it is to be a guardian. Quite spontaneously my inner self reverberated with the primordial heart centre so strongly that the Mother Earth couldn't bear my heartache, but it's too much when one after another my friends give their lives for me and Daish Shaktay.'

'I know it doesn't help at this point in time,' I said cautiously, 'but another thing we learnt in Sasrar is that a great soul like Danard will be reborn very soon. I apologise if I'm speaking out of place.'

'You're not; you're just helping me to face the truth. I know he'll be back, far more than you do,' Rajay smiled for the first time in a week. 'You two, give me vibrations to restore my inner joy, because I've got a country to run.

You shouldn't have felt uneasy about coming up here - I value your friendship so much.' We did as he asked and the next day he was his usual self again.

Although Rajay was still weak, he relished life once more, and if he continued to miss Danard bitterly, no one knew it. In many ways his death was like the stone in the pond that sets off the ripples right to its edges. Everyone noticed the exact correlation between the timing of the eruption, the earthquake and the news of his death being given to Rajay. Messengers were sent to the

towns and villages to tell the news of Danard's great victory and his noble end, and soon it was not only in Daish Shaktay that people knew the saga. All over the territories of the ogres: in Luker, Wattan, the lands north of Mattanga and the many islands in the Eastern Ocean under their domination, people were saying, 'That Danard was only a farmer's son, a partisan. If he could do the impossible, why not us?'

When Moozand returned from his hunting trip three days after the catastrophe he was horrified at what he saw - the still smoking volcano and no Gap Fort. He went to a nearby village and learnt that High Plains Fort had also been destroyed, Tiger's Head was lost and Offlen and his followers dead, so he decided to visit Rajay at Malak Citadel. Even though his father had turned into an ogre, Moozand had no traces of ogrishness in him, because his nature was not like that of the cruel rulers of Mattanga, and if the inner person was humane the outer body remained so too.

He arrived at Malak Citadel with a small entourage; his escorts were mostly his huntsmen, because the other Mattanga men were nearly all dead. Moozand was polite and humble towards Rajay and respectful towards Queen Jansy. Despite his reputation as a pleasure loving wastrel there was something sincere and likeable about his almost childlike nature. When he was alone with Rajay the reason for his visit emerged.

'Sire, by force of arms and the help of the powers that rule the elements, you have gained independence for your country. My sister Princess Zulani and I both worship your Goddess of Daish Shaktay and have both had our Trees of Life awakened. We understand that the worship of the Crocodile God, with its emphasis on human sacrifice and revenge, is such a perversion of religion that it must enrage the divine. Since my father's people began worshipping the Crocodile God they slowly became ogres. My sister and I know full well that my father has no right to lord it over this part of the world.'

Prince Moozand had been sitting at a safe distance from Rajay and two armed guards were standing at the door. Rajay did not comment on this speech, coming from someone who was supposed to be his enemy, but dismissed the guards and invited Prince Moozand to sit on his divan as he would a close friend.

'I'm not a fighting man like your brave Danard,' Moozand went on. 'I enjoy a thrilling chase through the forests after a boar or deer but I simply wasn't made to be a ruler of men. Please allow me to leave Daish Shaktay in peace. My father may easily kill me, but I'm going back to Mattanga to advise him and his people to leave this continent and return to the islands where they came from.'

'Do you think I'd have you sitting here beside me, with no guard in the room, if I intended to give you a hard time? Your wish is granted. Also, my friend Namoh will take you to look at some of our fine horses, so you can select one as a gift. I would take you myself, but my health is not good at present.'

Namoh took Moozand around Rajay's stud farm down in the valley. They chose carefully, because Rajay told Namoh to give Moozand a strong, sure-footed horse for hunting wild animals. They selected a snorting young stallion, who soon succumbed to the lure of caked sugar. Then they went on to the kennels, where they discussed the breeding of hounds. Rajay loved dogs and had some large ones at the Citadel - watchdogs, which had been trained by Ekan. Moozand politely hinted to Namoh that his hounds were of a finer variety than Rajay's and he would send some puppies to improve Rajay's stock. Once everyone at Malak Citadel had overcome their initial revulsion towards him as King Karlvid's son, Rajay's friends found his simple nature irresistible. After he left Rajay was more pragmatic.

'Danard has won Daish Shaktay for us.'

When Moozand left for Mattanga the following week, he sent Rajay the promised puppies - a whole clutch of them, with a letter saying that Rajay could also keep the dog handler. He had been taken in some battle and although he was outstandingly good with animals he had suffered from a head injury and had lost his memory of anything prior to his capture. He had reddish hair and the coppery tinted skin of the people from the northeast of the continent, but spoke with the accent of Daish Shaktay and had threatened to kill himself when told Prince Moozand was taking him back to Mattanga, so Moozand, a kind soul, left him behind with the puppies.

Rajay was curious to meet this fellow and sent a servant to fetch him. The servant was new to the Citadel and as he and the dog handler were crossing the yard, some of Rajay's watchdogs saw the newcomer. They bounded up to him and gave him such a welcome that the unfortunate man was bowled over and hit his head quite a crack as he fell. He lay on the ground for some moments and was very dazed when he sat up.

'Where am I?' he said, in a puzzled tone of voice as the servant helped him to his feet.

'You all right? Come on, the king is waiting.'

'This is Malak Citadel. Is Rajay here? It's so long since I saw him.'

'You'd best address him as Your Majesty when you meet him. You're nothing but a kennel hand. Only his friends call him Rajay.'

'But Rajay *is* my friend - he and Danard and the others.'

'Listen,' added the servant brusquely, 'I don't think you know who you are. They said you'd had a bad knock on the head. Do yourself a favour - keep quiet and only speak when you're spoken to. His Majesty is a great and patient man, but there are limits to anyone's tolerance, even his. Don't mention Captain Danard. He's dead; killed in action and it almost broke our king's heart.'

The dog handler put his hand to his head, perplexed and disappointed. He pushed the hounds away, because they continued to welcome him unsparingly, and followed the servant into the main building.

'You wait here,' commanded the servant as they reached the door of Rajay's living room. 'Brush the dust off your clothes. You look like a vagrant.' The servant went in to Rajay, who was working with Lee and Namoh.

'With respect, sire, the man who brought the puppies is a bit mad. Says he's a friend of yours. He might suddenly turn violent or something. Are you sure you want to meet him?'

'Yes, I feel I should. Namoh, go and get him. He might be nervous - try and put him at his ease.'

Namoh went out and saw the man looking at his reflection in a mirror in the hallway, tidying his hair. He didn't see Namoh, who quickly returned.

'What's the matter? You look as if you've seen a ghost,' joked Lee as Namoh came in.

'I have,' murmured Namoh, stunned. 'It's Ekan!' Rajay went out, Ekan turned and they embraced each other warmly.

'What happened?' said Ekan. 'I fell over in the yard and my head is so painful, but before that, I don't know. I'm so befuddled.'

'Come in. I can't believe it's really you!' beamed Rajay. 'This is miraculous!' Ekan also embraced Namoh warmly and sat with Rajay on his divan, much to the amazement of the servant. Slowly the mystery was pieced together. Ekan had been taken as a prisoner to Mattanga, despite his wounds. However he had lost his memory and only remembered how to train dogs, which he did very well, so was sold as a slave to a high ranking official, who in turn sold him to Moozand. When Moozand brought him to Daish Shaktay he vaguely recollected having been there before.

Dr Belsanto was summoned and said he couldn't do much but suggested we gave Ekan spiritual healing. By now the doctor had seen so many good things happen when we used the vibrations that he recommended all his patients to do this after he had looked after the physical side of their ailments. After some days of the best we could offer him, Ekan became almost normal again and the watchdogs were given large marrowbones as a reward.

CHAPTER 6

THE CIRCUS OF DOOM

Robin, Ahren and the other members of the circus reached the outskirts of Mattanga. Already rumours had preceded them and they gained permission to have a procession through the streets to advertise the show. First went the small and raucous band, made up of some of Luth's men. They were also acrobats and led some of the more monkeyish looking inhabitants of Luth's home city of Vandargar, who were pretending to be performing monkeys. They were followed by the tigers, nobly imprisoned in cages on bullock carts. They gave the odd snarl, but mostly slept through this humiliating experience. Finally came Robin and Ahren riding their magnificent flying horses, followed by the other two. Robin had insisted that Ahren disguise himself and yet again he had bleached his face and dyed his hair.

There were a number of bloodthirsty spectator sports practised in Mattanga, such as bullfighting, so it was easy to rent a building for the circus which would keep the audience safe from the tigers should they run amuck. They took an amphitheatre which had lodgings and animal houses attached, so everyone could stay together. Luth's local cell arranged the publicity: a town crier was hired, advertisements were placed in the paper and posters stuck all over town.

The opening day was a sell out. There were nobles and their ladies in the expensive seats in the shade and various other levels of society, as their pockets allowed, took the other seats, right down to the vast underclass of Mattanga who sat high up in the sun. The intention was not to make money, but Robin said that if people were allowed in for nothing it would look suspicious. The rates were low enough to draw the masses, but high enough to look genuine.

First the band played stirring music loudly and slightly out of tune, to rouse the audience. The first act was a clown show with the monkeys as clowns - very popular with the children. The second act was Athlos's lithe, rubbery and incredibly strong troupe. They did an acrobatic act worthy of professionals who had been at it all their lives, then demonstrated some scary knife throwing and many of the ladies cried in shock as the lethal knives narrowly missed the men's bodies and hit the wooden board behind them. Ahren decided he'd got it easy compared to Athlos's men.

After this it was back to the monkeys again, who doubled as jugglers and even did amazing feats of juggling while on a tightrope. The monkeys also did an act of 'intelligence' proving they could read and even write - some letters and short words in the sand. This was no problem for them; although they looked very monkeyish they had the same intelligence as humans. In many cases they were much wiser because they were not so aggressive and self-destructive. However the audience didn't know this and were suitably impressed.

Soon it was time for the intermission, with refreshments and cooling drinks laid on by another cell of Luth's men posing as vendors. The food and drink had been supercharged with vibrations. This was done by a person who had an awakened Tree of Life making a number of bandhans over the food or drink, until it radiated coolness. If the person who ate the food was positive, they would like it very much and it would help their physical health and spiritual growth. If they were very negative it might not have that effect. Still, as Robin had said earlier, 'Try anything, because there must be some good people here, hidden away among the ogrish ones.'

After the intermission came the tigers. Ahren was the tiger trainer and most of them were old friends of his. He had a whip for show, but was actually controlling them with his voice, his attention and his Sasrar key. He hoped they wouldn't decide to mischievously do away with a few ogres in the audience while his back was turned, but they played the game perfectly.

They stood on their hind legs, put up their paws when asked, followed Ahren when he ordered them to and knelt before him. They played ball with him, caught a large red ball in their fore paws and even threw it to one another. When he put his fingers up they would swish their tails the required number of times: two fingers two swishes and so on. As a finale he asked one large tiger to come up to him and open its mouth, and he put his head inside it, looking as if he was inviting a quick and nasty death. The tiger knew what it had to do and afterwards Ahren stroked its ears in thanks. The applause was tremendous.

The last act was the flying horses. Robin entered the arena first, on his powerful and faithful steed Yamun. The shining white animal walked into the arena, unfurled its golden wings and snorted through its nostrils as it looked at the assembled audience. Robin patted him and asked him to fly up to the height of the top of the highest seats, where he hovered. Two other horses, Tama and Misippa, came in and also took off and hovered above the audience. Robin took some apples out of his pockets and threw them at the two riderless horses, who caught them in their mouths. He had Yamun pretend to play a game of tag and catch me if you can with the other two for a short while and at one moment Robin fell off Yamun. This was part of the act and as he fell Tama caught him in mid air by flying underneath Yamun at exactly the right moment, so Robin fell neatly onto her back. She dipped as he fell on her but then slowly rose again.

The three horses landed and Ahren appeared on his horse, Zamba. He had his bow and a quiver of arrows on his back. One of the acrobats came into the arena and with a large catapult shot more apples up into the sky, but this time Ahren shot them in half with his superbly aimed arrows, sitting on his flying horse as it hovered above the audience. Next he stood up on his flying horse and did the same thing standing on its back, with the ground quite far below. More ooh's and aah's from the crowd, because if he had fallen off that would have been the end of him.

Finally Ahren and Robin both flew into the sky on their horses and again stood on their backs while they dived and swooped. What the audience didn't know was that the horses could feel whenever their riders slightly lost their balance, and moved to compensate and put them right again. It looked awe-inspiring from the ground and the applause was deafening.

Later, Robin and Ahren thanked everyone profusely who had been in the show. All the humans and monkeys were asked to make a bandhan of request that they might somehow get an invitation to perform in front of the court, because that was where the worst ogres were, and that was where the horses needed to be seen and put their feet, and hopefully activate the power of positive destruction.

The next day Robin and Ahren went for a walk and found a stylish little eating-house owned by a man from Chussan. They avoided the Mattangan eating-houses because they had been warned to be careful of the menu - Mattangans ate dogs, cats, snakes and all sorts of meat most people didn't touch. This place had just the sort of food they both liked, and Robin sent a boy who worked there back to the arena to tell Luth's men to come and join them. They had made an embarrassingly large amount of money on the previous evening, so decided to get rid of some of it by taking everyone out for a good meal. When the men arrived, with them were two ladies, veils modestly covering their faces. Ahren and Robin noticed heavy gold bangles on their wrists, and the enormous jewels in their rings said 'money' and 'status' in no uncertain terms.

'Please join us,' Robin invited them, standing up.

'Thank you. We mustn't stay too long,' replied one.

'Could we talk somewhere more private?' said the other.

Robin asked the proprietor if there was a room where they could be alone and the four of them were shown into a small parlour. He ordered cooling drinks all round, the owner closed the door behind them and went to get the order. The ladies pushed back their veils, revealing themselves as polished and elegant. They were both young, had the soft skins, elaborately dressed hair and carefully applied make up of people who led a life of ease. The first to have spoken had coppery-brown hair, strong features and a coppery hue to her skin. The second had deep reddish-blonde hair, a pale honey skin, dark blue eyes, delicate features and a soft, musical voice.

'How may we be of service to you?' inquired Robin politely as they sat down. In answer the blonde lady started to make a bandhan of request on her hand.

'We saw your performance. It was brilliant.' She went on making the bandhan as Robin and Ahren watched, curious. 'We came to see you because we felt your subtle selves. They're excellent, and your animals - incredible! Who are you?'

This was not what Robin and Ahren expected within a few days of arriving in the enemy's capital. The vibrations of the ladies weren't totally cool, but they had certainly received their awakening.

'May I ask how you got your Trees of Life awakened?' Robin asked. 'I can feel your vibrations and although you do have some problems, which, I hope you don't mind my saying, is hardly surprising if you live in Mattanga, we're all on more or less the same level of awareness.'

'My name is Clary of Wattan,' said the chestnut haired lady. 'I was the fiancée of Sarn Lionheart, the son of Vittorio Lionheart. Sarn has disappeared, but before he did, he had his awakening from some people from Daish Shaktay. I had mine from a friend - she was captured by Rajay Ghiry's soldiers near Port Volcan.' Ahren prayed Sagara Samudra would not recognise him if she saw him disguised with mid brown hair and a bleached skin.

'Who were the people from Daish Shaktay?' said Robin.

'Quite important,' replied the blonde lady. Robin had more sense than to pry further.

'Could you get us an invitation to perform in front of the court?' Ahren asked, ever optimistic.

'Yes, I'm sure that could be arranged, but don't tell anyone you met me and don't react if you see me at the show. You didn't answer my question. Who are you and what are you doing here?'

'We're from Chussan and we're doing something which will help anyone who has an awakened Tree of Life,' explained Robin.

That evening a formal invitation arrived: a command to perform in front of His Excellency King Karlvid and his courtiers, in the palace amphitheatre, two days hence. The next evening a messenger arrived and asked if the lady they met the day before could talk to them again at the eating-house, at midnight.

'Come in,' said the blonde lady, alone this time, but outside the door were two ferocious looking bodyguards with drawn swords.

'Good evening, Madam,' Robin began courteously. 'Thank you for arranging the invitation. How did you manage it, if I may ask?'

'The king is my father, but whatever my relationship with him, my heart is given to the cause of freeing Daish Shaktay and helping Rajay Ghiry in any way I can. I heard he has indeed won his independence, with the help of the

Mother Earth herself.'

'We heard the same thing,' replied Robin blandly, as if this was mere small talk.

'Is it safe for you to be here, talking to us like this, Your Highness?' said Ahren.

'Yes and no. I have my bodyguards outside the door, and more in the street, but my father would be furious if he knew I was out this late at night and in such a lowly part of the city. We court ladies keep away from the common people and don't usually appear in public, especially alone with men. However, I get the feeling you're not quite what you seem?'

'Your Highness,' Robin assured her, 'we're both very ordinary. Please believe me when I say we're doing something to help all the good people in this world.'

'I do believe you and that's why I'm here. My father wants to capture your flying horses tomorrow. He'll arrange for you to be killed. His men will do it when you take a final bow in front of him, to accept the gold he'll offer you. He's assuming that unlike Rajay Ghiry, you *will* bow down before him,' she smiled, remembering that fateful day when she had been so impressed by Rajay's forthright behaviour.

'Thank you, Your Highness, for that extremely important information. It wouldn't be in your father's interest to harm those horses,' advised Robin.

'My father has done a great many things recently which have not been in his interest, but that's no affair of mine. He's no longer human so I feel no allegiance to him any more. I must leave now. I hope we meet again one day in a situation where we can be more open with each other.'

'Don't forget to put on a bandhan of protection before you leave.' They were members of a very exclusive club.

'I will. Good luck, and if you manage to escape, and happen to see Sarn Lionheart on your travels, tell him Clary is waiting for him. He could have trusted her and told her what he was doing. She was pretty cut up when he took off like that, until I had her ask a number of questions on the vibrations.'

'The vibrations always tell the truth. Sometimes we hide that from those who matter to us, to protect them.'

'The net is closing in around us,' she said nervously. 'My father has already murdered some members of our family who've displeased him. He's quite capable of doing so again. Do you know anyone in Daish Shaktay who could help us, if my father discovers Clary and I have changed sides, and have to flee?'

'Yes, maybe,' Robin was silent for a few moments, as if thinking. 'She's called Asha Herbhealer. She lives at Malak Citadel. Give her this ring, or if she's not around, get it to King Rajay. They both know it well.' Robin took my ruby and sapphire ring off the chain around his neck and gave it to the princess. 'And if you do have to escape, there's a man working in your father's kitchens, called Vern. He's in the service of King Rajay's spiritual master Luth and he'll arrange for some partisans to escort you. Show him the ring.'

'Thank you. Thank you a million times. Now we understand each other better. Goodbye,' she stood up and left.

'Neither Asha nor Rajay are going to be too pleased when they find out you've given that ring to Karlvid's daughter,' Ahren observed, after she had gone.

'I know it looked a bit odd, but I checked everything I said and did on the vibrations,' Robin assured Ahren.

'OK, but what do you make of her warning?'

'She's given us information to save our lives. Give me time to think it through, and you try and have some brainwaves. Between us we'll come up with something.'

They laid their plans carefully and the circus made its way to the royal palace as if no one suspected anything. The private amphitheatre was as packed as the public one had been, because it was known that the performance in front of the king and court was going to be tremendous. The music was even more stirring and the flying horses appeared at the beginning in a procession round the amphitheatre, their hooves stamping the ground proudly and, Robin knew, angrily. With his intense sensitivity, he felt the Mother Earth and the powers within the primordial Tree of Life starting to react, as if she was finally shuddering in pain at the evil of the ogre peoples and was soon going to do something about it.

The acrobatic act and monkey's turns were even better than before and the knife throwing performance was even more hair-raising. After the band had played and Luth's men had done their turn, they bowed and left. They didn't just leave the amphitheatre, they left the palace and reverted back to half clad monks with begging bowls, skulking in the shadows of the temples, and later made their way in ones and twos out of the city towards the hills to the west. This time the refreshments had been given out by the staff of the palace and Robin had bribed them heavily to make the interval last as long as possible. By the end of the intermission the band and the acrobatic troupe had ceased to exist.

Next came Ahren and his tigers. He was wearing a striking red satin coat, which set off his carrot coloured wig and covered his already dyed brown hair. He looked suitably eccentric as he risked his life, so the onlookers thought, even though the spectators were in far more danger than the tiger trainer, if they did but know it. Princess Zulani was sitting with her friends Clary and Sagara.

'It's him!' whispered Sagara when she saw Ahren, looking unmistakably Ahrenish with his snub nose, despite his disguise.

'Who?' replied Zulani, sitting next to her.

'The tiger trainer - he's one of the boys who awakened my Tree of Life when I was captured near Port Volcan.'

'Whatever are they doing here?' Zulani fingered my ring, which she was wearing under her clothes on a chain. 'Let's watch, this looks as if it's going to be good. I've got a feeling these tigers aren't quite what they seem either.' She had heard stories of the guardian tigers of Daish Shaktay and began to put the pieces together, but said nothing to her friends. She was highly intelligent, had been brought up to court intrigue and statecraft, and knew when to be discreet.

This time Ahren rode one of the tigers as well and it gave a few snarls to make it appear more scary. It was snarling at the horrible vibrations emitted by the king and those near him, and Ahren had to stroke it gently on the shoulder to stop it bounding at the king and ripping him to bits. His act finished amid tumultuous clapping - partly because he was still alive to accept it, and he signalled to the tigers to leave the arena. They went back to their cage, but only until all attention was on the flying horses, because the cage guard was a member of Luth's order who worked in the palace, and he soon opened it to let the tigers out.

The monkeys jumped onto their backs and they bounded across the pleasure gardens, scattering terrified tame deer, and made their way down to the nearby river where they swam across and clambered out onto the park at the other side. None of the 'sacred' crocodiles in the river dared approach these fearful, spiritually powerful creatures, who guarded the monkeys as they swam. They ran through more pleasure gardens surrounding nobles' palaces, out of town and inland, back to the mountains of Daish Shaktay and Luth, far away in his hermitage.

In the amphitheatre it was the turn of Robin, Ahren and the flying horses. They gave a stupendous performance then briefly dismounted and Robin gave Yamun, his horse, a silver apple with golden designs on it. The horse took the silver stalk in its teeth.

'Go and present this to His Esteemed Highness,' said Robin in a loud voice. The horse took off, hovered above the royal enclosure half way up the side of the amphitheatre and placed it in the lap of the amazed King Karlvid. These horses could levitate as well as fly, which astonished everyone in the audience. The horse even allowed himself to be patted after presenting the apple, but Robin could see him shudder from the negative feeling Karlvid emitted. 'Yes,' Robin thought with a rush of adrenalin, 'that should do it.'

Then the finale: Robin and Ahren had the horses fly higher, while they stood on their backs, and they turned and swooped as the two young men balanced precariously. King Karlvid clutched the silver apple. His spies who had watched the rehearsal in the afternoon told him that after this, the two on the flying horses would land, dismount and bow before him. They would then, as had been promised, accept a large amount of gold and jewels. At that moment the men who were presenting the treasure would kill Robin and Ahren. Others would grab the horses and put ropes over their backs and wings to stop them flying off.

However, at a signal from Robin, instead of flying down to the arena, he and Ahren dropped onto their usual sitting position on the hovering horses, and before anyone had grasped what was happening, all four flew higher and higher, and their great golden wings carried them to safety.

By the next morning the horses, seen by many as they flew through the night skies above Mattan Province, reached some uninhabited hills to the south of Nardy. The exhausted riders almost fell off the utterly spent animals in a forest clearing and they all drank from a stream. Ahren noticed the horses were standing with their feet in it after they had finished drinking.

'That's a sensible idea,' he looked at them. 'The vibrations of Mattanga were so awful, I feel ill. I'm going to put my feet in the stream too, and ask the water element to draw out the negativity I picked up, especially last night.'

Robin and Ahren soaked their feet in the water along with the horses. After some time Ahren put his attention on his hands. 'My hands and fingers are cool again so I guess I've washed off the inner dirt of Mattanga. I wonder how Clary and that princess manage there now they're aware on the subtle level.'

'Perhaps they don't,' said Robin. 'That's why I gave her that ring, to help her get to Asha or King Rajay.'

'I wonder what her name was.'

'Princess Zulani. I asked around - carefully, so as not to betray her. Apparently she kept delaying Karlvid from murdering King Rajay when he was a prisoner there.'

'She's quite some lady, even though she's so young. She reminds me of Asha – the same way of doing things you'd never expect of a girl, but somehow she gets away with it. It's a pity we couldn't have rescued her and her friend; because they deserve to come to Daish Shaktay.'

'Let's make a bandhan that something works out for them,' suggested Robin, and they both did so.

'It's really cool! Let's hope that ring does the trick.' They were now sitting by the stream relaxing on the grass. 'Hey, we forgot to bring anything to eat.'

'I've got some crusts in my shoulder bag; they were for the horses,' Robin gave Ahren some and they munched the stale bread. 'Let's sleep a bit, and then we'll go and shoot some game. We've got our bows and arrows, and our knives, and I always have my firebox in my pocket. We'll live off the land for a day or two.' Robin lay on his back and stroked his horse, which came to nuzzle him.

'I'm looking forward to telling Rajay how easy it was.'

'We don't yet know what's going to happen as a result.'

Robin was apprehensive about my ring. He was extremely honest, and by giving it away knew he had abused my trust and possibly got me into deep trouble with the King of Daish Shaktay. The astrologers had told Robin that despite his youth, Rajay Ghiry was one of the senior guardians of Navi Septa, and he did not want to start off their relationship on the wrong foot.

'It'll take about two days to get to Malak Citadel,' Ahren yawned and went to sleep, relaxed as a baby. Robin considered what Ahren had said about Lady Clary and Princess Zulani – knowing he had a way of getting right to the truth of the matter, often unintentionally.

CHAPTER 7

NAMOH AND LEE, AHREN AND ROBIN

Namoh and Lee sat in the shade of the orange grove outside the walls of Malak Citadel, a few days after Moozand had paid his visit.

'Let's ask Rajay,' began Namoh, 'whether we can take the Northern Regiment and try and recover those forts he had to win for Mattanga with Lionheart. Will you come with me if he agrees?'

'Of course, if he does,' replied Lee doubtfully. As Danard had been killed taking Tiger's Head Fort, Lee reckoned that Rajay might not want his brother risking the same fate so soon after. Namoh picked this up.

'If Danard could take Tiger's Head, then by the Grace of the Goddess, we should be able to succeed north of the Shaktay River.'

They asked Rajay and he agreed, with the proviso that they should try to negotiate with the lords of the forts, and to be sure to avoid bloodshed if possible, being as he wanted these forts and the people in them as allies and loyal subjects, not bitter defeated enemies. Lee and Namoh gave their word, set off with Rajay's blessings and went first to Bart Charval's home. Bart invested all the money he made fighting and serving Rajay in land and had recently bought some with a disused fort on it, to convert into a comfortable home for his wife Kanta, their growing family and their ever more numerous staff. Bart was already well on the way to achieving Rajay's aims. Through the use of diplomacy and a considerable amount of gold that Rajay had given him for bribery, he had managed to get oaths of allegiance from the commanders of two of the four forts which Rajay and Vittorio Lionheart had captured.

Lord Chandan of Jewelton refused to cooperate and was determined to remain independent. This was formerly the northern frontier town of Daish Shaktay and Rajay intended it should be again, because then he could keep the high road safe for traders, travellers and people trying to get to Sasrar. Lord Chandan had recently taken to taxing Daish Shaktay merchants using the high road very heavily, which gave Namoh a good reason to retake the town and surrounding lands. Bart called in the help of his local troop and Count Zaminder also sent four hundred soldiers on horses with his son Bukku.

Namoh and his regiment settled in to besiege Jewelton before Bart and Bukku's men arrived, and the sentries on the walls reported the force was not that large. Lord Chandan decided to ride out and defeat the Daish Shaktay troops, being as he had done so before. He led his small but competent army, but as he did, Bart and Bukku Zaminder appeared and turned the battle in Namoh's favour.

Lord Chandan was brave, but his years told on him and he died, as much from heart failure as anything else. Namoh prepared to enter the town, only to find another force come out against them led by Chandan's wife, determined to avenge her husband. She fought like a cornered tigress and only when surrounded by at least twenty soldiers of the Northern Regiment would she surrender. She was much younger than her husband and a very beautiful woman, as well as being fearless.

Namoh, Lee, Bukku and Bart were elsewhere on the field when she was captured and taken to a tent where the soldiers mocked her, making her entertain them like a dancing girl. They laid their razor-sharp swords edgewise on the floor and made her dance between them barefoot. If she stopped they promised worse for her and if she stumbled on a sword her wounds would be cruel. Lee heard coarse laughter and came into the tent when Lady Chandan was about to drop from exhaustion.

'Stop this at once!' roared Lee.

'Isn't this a pretty punishment for daring to oppose us?' jeered one man.

The soldier who had made her dance was taken to Namoh's tent, along with Lady Chandan. Lee had her wait outside with a guard while he dealt with the soldier.

'What possessed you to treat such a brave lady in such a shocking manner?' demanded Lee in despair.

'We defeated her, so why not have some fun and make her pay a little for her arrogance?'

'Haven't you heard of the Goddess of Daish Shaktay and don't you believe that all virtuous women are made in her image?'

'I'm not too bothered about that sort of thing.'

'Don't you know King Rajay's policy towards women? Every single one is to be treated like his mother or sister.'

'I've heard it, but surely it's only talk.'

'Don't you know that any soldier found with a woman in his tent on campaign is instantly court martialled?'

'This is different.'

'You're a disgrace to our cause.'

At this point Namoh came in and took over: 'If I were the king I'd punish you heavily right now, but I'm only his commander, so you'll explain your

288

behaviour in front of His Majesty when we get home, and meanwhile you'll be a prisoner.'

Next he called Lady Chandan in. She wondered bleakly what her fate would be in front of Namoh, if the others had used her so badly.

'Madam, I have something to ask of you,' he pleaded.

'Go ahead - I'm helpless,' she replied glumly.

'Lady Chandan, on behalf of my king I want to ask your forgiveness and beg you to accept my sincere apology for what happened just now. As I was elsewhere I wasn't able to see that my men treated you with dignity, as befits your station. I'd like to recommend to King Rajay that you become the Mayoress of Jewelton, now it's going to be part of Daish Shaktay again. Your town will prosper greatly when you join us.'

Lady Chandan, who was little older than Namoh, burst into tears, then composed herself somewhat and answered, between sobs. 'I came before you with hatred in my heart, but now I understand your king and how he has made all his commanders as honourable as him. I realise that my people will be much better off if we have the protection of a strong king and a larger nation state.'

Lee and Namoh's sense of chivalry had achieved what two battles had failed to do. They had got the cooperation of the ruler of Jewelton, so the town could again be the northern frontier outpost of Daish Shaktay. Lady Chandan knelt before Namoh and her thick, curly brown hair, which had come loose during the enforced dancing, tumbled on the ground. He was embarrassed and told her to get up; he knew Rajay did not encourage this sort of subservient behaviour.

At Malak Citadel there was much excitement as one evening Robin, Ahren and the four flying horses landed in the yard of the fort. The watchdogs barked loudly and the men-at-arms ran up, but relaxed when they saw Ahren. Saber Rizen, Amber's husband, happened to be on duty.

'I don't know what you'll get up to next!' he slapped Ahren on the back as he dismounted. 'These animals are unbelievable! Good to see you! Was it a success?'

'Yes I think so,' said Ahren cautiously. He wasn't sure how much Saber knew about their project in Mattanga. 'This is Robin, my friend from the north.'

'Pleased to meet you,' Saber greeted Robin. 'His Majesty and Asha will want to see you both as soon as possible.'

'Thank you, but where can we put the horses?' asked Robin.

'There are some elephant stables in the fort,' Saber looked at the horses' enormous wings, which they had not yet folded up. 'They'll do for the night and then tomorrow the horse farm is the best place.'

I was at that moment serving supper to Rajay and Queen Jansy. The guard on duty announced Ahren, Saber and Robin, and Rajay stood up to welcome them. The broad smiles on Robin and Ahren's faces said it all as they walked in the door. Ahren went up to Queen Jansy and greeted her respectfully, then introduced Robin to Rajay.

'So, you're the new member of our team,' Rajay gave Robin a knowing look and he smiled, well aware of which team Rajay was referring to.

289

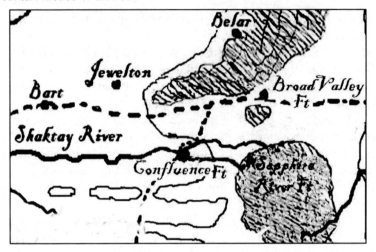

'You've arrived just in time for supper,' the queen invited them. 'Asha, tell the servants to bring more food.'

'What news from Mattanga?' began Rajay.

'It was a wonderful circus,' said Ahren.

'You were the star turn, Ahren,' added Robin modestly.

'And? You didn't risk your lives solely to amuse Karlvid. We all know that,' laughed Rajay.

'It's difficult to say, Your Majesty,' Robin continued, 'but if my experience is anything to go by, within a couple of weeks the power of positive destruction will start to show itself....'

They told the whole story – well, not quite the whole story. Later Robin wanted to check on the horses, so Ahren and I went too. Not only had Saber made sure they had been given the best of everything, but had also posted two guards near their stalls, because he realised the enormous value of these animals. Afterwards we three, Ahren, Robin and I, sat outside on a stone bench and one of the sentries came over.

''Evening, Miss Asha. Mr Ahren, good to see you back safely. Everything all right in the elephant stables, sir?' he asked Robin.

'Yes, fine.'

'Us guards are looking forward to seeing your flying horses. I'd never believe it was possible for horses to have wings.'

'I'll take them out exercising tomorrow, and you can see them then, but they need to rest now.'

'Quite so, sir,' and he went on round the yard.

'You and Ahren might have solved Rajay's whole problem with the help of the flying horses,' I congratulated them.

'Here's your ring,' said Ahren, taking my gold four petalled one off the chain with the Sasrar key on it which was around his neck. He returned it to me. 'It certainly brought us luck!' I looked at Robin, expecting him to give me back the other one.

'I must ask your forgiveness for something,' he looked at me uncertainly. 'Your ring ...'

'What happened?' I thought he was going to say it had got lost.

'I had to lend it to someone.'

'Who?'

'A very brave lady, the youngest daughter of King Karlvid.'

'But Robin, she's the enemy! That ring was given to me by the king of this country and he's the bitter enemy of Karlvid. What's Rajay going to say when he finds out? I told him I'd lent it to you and he was fine with that, but....I trusted you with that ring.' I was mortified. I couldn't believe this of Robin. I got up and began walking across the yard, tears in my eyes. It wasn't the ring; it was the fact that he could casually give such a precious gift to the enemy.

'Please, listen,' Robin came running after me. 'I had to lend Princess Zulani that ring. Are you aware that she saved King Rajay's life?' I stopped walking and looked at him. 'Furthermore, she saved Ahren's and mine by warning us how Karlvid planned to murder us. Plus, she did so at considerable risk to herself.'

'Look, I stay with Saber and Amber. Let's go there and you can tell me everything. Ahren, you come too.' I was still uneasy, but realised that if one involved oneself with people like Robin and Rajay, none of the normal rules applied. Detachment and trust were the only way to relate to people like them, who thought and acted for the collective good, or for others, and never just for themselves.

Amber insisted Robin stay with us; I got a room ready and Amber lent him some of her husband's clothes, then Robin told us more about Zulani and Clary. Gradually I softened and he was relieved. We had always got on well and had a great deal of respect for one another. Later Saber came back, and Amber and I left him, Ahren and Robin well after midnight, talking guerrilla warfare and the training of flying horses. By that time I was looking forward to meeting Princess Zulani and hoped she would make it to Malak Citadel, preferably with my ring. However I understood why Robin had given it to her.

Soon it was common knowledge that some extraordinary animals had arrived. Robin was much in demand showing them to everyone in the district, which he did by taking them for flying exercise. He and Rajay related to each other as if they had known each other for ever and the many meditation groups in the area all wanted Robin's deep wisdom about the Tree of Life, because he was much more experienced than Ahren, Lee or me.

Meanwhile, up north, Namoh and Lee, with a cavalry force, pressed on to the last fort which Rajay wanted back as part of Daish Shaktay. This was Broad Valley Fort, dominating the pass that carried the high road from the centre of the continent to Mattanga. A message came from Luth's men in Mattanga that the ogre king himself, in a last attempt to reconquer Daish Shaktay, was going to invade it. He and his army would come via Broad Valley Pass, because the fort there was manned by his vassal. Luth's men also reported that he was unwell and looked even more like a crocodile.

Namoh and Lee advanced towards this fort as fast as possible, because they wanted to regain it before King Karlvid could reach there. Namoh sent a letter to the commander with an offer to either surrender or become an ally of Daish Shaktay. He knew that if he could gain control of it before King Karlvid arrived he would have a good chance of holding the pass. The commander of this fort had heard about the chaos in Mattanga and the victories of Rajay, and, like the Lionheart family, wanted to dissociate himself from the Mattanga Empire. Consequently he was only too happy to surrender, especially when Namoh explained that there would be a good chance of his continuing to be commander, as long as he helped outwit King Karlvid and his approaching army.

Namoh's intuition was right, because the following morning Karlvid's army was espied in the distance, coming up the pass through the mountains from Mattanga. He quickly made his plans and then, almost at the same time, a lookout on the back watch tower noticed another force coming from the west - it was Commander Odain, who had hurried from Confluence Fort with another two thousand men, because he had fortunately also received the report that Karlvid was on the way. A messenger galloped out and told Commander Odain what was going on. Namoh left the red and black flag with the bleeding skull, the Mattanga standard, flying on the fort's flagstaff, and as the army of the ogres and men came closer they saw what they thought were the sentries of their vassal on the walls, but the gates were closed even though it was only afternoon.

'Open the gates!' asked the envoy from Karlvid.

'We have a fatal fever here. You can't come in; go and camp down by the river, because there's water there,' replied the sentry.

'We also have many people with a strange new fever.'

'Describe it; maybe we have the same,' continued the sentry, a faithful man of Namoh's bodyguard.

'It started after a travelling circus visited Mattanga. Many who are transformed worshippers of the Crocodile God, that some call ogres, and people who sympathise with them get it. They shrivel and die, but before they do they look like the bleeding skull on the standard. It's terrible.' What he didn't say was that Karlvid and half the army had it.

'We can't let you in. Our fever is different, and if we do we might catch each other's diseases.'

So the army, with its rich baggage train, artillery, elephants, horses and all the remaining gold that Karlvid could lay his hands on - to reward his followers when Rajay Ghiry was dead at his feet - made off towards the forest and the river. As soon as they were out of sight of the fort, the front and back gates were flung open and out poured the Daish Shaktay cavalry, led by Namoh, Lee and Bart.

They attacked the rear and Commander Odain, hidden in the forest, prevented any of the Mattanga forces from reaching the much-needed water. The soldiers of Mattanga had shining armour and rich uniforms, but many were sick and dying. Although a few ogres had begun showing symptoms of the disease before the army left Mattanga, no one then realised how serious it was. Karlvid was the first person to have contracted it, but he was strong and had a great will to live. Many of the Mattanga soldiers hardly had the energy to draw their swords or shoot their arrows or guns at the soldiers concealed in the trees at each side of the track down to the river. Odain had not allowed any of his men to open fire until all the Mattanga troops were inside the wood.

Those who were still alive when they reached the valley where the river flowed met a fierce cavalry under Bukku Zaminder, who had also come to help. Within a short time Karlvid, himself wounded, summoned those who remained alive and intended to flee back to Mattanga, but suddenly he collapsed and the disease finally killed him, there in the forest. The rest of the Mattanga army took to their heels, their baggage abandoned, and Namoh ordered his soldiers to let them go.

Most of the spoils were taken to Malak Citadel by Lee and Namoh. A generous portion was allotted to Bukku, for his father Count Zaminder, to make up for the heavy tribute he had been forced to pay for years, and enough gold was given to Bart to rebuild his fort in fine style and reward his fellow farmers who had fought alongside him. The disease had got a name: Silver Apple Fever, because anyone who touched that fatal but beautiful silver apple which had been presented to the king at the circus and had any ogrish tendencies caught the fever and passed it on to others.

When Namoh and Lee returned to Malak Citadel, Rajay congratulated them publicly and then asked to see them alone.

'Did you carry out my instructions to the letter, not to kill any more people than was absolutely necessary?' he began.

'Yes, but on the whole, we were lucky that everything went so easily,' said Namoh.

'I was impressed by the way you handled Lady Chandan.'

'Anyone who has the slightest understanding of what you're trying to achieve would have done the same.'

'I lambasted that soldier who abused Lady Chandan and dismissed him from the armed forces. I've taught you all I can about guerrilla warfare, and fighting in general, but let's hope all that's over now, at least in this part of the world.

'Oh – Witten is delighted at the amount of gold and other booty you brought back. Everyone who went with you will have a share, not least you two. I said we would bankrupt Mattanga, and it looks as if we have. I doubt there is anything of value available from there any more.'

However, Rajay was wrong.

CHAPTER 8

REFUGEES

The Silver Apple Fever was awful for the ogres, and the whole society of Mattanga fell to pieces. The poorer people fled to the countryside, slaves abandoned their sick owners, soldiers walked off the job and Princess Zulani and Clary decided it was definitely time to leave for Daish Shaktay, as law and order were fast breaking down. Zulani contacted Luth's man in the palace kitchens, and he arranged for some armed monks of Luth's Mattanga cell who knew of her good deeds to accompany them.

By great good fortune they met up with Prince Moozand, Zulani's brother, on the road out of Mattanga and he immediately turned round and went with them. Zulani and Clary had brought a fair amount of jewellery and money with them, had good riding horses and extra ones for their luggage. The monks who were guarding them heard there were a number of Mattanga soldiers on the high road behaving like brigands, so they avoided it. They took a smaller road that led southwest through the mountains and some days later were met by a patrol of Daish Shaktay troops. Luth's men convinced them that the three travellers were innocent refugees and the patrol agreed to escort them to their fort, where they could ask the commander for permission to enter Daish Shaktay. The monks returned to Mattanga to find more people in need of their help.

Moozand disguised himself as a merchant. He had undergone a complete loss of self-confidence, and although Zulani and Clary constantly gave him vibrations and tried to reassure him, nothing could remove his feelings of guilt and depression. Zulani hoped her brother would get over this and that Rajay Ghiry would forgive him for having been born into the family of the enemy, especially as the King of Daish Shaktay had been so friendly to him before. All went well until they reached Sapphire River Fort and asked if they could stay the night, assuming there would be no problem.

'I'll have to ask the commander,' the sentry on duty was uncertain.

'Why should we take you in?' the commander complained when he arrived. 'You look like rich people, so you'd be on the side of Karlvid of Mattanga. You cannot pass into Daish Shaktay. Our king has spent the last four years getting rid of your lot.'

'Please sir,' begged Princess Zulani, 'I have a token. Your King Rajay knows this ring.' She hoped and prayed it would convince him, because they were in the mountains and not only was there nowhere else to stay, but in this wild country there would be ferocious beasts and possibly outlaws. She took out my ruby and sapphire ring which Robin had given her. When the commander saw it his mood completely changed.

'I know this jewel!' he exclaimed. 'His Majesty had it made when he was up here, for a brave and clever young lady, who has great spiritual gifts. 'You can certainly stay for the night.' Zulani didn't have any idea what she would have said if he had asked if she was the young lady the ring was made for. He luckily assumed she was. She, Clary and Moozand had to give an awakening programme to the entire garrison the following morning, but it was a small price to pay for gaining entry to Daish Shaktay.

That same night, by coincidence, a lone traveller arrived at Malak Citadel and stayed in a hotel in the town. The next morning he made his way up to the Citadel, asked to see the king and gave his name as Sarn Lionheart. Sarn was wearing seaman's clothes, and when I saw him coming across the yard I thought he was one of Zafan's pirates, but when I was told who he was, I took him straight up to Rajay.

'What happened to the jewel merchant?' Rajay teased when they had embraced each other.

'Oh him?' laughed Sarn. 'He only lasted a day or two. That slave guard was such a tiresome chap, but a jewel merchant has to have one. He was always in a fight with someone or other. I gave him his freedom and told him to go, but really I was the one who had my freedom from him. And slavery is not right, as you well know.'

'That's true, but what happened next?' asked Rajay, amused by Sarn's carefree attitude to life.

'I changed my disguise, and at the next port I met a man who told me about an island in the middle of the Sea of Illusion, where there was a very wise teacher, and he encouraged me to go and spend some time with him. This man had been at school there, but he was certain I could go for a short while, even though I'm grown up. I was dubious, what with all the terrifying stories about that part of the world, but I went, because the vibrations were very cool to do so. To cut a long story short I went to Theon's Island and he and his excellent son Mazdan put some sense into my addled head. While there, I realised I so much to learn about life, but I'm on my way home now.

'I hope my fiancée has waited for me and I'll be able to find her, because I've heard Mattanga is in turmoil. She's the only surviving child of the vassal lord of a province near Mattanga, and my father is heir to a large amount of land taken from us by the ogres in Mattan province itself. I'm going to try and win all those lands back again.'

'Sarn, I strongly suggest you stay here until everything has settled down. Take my advice: keep away from Mattan province right now.'

'But Theon told me to go back there.'

'Let it all work out naturally before you try to do anything. Theon would go along with what's happening in Mattanga, I assure you.'

'He did say you're to be my overlord. He was quite definite about that.'

'I won't get in the way of your freedom, but if you want my help and advice, I'll do my best.'

'I'd appreciate that.'

'I'm sorry Sarn, your father died. If he hadn't died naturally, Karlvid would have killed him for changing sides.' Sarn was silent for a few moments, and great sadness came over him, but then he collected himself.

'I knew he was ill and that I probably wouldn't see him again. The doctors warned him.'

Rajay asked me to fetch the pendant of the Lionhearts, which had been returned to him by one of Luth's men after Vittorio's death. I went to Queen Jansy and asked her for the jewel, because it was stored in her personal safe. I brought the inlaid enamelwork casket that contained the treasure and Rajay took it out and gave it to Sarn.

'You are now its owner, but never forget, it is the Goddess, whose image is on the pendant, who is the real owner of these lands. She is behind all our victories, and we must lay everything at her feet. If you always do that, you'll be as successful as I have been.'

The night before they reached Malak Citadel, Moozand, Clary and Zulani stopped at an inn. As they waited for their supper in the parlour, sitting in the shadows, they listened to the locals.

'I met the king yesterday,' began a businessman returning from a conference at Malak Citadel. 'He's a fine young man. We don't realise how lucky we are to have someone like him looking after us.'

'Oh, I think we do. I heard he's going to get married soon,' said the innkeeper's wife, bringing in some plates.

'They say it may be Valya Northwestern's youngest sister,' went on the businessman. 'It's bound to be some good Daish Shaktay girl. That Karlvid brute was going to force him to marry one of his horrid brood, but he's well out of all that.' Zulani put her scarf over her head to hide her blonde hair and prayed no one would recognise them.

'That's for sure!' said the innkeeper, coming in with a braised goose in a sauce of tasty vegetables and fragrant herbs.

'No, you don't understand,' contributed a lady who was sitting with her husband and three sons. Zulani could feel from her vibrations that she had been given her inner awakening. 'Our king is a saint as well as a king. He'll marry one of the other saintly ones that we're blessed to have in this part of the world.'

'You mean that girl – Asha Herbhealer - who came originally from

Teletsia?' put in a young man who had also had his awakening, judging by his vibrations.

'No, not her. Rumour has it that there are others who are somehow different, superior in some way....'

And so the matchmaking went on.

They all loved their king and hero and wanted the very best for him. Zulani was a little scared at the thought of meeting him, and hoped that by then he might have a fiancée or wife by his side, who would make it easier, if she was kind and forgiving. Zulani put her attention on the goose, enjoyed the excellent Daish Shaktay cuisine and tried not to think of her uncertain future. She had been brought up to suppress her feelings, but found it hard where Rajay was concerned, because she could never forget that fateful gathering where he had defied her father with his disarming and beguiling courage. His smile on that day had changed her for ever.

The next evening, I was in the town below the Citadel, in the Covered Market. It was dusk and we were having an awakening programme. A number of the regulars were there and a crowd of new people, because many visitors came from all over the country these days to see Rajay, Witten, Deradan or one of the others who were helping them. Lee was at the front demonstrating various cleansing techniques, as we had finished the first part of the programme that involved singing, dancing and the actual awakening. Ahren and Robin had gone to another town to do a programme that night, on the flying horses. I was walking around at the back, talking to new people. I noticed some travellers on horses arrive in the square, but in the gathering dark could not see very well. One of them, a girl with blonde hair, walked towards me.

'I'm looking for Asha Herbhealer,' she began. 'Someone said she's here.'

'I'm Asha.'

'I was told if I gave you this ring, you'd help me,' she went on, uneasy. I looked at my sapphire and ruby ring and couldn't help it; I put my arms around her and hugged her.

'Princess Zulani, how can I thank you enough? You've saved the lives of some of the most important people in my life.' She smiled, somewhat comforted.

'It was nothing, and I'm not a princess any more, just an exile begging for help. My brother Moozand is here too. I only hope His Majesty isn't going to throw us into jail or banish us.'

'Far from it. Robin told Rajay about how you helped him and Ahren, and everyone's been speaking so highly of you,' I reassured her. 'I'll get my cousin, who's over there, and we'll go up to the Citadel to find Rajay.' As I walked over to Lee it came to me that even tired and in travel stained clothes, Princess Zulani was very good looking - an unassuming beauty with a kind smile. Lee joined us and we walked up the hill together, leading the newcomers' horses.

'Rajay is working at the moment. After that he'll have dinner with Queen Jansy,' said Lee. 'Would you like to wash and change first, before coming to meet him?'

'Yes, indeed,' replied Moozand. 'I'd not want His Majesty to think we're complete tramps, even if we do come as refugees.'

'Prince Moozand, please come with me, and the ladies can go with Asha to the house of Saber Rizen, the Captain of the Guard, where Asha lives,' Lee continued. 'I could take you all to the state guest rooms but they're not prepared, so tonight, if you don't mind, we'll have to be more informal.' Zulani and Clary smiled at each other. It didn't *seem* to be a prelude to the dungeons, but they didn't want to raise their hopes too much.

Lee went off to the young men's apartment with Moozand and I took my exalted guests to Amber's house, which was roomy, clean and friendly, but not a palace. I hoped the princess and her companion would be happy there. As was her style, Amber bustled about helping and some time later two extremely elegant ladies emerged. I couldn't believe the transformation! Zulani especially looked stunning, in a green silk dress embroidered with seed pearls, which set off the magnificent emerald and diamond jewellery she wore. The way she looked now, I could never embrace her as informally as I had down in the square and felt perhaps I had behaved wrongly. I told her companion Clary, formerly Sarn's fiancée, that Sarn was here, and picked up that she was not impressed. Lee came to tell me the visitors had been invited to dinner with Sarn, Rajay and Queen Jansy. He took me into Saber's study, always the place for private conversations.

'I just spoke to Rajay – alone in the passage outside his mother's living room,' Lee began. 'He looked quite unsure of himself and said, "Lee, give me a bandhan of request. I've got to get this one right," but before he could tell me more, Prince Moozand came to ask me if Princess Zulani was happy over here. What do you make of that one?'

'Haven't a clue. Princess Zulani is fine. She's so nice, you wouldn't believe it.'

We took Zulani and Clary over, and when we arrived at the large central building the guards bowed and a footman preceded us. As we reached Queen Jansy's living room, she and the others stopped talking in the way people do when they don't want the newcomers to hear their conversation. At a gesture from Rajay the footman backed away. Lee and I waited at the door and Rajay beckoned us to come in.

'Forgive me if I interrupt,' Lee said cautiously, 'but I would like to present Princess Zulani of Mattanga and Lady Clary of Wattan.' Sarn immediately got up. I looked round and noticed Clary was waiting in the hall; her courage had failed at the thought of having to face Sarn.

'This is better and better,' Rajay stood up and said, with a smile like the rising sun, 'first Prince Moozand and his sister, and – eh – Sarn's fiancée.'

'Where's Clary?' asked Sarn, concerned.

'In the hall,' I whispered. 'She feels you abandoned her. She was also having an awful time in Mattanga.' Sarn had heard about some of this from

Robin, but thought she would have understood by now why he left her so suddenly, and without saying anything.

'Go and talk to her in private,' Rajay suggested. 'I'm sure you'll smooth things over. Go on! Don't keep her waiting any longer!' Sarn went out, apprehensive.

Princess Zulani paused at the door. It was a tense moment. On one hand she was in front of her father's greatest enemy, the Mountain Mouse, and on the other she was about to meet the young man she had pledged herself to serve from the moment she first saw him. Would Rajay Ghiry protect and help her? She had heard how gallant he had been towards her friend Sagara Samudra and prayed he would treat her with the same magnanimity. That was why she had taken special care to look her best. She was dressed in the one court dress she had brought with her and was wearing her finest jewellery.

Rajay stood up to welcome Zulani. He had also dressed smartly, for a completely different reason. He wore a red silk turban with a large pearl and sapphire jewel in the front, a sleeveless brocade surcoat in blue, with gold embroidery, over an embroidered white shirt of the finest cotton, and thick red silken trousers. He looked resplendent - the young, victorious king. Zulani tried to look confident and dignified as she knelt before him.

'Princess Zulani, I'm honoured to meet you,' he began. 'Don't kneel - I should kneel before you, being as you saved my life. At last I can thank you!' and he indicated to the divan where his mother was sitting. Rajay glanced at Zulani and for a moment coolness flowed through the room despite there being no breeze. They both looked extremely elegant, these scions of two important royal families. Queen Jansy spoke to Princess Zulani for a short time to put her at her ease, but soon came to the point.

'My son would like to speak to you in private,' and she and Moozand went to the dining room at the other end of the hall. Sarn and Clary were in the garden, hopefully resolving their differences and misunderstandings.

The door was closed and they were alone. Princess Zulani was desperately nervous but assumed she was hiding it well: the sophistication of Mattanga was meeting the rustic but subtle power of Daish Shaktay. Rajay was not his usual confident self either; he was much more at home with his partisan friends than with this elegant princess and had no idea how to tackle the challenge before him. Unbounded love for all that was good flowed always flowed from his heart and he directed it towards Zulani in an effort to put her at ease, because he felt her inner nature and was aware of her fear; it was giving him pain in his own heart centre. He took a deep breath and began.

'I hear the first thing you did on entering our land was to give awakening at the Sapphire River Fort. I wish all travellers would do that,' Zulani stared at the floor, unable to think of how to reply, so he went on. 'My mother, and those of us who govern this country, have decided that we will definitely allow you and your brother to stay here for as long as you want, and we will make sure you are well cared for in every way.'

'I am truly grateful, Your Majesty,' Zulani looked up. 'We have nothing except what we brought with us. I have a few jewels, and my brother has some gold, but that is all.'

'That side of things can easily be arranged. But on a lighter note, in the fairy stories, the prince saves the princess and they live happily ever after, but in our case, it's the other way round. You helped save my life and later gave vital information to my friends, which saved theirs. That's got to be a good beginning to our relationship,' Rajay smiled and noticed she was starting to relax. From her side Zulani remembered what her friend Sagara had said about him, that once the dreaded Mouse started speaking to you, it was difficult to resist his charm.

'As you well know, at one point your father wanted me to marry you. Your brother and my mother are totally in favour. If you would consent to be my wife....'

Rajay decided he should be formal. It was difficult, because he was a spontaneous young man, and knew from asking the vibrations that she was very suitable. He was aware she might not see it that way, as he and his allies had defeated her father and destroyed his empire. He would never force her to marry him, even though he could, as she was virtually his prisoner.

'Your Majesty, I came as a refugee and you're offering me a kingdom, but I'm nothing any more...' As far as Zulani was concerned, kings married to create alliances or to strengthen their power bases and never bothered about the daughters of defeated enemies.

'With you by my side, if we could always put our people's needs first we could make this country truly great,' Rajay continued, thinking her caution was a mere formality.

Zulani felt a constricting fear overwhelm her at the thought of becoming a queen, because queens in Mattanga were often put aside for younger or more politically expedient matches after a few years. They were sometimes poisoned - her mother had been killed in this way. She assumed she had escaped all that when she ran away from Mattanga.

'I – I don't know. This isn't what I expected – I'm so confused. No, it's not possible,' she mumbled.

'I shouldn't have sprung such a question on you so soon. Take some time to think about it.'

'No, please don't force me. I'm finished with all that, I just want to live a simple life.'

Rajay noticed, with dismay, her worried expression. He was disappointed, and sadly presumed she was utterly prejudiced against him, and he could hardly blame her. When the idea of marriage had been mooted in Mattanga he had been filled with dread, but later heard of Zulani's beauty and her pleasant nature. As the time had passed and he heard more and more good things about her, he regretted the way events had turned out. Now here she was, in front of him, and his heart had gone out to her the moment she had walked in the room, but she had definitely refused him. He rang a bell to end the interview, and a footman entered the room.

'Her Majesty bids you come and have dinner when you are ready,' he said, breaking the tension.

'Madam, please come and eat. You must be very hungry,' Rajay bowed to her, seated on the other divan. She stood up and together they walked to the dining room in awkward silence. As he entered he shook his head almost imperceptibly at Queen Jansy and Prince Moozand, who looked at each other anxiously.

Rajay talked rather more than usual during the meal but Zulani was completely tongue tied. He was acutely conscious of her discomfiture and was eager to make everything as easy as possible for her, so after they had finished eating he called for the court musicians to play for the guests. However she said she was very tired and wanted to return to Amber's house. A guard was called to escort her, but when they were in the yard she asked if there was a temple in the fort. He took her to the small one near the herb garden.

'I'll make my own way to the Rizen's,' she told him. 'Thank you for your help, but you can go back to your post.'

Zulani went into the shrine room, knelt and sat down. There was a statue of the Goddess of Daish Shaktay and behind it, against the wall, a relief sculpture of the Tree of Life, in which all religions had their place. The seven subtle centres, flowers made of inlaid jewels, were worked into it and the tree had leaves of gold and a trunk of burnished silver. The temple was decorated with bunches of fragrant flowers in fine porcelain vases and there was a light but serene feeling. Once alone she burst into tears.

I often went into the temple in the evening, not only to meditate for a little while, but also to check that the flowers were fresh and everything was clean and neat. Imagine my surprise when I walked in and saw Princess Zulani sitting cross legged on the richly patterned rug in front of the statue, sobbing uncontrollably.

'Oh Asha, I'm such a fool!' she groaned, 'Rajay proposed to me, but I was in such a state, I refused him!' I sat down next to her.

'Rajay is the kindest, most considerate person in the world, and I'm sure he'll understand,' I comforted her. 'But, if it isn't too personal a question – why did you refuse him? It's well known he wants to marry soon, and every girl in Daish Shaktay would give anything to be his wife.'

'Kings marry for diplomatic reasons, and I'm of no value in that way now. In my country someone with no status, like me, even if I did marry him, would just become a minor wife, no better than a concubine, and would probably be cast aside completely after a short time. My mother was...'

'But Rajay's not like that. You don't know how he's been praising you. At times I wondered if you'd both secretly arranged something in Mattanga.'

'Really?' Her face lit up.

'Yes. Now let's do something together. Let's ask the vibrations: "Is Rajay the right husband for you?" See, it's blowing cool. Don't you feel the same?'

'Oh my! It's a gale on my hands!'

'So you mustn't worry. Something will work out. Rajay has made a number of vows, and one of them is to protect and respect women. Please, if you don't mind, stay here for a little while and I'll be back shortly. I have to do something first. Then we'll go back to Amber's house and have a nice soothing tisane together. Is that alright?'

'Yes, of course.'

I went over to the main building as quickly as I could, and heard the musicians playing in the large reception room. There was a footman outside the door, and I whispered to him that I needed to see Rajay urgently. He took in the message and soon Rajay came out.

'Forgive me for intruding, but Princess Zulani is in the temple, desperately unhappy that she refused your proposal. She may look like an elegant princess, but there's a very insecure girl under the jewels and silks. Talk to her like you always talk to me – as a friend, not as a king. You can be quite scary sometimes, although you don't mean to be.' I knew I was being extremely brazen speaking to him like this, but Zulani's whole life was at stake.

Luckily Rajay smiled, in fact he laughed. 'If you say so. You found me a navy, so maybe you can also help me with a wife.'

'You'd better go quickly,' I urged him. 'We checked on the vibrations – you're completely right for each other.'

'Remember when we did that in the Watch Tower Pavilion together? Let's hope it works out as well as it did for Valya,' he left, almost running.

Zulani heard someone come into the temple and saw to her surprise it was Rajay.

'Don't let me disturb you,' he said, after kneeling in respect to the statue.

'You're not – I mean, this is your temple – your country. Forgive me, I've been so ungrateful.'

Rajay decided to try once again, and if she still wasn't responding he would have to reconsider one of the Daish Shaktay girls, even though the vibrations were not so strong, and even though Zulani had completely captivated him. He threw convention to the winds, because the formal approach wasn't going anywhere. He looked at the statue of the Goddess of Daish Shaktay and the image of the Tree of Life, said a silent prayer and sat beside her.

'Forget you're a princess and I'm a king. When you came in the door of my mother's living room, I felt such gentle, altruistic love shining out from your subtle heart centre. Your Tree of Life is so strong; aren't you also aware of mine? Couldn't we share this joy?' he finally struck the right chord. Zulani had admired, even idolised Rajay for months and her suppressed, confused and conflicting emotions poured out like a dam bursting.

'From the first moment I set eyes on you in Mattanga, I knew our fates were intertwined,' she paused, as if groping for the right words.

'I've realised that too, but only this evening. I owe you my life, but will you accept my respect and love, as a young man who knows he's met the lady he wants to share his life with?'

'Yes. I promise you I'll always try to be a good wife and queen.'

'I'm deeply honoured.' Rajay noticed the tears streaming down her cheeks. 'Take my handkerchief. Are you all right?'

'Oh yes! It's - it's all been too much....' She took the handkerchief and dried her eyes, looked down in shyness and did not see his radiant smile. Then she made to give it back.

'Keep it – the first of many gifts to you,' and he gently took her hand in both of his. This seemingly sophisticated and resilient princess was in reality like a fragile flower, beautiful but delicate and vulnerable. His first instinct was to take her in his arms to calm her and show her his affection was genuine, but he was cautious and a little reserved with women he did not know, even if she was now his fiancée. 'May I make one small request?' he continued.

'Indeed.'

'I promise you, in this sacred place, that I'm going to look after you as well as I can, for the rest of my days, but if you aren't at peace neither am I, because I feel your subtle self, and will do so all the more when we're married. So please, don't be afraid any more. And most of all don't be afraid of me. Sometimes I have to be strong, even fierce, because - as you know I've just fought a war to unite this country, but I'll never, ever be like that with you.'

'I'm sure you won't. Asha told me about your vow to protect women, and I trust you completely.'

'I didn't do a very good job of proposing to you, earlier,' Rajay chuckled.

'It was perfect – it was my reaction that wasn't.'

He let go of her hand and they sat in silent peace for a while, after which he offered to walk her back to Amber's house. He wasn't capable of small talk and Zulani would never start a conversation with someone of Rajay's status she hardly knew, so neither of them said anything. As they walked across the yard and round the corner of the barracks, quiet now except for the occasional sentry marching around, they were thinking similar thoughts. Zulani realised Rajay was utterly delightful, whereas he was overjoyed that she was way beyond what he ever imagined could be his good fortune.

He understood a dream he had the night before: he was in a large hall with all the guardians and one of the older ones told him that from now on, young guardians should try to marry people of Navi Septa who had received their inner awakening and were well meaning and sincere. The next day Zulani had arrived.

As they walked he put his attention on her heart centre to clear the weakness caused by her dreadful father.

'Better now – less anxiety, isn't there?' he suggested as they reached Amber's door.

'Yes, My Lord,' she replied, bowing her head and putting her right hand on her heart in humble agreement.

'Good night, My Lady – but – call me Rajay. All my friends do – and you've been my friend for months, even though we didn't meet until today.'

CHAPTER 9

ANOTHER SURPRISE

Rajay worked tirelessly as king, counsellor and arbitrator, but he also liked to have a good time, and the following morning he had gone to the horse farm early, with Robin, Lee and Ahren, to ride the flying horses. He was down there whenever he had a moment to spare from the never-ending administration. I had given my horse permission to carry him because the flying horses would carry their owner, or anyone the owner instructed them to. Tama neighed with delight whenever she saw him coming, and I was tempted to give her to him, except it might have hurt Robin's feelings. Meanwhile I was in Queen Jansy's apartment, serving her breakfast.

'It's time to have the coronation, don't you think, Asha?' she said.

'Yes, Madam, that's what the townsfolk are saying.'

'In Daish Shaktay the king must have a wife before he is crowned, and she's arrived at just the right moment.'

'Princess Zulani?'

'Indeed. Without her we might not still have a king to be crowned. I can't believe such a flower can come out of that wasteland of Mattanga! When Moozand arrived last night, Rajay said to him, "I've got to have the coronation soon and for this I need a wife. She must be spiritually deep, patriotic towards our country and able to be a dignified queen. From what I have heard about her, your sister fulfils all these criteria." Rajay would have married whoever would best help him carry out his role as King of Daish Shaktay, and see how he's been blessed! Isn't she the perfect princess?'

Within a day or so it was round the entire country that Rajay was finally to be crowned king, and was getting married to the daughter of his enemy, who had nevertheless saved his life. He personally thanked me for my little part in the drama.

'I said he'd finish up marrying Karlvid's daughter,' Namoh commented. 'I told him that when we were in Mattanga but he wouldn't believe me.'

'Don't be too sure about that,' replied Witten, 'he listens to everyone's suggestions, especially ours.'

The day after that I was cooking in the Rizen's house. I had invited Robin, Lee and Ahren and some of Amber and Saber's friends to lunch. Amber was upstairs, because by now she had had her baby and the little boy needed her attention. Princess Zulani had gone to stay in Queen Jansy's apartment along with her friend Clary. Amber's enthusiastic but clueless soldier servant had gone shopping for some dessert from the cake shop down in the town - anything to dissuade him from wanting to help cook. Some time after he left Robin walked in; he heard me in the kitchen. He and Rajay had been with the flying horses all the morning.

'Oh, hi, Robin,' I began, standing over the iron stove. My hair was tied up under a scarf and I was wearing an old apron over my clothes. 'Sit down. I must go on cooking or we won't have anything to eat.' Robin relaxed in the rocking chair in the corner of the kitchen. 'Would you like something to drink?'

'Yes, thank you.' I gave him a glass of water with a squeeze of lemon and a little honey in it, the water from the earthenware crock in the larder, which kept it cool even on the hottest days, and he smiled at me. Robin often smiled but there was something different about him today. I went back to the cooking. 'I need to have a few words with you, but I can come back when you're not so busy,' he went on.

'Please stay. I much prefer cooking with someone to chat to. Hand me that knife, will you?'

'Stop cooking for a few moments.'

Robin came over to me, took the large pan from my hand and put it on the side of the hob. I knew him when he was like this - he had something to say and nothing was going to deflect him. We sat opposite each other at the kitchen table.

'Some of Rajay's friends want to find themselves wives now the country is at peace. Your name has been mentioned more than once.'

'You know I won't settle down until we've tried to do something about Teletsia. Also I've tied brotherhood bands on nearly all of them.' Robin was silent and my mind was on the lunch, or lack of it. I got up and went back to the cooking. Saber would come in soon wanting food and the other guests too.

'If someone asked you to marry him who'd help you with Teletsia, would you accept?'

'That would entirely depend on who it was! Marriage is for life, not just a quick fix to help my country.'

'Come here again - no one will mind if lunch is a bit late.'

'All right, let me finish the vegetables.' I did so then sat down. Robin looked on with amused curiosity; it was some time since he had seen me being domestic.

'I'd go back to Teletsia with you. For as long as it takes, and then we could live wherever seems best for both of us.'

'Robin, am I really hearing this?'

'Yes, and you've no idea how important it is to me to help you with Teletsia. Marry me, Asha.' I felt a gust of coolness flowing over my whole body as the all-pervading power confirmed Robin's proposal.

'Yes, a thousand times yes!' The words came out spontaneously, but from somewhere deep inside me.

Unaware of what was happening, Amber wandered into the kitchen to see how I was getting on. Robin got up to leave and I went back to the stove, my heart exploding with joy. Later Lee came into the kitchen where I was alone, as Amber was entertaining the guests in the living room. He had found Robin sitting in the Citadel garden, bemused, and had managed to get out of him that he had proposed to me and I had accepted. Lee was delighted and as my closest relation present had given Robin his necessary consent, but insisted on getting the approval of Rajay, who was in a way the head of our family at that time. Rajay wasn't surprised, gave the approval and Robin asked him if he could buy a ring for me, with some of the gold he had managed to bring back from the profits of the Mattanga circus, because Lee told him the Malak Citadel vaults were full of jewellery from Port Volcan and other places. To this Rajay replied, 'Robin, you've risked your life for our country, so the least I can give you is a beautiful betrothal ring for Asha.'

He reappeared and brought Rajay with him – an unexpected but most welcome extra guest. Robin took me into Saber's study and closed the door. Lee and Rajay knew what was going on and tactfully deflected attention away from us, especially Rajay. It was easy as everyone looked at him when he came into the room.

'There's more to this - I'll try to be honest with you,' Robin began when we were alone.

'But you've always been totally sincere.'

'As far as possible, yes. Last night, Queen Jansy called me and asked me my plans, and I explained I had a feeling I was going to be needed in more countries than Chussan and here. To my surprise she said, "Robin, marriage is in the air at present. Asha turned down Valya because of her vow to Teletsia, but if you'll help her with it she might accept you. Don't waste any time because Rajay's companions are looking for wives now." I told her that although I'd never thought of you in that way, someone did once say we'd be good for each other.'

'Who was that?'

'Mrs Pea-Arge, the astrologer's housekeeper, a wise old bird if ever there was one.'

'Indeed! Why did we never see this until now?'

'Does it matter? You've been very dear to me from the moment I first set eyes on you, but in a different way. I've always wanted to look after you.' Robin put the magnificent diamond and ruby ring on the middle finger of my left hand, the betrothal finger, and embraced me warmly. I now understood his excessive concern for me, which had sometimes led to our having disagreements. 'Let's show the others your ring. Lee and Rajay were worried that it might be too large. Is it all right?'

'It's perfect, like everything else today.'

Rajay gave us his blessing and lunch turned into quite a celebration. After everyone else had gone he had a few words with us two.

'You've got yourself a fine husband but don't you both go doing too many bold and daring things!' he joked. I smiled, and thought, 'You're hardly the one to warn against courageous deeds!'

'Your bold and daring nature is what I've always found so endearing,' Robin admitted after Rajay had left. 'I've often had to pretend to disapprove but that's not how I felt. My heart would sing for joy when you defied convention and risked your life for what you believed in. Here, your work with awakening people has been easy and the fighting has been conventional, but in Teletsia it will be a subtler battle and I'll help you there. Also, here people have Rajay as a figurehead to follow but in Teletsia it may have to be you seven.'

Later my duties took me to see Queen Jansy. She smiled as I entered.

'Happy, my dear? Our young men are - one better than the next - but Robin's the right husband for you.' She looked at my hand. 'Splendid ring! I told Rajay to make sure they chose you one worthy of the treasury of Daish Shaktay.'

The only thing that marred my joy was something Lee said: 'Deradan came to me yesterday and asked if he might have a chance with you. I told him you didn't want to marry yet.'

'I didn't, but I feel so right about Robin. I'm sorry if I've hurt Deradan – he's the second of Rajay's friends I've done that to.'

'What will be, will be. Don't feel bad.'

But I did. I don't like hurting people.

That evening there was a meeting in the Council Chamber. Luth was there, and he, Queen Jansy and Rajay had the places of honour. Princess Zulani was sitting with her friend Clary at the back of the room; she had asked not to be in the limelight just yet and Rajay respected her wish.

'There are one or two things to decide,' he began, 'and as in Sasrar the collective vibrations will guide us.'

'Firstly, Rajay must be crowned,' said Luth, and a strong breeze blew through the chamber without anyone having to feel anything on their hands 'and he has to be married before that.' Again we all felt the coolness flow.

'A wedding is a social function,' Rajay took over, 'to be witnessed by members of my community, my friends and those who've helped me free the kingdom. There are two other impending matches. Would the people concerned like it if we all got married together?' Clary hadn't quite forgiven Sarn for taking off without telling her, and Robin and I had not even thought of our wedding.

'About you two,' Rajay turned to Sarn. 'In the past the Lionheart family was very powerful in Mattan and Clary's father, now sadly dead from the fever, was the vassal of Wattan, a province of the Mattanga Empire. I've had messages from Master Theon, who's certain you two have the ability to govern that area.' Sarn wasn't sure about this and his expression betrayed his thoughts.

'You need the support of your fiancée, young man,' said Luth testily. 'Marriage will do you the power of good. You're the second couple.'

'Would you like to stay with us for a bit and learn how to run a country properly?' asked Rajay.

'Whatever you say,' replied Sarn. Clary looked uncertain. At this stage she wasn't convinced that Sarn would ever settle down and face his responsibilities.

'You can have the Daish Shaktay army to restore order in Mattanga once the disease has run its course. Someone's got to rule Mattanga. Prince Moozand,' Rajay nodded at him, sitting at the back, 'positively refuses to have anything more to do with politics.'

'I never want to see Mattanga again,' said Moozand, 'but I'm very grateful for your offer to be your bailiff of the lands those treacherous nobles owned, the ones who were with Duratman Offlen.'

'Your first job,' continued Rajay, 'is to divide those estates up into smallholdings and to give a piece of land to every man who fought for me, if they don't already own enough to support themselves.

'Asha and Robin, would you like to get married with us as well?' I looked at Robin.

'We'd be honoured,' he said.

'So that's settled. While everyone prepares for the celebrations, I'd like you, Ahren and Lee to go round the country, so the flying horses can put their feet all over the land and any serious wrongs can be exposed. I'm hoping you'll lend me your horse, Asha, so I can go too.'

'I'm sure Tama would be proud to carry you,' I replied.

'Thank you. Any other business?' He looked around the room. 'No? That's it then.'

Clary was overwhelmed.

'You have to get used to Luth and Rajay,' I advised her as we left. 'They don't allow people to make a mess of things. Whatever they want you to do, do it. They're guardians and totally in tune with the flow of creation. Plus Sarn is a really good man; you're lucky to have him.'

CHAPTER 10

THE TOUR OF THE COUNTRY

Moozand went off on a pilgrimage to the Temple-in-the-Mountains. It didn't matter how much we told him he should just ask for forgiveness at the temple in the town and stop worrying about his appalling relations, virtually all now dead, he was determined to go. We gave him invitations for the forthcoming celebrations to give to the Zaminders and Persheray's family when he passed Belar, also Pulita and her parents the Belar grocers, the village headman Pahari and even Baktar the saint, if he could find him.

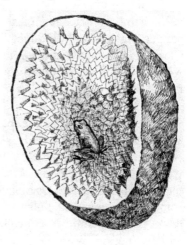

Rajay was getting to know Zulani. It was touching to see the great warrior, confident strategist and powerful statesman so gentle, tentative and caring. Clary was trying to come to terms with her future role as First Lady of Mattanga, but was still uncertain, and if Sarn could actually do something constructive and practical it would reassure her. Her father had administered a whole province, and even though he had been ruthless and cruel, he did know the meaning of a hard day's work. She tended to measure Sarn against him and to have him doing nothing at Malak Citadel did not increase her faith in her fiancé. Rajay asked Sarn to go up north with Witten, to sort out some administrative details in Jewelton, beyond the Shaktay River. Then he took Lee, Ahren and Robin, along with the flying horses, on a trip round the kingdom. Meanwhile Queen Jansy, Deradan and the rest of us arranged the weddings and coronation.

Before he left Rajay had a quiet word with me. Although he realised that Zulani had enormous courage he could feel that she was still suffering inwardly from her traumatic past and told me he had suggested to her to ask me how to clear the effects of this from her subtle system. He warned me that she still had some fear, both of him and of life in general. I was honoured that he had taken me into his confidence and did my best. Now his country was won he had more time to put attention on our inner wellbeing, and once or twice advised all of us in that direction.

When the men had gone I spent some time with Zulani and despite our utterly diverse backgrounds we got on well. I arranged for the best dressmaker in town to visit her, introduced her to the staff of the Citadel, found her a lady's maid and generally made her feel at home. She often came and helped at the awakening programmes, and Queen Jansy was instructing her about how things were in Daish Shaktay from the point of view of a queen. Understandably, Zulani was happiest when we sat in the Citadel garden in the evenings and delighted her with stories about Rajay. Ekan would tell her about his love of animals, Namoh of his brave exploits and Deradan how hard he worked at the endless task of running the country, and how no one was too unimportant to have an audience with him. I could see she longed for his return.

Clary spoke to Namoh, who had nothing but praise for Sarn. He was much respected as being part of the team who had delayed Karlvid from murdering Rajay, thus giving him time to escape. Rajay's friends understood Sarn's casual attitude to life; they had all learnt to be outwardly carefree in the face of grave danger. Namoh had no doubt Sarn was the same and his flippancy towards Clary in Mattanga had been his way of hiding much more serious emotions within. Namoh did as much as anyone to patch up the relationship between the two of them.

Wherever the four young men arrived on the flying horses, it would create a tremendous stir, especially when it became known that one was the king. Nevertheless, they had their weapons with them and the three from the north were Rajay's bodyguards. When folk discovered that the two youngest were the partisans from the legendary kingdom of Sasrar and the fourth had done something magical to finish off the ogre peoples, everyone wanted to meet them. Giving people inner awakening was unbelievably easy after that sort of an introduction. With the presence of the horses many wrongs came to light and because Rajay was actually there he could resolve them quickly.

On the way back to Malak Citadel, the four on the flying horses saw a big road works project below them. They landed the horses and went up to the road gang that was cutting away a hillside and making the main road to the south straighter. The gang had not noticed the flying horses, which were out of sight by now.

Rajay walked over to where the men were working. At first they thought he was a curious nobleman or a rich merchant, but someone recognised him and all work came to a stop, because everyone wanted to thank him for freeing the country. They also congratulated him on his engagement, because the stories about Zulani's part in Rajay's escape from Mattanga were well known, as were the reports of her beauty. She was already 'their' queen. As always,

Rajay's heart was warmed by these simple folk who did this grindingly hard work. He called for Ahren to bring his backpack and handed out a silver coin to each of the fifty road workers, and a small gold one for the foreman. As he did so he mentioned to Lee: 'One advantage of being king is that now I have the money to do this sort of thing, and these people are so grateful.'

Two workers came up, heaving a perfectly rounded stone.

'What's this?' asked Rajay as they dropped it in front of him.

'Your Highness, stones of this type, when broken open, are hollow and lined with gems or crystal,' said the foreman.

'Can I try?'

'Yes indeed, sire. That's why we brought it to you. It's not hard if you'll let us show you how,' replied one of the men, a skilled mason.

They all crowded round. Was it going to be valuable amethyst, or one of the more common stones lined with rock crystal? Rajay took the mallet and chisel and hit it exactly as the mason instructed. The rock broke open and the inside was lined with deep purple stones, amethysts of the finest quality, but this was not what they were all looking at, when there was a cry of amazement from the onlookers. The inside of the rock was like the outer side, without crack or flaw, so that even air could not enter before Rajay had smashed it open. There, sitting in the middle of the amethysts, blinking in the sunlight, was a yellow frog, apparently sprung full grown from the jewels.

'Wherever did that come from?' the foreman was surprised.

'What a miracle! I may be king and able to give all of you money, but this little frog is telling me that even the king, and especially the king, must never forget that the divine creator is the real doer of all deeds, great or small. He, or She, can make frogs out of crystal, and we are nothing more than instruments. If I have the power to be generous and can give out gold and silver, it's because I'm blessed in that way.'

Rajay briefly bowed his head and put his right hand on his heart, and everyone was impressed at the modest way he had interpreted the wondrous phenomenon. It did more to endear them to him than any coins or crowns or titles. He turned round, as he heard Tama, my flying horse, come up behind him, whinnying and very agitated. The road workers were astonished to see her and drew back in apprehension, especially when the other horses appeared too.

'Asha may need us,' Robin said nervously. 'I know these horses and Tama wants you to get on her back so we can leave. I think Asha has called her, and she wouldn't do that unless she was in great danger.'

'We must go fast; I feel fear from her,' Rajay agreed.

I was indeed in bad trouble. I often walked down to the orange grove outside the town in the late afternoon and would sit under the trees and read a book. On this particular afternoon I heard a group of people approaching and about ten men came down the track towards me. They were dressed as travelling merchants, and armed, and had terrible vibrations.

'That's her. That's the Teletsian sorceress! Be careful! She has great powers!' I ran off, making a bandhan on my Sasrar key to call my flying horse, hopefully bearing Rajay on her back. I also managed to whistle through the key to call the tigers. The men were gaining on me as I dodged in and out of the trees, and soon one of them caught me. They bound my arms behind me and forced me to hurry on, in the direction of the woodland beyond the grove.

'Who are you? Where are you taking me?' I gasped.

'You'll find out soon enough,' snarled one, brandishing a cruel knife as he ran beside me.

'You're going to be sacrificed to the crocodiles. We're delivering you to someone who bears you quite a grudge,' said another.

'It was because of your sorcery that he got sold as a slave. Luckily some of his friends bought him and freed him, after he'd done a nasty stint in the coal mines.'

'The priests in Mattanga who are still alive say if you can be sacrificed to a crocodile, the Crocodile God of Mattanga will hear their prayers and bring their chosen ones, that you call ogres, back to life.'

'Why me?' I cried in despair, as they forced me to run on.

'It was your young man as gave the fatal apple to King Karlvid, wasn't it? I wonder what your Mr Robin will say when he finds his lady's been fed to the crocodiles, eh?' he sneered.

I knew where they would take me. There was a largish river some way from Malak Citadel and it did have a few crocodiles in it. Just when we all thought everything was all right and we could live in peace! I wondered if by any chance they were raving lunatics playing some macabre game, but no. I was forced to run on and on, deeper and deeper into the wood, and after some time evening came. We reached a clearing and there was the priest who had got himself sold as a slave. I was dropping from exhaustion and they threw me on the ground and went up to the priest, who was rubbing his hands in glee. Two men stayed with me and drew their swords.

'Please, can you untie my hands? I can't get away and the rope is so painful,' I moaned.

'Yes, I suppose so,' said one man as he cut the ropes binding me. 'When the three moons come up you're to be thrown in the river.'

I put my hand to my neck. My key was under my clothing and as I touched it I felt great courage. I remembered how Lee had used his at Gap Fort to kill the man chasing him. I was only allowed to use this power if death faced me and there was absolutely no other way out. One of my tormenters was standing behind me, a drawn sword in his hand and the other one was by my side, also with a sword, but a little way off. I pretended to scratch my neck. Slowly I put my index finger in the little indentation at the back of the flower, brought the key out from under my clothing and prayed. There was a blinding flash as the key changed into the shining discus with a serrated edge and detached itself from the chain around my neck. These keys were pure, concentrated vibrations.

The discus flew from my finger, beheading the men closest to me. It was horrible to see and I felt nauseous, heard a singing in my ears and passed out. As I did so I heard the noise of great wings and saw a flicker of silver in the skies reflecting the light of the Moon of Compassion, which was now rising.

'Whatever's happened?' cried Rajay, arriving on Tama. He jumped to the ground, drew his sword and fearlessly prepared to fight, whatever the odds were against him. Lee and Ahren were right behind him.

'There's Asha!' Robin was desperate. He slid off his horse, could not see anyone attacking Rajay and ran over to me, lying on the ground. 'Why did it have to come to this?' he groaned in anguish. He took my wrist to feel my pulse, relieved to find it perfectly normal. I woke up when I heard his voice.

'They're dead, every single one of them. Beheaded!' shouted Rajay, increasingly puzzled. He looked around the forest clearing at all the blood and corpses.

'I always faint at the sight of blood,' I gasped, still feeling dizzy, and smiling weakly. Robin sat on the ground looking carefully to see if I really was all right. Rajay walked around, sword in hand, looking at the headless bodies. He found my key, picked it up, came over to me and sheathed his sword.

'Your key, Asha. You *must* be more careful,' he said sternly, putting my Sasrar key in my hand. At this moment a tiger also came bounding up and knelt at my feet. I stroked it, thanked it and told it apologetically that I didn't need it any more. My rescuers stood before me in a row: four powerful fighters, one tiger and four flying horses. They wanted an explanation. They were silent and only the river, a night bird and the crickets chirping made any sound.

'I got kidnapped,' I began lamely. 'Then, with my key, I was able to call the horses and the tigers. I managed to free my hands and used the key as the fiery discus and it killed all the men who had caught me. They were working for that priest you sold as a slave, Rajay. His body is there somewhere, if you care to look.'

'I don't, but I can quite believe it. I'll send some men to cremate these scoundrels tomorrow. They don't deserve it but I don't want this forest polluted.'

'So, you called for the guardian animals of two areas of the world and for four of the most feared warriors in Daish Shaktay to save you,' Lee commented, 'including the king, but having done this, you finished off your kidnappers by yourself!'

'It just sort of happened,' I smiled nervously, feeling an absolute idiot.

'Let's be grateful you're safe and sound,' Rajay reassured me. 'The powers we've been given are quite awe-inspiring.'

'Let's get out of here. Lee, help Asha up behind me,' Robin asked. 'Yamun will have to carry us both this evening, if he doesn't mind.'

'Can we go to that hill, where there are no trees?' suggested Rajay. 'There are very strong vibrations coming from it.' We flew the horses up to a rocky hillock. The tiger was standing nearby and wanted to show Rajay something so he followed it, and right on the top he could see a natural design in the rocks of a twelve petalled flower. 'This hill is the very point where the power of the heart centre radiates out of the Mother Earth! Test what I say.' We did and it was very cool. Even on this warm night, a cool breeze was gushing out of the rocks. 'What a strange chance has led me here. I thought I knew every nook and cranny of my land, but this is a revelation. Let's kneel in gratitude that we're all safe, and for letting me find this spot. I'll have a temple built here and then my people can come and actually feel this flower of the Tree of Life.' We did as he asked and gave thanks, none more than me, for having been saved yet again by this wondrous power, channelled through a Key of Wisdom.

'So,' concluded Rajay, getting up, 'even the worst scenes in the drama have a silver lining!' We looked out over the forest. 'Let's give you some vibrations, and this is the ideal place to heal your heart centre, which is a bit damaged right now.' He was perfectly accurate, because I was still in shock. The four of them directed the vibrations coming from the stones on the ground towards my heart and soon I felt fine, with all of them doing what they did best - resolving problems with confidence in the all-pervading power, and a great deal of patience with people like me, who were incapable of keeping out of trouble.

Although it had been a ghastly experience it was magical to return to Malak Citadel gliding through the night sky, sitting behind my fiancé on his flying horse. When we arrived the horses came down in the yard of the fort and a relieved Saber ran up. He had only recently sent out search parties for me, because he assumed I was spending the evening with the Ricemaize family in the town, as I often did. Zulani, Queen Jansy and the others came out and soon everyone was talking to everyone. After thanking Saber for his concern I bid my rescuers goodnight and crept off to my room in Amber's house. Robin, Lee and Ahren went with Rajay, as they were all staying in the central building, in the young men's apartment.

CHAPTER 11

CELEBRATIONS

Three days before the wedding the guests started arriving and when the Aydriss family came they were invited to a meal with Rajay in Queen Jansy's apartment.

'Asha, come out into the garden,' Rajay asked me after they left, and we stood in the shade of an old fruit tree. 'Can you arrange a meeting between Witten and Pearl? She's completely different.'

'Witten asked me if the Aydriss family had arrived. Could they get married with the rest of us?'

'We can try. But is he still interested?'

'Yes, I think he is. His very shyness and his disappearance when he saw her crossing the yard gave him away. I'll do my best.'

'I leave it with you. There's another thing, too.'

'What's that?'

'Are you aware that Deradan has long admired you, and he's very down to see you swept away by your dashing Robin?'

'Yes, I knew, but there wasn't much I could do about it.'

'All my friends are so courageous and committed to their ideals and they see those qualities in you. It's a good thing you tied brotherhood bands on most of them, otherwise they'd all have wanted to marry you! One of the problems with this country is that the educated women are traditionally very timid and retiring and often suppressed by their men, or hide behind them. You and Zulani, and also Melissa, are a breath of spring – so refreshingly different. I've got so many ideas as to how to transform our women once Zulani is my queen - I know she's going to set a great example. Anyway, let's see if we can find someone for Deradan. There are some very eligible young ladies here at the moment. Keep your eyes open.'

'Will do!'

It was great to hear Rajay talk like that about women and more so about Zulani. I wondered if she knew how he had a remarkable way of getting people to do things they never thought they were capable of, and what he had in store for her.

I gave a bandhan of request for Deradan and did a bit of diplomacy with Witten and Pearl, with the result that they were both delighted. She had been diligently doing the treatments to put herself right, and although she did still occasionally get a bit crabby she was vastly improved. Witten had been feeling left out as he was the oldest of Rajay's companions, and Rajay had promised to help find him someone suitable once the country was at peace - he had seen all the wedding preparations and assumed he'd been forgotten in the excitement. Rajay never forgot about anyone but wanted to make sure about Pearl before saying anything. He and I had another short, private conversation and he mentioned that strangely enough, it seemed that his criticism of Pearl, which had made Witten cautious, had forced her to look at her shortcomings, and might have been a good thing. So it was we were four couples three days later.

I was to wear pink, my most flattering colour. Zulani had a magnificent robe of red and gold, as befitted the future queen of the country whose subtle centre was red. Clary, with her dark copper coloured hair, chose brilliant blue, because she and Sarn would be ruling lands by the sea. The tailor frantically made an elegant robe of rich green satin for Pearl. She knew about the subtle system by now, and explained it like this.

'Witten is going to be Rajay's Finance Minister. The subtle centre which governs material prosperity is the third one, and its colour is green. So that's the colour for me.' She was tall for a woman and carried herself well. With her long straight dark hair, dark olive skin and regular features she was the most dignified of all of us.

Queen Jansy told Pearl, Clary and me to borrow any jewellery we liked for our weddings and Deradan took us deep into the vaults under the Citadel. It was a bit awkward; I could feel his sadness and knew why. We could hardly believe the wealth that was there, all carefully itemised and stored away. Zulani was not with us because there was traditional jewellery for her to wear.

'This is the collateral of our country,' Deradan told us, 'but don't let anyone know how much there is! You're all going to need a simple crown, for starters.' He led us into a small room and opened some of the locked chests. We looked in wonder.

'May I make a suggestion?' Pearl asked.

'Go ahead,' I said, confused by the enormous variety of crowns and tiaras.

'Tomorrow is primarily Rajay and Zulani's day. We three should choose unpretentious jewellery so as not to outshine our future queen.'

At that moment I knew why Witten had chosen Pearl as his bride. Here was one Finance Minister whose wife would never enrich herself at the country's expense, because she had inherited the famous integrity of the Aydriss family. When Queen Jansy saw the modest jewellery we had borrowed, she told us to keep what we were to wear as wedding gifts.

The weddings, which were held in the castle yard, were similar to Valya's. Traditionally the couple would have their immediate family sitting round the fire with them. Rajay's family included his mother and those of his friends who were not themselves getting married, and with them was Moozand. I had Lee and Ahren, Mr and Mrs Ricemaize, and Heeram Milkfarmer and Coral Aydriss from Crossings Fort, who had done so much to help with my awakening work. Amber and Saber Rizen, my generous hosts for over a year, completed my Daish Shaktay family.

Rajay had always known he would have an arranged marriage but did not expect his bride to be a radiant and charming princess who had saved his life and dedicated herself completely to his cause. Zulani was in a daze; the most selfless and great-hearted man she had ever met was to be her husband. It was a marriage made in heaven for two people who richly deserved each other.

Witten returned with Sarn from their working trip with such good reports of the young Lionheart that Rajay had no doubts he was ideal for Mattanga. Clary forgave him and understood that when he left Mattanga without warning, she was free from being involved if anyone questioned her as to where he had gone. She had made the risky journey to Daish Shaktay to help her friend Zulani, and certainly not with the intention of meeting up with Sarn. Now she had a much more mature young man as a husband. Witten had always only seen the good side of Pearl and she had surrendered completely to the power of the subtle vibrations to improve her nature.

Robin had risked much to help resolve a desperately serious situation in a country that was not his concern, and what a blessing that he and the people in Sasrar had showed me again and again that I should always trust the

vibrations, which had enabled me to wait for the right husband. We all finished up with the partner who was best for us and had done so by putting something more than our smaller selves first.

The guests included many people who had helped Rajay. Luth's monks, Rajay's often unseen helpers, came tramping down the roads of Daish Shaktay and were offered warm hospitality wherever they stopped to rest. Sim Patter came from Midway Manor and the partisan schoolmaster from near Santara. There was even a rough looking foot soldier the guards initially refused to let in, until he explained that he had helped Rajay escape from the village lockup on his way back from Mattanga and had been offered a place in Daish Shaktay by the king himself. Eventually the whole of the courtyard was full and nobody was turned away.

Rajay and Zulani tried hard not to dominate proceedings but it was unavoidable and we were honoured to be there with them, as group after group came and gave their congratulations after the ceremony and Zulani met hundreds of her future subjects. Many had brought gifts and one of the most touching was from a road gang foreman, on behalf of the Guild of Road Builders. It was an amethyst lined stone, partly opened, and inside was a small silver model of a frog. There was also a hand painted rolling pin, presented by an elderly farmer's wife who had come all the way from the Eastern Mountains. She had been personally invited by Rajay.

As the weddings were held outside, the Great Hall could be got ready for the coronation some days in advance. Two thrones decorated with gold and jewels were placed on the dais and carpets and tapestries were spread everywhere. A damask canopy was placed over the thrones and surrounding them were symbolic objects of kingship and authority: fish heads of gold for Daish Shaktay's navy, the scales of justice, a bundle of rods symbolised the power of the army and horse tails for the cavalry.

Queen Jansy had long hoped for this coronation, because once Rajay was crowned none of the other noble families of the country would dare oppose him. The ceremony was to be performed in the traditional manner and Bargu, a learned priest, came all the way from the Temple-by-the-Sea, where the aspect of the Divine Power who had come to earth as a warrior and king was worshipped. Bargu insisted everything was done precisely as he instructed and more than once during the rehearsal threatened to go home when most of us could not get our parts right.

More guests arrived: noblemen and leading citizens of Daish Shaktay, priests from temples all over the country, ambassadors from far off lands and even some guardians – Prince Roarke, Prince Osmar and Princess Neysa. Also present were Mazdan, representing his father Theon, Zafan, Zafeena and the 'pirates'. Zafeena looked sophisticated and wore gowns sewn with magical jewels from the Emperor's Island, her thick dark hair done up under a golden tiara, completely unlike her usual homespun and slightly dishevelled self.

The day of the coronation arrived and in the morning was the purification ceremony for Rajay. He was dressed in white cotton garments; this was a symbolic washing off of any sins he might have committed during his conquests. In the courtyard, in the presence of all the guests, Rajay had water poured over him from the sea and rivers in and around Daish Shaktay.

The crowning ceremony was in the evening. The Great Hall was festooned with flowers and lights burned in all the windows. Jewellery had been taken out of vaults and everyone wore brightly coloured new clothes. Rajay and Zulani sat on their thrones: gone were the freedom fighter and the refugee and in their place were two regal figures, dressed in silks, gold and jewels. Musicians played – auspicious shennaies – a raw, commanding instrument which suited the occasion perfectly, and choirs of children sang, thanking the divine power that the country was now free.

At this point events took off in their own spontaneous direction; as always when Rajay was involved nothing happened quite as expected. Luth walked in the back of the Great Hall and Rajay immediately asked him to come up onto the dais. Rajay and Zulani stood up, and Rajay knelt at Luth's feet and offered him the throne. He refused it, but sat in the front row with the other guardians.

Bargu, flustered at this departure from convention, asked me to come forward, as had been planned. I was given Rajay's sacred sword and placed it at his feet, and then he and his wife knelt before it, showing he was only an instrument of the divine force. Next Rajay's companions came up and Ahren and Lee made the number up to seven, and they each presented Rajay with a gold plate full of the jewels which corresponded to one of the subtle centres. The plates were placed in front of the sword, to signify the fact that Rajay's whole being was surrendered to the power which ruled these subtle inner centres. Rajay and Zulani stood up, and their cloaks were tied together at the base, a symbol that both the strength of the man and the compassion of the woman were needed to rule the country well.

Suddenly the doors at the back of the hall opened and the moons' light streamed in. Everyone turned as Queen Jansy entered, in a red damask dress, resplendent with gold jewellery. In one hand she carried a jewelled key and in the other a golden rod with a golden flower on top. She was riding a tiger with a golden collar around its neck and it was followed by eleven others. The guests gasped in terror as they padded in but Luth stood up and calmed everyone, explaining that these were the guardian animals of the country and not to be feared. Slowly panic subsided.

The tigers walked up to the dais and knelt before Rajay in the open space in front of the thrones. Bargu was fast becoming resigned to the fact that the Ghiry family had a way of turning convention on its head and doing things their way. He nevertheless backed away, mortally scared. Zulani handled this first test of her life as Queen of Daish Shaktay very coolly, and smiled graciously at the tigers without outwardly showing any fear. Queen Jansy went up onto the dais and gave Rajay the jewelled key.

'I do not need this key any more,' she said, 'I am going back to my own country, so you can give this to your wife, who will no doubt use it wisely.'

He took his own key out from under his clothing so it could be seen by everyone, and put the second one around Zulani's neck, to indicate that she was his partner in every way. Queen Jansy gave Rajay the golden rod, the sceptre of Daish Shaktay, to hold, and said in a loud, clear voice: 'This was entrusted to me by your father, my husband, when he left this land, and asked me to administer it until you grew up. This is for you. It represents the inner Tree of Life.'

Finally Bargu called for Luth and the old monkey man mounted the dais. He was given the crown of the country and placed it on Rajay, and put another one on Zulani. The musicians played once more, a thousand voices sang, and everyone, including the tigers, stood up. Bargu offered prayers for the long life and good health of the king and queen, and Robin, sitting next to me, whispered that Rajay was so calm, so still, but so totally in command.

Rajay was aware of the qualities of the subtle centre of the heart radiating through him – courage, confidence and responsibility, love for his family and people as their king, as a father, brother and husband, and a peaceful, detached ecstasy radiating from the left part of his heart centre, the joy of the spirit. He felt deep gratitude for the aspect of the divine he worshipped in this lifetime – the goddess of Daish Shaktay.

He called his five companions and others, and honoured them with titles and gifts. Bart Charval was to become overlord of the land above the Shaktay River and Athlos was to be Commander-in-Chief of the army, and Rajay quietly suggested it was time he gave up being a monk and also got married. He gave gifts to numerous others, from Dr Belsanto to the farmer's wife with the fearsome rolling pin. This took time, and meanwhile there was excellent music in case anyone should get bored. There were gifts to and from the visiting guardians and when they came up to Rajay there was a sense of serenity and shared joy as they interacted not only with speech but also with their powerful vibrations.

The evening continued with a great feast served in the castle yard and everyone in the town was invited. Lastly there was a tremendous firework display and the guns boomed from Malak Citadel Fort announcing that the Mountain Mouse, Rajay Ghiry, had fulfilled his vow to free and unite Daish Shaktay.

CHAPTER 12

NEW BEGINNINGS

The next morning Rajay invited us from the north to meet him in the Watch Tower Pavilion. Zulani was with him and he was looking over the orders for the day with Deradan, who was unusually cheerful. I assumed it was because Daish Shaktay was finally settled, along with Rajay's personal life.

'There's a delegation from the state owned gold mine in the Eastern Mountains,' said Deradan. 'The union leaders want to ask you if they can run it as a Worker's Cooperative. They're nervous about approaching you because the present boss may lose out. I said you might welcome the plan, but there is one problem.'

'What's that?' asked Rajay.

'They must go back today or they'll lose their jobs.'

'They won't, if the proposal is good. On the contrary, they'll get big promotions from me personally,' continued Rajay forcefully. 'It has to be a better way of running our gold mines than that harsh Mattanga sympathiser who's in charge now. Who else?'

'Professor Sagewell, from the University of Falton, wants to base the whole education system on the wisdom of the Tree of Life.'

'I'll see the folk from the gold mine in the Council Chamber now and have lunch with the professor.'

Deradan left to make arrangements.

'So, how did the coronation, go?' Rajay asked the rest of us.

'It was great! Tremendous vibrations and enough drama to keep everyone in gossip for the next year,' observed Lee drily.

'Poor old Bargu, it was a bit too much for him when the tigers came in!' Rajay joked. 'My wife and queen on the other hand handled the incident perfectly.'

'It was a good thing I was tied to Rajay's cloak at the time or I'd have run off in terror,' Zulani admitted. 'By the way, Deradan has seen a young lady he wants to meet.'

'Who?' I asked, understanding his changed mood.

'Zafeena, Zafan's sister.'

'She grew up at the court of the emperor but has also lived in the jungles, so she'd fit in perfectly here,' I mused.

'That's what Zulani and I were thinking,' agreed Rajay.

'At the firework display, Robin and I were sitting next to Zafan and Zafeena,' I added, 'and she told me she's asked her brother to find her a husband. Zafan has met Deradan and speaks very highly of him.'

'We'll leave it to you, because you know everyone concerned,' Rajay looked at me knowingly. 'Also, at dinner last night, I discussed the mass awakening programmes with the visiting guardians. They'd like to see how you do them. Could you organize one in Santara, on your way home?'

'It'd be a pleasure,' said Robin.

'I must go and see these miners. Come,' Rajay turned to Zulani, 'I'm hoping you're going to help run our country from now on.' Her expression was one of surprise and delight. No Mattangan queen had ever been asked anything like that. 'I'll need a lady's input, especially as my mother is going back to her homeland, now it's no longer a colony of Mattanga. The people there have asked for her help.'

In the evening we had a hastily arranged party. The visiting royalty, Luth and Sarn were with Rajay and Zulani, and the rest of us met at the Rizen's. I told Zafeena that Deradan wanted to meet her. She was not sure about him because he looked so staid and worked with dry documents, even though the vibrations were cool when we asked if they were right for each other, and I assured her he had many excellent qualities. At the start of our party Zafan introduced Zafeena to Deradan, and the three of them talked rather stiffly, because Zafeena was very bashful and Deradan more so. Then we had supper.

After that it was time for the music. Ekan and Saber played and sang some folk music on the wooden xylophone they had borrowed from the Guards' Common Room, accompanied by Namoh on a drum and Lee on his flute. Somehow the strange combination of instruments worked. Then Robin pushed Deradan to the front and he knew this was his chance to win Zafeena. His face lit up as he sang his own poems in a deep, powerful voice, and his fingers flowed effortlessly over his stringed instrument as he played his unforgettably beautiful melodies. He touched our hearts when he sang about the fallen heroes, Danard and Varg-Nack, and we smiled at those telling of Rajay's outrageous exploits, wittily captured in verse.

Zafeena was sitting next to Heeram Milkfarmer, because they had met at the supper beforehand. Although Zafeena had been brought up at the Emperor's court, she was more at ease with someone from a simpler background than the courtiers of Malak Citadel, having spent the last few years in the jungles with the 'pirates'. She did not know that everyone there had either been a partisan or was very easy-going, because Rajay abhorred snobbishness and arrogance. Heeram was in on our plan for Zafeena and Deradan, and between his songs Heeram whispered to her that Deradan was also renowned for his defiant bravery. Zafeena saw him in a new light and realised she mustn't be put off by his clerical appearance. After he finished, we played some fast, rhythmic music and everyone was up and dancing. I noticed Rajay and his party enter.

'Hope you don't mind our gate-crashing,' he came up to me. I replied that it was an honour. 'How's the matchmaking going?'

'I'm not sure, ask Heeram.'

Rajay made his way across the crowded room to her, at that moment dancing with Dr Belsanto's chubby six year old daughter and mischievous looking nine year old son. He asked her to come into Saber's study.

'How's my rock climber?' he laughed. 'I meant to apologise for making you do that climb again – I shouldn't have forced you.'

'That's alright, Your Majesty, as I said at the time, it was nothing compared to what you've done for us.'

'OK then - but what about Zafeena? Do you think she'll accept Deradan's offer? I hope so, because he deserves someone special. He'll be a very devoted husband.'

'Well, they both want to get married, and they're both fine people from similar backgrounds, so that's a good enough reason for them to go ahead, isn't it?'

'Yes. I wish everyone saw life as simply as you, Heeram.'

Rajay chatted to her about her work of awakening people's Trees of Life. The change in their relationship, from when he had first met her at Crossings Fort, was vast. There was a confidence in Heeram and a breeziness about Rajay I had never seen before.

By the end of the evening Zafeena was completely won over by her serious looking suitor, who nevertheless had an awesome reputation as a warrior, a chivalrous manner and was an inspired musician and poet. Deradan immediately found a kindred spirit in Zafeena, who despite her present elegance could live rough in the jungle to help the cause of peace and justice. They announced their engagement the following day.

A few days later, one of the biggest ever awakening programmes took place in Santara. Prince Roarke was the lead musician and Princess Neysa one of the singers. They were so accomplished we were put to shame! Hundreds of people sang and danced with us, felt the inner joy and cool breeze. Rajay and Zulani came too and afterwards we all spent a long time with the enthusiastic new people.

The next morning we left, and beforehand Rajay and Zulani invited Robin, Ahren and me to join them for breakfast on a roof terrace which looked over the town, and on the far hills I could see Tiger's Head Fort. I caught Rajay's eye; Tiger's Head would always have sad memories for him.

'Rajay wants me to redesign this palace,' said Zulani, looking at some papers on the table, 'and to bring some of our craftsmen from Mattanga. He's made this country peaceful and he wants me to make it more beautiful.

Mattanga was built with slave labour, whereas here we'll make careers for people while they work for us.' We looked at the imaginative designs, drawn by Zulani. I smiled - within two weeks of their marriage Rajay was turning his wife into an architect. 'I've tried to show what some of our nicer palaces in Mattanga are like and made some sketches, and now my husband has got me doing a full scale design job!' At this moment Lee arrived.

'Come in. Breakfast?' Rajay asked.

'No thanks. I've got a request from some people for an audience, and they're waiting for an answer downstairs.'

'Tell me.'

'There's a violent disagreement between the Federation of Fruit Farmers and the Santara Beekeepers Guild. The farmers are demanding payment from the beekeepers because they say most of the honey comes from the fruit blossom and the beekeepers say the farmers should pay *them*, because the bees put up the yield of fruit when they pollinate the trees.'

'Back to work! First we spend years fighting to get freedom for these folk and now I'm going to have to spend more years persuading them not to fight each other.'

'If they could all get their awakening maybe their hearts would open and they'd be grateful to Mother Nature for the wealth she gives and not always trying to grasp that bit extra.'

'Give it time,' sighed Rajay, 'now the country is at peace, I can make sure that everyone who wants it has their Tree of Life awakened. I'll try to train my friends and the others who've helped in the freedom fight to run the country so I can attend to subtler matters, then the citizens of this land will hopefully learn to allow the all pervading power to make their decisions. If they could simply ask the vibrations what to do and abide by that, I wouldn't have to spend half a morning sorting out these foolish beekeepers and fruit growers. This land belongs to the people who live here, but they have to be responsible enough to look after it. Anyway, that's not your headache. We must say goodbye, until we meet again. Robin, let me know if you need help with Chussan.'

'I'm sure we'll soon have a new government there. Teletsia is a greater problem.'

'Too true.'

Rajay embraced Robin and Ahren affectionately. I was about to make the formal gesture of respect to him, because although he would protect every woman with his life, he would generally only touch his mother and wife.

'Rajay, break your own rules for once and bid Asha goodbye as you would a real sister,' said Zulani. So first she bid me a fond farewell and then Rajay took me in his arms, and I felt one of the guardians of the heart centre of Mother Earth enveloping me with the tender power of the great king he had become. His love and gratitude as a brother flowed through every pore of my being. I felt his sense of protection not only for us present, but also for the whole of

Daish Shaktay and was also aware of that highest love emanating from him: that divine, detached bliss that is reflected in us as our spirit. It was a momentary experience, but one I would never forget.

'Thank you all, from the very bottom of my heart, for helping me win back my country, and in other ways too,' he looked at me. 'I'm always in your debt and here if you need my help. This country, as we know, is a part of the fourth subtle centre on the Mother Earth, so it's only fair that I help you with yours, which is the seat of the first centre.'

'That's very noble of you,' said Lee.

'Not as noble as what you did when Comeni tried to kill me at Midway Manor, or what Ahren did to save me from that mad young man at Port Volcan – and all the other times you've risked your life for Daish Shaktay. And what with Asha's ideas and everything else, it would be a chance to even things up a bit.'

I now understood why we had come to Daish Shaktay, and how it would help in the fulfilment of our more long term mission, that of freeing our own country, if we had someone of the calibre of Rajay with us. I wondered if that was what the astrologers in the mountains of Chussan had had in mind all along.

Later I asked Robin how he felt when Rajay embraced him. He described the experience – identical to mine. Ahren just commented, 'It was fantastic - but don't you always feel like that inside?' which told Robin and me what sort of a person Ahren, the formerly wild and uncouth farm boy, had become. We left the palace, the flying horses were waiting for us in the yard at the back and with ours was Lee's, and Namoh was standing by his side.

'I'm coming too,' he said. 'Lee has lent me his horse, because he's staying here. I've wanted to go to Sasrar ever since Asha first gave me my awakening, and Rajay is right behind the idea – he's given me a year's paid leave.'

We finally arrived back in Chussan and when we reached the astrologer's house we trooped into the kitchen, where Mrs Pea-Arge was, as usual, presiding over her domain.

'I took your advice. Meet my wife!' Robin put his hand around my shoulders.

'So that's why you went to Daish Shaktay. I'm glad you didn't lose her to one of those southerners,' she observed.

'It was the king of those southerners who suggested the match.'

'Well in that case, he must be a good king,' she replied, with her rather idiosyncratic approach to logic.

'He is,' Namoh added, and introduced himself.

'Where's Lee?' Mrs Pea-Arge looked around for him and was momentarily worried.

'He's stayed in Daish Shaktay; he's learning how to run a country – he's working for King Rajay,' I explained.

'That might come in handy – and Ahren – quite the young man now! I'm sure you've learnt how to fight from this king.'

'Yes, or I wouldn't be here now, and he's promised to help us put Teletsia right.'

Deradan soon married Zafeena and her brother Zafan often came to Malak Citadel to advise Rajay on naval matters. Shortly before we left Daish Shaktay, Valya and Melissa, and some time later Rajay and Zulani became the parents of boy babies. I asked the vibrations and it was very cool; I was absolutely certain that the great souls who had been Varg-Nack and Danard were back to enjoy the beautiful country they had given their previous lives to set free. So Queen Jansy's promise, that Danard would be a part of their family for ever if he could win back Tiger's Head Fort, came true, in a way.

Lightning Source UK Ltd.
Milton Keynes UK
UKOW021032221011

180760UK00001B/25/P